Forgotten

Jane Blythe

Bear Spots Publications
Melbourne Australia

bearspotspublications@gmail.com

ISBN: 0992418054
ISBN-13: 978-0-9924180-5-2

Cover designed by QDesigns

PROLOGUE
FIVE YEARS LATER
FEBRUARY 19TH

5:32 A.M.

It was so quiet out this early in the morning.

Peaceful and tranquil.

The sky was just turning white and it wouldn't be long before the sun rose sending golden fingers curling across the land. This was the best time of day, when the world hovered, half stuck, between night and day. A time where it felt that anything might happen, like magic hung in the air and if you could just figure out the right word to unlock it then all your dreams could come true.

Arising each morning in the predawn, rushing out to the woods, wishing that this morning might be the morning where things would be different, where miracles might happen.

Legs dangling in the gentle pull of the creek, enjoying the feel of the icy water that made skin tingle. Loved it because it was a feeling and there hadn't been too many of those lately. The little stream twisted and turned through the woods, tumbling over smooth stones, gurgling softly to itself, like it didn't have a care in the world. Tiny fish darted this way and that beneath the surface, dancing in the moonlight, the sunlight, the half-light, always zipping about merrily.

As the first hints of sunrise shone down between the trees the birds begun to awaken, chirping sleepily as they rose from their nests to greet the day. Reluctantly pulling legs out of the water, watching as the little drops raced down to the tips of toes before splashing to join the throng in the creek below. Wiggling toes to try to warm them, then jumping up and stomping around until at last the biting cold was gone leaving normal legs and the usual sense of deadness.

Beginning the trek back to the house. The others would be waiting, worrying, it was a stressful day for all of them. Five years today since it had happened. Five long years since that fateful day. Five years since their lives had been irrevocably changed.

FEBRUARY 9TH

5:11 A.M.

'Just a little further' she thought to herself. She couldn't shake the feeling that something was wrong. She didn't know what it was. It always made her uncomfortable running alone in the park at this time of the morning, but she didn't have a choice. She hadn't made any friends since she'd moved to the city two months ago, and she spent almost every waking minute at work. She wanted to make a good impression. She wanted her father to be proud of her, and he had pulled a lot of strings to get her this job.

It was a typical winter's morning, even in the dark you could see that the sky was piled high with deep, thick clouds, they were in for another grey day. There hadn't been a lot of snow this winter, but enough to lightly dust the world with a light layer of white, although to be honest the snow was now more slushy grey than bright, fresh white.

Natalie Jannes hated winter, hated the cold and the snow. Her body was aching for the gentle warmth of spring, the fragrant flowers, the soft fluttering breeze, the endless blue skies, the tingling feel of the sun on her skin. She much preferred a carpet of delicate pink and white blossom petals than the wet, slippery flakes of snow. In fact, she had started a countdown, only thirty-nine days to go. Still it was probably cheating to not count today since it was only five o'clock in the morning.

Natalie shivered.

There was that feeling again.

She heard a twig snap and took a quick look over her shoulder, but once again saw nothing. She started to jog a little faster.

Another couple of minutes, she reassured herself for what seemed like the hundredth time, and she'd be back to the road, then another minute or two to get to her apartment. Then she's take a shower, have a quick breakfast and check to see if there was an email from . . .

She frowned. Up ahead something white lay at the side of the road. It was too big to be trash, and it kind of looked like a . . . a body.

Gasping, she broke into a run and sprinted quickly to the stranger's aid, her cell phone already in her hand. Reaching the body, Natalie saw it was a young woman, wearing only a thin white shirt and mauve skirt, despite the February cold, her bare feet were scratched and scraped. Bending down she touched the girl's ice-cold neck to check for a pulse, and let out a sigh of relief when she found it, quickly dialing 911.

"911, what's your emergency?" the operator asked.

"There's a woman in the snow . . ." she began breathlessly.

"Is she breathing?" the woman on the other end of the phone spoke in an impossibly calm voice.

"Yes," Natalie confirmed shakily, "and she has a pulse, but she's so cold, she's just lying here in the snow and she's only dressed in a shirt and skirt . . ."

Interrupting her babbling, "can you tell me where you are?" the operator asked.

"In the park, we're in the park."

Continuing in her steady voice, so unlike Natalie's own, the operator moved on to her next question, "can you see if she has any injuries?"

"I . . . I can't tell," Natalie stammered looking down at the young woman who lay so still. "She's lying on her stomach, I can't see anything but . . . her feet, she doesn't have any shoes on and her feet are cut."

"Alright, I'm going to explain to you how to turn the woman over carefully, in case she has a neck injury," the operator explained.

Following the 911 operator's instructions Natalie flipped the unconscious woman onto her back. The young woman had a tangle of golden curls obscuring her face, and Natalie gently pushed them away to reveal a gash across the girl's temple and a split lip. There was no blood on the woman's white shirt, but when Natalie lifted the young woman's hand, intending to check the too still girl's pulse again, when she let out a horrified gasp. The young woman's wrist had been rubbed raw. Quickly, Natalie leaned over her motionless body to check the other wrist, it too was red and enflamed. On instinct she turned to look at the girl's ankles, she was appalled, but not surprised, to find them in the same condition. Shrugging out of her coat to cover the young woman who looked unnaturally pale, almost translucent, in the snow.

Praying that an ambulance would arrive soon, Natalie was about to retrieve her phone and update the 911 operator on what she had found when the young woman beneath her began to stir. Taking the girl's hand, and putting on her brightest, most reassuring voice, "hey, my name's Natalie. You're going to be fine, an ambulance is on its way. Can you tell me what happened?"

The young woman had large dark blue eyes, and for a moment they stared up at her before taking in their surroundings.

When the girl said nothing Natalie tried again, "can you tell me your name?"

Blue eyes growing wide and panicked, "my name!" the girl's voice was hoarse but there was no denying the underlying terror. "I can't remember my name!"

Natalie looked at her in shock, taking in the girl's sparsely clad body, her bare feet, her raw wrists, and the terrified eyes that stared up at her, begging for help. But Natalie didn't know how to help, feeling very inadequate she pasted on what she hoped was her most reassuring smile and reached out to smooth the young woman's matted hair. "Everything's going to be okay," she whispered, the words sounding hollow even to her own ears. But it didn't matter, the dark blue eyes fluttered closed and the girl sank back into unconsciousness.

* * * * *

6:04 A.M.

Striding through the park, Detective Parker Bell shivered as he ducked under the police tape and made his way over to where his partner was talking to their only witness in what was shaping up to be a most bizarre case.

A Jane Doe had been found, unconscious, with injuries that pointed to her possibly being a kidnap victim. To add to the drama the young woman was apparently suffering from amnesia and could not remember her own name, let alone what had happened to her.

Parker sighed, more drama was not what he needed right now.

Passing the ambulance just as they closed the doors to take the mystery woman to the hospital, they would head there next, when they finished up with the witness. Hopefully by the time they joined her at the hospital and she woke up again the young woman would remember something, anything, at the very least her name.

Sighing once again as a blast of freezing air seemed to pass straight through his coat. Rearranging his scarf, Parker started to walk more quickly towards where his partner was interviewing the woman who had stumbled upon this unusual scene.

"Did you see anyone else while you were jogging?" he heard Skylar Wyatt ask as he approached.

The young lady shook her head, her long russet colored ponytail swinging with each shake. She had on no coat, and shivered in the cold. "No, I never see anyone else out at this time, but . . ." she trailed to a stop.

"But what?" Parker asked as he came up next to her, taking off his own coat and draping it over her shoulders.

Wyatt turned to look at him, mild surprise flickering in his emerald green eyes before he raised a questioning eyebrow. "Natalie, this is my partner Detective Bell."

Ignoring Wyatt's probing stare, Parker held out his hand and the woman took it, looking at him with big, distracted, brown eyes, then she glanced in the direction the ambulance had gone. Shaking her head again, this time as if to focus her thoughts, she turned back to look at him, "thanks for the coat, I gave mine to . . . the girl."

"You're welcome. But what?" Parker repeated his question hoping to refocus the obviously shaken young woman. "Before you were saying that you never see anyone when you go jogging at that time, but . . ."

"But this morning something felt wrong. I kept getting shivers like someone was watching me, following me, but every time I turned around there was no-one there," Natalie shivered again and he assumed she was reliving the memory.

"Thank you. You've been very helpful," he told her.

Exhaling in obvious relief, but wanting to check he was sure, "you mean I can go now?"

"Yes, we have your details and we'll contact you if we need to clarify anything. And thanks again, she was lucky. She could have laid there in the cold for hours if you hadn't found her, or someone less . . . ah . . . helpful could have stumbled across her."

Natalie nodded and shot him a grateful glance, "I'm sorry I couldn't be more helpful, but I really didn't see anything. Just her."

"You've been great, very helpful," Wyatt reassured her. "We'll get an officer to take you home," he added gesturing to a young police officer that came towards them.

Natalie took off his coat and handed it back to him, "thanks again."

Watching Natalie Jannes leave when Parker turned back to face his partner he saw Wyatt was watching him once again with a reproachful frown.

"You got here quick," his partner pointed out. "You spend the night at the house?"

The house Wyatt was referring to was the home in which Parker had grown up. He and his twin sister Matilda had spent the first ten years of their lives bouncing from foster home to foster home, until after a particularly horrible placement they were adopted by Luka and Laura Bell. The Bell's had recently lost their seven year old son Taylor to cancer and were looking not to replace their child, but to offer a home to another child in need. Parker quickly grew to love the Bell's but things hadn't gone as smoothly for his sister.

The reason Wyatt was enquiring as to his living arrangements, was because Parker and his wife Tessa had been having problems ever since Tessa had been forced to confront her past in order to save seven little girls. That was five months ago. Ever since it seemed that every time they were together all they did was fight and Parker had taken to spending most nights at his old house rather than at Tessa's mansion where they had been living before things had begun to fall apart.

"Well did you?" Wyatt pressed.

"Yes I did, not that's it any of your business," Parker snapped. When the Bell's had adopted him and Matilda, he had quickly become good friends with Skylar Wyatt, his fifteen-year-old next-door neighbor. Now twenty two years later they were best friends as well as partners, which Wyatt thought gave him the right to meddle in Parker's affairs.

"You two are impossible," Wyatt huffed as he rolled his eyes. "You know someone has to make the first move."

"Why don't you tell Tessa that," Parker was aware he was sounding more like a petulant child than a thirty-two year old police detective.

"I have," his partner snapped, "and she's just as stubborn as you are."

Wyatt was the youngest of five boys, during her pregnancy his mother had been positive that she was finally going to get a daughter. Although she loved all her sons, she was so disappointed not to get a girl that she decided to stick with the name she had chosen when planning for a little girl, and so Skylar Wyatt was born. Growing up Wyatt had been aware of his mother's disappointment with his gender, and around thirteen had decided to rebel, part of that was refusing to use the name she had chosen, he had started using his surname instead. The only person, bar his mother, who Wyatt allowed to call him Skylar was Tessa. Parker's best friend and his wife had become good friends, more like surrogate brother and sister, and Parker knew how upset Wyatt was about his and Tessa estrangement.

Apparently deciding that he wasn't going to get anything out of Parker now, Wyatt sighed, "come on, let's go to the hospital."

Following his partner to the car Parker surveyed the park he had loved as a child. It seemed like only yesterday that he had been here, spending hours playing baseball with his friends, riding his bike, rocketing around the playground. How quickly things could change. Just six months ago, he and Tessa were happily married and planning their future. Now he didn't know what that future held.

* * * * *

7:15 A.M.

"Parker didn't sleep here last night, huh?"

Tessa looked up from the bowl of cereal she was eating, or rather playing with, to glare at her older brother.

"I can't even remember the last time he slept here," Daniel continued, taking a seat across the table from her.

"Daniel," Tessa cautioned, tucking her white blonde curls behind her ear to frown at her brother more easily.

"You know if he's going to leave he should just do it, this backwards and forwardsing isn't fair to you."

"I'm . . ."

"Fine," Daniel finished for her. "I know, you're always fine, and it's always a lie."

"Really, Daniel, I'm okay and I don't want to talk about it," she returned to her breakfast, deliberately eating a few mouthfuls of the cereal, which had turned to mush in the milk.

Her brother lasted about a minute before he began again. "I don't get that guy," Daniel shook his head to emphasis his disbelief. "He pushes you into telling him what happened to you and Eleanor, something he's wanted to know since he met you, then once he knows that you were raped and forced to kill someone he decides he can't handle it and splits?"

"It's more complicated than that and you know it," Tessa told him sternly. To be honest she herself wasn't sure exactly what had happened between her and Parker. At first, it had started with an argument about where they would live after Parker was released from the hospital. He had wanted to move back to his old house, she had wanted to remain here on the estate she had inherited from her grandparents. Parker hated her house because of what had happened there a few months ago, she couldn't face his house because of what had happened there a few months before that. Then it had expanded to include Parker's actions in the days following her confession and her refusal to tell him the reason she had let a child trafficker go. Now it had blossomed to incorporate anything and everything.

"I'm going to talk to him . . ." Daniel began.

"Don't, Daniel, it'll only make things worse," she told him. Her brother and her husband had gotten off to a bad start, things had picked up for a while, but quickly rolled back downhill last September.

"Make things worse? Parker's walked out on you, how can things be worse?"

"You're giving me a headache," Tessa moaned, she'd been having a lot of headaches recently. "I really don't want to talk about it anymore."

Daniel didn't say anything, just stood, crossed to the cupboard and retrieved some painkillers. "Here you go," he said gruffly, setting the pills down on the table, but the look he gave her was tender. "When do you want to talk to Winter?" he asked, changing the subject somewhat reluctantly.

Wanting to answer never but knowing that at some point they needed to tell their niece the truth about her paternity. Sixteen-year-old Winter had been living with her for over a year, ever since her mother, Tessa and Daniel's older sister, had died. Tessa had been putting off revealing to Winter who her biological father was. First it was because she was waiting for Parker to recover, then it was because she was waiting for things to settle down between them. Now it was apparent that things weren't going to calm down between her and Parker so it seemed she was out of excuses.

"Tessie, we have to tell her," Daniel prodded.

"I know."

"Is Parker still going to be here when we do it?"

"He said he would," Tessa shrugged. Whatever problems she and Parker were going through, he loved Winter and he knew how devastated she was going to be when she found out the truth, he'd be there.

"Yeah, well, he said a lot of things that turned out not to be true, like he told you nothing would ever make him leave . . ."

"Daniel," she sighed wearily.

Throwing up his hands in surrender, "okay, okay, okay, but I think we should make a time to tell Winter, we can't put it off any longer, it's not going to make it any easier for her . . . or for you."

"I'll be fine," she assured him, quickly standing to clear the table so he wouldn't catch the tremor in her hands. "Lets just focus on Winter." Tessa could feel Daniel's eyes on her as she loaded the bowls and glasses into the dishwasher. She knew he was still hurt that she hadn't called him when everything happened last September. She had told him the whole story after he'd showed up in her hospital room, but she knew that hadn't alleviated his disappointment that once again she had shut him out. However, she didn't want to think about that now, so putting on a chirpy smile she turned to face her brother, "so how are things going with you and Matilda?"

Daniel's usually pale cheeks instantly turned bright red. "Fine," he answered shortly.

Her brother had been dating Parker's twin sister for about eight months, much to Parker's distaste, he did not approve of Daniel as a suitable partner for his sister. While she was going through hell a few months ago, confessing to Parker what had happened when she had been kidnapped at the age of eleven, Daniel had been on an overseas trip with Matilda, and the two had come back closer than before. Tessa hoped things worked out between them, especially after everything Matilda had been through during her years in foster care. "And . . ." she poked, amused by her brother's embarrassment.

"And what?" he snapped, covering his discomfort with irritation.

"And do I hear wedding bells in the near future?" enjoying not being the one in the hot seat for once.

"Not right now," Daniel said tightly.

"Come on, Daniel, she's crazy about you, everyone can see that," Tessa ruffled her brother's curls, a slightly darker shade of blonde than her own.

"Cut it out," he growled.

Beginning to laugh, "don't like it when the shoe's on the other foot huh? You're happy to throw yourself into my business but don't like it when I return the favor?"

"Fine, fine, you made your point, I'll try my hardest to keep out of your relationship with Parker." Her brother's face softened and he grabbed her hand, "I just don't want to see you get hurt again."

"I know that, Daniel, but I'm a big girl and I can take care of myself," to emphasize her point she gently tugged her hand free. "Winter has tests today and tomorrow how about we tell her the day after that, the eleventh."

"Yeah, okay, sure," Daniel sounded disappointed, Parker wasn't the only one who wanted to know more about the mysterious child trafficker whom she had refused to turn into the police.

Pausing at the kitchen door, "Daniel."

"Yeah," he looked up at her from the table.

"Seriously, you should think about proposing to Matilda. You really love her and she really loves you, nothing is more important than that, besides you two really do make a great couple."

* * * * *

7:42 A.M.

Parker hated hospitals, hoped he had seen the last of them after being shot last fall. They were too white, too sterile, with that overpowering antiseptic smell and that busy bustling commotion. It wasn't just his own stay in the hospital that made him hate them so much but all the times he'd sat at Tessa's bedside here, and right now thoughts of his wife left him feeling utterly confused.

Stomach grumbling, Parker wished he'd had more to eat when he and Wyatt had stopped for breakfast on their way here. He'd skipped dinner last night, worked late and convinced himself that was the reason he hadn't driven out to Tessa's country estate. He was just about to tell Wyatt that he was going to head to the cafeteria to get something when he spotted a familiar face. "Beth, hey."

Elisabeth Bennett smiled back at him, "hey yourself."

"What are you doing here? I thought you were still on maternity leave." Elisabeth was a psychiatrist who regularly helped them on cases and two months ago had become a proud first time mom to baby Lucia. Although he'd met the infant once or twice he couldn't help but feel a twinge of jealousy every time he saw a baby and it's happy parents. Several months ago Tessa had suffered a miscarriage, if it had survived their own baby would now be a month old. Parker often found himself wondering if he and Tessa could have avoided the problems that now plagued their marriage if they hadn't lost their child. "There's nothing wrong with the baby is there?"

"No, Lucia's fine," Elisabeth assured him, radiating joy at the mention of her tiny daughter, "perfect in fact. J.J. called me," Elisabeth explained, referring to his boss Lieutenant Jacob Jacobson. "He told me about your case, thought I might be able to help with your Jane Doe. Hey, Wyatt."

"Hi, Beth," Wyatt came up beside them and gave the psychiatrist a quick kiss on the cheek. "What're you doing here? Lucia okay?" Wyatt had two kids of his own, eleven-year-old Sam and six-year-old Stacey. Wyatt and his wife Casey had also been through the trauma of losing a child when their three-year-old daughter Serena had been killed in a car accident.

"Baby's fine," Parker told him. "She's here to help us with Jane Doe," he found himself struggling to get those words out. The term Jane Doe reminded him of John Doe, the pseudonym of the child trafficker who had abducted Tessa when she was eleven and started the chain of events that had led to his current situation with his wife. "Have you spoken with her?" he asked, still hoping that the young woman had by now remembered who she was and what had happened to her that left her lying unconscious, in the park, in the snow.

Hesitating, "well I've seen her, but I haven't spoken with her," Elisabeth replied.

"Is she still unconscious?"

"No. She regained consciousness not long after she arrived," the psychiatrist elaborated. "They checked her out in the ER, she has some cuts and bruises but nothing too serious. She's suffering from mild hypothermia, which is to be expected considering the way she was found, also mild dehydration. They did a CT and an MRI but they didn't find any serious head trauma, and so far I haven't been able to coax her into saying anything."

"She hasn't said anything yet?" he repeated a little surprised. At best Parker had expected the girl to wake up with her with her memory back and hysterical about what she'd been through, or at worst without her memory and hysterical that she didn't know who she was.

"She's very timid, very scared and overwhelmed right now," Elisabeth explained. "We did ask her a few basic questions to see if she had regained her memory, asked her to nod or shake her head in response, and it seems she still doesn't remember anything."

"Is the amnesia caused by a head injury?" Wyatt enquired.

Shaking her head, "no, we didn't find any evidence of an injury severe enough to cause damage to the brain. It's more likely caused by psychological trauma. It's called dissociative fugue, it's where someone is unable to recall some or all of their past, and its usually temporary."

"What's her emotional state like? Can we talk to her?" Parker asked.

"All things considering she's pretty calm. You can see her but I can't guarantee she'll say anything," Elisabeth told them. "This way," she led them down the hall, stopping outside a room, inside which their Jane Doe lay on a bed. The wounds on her head and wrists had been bandaged, her eyes were closed and she looked like she was sleeping.

"Can we go in?" Parker asked.

"Yes," Elisabeth nodded, "but before we do I just want to make a few things clear. I want to keep her calm at all costs, if she gets worked up you two are out of there. Try to keep your questions to ones with yes or no answers, I don't think she's going to be speaking." Once they both nodded Elisabeth added, "I'll go in first since I'm a familiar face."

Slowly Elisabeth opened the door and stepped inside, Parker and Wyatt followed, making sure to keep behind the psychiatrist. At the sound of the opening door the young woman turned her head her eyes springing open. Parker couldn't help but stare at her. She reminded him of Tessa. Her curls were a darker, more golden blonde than his wife's, her eyes a darker shade of blue, but he couldn't deny that the resemblance was uncanny.

As the young woman studied them, Parker saw recognition flash through her face as she noted Elisabeth, but when she looked himself and Wyatt up and down her eyes grew round and terrified, her breathing growing rapid.

Hurrying to the girl's side Elisabeth sat on the bed next to her, "honey, what is it?" She gently turned the girl's face towards her, "what's wrong?"

In response the young woman lifted her hand and pointed towards them.

At first Parker thought the girl was indicating that she was scared of them because they were police officers, and wondered whether maybe it was a cop hurt her, but then he followed the direction of her gaze and noted it settled on his waist. Slipping out his gun and holding it up, "is this what you're afraid of?"

The young woman nodded her terrified eyes fixated on the gun, as her breathing quickened even more Elisabeth once again turned her face away. Stroking the girl's hair she soothed, "hey, it's going to be okay, just try and calm down." Then to him and Wyatt she said, "I think you better put those away if you want to get anything out of her."

Handing his gun to Wyatt, who quietly ducked out of the room, Parker crossed over to the bed, pulled over a chair and sat beside the young woman.

"This is Detective Bell," Elisabeth introduced him. "He's a police officer and he's here to help you, okay?"

The girl nodded and observed him cautiously.

"And this is Detective Wyatt," Elisabeth added as his partner re-entered the room, minus the guns. "They're going to ask you a few questions, is that okay?"

Again the girl nodded, twisting one of her golden curls around her finger, but when Elisabeth moved to stand the young woman turned her gaze from the detectives to the psychiatrist, her eyes panicked.

"It's okay," Elisabeth soothed, taking the girl's hands. "I'm not going anywhere, I'm not going to leave you, I'm going to be here the whole time. You just let me know if you want them to stop." Elisabeth smiled reassuringly then turned to caution him and Wyatt, "take it easy okay."

Giving her a warm smile, "my name's Parker, are you feeling okay? Are you in a lot of pain?"

She nodded then shook her head.

"Any luck remembering your name?"

A shake.

"Can you remember anything about your home or your family?"

Another shake as she began again to twist her hair around her finger.

"Can you remember what happened to you in the last few days?"

Gaze dipping to her bandaged wrists, then up to Elisabeth who gave her a reassuring smile and an encouraging nod, before settling on him once again, she gave another shake.

"Do you know who hurt you?"

The girl turned her head to stare out the window, a single tear slowly rolling down her cheek, turning back to Parker she shook her head once again, then closed her eyes and rested her head back on the pillows.

Elisabeth lifted the girl's wrist to take her pulse and turned to Parker, "I think that's enough for today."

Parker nodded, then laid his hand on the girl's cheek, she opened her eyes to look at him. "We need a name to call you, until we figure out your real name," he couldn't stand to think of the young woman being referred to as Jane Doe. "I was thinking maybe 'Hope', that way none of us will give up hope of finding out who hurt you and getting you back to your family. Is that okay?"

A smile lit the girl's face, the first smile he had seen, her dark blue eyes shimmering with unshed tears, and she nodded.

Stroking the young woman's hair, "I'll be back in a minute okay, try and get some rest."

Squeezing her hand, Parker stood and followed Elisabeth to the door, Wyatt on his heels, he gave the girl one last reassuring smile before softly closing the door behind them.

Once they were outside Wyatt asked, "how long are we thinking that her amnesia is going to last?"

"There's no way to tell," Elisabeth answered. "Hopefully in a day or so when she starts to feel safe her memory will come back."

"Hopefully," Parker echoed, hoping it would be end up being less time. "Maybe we should head back to the station and start going through missing person files, see if we can identify her," he said to Wyatt.

His partner nodded. "Call us if she starts to talk," Wyatt said to Elisabeth, "or if she remembers anything."

Elisabeth nodded, "of course. Good luck."

As the psychiatrist went back into the room to sit beside the sleeping girl, Parker and Wyatt headed back to the station, hoping to find something to give them a lead in this most bizarre case.

* * * * *

11:50 A.M.

Shadows.

Everywhere she turned there were shadows.

She was walking through a city, she wasn't sure which one, and everyone around her was just a shadow. She couldn't see their faces, she couldn't see their bodies, she couldn't tell if they were men or women, young or old, all she knew was that everyone had turned into a shadow.

Pausing in front of a building, she wasn't exactly sure whether it was a shop or a business, maybe it was even a house, she caught sight of her reflection in the window. Or rather the lack of her reflection. It seemed that she too had morphed into a shadow.

Spinning in circles desperately seeking a real person, someone, anyone, she didn't care she just didn't want to be alone anymore.

Then she was running, as hard and fast as she could. She wasn't sure where she was going she just knew she had to hurry to get there.

As she ran the shadows chasing her began to slowly gain, getting closer and closer until their wispy black hands were grabbing at her trying to hold on, trying to pull her down, but she twisted and turned, managing to break free.

Next she was standing on a vast black landscape, there was not a tree or a building in sight, neither was there a single person, shadow or otherwise. The sun shone brightly from the black sky highlighting the fact that she was so completely and utterly alone. As her loneliness grew, the sun began to move towards her, coming slowly at first then quicker and quicker until she scrunched herself down onto the smooth black ground and waited for its impact.

When nothing came she blinked open her eyes to find herself

in bed, in a hospital room, and she remembered that she didn't remember anything.

She recalled waking up in the park with the horrible realization that she didn't know who she was or how she got there. She recalled waking again this time here at the hospital, there had been a doctor, a psychiatrist, there. The lady's name was Dr. Bennett and she had stayed with her all morning, her constant presence had become comforting, a sort of rock to cling to in the empty world her life had suddenly become. The psychiatrist had even stayed with her when the police had spoken with her, the woman's quietly encouraging demeanor had given her the strength to answer their questions.

Not that she really had much to tell them.

She liked the police detective who had asked her the questions. He had thick black hair, and glowing gold eyes that seemed to exude empathy and understanding. He had been patient and kind with her and he had given her something to hold on to; hope. She liked the idea of calling herself Hope, it wasn't her real name but it couldn't be any better than the name she'd been given at birth.

Climbing from the bed, Hope noticed that the psychiatrist was still there, dozing in a chair. Bypassing her Hope headed for the closed door that she assumed led to the bathroom. There was something she needed to do in there, and it wasn't using the facilities. She needed to see herself, needed to see what she looked like, maybe that would finally spark some sort of memory in her addled brain.

So far, she hadn't thought about the events that had led to her being here. Hadn't thought about her bandaged wrists or the cause of her headache, hadn't thought about who had caused them.

Flicking on the light inside the bathroom she pushed the door the rest of the way open and hovered there, wanting to go in but not sure how she would feel if she couldn't recognize her own face. Before she could change her mind Hope took a deep breath and jumped in front of the mirror. Golden curls framed the face that looked back at her, the skin was tanned, a dimple on the left cheek, and dark blue eyes that stared back hollowly.

It was a face she could have sworn she had never seen before.

It didn't raise even the smallest hint of familiarity.

Hope focused all her energy and stared at the mirror willing herself to remember something, anything.

"Is everything okay?"

Spinning around to see Dr. Bennett standing in the doorway studying her with dark brown eyes, her long chocolate colored hair was pulled back in a ponytail, her smooth olive skin marred only by a long snake of a scar that crossed her left cheek. Frustrated, Hope wondered why she could remember this woman's face and yet her own was like that of a stranger.

"Is everything okay?" Dr. Bennett repeated with an easy smile on her pretty face.

Earlier Hope had been too overwhelmed, too disconcerted at being so alone in the world that she didn't even have herself, to talk, but now she wanted answers. "Why can I remember your face but not my own?" She'd been hoping her voice might lead her to recall something, but once again, it may as well be a stranger's voice.

If Dr. Bennett was surprised to hear her talk she didn't show it. "Your brain wasn't damaged so it is capable of creating and retaining new memories."

"But not of recalling old ones," Hope couldn't stand to look at her face in the mirror any longer, and stormed past the psychiatrist back into the room, tucking herself back into bed.

Dr. Bennett took her time, turning off the bathroom light and closing the door before returning to her chair beside the bed. "Your memories will come back when you're ready," she said gently.

"You mean I've forgotten on purpose?" Hope asked.

"Not *on purpose*," Dr. Bennett clarified. "Your brain is trying to protect itself so it's locked away your memories, but they're still there somewhere, and when you're ready it'll come back to you."

"You think my brain is trying to protect me so it made me forget what happened?" Hope couldn't stop her gaze from falling to her bandaged wrists. "To forget who hurt me?"

"I think so," Dr. Bennett nodded.

"Then why can't I remember who I am?" she demanded. "If my brain is trying to protect me then I understand why I can't remember what happened, but why can't I remember who I am? How does that help me? It just leaves me all alone."

"I know it's hard but you're just going to have to be patient," the psychiatrist soothed, taking her hand and giving it a reassuring squeeze.

"Do you think that someone I know hurt me?" Hope's mind was spinning at a million miles an hour. "Do you think that's why I can't remember who I am? Because someone close to me is the one who hurt me?"

"Possibly," the doctor agreed with a look that told Hope the thought had already occurred to her.

"It's so frustrating," Hope moaned, pulling her hand free to ball them into fists. "I don't even know how old I am, or . . ."

"Late twenties to early thirties," Dr. Bennett inserted. "Sorry I can't be more specific."

Finding her anxiety ease a little at the knowledge of her approximate age, "thank you."

"And Detective Wyatt and Detective Bell are going through missing persons records right at this second, they're going to find out who you are," Dr. Bennett reclaimed her grip on Hope's hand.

"They were the detectives who were here before right?" she confirmed. When the doctor nodded Hope added, "they seemed nice."

"They are, and they're good at their jobs. They'll find who you are and they'll find who hurt you, you can be sure of that."

"Can I ask you a question?" Hope asked studying Dr. Bennett's beautiful face and warm, easy smile.

"Of course."

"How did you get that scar?"

The psychiatrist's eyes clouded over but her smile stayed in place, "I was attacked by a criminal I was interviewing," she answered shortly. Then with a sigh continued, "he was a sociopath, he wanted to escape from prison, he slashed my face to distract me and then stabbed me in the stomach. He never even made it from the room."

"You remember it?"

"Every horrible little detail," Dr. Bennett couldn't hide her shudder.

"But you got through it right?" Hope pushed. "I mean you're happy now right?"

Her face brightened into a huge smile, "yeah, I'm married and we just had our first child two months ago, a little girl, Lucia." Growing serious, "you'll get it all back, you'll remember who you are, we'll find your family, and one day this will all seem like just a horrible nightmare."

* * * * *

2:13 P.M.

Rubbing his tired eyes, Parker pushed the computer mouse away and turned to look at Wyatt, "I'm not finding anything, how about you?"

Turning away from his own computer, Wyatt sighed, "nothing. Not a thing. If someone's reported her missing, I'm not finding her file."

Leaning back in his chair and propping his feet up on his desk, "I think we're going to have to check missing person files from across the country," Parker replied. "If she was abducted it could have been from anywhere."

"It's going to take us hours to go through missing person reports for the entire country. And she might not have even been reported missing," Wyatt sounded tired and annoyed, like it was Parker's fault that they hadn't found anything.

Struggling to keep his own temper in check, he knew Wyatt wasn't really bothered that they hadn't found anything yet; neither of them had really expected to. His partner was still annoyed with him about the whole Tessa situation. "I know that," Parker replied, vowing to stick to the case and refuse to be drawn into another argument about how he was handling things with his wife, "but I don't think we have a choice. So far we have nothing to go on, no leads, no . . ." he trailed off as he saw Marty Jenkins the head of the crime scene unit enter the room.

Marty walked over to them, "hey, Parker, Wyatt, quite a case you two have got here."

"What's with your eyes?" Parker asked, frowning as the CSU tech blinked his eyes furiously. "And where are your glasses?"

"I got contacts," Marty replied, his fingers brushing at his cheeks.

"It doesn't look like it's going too well," Parker continued, amused by the scientist's obvious discomfort at his new contact lenses. "What possessed you to do that?" For as long as Parker had known Marty Jenkins the man had worn thick, black rimmed glasses, framing his serious grey eyes, and perched on a narrow, beaklike nose, Parker had always thought Marty looked like a thoughtful owl.

"I uh, um . . ." the usually incredibly rational Marty stammered.

Intrigued, "what's going on with you?" Parker asked.

"Uh, I uh, I . . . I met someone," Marty's pale cheeks flushed a deep red.

"A girl someone?" Wyatt joined the conversation.

Managing to turn an even darker shade of red, Marty nodded.

"Really? That's great," Parker beamed. Marty had been a

widower for close to twenty years, and for as long as he'd known him the CSU tech never dated, and as far as anyone knew didn't even have any hobbies outside of work. "What's her name?"

Clearing his throat, "her name's Rachel." Marty resumed rubbing at his eyes. "I met her at book club."

"How long have you been dating?" Wyatt asked.

"About a year."

"A year?" Parker exclaimed. "Why didn't you say anything?"

Shrugging uncomfortably, "after Kelly died I didn't think I'd ever want to meet anyone else, but then Rachel came along and I fought it for a while but she didn't give up and in the end I realized that loving Rachel doesn't mean that I stopped loving Kelly. Besides you always have enough drama going on I didn't want to add to it," Marty shot a pointed look his way.

Apparently Wyatt wasn't the only one with an opinion on the state of his marriage. Scowling at Marty, he didn't understand why everyone couldn't just leave well enough alone. "Do you have anything helpful for us related to the case?"

Rolling his eyes, "from the wounds on her wrists and ankles," Marty began, "I found a few rope fibers. I can try to match it to a specific type or brand of rope but I'm thinking that won't end up being too helpful."

"The doctors said she was suffering from dehydration and starvation, so maybe someone took her, tied her up and left her," Parker mused aloud.

"The doctors said it was hard to tell from her level of dehydration how long she's gone without water because it depends on the environment in which she was being kept," Wyatt added for Marty's benefit.

"Did you find anything else?" Parker queried.

"We found a couple of hairs on her clothes that didn't belong to her. We won't be able to get DNA off them but the hairs were brown and short and definitely human," Marty explained. "So I'm thinking probably male, and most likely from whoever tied her up.

The only thing we found under her fingernails were fibers from the ropes. There were no drugs in her system. And we didn't find anything else, no fibers or fingerprints on her clothes."

Scrutinizing the CSU tech, there was something he hadn't shared with them. "But . . .?"

"Well . . ." Marty paused and looked uncomfortable.

"What is it?" Parker prodded.

"They did a rape kit on her when she was admitted to the hospital . . ." again the scientist paused, his eyes looking anywhere but directly at them.

"And did they find anything useful?" he raised a hopeful eyebrow and tried not to think about whatever horrors Hope had been subjected to.

"They found something, but not DNA," Marty clarified.

"Well what was it?" Parker wanted to shake the answers out of him.

"They found traces of . . ."

"Of . . ." Parker prompted, waving a hand to speed him up.

"Traces of gunpowder residue," Marty finally finished.

He and Wyatt stared at the criminologist, dumbstruck.

"Gunpowder residue?" Parker wasn't sure he'd heard right. "Like from a gun?"

Marty nodded.

"She was raped with a gun?" Wyatt clarified disbelievingly.

Marty nodded again.

Parker rubbed his eyes wearily, he hated rape cases even more since he had found out the truth about what had happened to Tessa when she was a little girl, and it sounded like Hope and been put through hell by whoever had abducted her. "No wonder Hope can't remember . . ."

"Hope?" Marty interrupted, puzzled. "I thought the girl didn't remember anything. Did she remember her name?"

"No, she hasn't," he replied. "But we can't just call her Jane Doe."

Casting him a sympathetic look, "because of the whole John Doe thing," Marty nodded.

Hating that he was so obvious, "it gives her something to hold on to, something to make her feel more normal," Parker inserted.

Nodding understandingly, "I'll see what I can do on the rope," Marty told them. "Maybe we'll get lucky and your guy used something high end, something that's harder to buy."

"But you don't think that's likely?" Wyatt asked.

"We can always hope," Marty grinned as he started for the door.

"Hey, Marty," Parker called out.

Pausing, "yeah?"

"Congratulations, I'm really glad you found someone."

"Thanks," the criminologist's grin broadened before growing deadly serious, "and, Parker, call Tessa."

Bristling instantly, "why should I be the one to make the first move?" he demanded. He was so tired of everyone assuming that Tessa was always the victim, when she was the one causing all of their problems. She was the one continuing to shut him out and refusing to be honest with him.

"Because if you don't you're going to live to regret it."

* * * * *

11:26 P.M.

Tessa had hoped that a run might clear her head enough for her to be able to get at least a couple of hours sleep tonight.

Ever since she had witnessed her best friend's murder at the age of eleven and been forced to stab a man in order to escape she had had problems sleeping. As a child she would often creep into her big brother's room after he had fallen asleep to spend the night huddled on the floor at the end of the bed.

Her nightmares had eased a little after she and Parker got

together. They never completely went away, but his comforting presence in the bed beside her had sent her bad dreams ebbing to the back of her mind and her sleep. Now that Parker barely slept here anymore her nightmares had come raging back and she found herself unable to scrounge more than an hour or so of sleep per night.

Enjoying the cool night air on her face as she jogged. Tessa was a running fanatic, every day, rain, hail or shine she always made time for a run. Her obsession had begun when she was a teenager, already well and truly paranoid by then, with good reason, and at only five foot tall Tessa knew that to have any chance against an attacker she had to be fast and strong. Now at twenty-seven she still ran each day like clockwork and if something sprung up and prevented her from fulfilling her daily routine she found herself getting all scrunchy inside.

Circling through the back of the estate that had belonged to her paternal grandparents, and where she and Daniel had moved with their mother, Emilie, after their father walked out on them. Both Tessa and Daniel had hated living here with Emilie, who spent most of her time locked away in her room, and their grandparents, who were cold and distant and always far too busy at work to spend any time with their grandchildren. Following their deaths, Tessa had inherited the estate from her grandparents and had moved out here after college. Unable to face living in the enormous stone mansion on her own she had moved into the cozy little cottage nestled in the woods behind the main house. Tessa had lived there until the place was destroyed in a fire.

Fumbling for her keys as she jogged along the side of the mansion, as she rounded the corner she was surprised to see a car parked in the driveway. Her surprise quickly turning to annoyance when she realized whose car it was.

"Hey, goldilocks," Skylar Wyatt greeted her enthusiastically as she came up behind him at the mansion's huge oak doors.

"What are you doing here?" she returned, not in the mood for another lecture today about what she ought to do with Parker. And Skylar was even worse than Daniel because unlike anyone else he actually knew all the facts. Tessa had definitely lived to regret telling Skylar the complete truth about Isaac Worthington. Well that wasn't entirely true. Skylar had been unbelievably understanding and supportive even though he didn't agree with her, but him knowing also meant he could use it against her.

"Well that's a lovely greeting," Skylar grinned down at her.

"If you're here to pester me again then I'm really not interested," Tessa let herself inside and let the door fall closed behind her.

Skylar caught it before it fully closed and followed her through the enormous entry foyer and down through the corridors to the kitchen, one of the few rooms in the mansion they actually used.

"Parker didn't sleep here last night," Skylar continued undaunted.

"Thanks for pointing out the obvious," she jeered sarcastically. "What would I do without you?"

"Probably starve yourself to death," he shot back. "Have you eaten dinner yet?"

"I'm not hungry."

"You still need to eat," Skylar began to rummage through her refrigerator in search of something for dinner.

"It's too late for eating," she complained, knowing it was a losing battle.

Skylar said nothing, just found some leftover lasagne and set it in the microwave to heat, then poured two glasses of soda. When the meal was ready, he dished it up and set a plate down before her. "Eat," he commanded.

Reluctantly Tessa took a few mouthfuls, but all the meal did was serve to remind her that her homemade lasagne was Parker's favorite meal. "Did he get my message?" she asked after forcing down a couple of mouthfuls.

"About Winter?" Skylar asked, already he'd wolfed down three quarters of his portion.

"Parker promised he'd be with me when we told her." Then so it didn't sound like she was incapable of doing it on her own she added, "you know so that Winter can get all the support she needs."

"What's this?" Skylar picked up an envelope that had been lying on the table beside them.

"A letter," Tessa replied, not wanting to discuss it further.

"This is from Lachlan Mountain," Skylar pressed. "Is he still writing to you?"

"Occasionally," she replied reluctantly. "Usually I don't even open them."

"What's he saying to you?"

Shrugging, "the usual. He loves me, he's sorry he hurt me, one day he wants to make it up to me."

"Should I be worrying about this?" Skylar was studying her anxiously, the letter still in his hand.

"No," she assured him. "Like I said, usually I don't even open them." Pausing, "Parker used to go through the mail, throw them out, but he's not here now, and I had already started reading it before I realized what it was."

Quickly getting frustrated, "I don't understand why you won't just tell him about Isaac," Skylar set his fork down.

"Shh," she hissed, looking around to check that no one was around to overhear. "The others are home, and I've already told you why I won't tell Parker." In fact she'd told him about a million times.

"I know, I know," Skylar scowled, "because he won't be able to let Isaac go, he'll hunt him down and you can't let that happen."

"Just let it go, Skylar," Tessa pleaded, she was tired, hopefully tired enough to sleep for more than a couple of hours, but if Skylar got her all worked up she'd be lucky to get any sleep at all.

"I can't let it go, Tessa," he said softly. "I'm worried about you out here all alone."

"I'm hardly alone," she retorted, "Daniel, Matilda and Winter are all here with me."

"You know what I mean, and I'm not the only one who's worried about you."

"You mean you're not the only one who's sticking their nose into my business."

"Casey said that she can hardly convince you to go out anymore," Skylar continued reproachfully. "She keeps inviting you over to our house for dinner or to go out shopping but you keep refusing. She said the only time she gets to see you is if she comes out here."

"That's not true, I go out," Tessa contradicted, although he wasn't far off, she had basically shut herself back up here on the estate just like she had before.

"You're being stubborn," he groaned. "For goodness sake just tell Parker about how Isaac saw you kill Jake and let you go, how you felt sorry for him and how he helped you with Dylan and kept Dino from killing you."

"I won't tell him, Skylar, he doesn't need to know any of that and I won't have him with me for any other reason than because he wants to be. You promised me you wouldn't tell him."

"I want *you* to tell him the truth," Skylar repeated.

"You promised," Tessa almost begged.

"Alright, alright," Skylar surrendered, "I won't say anything, but maybe it would help things if you weren't so stubborn about everything all the time. You can't live in Parker's house after what Lachlan did to you there, he can't live here at your house because of everything that happened here, why can't you two just buy a *new* house?"

"Because it's gone beyond that now," she replied. Things hadn't gone downhill immediately after Dino shot Parker, he'd been angry because he thought that she had gone off on her own after a killer once again, but at first their arguments had almost exclusively revolved about their living arrangements. Around Christmas they'd had a brief period of peace when Parker had found out, exactly how she wasn't sure, that she had been forced to go with Dino at gunpoint after he threatened two innocent children. The respite from their arguing had soon ended when he realized that she had deliberately let John Doe, aka Isaac Worthington, get away. After that things had quickly gotten worse, Parker had refused to stay in her mansion a second longer and their arguments had grown to the point where they couldn't spend two minutes in the same room together without finding something to bicker about.

"I'm really tired, Skylar," she announced. "I think I'm just going to head up to bed."

"Okay," Skylar looked concerned but decided not to disagree. "You go up, I'll tidy up down here."

"Thanks, Skylar," she darted out of his reach as he tried to grasp her hand. He reluctantly let her go and she weaved through the house to the room that she had used as a child. When she and Parker had first moved in here they had used one of the many spare rooms, but when he had left she had gone straight back to her old bedroom.

Tessa wasn't sure exactly what had possessed her to move back into the room she had hated as a little girl. Maybe it was to punish herself. She had known that if she got involved with Parker he would only get hurt, and he had ended up being shot. She had allowed Parker, against her better judgment, to convince her that things could be different, but it was starting to look like they were going to turn out exactly as she had been afraid that they would.

FEBRUARY 10TH

1:09 A.M.

Walking through the hospital's halls made him think of Tessa.

Of dragging her out of her burning cottage, then sitting all night in the hospital waiting to talk to her, just days after they met. Of finding her bleeding to death on the hospital floor after she was shot. Of the miscarriage. And the car accident. Of every time he had been scared to death that he was about to lose her. Parker wasn't sure he could do it anymore.

Reaching the nurses station he recognized the nurse from earlier and flashed her his identification. "Hi, I'm Detective Bell. I was here earlier, I'm working on the Jane Doe case. Is Beth still here?"

"No sir. Dr. Bennett was here most of the day, but she left about an hour ago to go home and spend some time with the baby. I can page her if you want."

"No, that's okay. No need to bother her. I'm gonna go sit with Hope for awhile."

"Hope. That's a pretty name."

"She's a pretty girl. How's she doing? Has she said anything yet?"

The nurse smiled, "yes she started speaking after you left this morning. Dr. Bennett spent the afternoon talking with her, trying to help her come to terms with things. Dr. Bennett was going to call you before she left, but when she saw how late it was she decided to wait till the morning. I think she thought you'd be home with your wife by now."

Catching the pointed stare the nurse gave him Parker

wondered if Elisabeth had said something to her about the state of his marriage or whether the nurse was just making a general comment about the fact that a husband should be home, in bed with his wife, at one in the morning.

Deciding it was just his guilt talking.

Elisabeth would have no reason to talk to one of the nurses about his marriage. He was just feeling bad about ignoring Tessa's calls earlier. He had got her message though. About the talk they needed to have with Winter. And no matter how strained things were between Tessa and himself there was nothing that would prevent him from being there for his niece. Or his wife. He knew how hard this was going to be for Tessa.

"Is everything okay?"

Realizing he'd zoned out for a minute, Parker gave the nurse a smile, "fine. Thanks."

Heading towards Hope's room, he made sure his gun was safely tucked away beneath his sweater, and couldn't help but shudder as he thought of what had happened to Hope. Quietly edging open the door he saw that Hope was fast asleep in the bed, golden curls spilling out across the pillow, catching the light from the lamp and glimmering like waves at sunset.

Walking slowly towards the bed, careful not to make a sound, the girl needed to rest and he didn't want to disturb her. Taking a seat beside the bed, he gently lifted her hand, it felt small and frail and vulnerable. Just like Hope.

As he watched her sleep, Parker wondered what it would be like to wake up one day with no memory of your past. He could only guess at how terrifying it must be. At how alone Hope must feel. It wasn't even like getting her memory back was going to make everything better . . .

Suddenly Hope's eyes sprang open, her breath came in quick gasps, her hands flailed as if to fight off an attacker.

Grabbing her forearms, "hey, hey," he soothed. "It's okay. You're safe now. You're in the hospital, you're safe."

Hope stopped fighting him but her eyes were still panicked, her breathing labored.

"Look at me, look at me," he held her face in his hands. "It's Detective Bell, you're safe now, everything's going to be okay." As her eyes looked into his, her breathing slowly began to return to normal, and he felt her relax in his grip. Setting her back against the pillows he asked, "you have a nightmare?" His own recurring bad dream had made a resurgence since he had moved out of Tessa's house. Probably his mind's way of reminding him just how much his life had changed since meeting Tess.

She nodded.

"Can you remember what it was about?"

A shake of her head.

"That's okay. Your memory *will* come back, you just have to believe that."

She studied him closely, as though evaluating the reliability of his words, then nodded slowly.

Parker smiled at her reassuringly, "get some rest."

Lifting her hand she placed it over his, "please don't leave me," she begged softly.

"I'm not going anywhere. I'm going to stay right here with you," he promised. He had made that exact same vow to Tessa after she had shot Dylan Riley, and he'd repeated it time after time in those first few months when he was trying to convince her to trust him, but in the end he had left her when things got tough. Attempting to assuage his guilt he convinced himself that he hadn't abandoned Tessa, he was simply giving her some space, waiting for her to learn to trust him.

Smiling back at him gratefully, "where's Dr. Bennett?" Hope asked.

"She had to go home."

"To see her baby?"

Parker nodded, "she told you about her daughter?"

"We talked for hours, about all kinds of stuff," Hope replied.

"It was really nice." Giving him a wry smile, "I may not know anything about my own life but I know plenty about Dr. Bennett's."

Amazed by the girl's strength, that she could still have a sense of humor after everything she'd been through was truly incredible.

"Anyway Dr. Bennett didn't tell me anything about you," Hope continued, watching him inquisitively, "tell me about your family."

"Well," Parker began, "I have a twin sister, Matilda. Our biological mother was a drug addict who lost custody of us when we were babies, and we never knew our father. Mattie and I lived in foster care until we were ten when we were adopted by a wonderful couple, Luka and Laura Bell."

"And you're married right?" Hope's eyes dipped to his wedding ring.

"Uh, right," he nodded, convincing himself that the fact he hadn't mentioned that to Hope didn't mean anything. "Her name's Tessa." Saved from having to add more when his cell phone began to trill, glancing at it he saw Elisabeth's name on the screen. "I have to take this," he told Hope who nodded. Ducking from the room he answered, "hey, Beth, what's up?"

"Sorry to ring so late, I hope I didn't wake Tessa," she apologized.

"Actually, I'm not at home," he told her. "I'm at the hospital."

"Parker," Elisabeth exclaimed, "how are you planning on fixing things with your wife when you spend all your time avoiding her?"

"I'm not really in the mood for a lecture," Parker stifled a yawn. "What did you want?"

Sighing irritably, "I didn't want you to worry about Hope. It was late when I left so I was going to call you in the morning, but then I thought you'd probably spend the night stressing about her so I thought I'd call and let you know that she started speaking."

"I wasn't planning on staying here," Parker was so sick of

feeling the need to be constantly defending himself. "I just came to check on her. She's been through a lot, I didn't want her to be alone."

"You mean like Tessa is?"

Angering, "Tessa's not alone she has Daniel and Winter and Matilda with her, Hope has no one."

"I asked you Parker, before you started on your quest to learn what happened to Tessa and Eleanor, I asked you if you could handle it no matter what you found and you told me you could. Well you got your answers, you pushed Tessa to relive the worst thing that ever happened to her and then you just up and left . . ."

"I didn't up and leave," he interrupted.

"How long has it been since you spent the night at home?"

"That mansion is not my home."

"You know what I mean. Days? Weeks? Months?"

"If Tessa would just tell me who John Doe is and why she's prepared to put everything on the line for him, then we could work things out." Changing the subject, "did you get a copy of Marty's report?"

"Yeah I did."

Parker could hear the cringe in Elisabeth's voice. "We'll find him, Beth," he assured her, "we'll find the man who did this."

After a long pause Elisabeth replied, "just don't let it be at the expense of everything you love," then she was gone.

He stood for a long moment, phone in hand, thinking about Elisabeth's warning. Parker didn't see any way that catching the man who had abducted Hope, tied her up and raped her could affect his relationship with Tessa.

Re-entering Hope's room he saw that the young woman had drifted back off to sleep, her hands tucked beneath her cheek, her mouth forming a small o, leaving her looking vulnerable and helpless. Settling into the chair beside the bed he gazed tenderly at Hope, and knew that he couldn't rest until he found out who had hurt her.

* * * * *

6:12 A.M.

Anastasia Vinciozo was beginning to seriously wish she had forbidden her boyfriend from bringing his dog with him when he had moved in with her six weeks ago. Already the dog had chewed all her table legs, dug up her backyard, tracked mud across her carpet, and destroyed two of her favorite sweaters. Not to mention the fact that since Frankie was almost always at work she ended up being the one who fed the dog and took it for its daily walks. Hence the reason she was out at six in the morning, being dragged along by the enormous Great Dane, as the icy wind curled it's way though her jacket to stab at her skin.

If she was honest though, Anastasia had to admit that GD, Frankie's idea of a joke to name his Great Dane, Great Dane, was starting to grow on her. She liked the way after dinner when she was watching TV he would come and rest his head on her knee, looking up at her with soulful brown eyes. Still she would like GD a whole lot better if he actually walked while on a walk instead of stopping every couple of steps to sniff around.

Still as sweetly irritating as the enormous dog was, Anastasia was infinitely happy that she finally bit the bullet and asked his owner to move in. After three failed serious relationships Anastasia had sworn off men, decided that she was happy to live out the rest of her years alone, convinced herself that marriage wasn't all it was cracked up to be, and attempted to move on with her life.

Then one night while out with a couple of her girlfriends she met Frankie Haber. Her friends had ditched her when they met up with a couple of cute guys. Still on her anti-dating kick she had refused to go with them, she had remained at the restaurant for one last drink when she had literally bumped into Frankie on the way to the ladies room. He'd struck up a conversation and despite her best efforts by the end of the evening she was smitten. From there things had gone from good, to better, to absolutely perfect, and then taking a big gamble she had asked him to move in with her.

Frankie had been surprised at first but had readily agreed, and within a week he had packed his stuff and settled in. It was like the two of them were made for each other, they seemed to meld together immediately, quickly learning each other's quirks and habits.

Hurrying the dog along, Frankie was due home from an overnight business trip at four this afternoon and Anastasia had a lot to do to prepare the romantic dinner she had been planning. Tugging on the leash to try and get GD to go faster but the dog was as big as a small horse and pulled her in the opposite direction when it picked up an interesting smell. GD paused at the top of a narrow set of stairs that led down to what Anastasia assumed was a basement apartment. Yanking on his leash to get him to move, the dog refused, steadfastly standing his ground.

"Come on, GD, it's cold and I've got things to do today," she sighed irritably.

Instead of obeying her command the dog lunged down the steps, pulling his leash right out of her hand, and began to paw at the door.

Uttering another irritated sigh, Anastasia trudged down the stairs after the dog. Just as she reached him he managed to push the door open and dart inside.

"Hello?" Anastasia called out to the occupants of the apartment. "I'm sorry about my dog. Your door mustn't have been properly closed."

Awaiting a reply, when she didn't get one she assumed the place was empty and pushed the door the rest of the way open and entered. Her breath caught in her throat as she surveyed the deserted room.

Someone had erected a metal pole that ran from floor to ceiling by the wall closest to the door, a pile of ropes lay beside it. Not far away sat a bottle of water and a plate of chocolate cake, of which GD was now wolfing into. A pair of shoes had been discarded in the middle of the empty room and a woman's jacket lay at her feet.

Before she realized what she was doing Anastasia was bending to retrieve the mauve jacket, as she turned it over she saw that is was streaked with blood. Dropping it quickly as though it were on fire, Anastasia realized that something terrible had happened in this room.

"GD, come," she called in a shaking voice.

The dog lifted a chocolate smeared face to look at her but was reluctant to leave its treat.

"Come," she repeated, her voice taking on a shrill, almost hysterical, quality.

This time the dog obediently left the chocolate cake to cross the room to her side. When he got close enough, she threw her arms around him, enjoying the safe, solid feel of the animal. Anastasia was reaching for her cell phone when she heard a shuffling noise behind her, turning around she let out an ear-piercing scream.

* * * * *

8:32 A.M.

The second morning in a row that they'd been out in the early morning chill. As he and Wyatt crossed the street, Parker hoped that this place would give them the answers they were looking for. Marty and his crime scene techs were already here and buzzing about. A couple of police cars were parked in the usually quiet street. And over in the corner stood a dazed woman with the biggest Great Dane Parker had ever seen, the top of it's head reaching to it's owner's shoulders.

He'd still been at the hospital when Wyatt had arrived to pick him up, and from the disapproving frown his partner gave him, Parker guessed that Wyatt and Elisabeth had been talking about him. Hope hadn't stirred during the night and he had managed to get a couple of hours of uninterrupted, dreamless sleep. When Wyatt had shown up, he had explained that someone had stumbled upon an apartment where Hope may have been attacked.

"You want to start with the girl?" he asked.

"Whatever you want," Wyatt answered shortly. On the way over here his partner had been tightly restrained, barely uttering a word, and Parker realized just how worked up about the situation between Tessa and him Wyatt actually was.

"Wyatt, I didn't deliberately not go home last night," he started to explain.

"You and that wife of yours are the most infuriating people on the planet," Wyatt complained.

Catching on, "you visited Tess last night huh." Parker couldn't quite hide his smirk, at least he wasn't the only one being harassed, it seemed like their friends were just as busy pestering Tessa as they were him.

Wyatt simply glared.

Growing serious, "you know I love Tessa, I'm not trying to hurt her, Wyatt."

"But you are," Wyatt turned his back and approached the young woman who was waiting nervously with the huge dog. "Hi Miss . . ."

"Vinciozo," the woman supplied, looking at them with round hazel eyes, "Anastasia. Was someone hurt in there? There was blood on the jacket and ropes on the floor."

"Miss Vinciozo, I'm Detective Wyatt and this is my partner Detective Bell," Wyatt made the introductions, ignoring the woman's questions for the time being. "Can you tell us what you saw when you got here?"

"I'm really sorry," the young woman began in a rush, trying to smooth down her frizzy blonde hair, which formed a fuzzy halo around her head. "I couldn't stop him, he ate all the chocolate cake, that's bad right? For your CSI people? I couldn't stop him, chocolate cake's Frankie's favorite so GD loves it too."

"Who's Frankie?" Parker asked.

"My boyfriend, this is his dog," the edgy woman answered. "I couldn't stop him," she repeated for the third time.

"What did you notice when you first got there?" Wyatt tried to focus her.

Taking a deep, steadying breath Anastasia Vinciozo began, "we were on our way home when GD started pulling me in the opposite direction," she absently patted the dog's head as she spoke, the giant creature leaning into her. "He stopped at the top of the steps. I tried to get him to leave but he's too strong and he pulled away from me and ran down to the door. I went after him but he got the door open, I guess it wasn't closed, and by the time I followed him down he was already inside. I called out in case someone was in there but when no one answered I went in to get GD, he was eating the cake . . ."

"Do you know it the cake was whole or if anyone had eaten any of it before your dog got to it?" Wyatt interjected.

Shaking her head, "DG was already well into it by the time I entered the apartment."

"What did you see when you did go in?" Parker asked.

"Well," Anastasia Vinciozo brushed hesitantly at her face, a face in which there were so many freckles it was hard to see any skin between them. "I saw the ropes first, they were lying on the floor at the base of that metal pipe. Then I saw the water and the cake that DG was eating. The shoes were on the floor near the jacket, it had blood on it, I picked it up, I'm sorry I wasn't thinking . . ." her apologetic eyes bounced backwards and forwards between the two of them.

While it was a minor setback from a forensics standpoint, Marty had already collected fingerprint and hair samples from the woman to eliminate anything she had left behind from anything their potential abductor may have left behind. "Don't worry about it," Parker assured her. "Did you notice anyone hanging around outside?"

"No, but when I was inside I thought for a second I wasn't alone. I heard a noise behind me but when I turned it was only some rats," Anastasia shivered at the recollection.

"But no one out here?" Wyatt confirmed.

"No one, we don't usually see anyone when we're on our walks, it's too early and too cold for most people. We're only out because this one's so big he tears the house apart if he doesn't get his walk," she stroked the dog's head fondly.

The huge animal looked up at Anastasia with doting eyes that reminded Parker of the way Tessa's dogs gazed at her with such open adoration. Despite the fact that Ladybug, a Dalmatian, and Buttercup, a golden retriever, had known him for over two years they still treated him with wary contempt, cautiously observing his every move to determine whether he would hurt their beloved Tessa.

"Do you often walk this way?" Wyatt continued.

Shrugging, "sometimes, it depends whether I walk mornings or nights."

"Have you walked this route in the last couple of days?"

Thinking for a moment, "yesterday morning, and then day two days before that," she answered.

"And you don't remember anything suspicious on either of those times?" Parker asked, wondering if she had seen either Hope or the person who had abducted her.

"Nothing out of the ordinary. Can I go home now?" Anastasia looked tired, and stressed, and edgy.

"Sure," Parker nodded, "take my card and call us if you think of anything."

Looking infinitely relieved Anastasia Vinciozo snatched the card, shoved it into her pocket and began to tug her dog in the direction of her house. Once she was gone, Wyatt started down towards the basement apartment, Parker tagged along behind him.

"Marty, can we come in?" his partner called when they reached the closed door, which had once been painted blue but now what paint remained was so faded it was almost white.

Seconds later the door sprung open and Marty peeped out at them, "sure, we're pretty much finished up in here," he held the door open for them to enter.

"You find anything in here?" Parker asked as he surveyed the room.

"Some fingerprints and hairs, we'll have to compare them to Hope's and Ms Vinciozo's but maybe we'll get lucky and some are from our kidnapper," Marty told them eagerly.

Marty and the other crime scene techs had already collected and bagged the ropes, water bottle, the plate with what was left of the chocolate cake, the shoes and the blood stained jacket. "Are we sure the jacket is Hope's?" he asked.

"It matched the skirt she was wearing," Marty replied, "same color, size and label."

Nodding as his eyes once again roved the dark, dank room. The windows were boarded up, the carpet had been ripped out and piled in a corner, the small kitchenette was missing its oven and dishwasher only the shelves and cupboards and sink remained.

Following his gaze, "the tap was dripping when we got here," Marty told him.

"Anastasia Vinciozo didn't mention that," Wyatt frowned.

"She was probably too freaked out about what she stumbled onto," Marty supplied. "This room is creepy."

"You think he did it on purpose?" Parker asked. "Left it on to torture her?"

"Maybe," Marty's narrow face growing serious. "If he did leave her tied to the pole, then the water and the cake would have been left just out of reach," moving around the room to demonstrate.

"So someone raped her and tied her up in here and then left her to die with the dripping tap to drive her crazy and the one thing she needed to live in front of her but out of reach," Parker mused, wondering what kind of deranged mind would do that to another human being.

* * * * *

2:45 P.M.

"Hi, Elisabeth," Tessa greeted the psychiatrist who was hovering by the nurses station. "How's Lucia?"

Narrowing her eyes, "what's wrong?" Elisabeth demanded.

Frowning innocently, "I don't know what you're talking about."

"I think you do," Elisabeth continued to eye her warily. "You never call my daughter by her name, you usually just ask how the baby is. And you never usually voluntarily start conversations with me since you hate psychiatrists."

"I talk to you," Tessa contradicted, she just found it hard to talk about and be around Elisabeth's little daughter since if she hadn't suffered a miscarriage her own child would be about Lucia's age. Elisabeth was right on the money though about her feelings for psychiatrists. Tessa had hated them ever since her grandparents had sent her to see one following Ellie's murder. They hadn't helped her then and neither had they helped her mother, who had been in a psychiatric hospital for the last fifteen years. In Tessa's opinion psychiatrists were full of talk but seriously lacking in action. However, even though she wouldn't admit it Elisabeth Bennett was starting to grow on her.

"You know Parker spent the night here at the hospital."

"Gee, Dr. Bennett, thanks for stating the obvious," she

snapped sarcastically. "How would I have ever figured that out without you?"

"Tessa," Elisabeth began with a pitying look that made Tessa feel very uncomfortable.

"Look I don't want to hear another spiel about how Parker and I are making a huge mistake and we're being childish and stubborn and blah, blah, blah. The bottom line is Parker wants something I can't give him."

"Can't or won't?"

"I'm really not in the mood for your psychological, semantic word games. Parker shouldn't have to know every little detail about my life for the two of us to be together. Besides, I don't see why everyone is lecturing me. Parker's the one who walked out on *me*. I'm still living in our house, he's the one who can come up with every excuse under the sun not to come home. Honestly between you and Daniel and Matilda and Casey and Skylar I am so sick of hearing what I 'ought' to be doing."

Raising an eyebrow, "Wyatt knows doesn't he?" Elisabeth demanded.

Blinking in surprise at the perceptiveness of the psychiatrist, maybe she hadn't given Elisabeth enough credit. "He was there the night Dino shot Parker. I was a mess, I needed to tell someone and Skylar was there."

"Tessa," Elisabeth started gently, "is keeping your secret about John Doe really worth risking things with Parker? Is it really worth losing him?"

Before she had a chance to protest and reiterate her rationale she caught sight of Parker and Skylar coming down the corridor, her husband slowed down when he noticed her.

"Skylar, Parker," Tessa greeted them when the two men finally joined her and Elisabeth.

"Hey, goldilocks," Skylar gave her a hug.

"Hi, Tess," Parker shot her an awkward grin as he gave her a quick kiss on the lips. "Sorry I didn't make it home last night."

"Oh never mind," she smiled indifferently. "You come home so infrequently these days it's a wonder I still remember what you look like," she couldn't help adding. "Elisabeth and I have just been having a great chat," Tessa goaded and was pleased when Parker's head swiveled to stare at Elisabeth, trying to gauge what had been said about him behind his back.

Parker had once shared her opinion about the pointlessness of the psychiatric profession but a couple of years ago he had been put in the situation where he had had to shoot an insane teenager in order to save his own life. During his mandated counseling sessions with Elisabeth he had been surprised to find that talking to her actually helped. So ever since they'd met Parker had been pressuring her to talk about her issues, as he called them, with Elisabeth.

"No need to stress, Parker," she smiled sweetly at her husband. "I didn't come here to see you, I actually came to meet your new best friend."

"You came to see Hope?" her husband's head snapped from Elisabeth to her. "Why?"

"Well I wanted to meet your new project," Tessa knew she was being childish but ploughed ahead anyway. "First there was Gina O'Hara, and we all know what a disaster that turned out to be. Then there was me, I guess the jury's still out on that one. Then there was Lila Abbott, which got interrupted thanks to Lachlan Mountain. And now you're onto the mysterious Hope," she finished with a huff.

"Feel better?" Elisabeth asked as Skylar and Parker stared at her in disbelief, since she rarely lost control of her emotions.

"Actually, yes," she confirmed then turned on her heel and entered the hospital room containing the next woman her husband was desperate to save. As she walked inside she got the distinct impression that the girl in the bed had just moments before been listening intently to the conversations happening just outside her door. While Parker, Skylar and Elisabeth trailed her into the room, she studied the pretty young woman. Between her golden curls and big dark blue eyes, Tessa could see why Parker was enamored with her, but looking into those eyes Tessa found herself instantly on edge. Amnesia was rare and easy to fake and even though she couldn't think of a good reason for this girl to pretend she didn't know who she was, Tessa's natural paranoid instinct was kicked into high gear.

"Hope, this is Tessa," Elisabeth sat on the edge of the bed beside the young woman and took her hand.

"Your wife?" Hope looked to Parker who nodded in confirmation. "Nice to meet you, Tessa, I'm . . . I'm . . . I guess I'm Hope."

Taking the hand the woman offered, Tessa wondered why she wasn't more concerned with the fact that she had no memories. "Nice to meet you too, Parker told you about me, huh?"

"Last night he was telling me about his family." Hope stared at Parker adoringly before ripping her gaze away to smile at Tessa, "thanks for letting him stay here with me last night. It was really wonderful not to wake up alone."

"Yes, it is awful to be alone," she smiled back, sensing Parker's uncomfortable squirm. "So you really don't remember anything? Your name, your family, where you're from? Nothing?"

"Dr. Bennett says it's because my brain is trying to protect me," Hope explained.

"Does she now?" Tessa was a little freaked out about the physical similarities between herself and this woman, and wondered whether that had anything to do with Parker's attraction to her. "So you don't have a clue what happened to you?"

"Tessa, can I talk to you outside for a second?" Parker interrupted before Hope had a chance to respond.

"Of course," she smiled sweetly at her husband. "Nice meeting you, Hope. I hope you get your memory back soon."

"Yeah, it was nice meeting you too. See you later," Hope

continued to smile.

"I'm sure you will see me later," Tessa returned as Parker got hold of her elbow and quickly maneuvered her out the door.

"What do you think you're doing?" he hissed.

"What do I think I'm doing," she repeated. "What do *you* think *you're* doing? Every time some pretty young woman who needs saving comes along you stop thinking with your head."

"Come here," Parker grabbed her arm and tried to pull her down the hall.

"Get your hands off me," she shrugged out of his grip.

With a frustrated growl, Parker picked her up, threw her over his shoulder and marched down the corridor, ignoring the shocked stares of nurses and patients.

"Put me down," she beat her fists against his back.

Finding an empty room Parker set her down inside and slammed the door behind them. "You are impossible," he snapped.

"That woman does not have amnesia," Tessa told him.

"How could you possibly know what's going on inside her head?"

"Exactly. You have only her word that she doesn't remember anything about herself or what happened to her. You've got your blinders on. Do you want this to turn out like the Gina O'Hara case? Where you end up making a mess of things because you don't want to see the truth?"

Parker flinched at the mention of Gina O'Hara, the insane teenager who murdered her father and framed her boyfriend and, had Parker not shot her, would have killed her newborn daughter and Parker. "You're the one who has a problem with the truth," he retorted.

Widening her eyes in disbelief, "how exactly do I have a problem with the truth? I told you everything that you wanted to know. I told you about Jake and Ellie and then once you got what you wanted out of me you just left. You were the one who brought everything back up. Everything that I'd worked so hard to forget. You brought it all up and then you just dumped me and left me to deal with everything on my own," frustratingly tears were pricking the backs of her eyes.

"I'm sorry," Parker's face softened and he took a hesitant step towards her. "I haven't left you. I'm still right here and I want to help you. If you would just tell me who John Doe is then we can put an end to this once and for all."

"And we're right back where we started," Tessa moved herself out of Parker's reach. "Why is it so important that you know who he is?"

"Why?" this time Parker's eyes widened in disbelief. "Because this man kidnapped little girls and sold them to pedophiles. Because this man kidnapped *you* and would have sold *you* to a pedophile if you hadn't escaped."

"I'm not having this conversation again," Tessa didn't want to think about Isaac right now, rubbing at her temples where a headache was pounding.

"You have a headache," Parker pronounced flatly. "I bet you haven't been eating or sleeping."

Shrugging in response, they both knew she never took good care of herself.

"You meant to kill him that night didn't you?" Parker asked suddenly.

"Who?" she queried although she already had an inkling as to where this conversation was heading.

"Dylan Riley, the night that he broke your arm, the night that Tanner was conceived, the night you tried to stab him to death," Parker was watching her with a sort of morbid curiosity.

"I had a raging fever," she reminded him. "I was delirious, I didn't know what I was doing. I don't even remember that night," she answered honestly, the whole evening was a blur. All she had known was that as long as Dylan was there none of them were ever going to be safe. "Why are you asking about that now?"

"It's that man's fault, that John Doe," Parker looked like he remained unconvinced. "I don't know why you want to protect him."

"I don't want to talk about that again," she repeated tiredly. Between Parker barking that at her every time they were in the same room, and Skylar badgering her constantly, she would be happy if she never had to hear about Isaac again.

"Fine," Parker sighed long-sufferingly. "I have to go talk to Hope anyway, we found the place where we think that she was tied up and held." Freezing at the door, "Tessa," he said gently now, "go home, eat something, and try to get some rest."

Before he went through the door she gave it one last shot to convince him to be wary of Hope, "she smiles too much for a girl with no memory." As the door thudded shut behind her husband she muttered, "be careful, Parker, please be careful."

* * * * *

6:29 P.M.

"Come on people, lets get started."

The assembled group quietened immediately as J.J. lumbered into the room and took a seat at the top of the table. The huge man looked the worse for wear after a long day, his thick brown hair stood out wildly, his beard was a mess and his eyes were bloodshot. J.J. was in his late fifties, had been a police officer his entire adult life and despite the stresses of his job he remained a family man, completely dedicated to his wife of thirty-five years, their four children and fourteen grandchildren. At close to seven feet tall and weighing in at three hundred pounds J.J. could be an intimidating character, especially when his famous unpredictable temper was in full swing. But, as Parker had seen on numerous occasions, he had a softer side that came out when he was dealing with his family, friends and victims.

"Okay, Marty, you start," J.J. commanded.

It had been a long day for him too and Parker was struggling to keep his focus on what was happening. His thoughts kept drifting back to his argument with Tessa at the hospital. Perceptive as always Tessa had known just what to say to hurt him and the comment about Gina O'Hara certainly had. Not that anything she had said was untrue. He *had* been blinded by the teenager's act, and he *had* wanted to save her, and it *had* almost all ended in disaster, but there had been no need for Tessa to bring it up. Still as frustrated as he was with her, he was almost equally as concerned. His wife had looked pale and tired, and he made a mental note to ask Matilda to make sure Tessa was eating enough and getting enough sleep.

"We found short brown hairs on the clothes Hope was wearing when she was found," Marty's voice finally shoving thoughts of Tessa from his mind. "They could be from whoever abducted her or from a friend or family member."

"And you can't get DNA?" J.J. boomed, dragging his fingers through his bushy beard.

"No, but assuming that the hairs are from the man who abducted Hope then at least you know he's a brunette. We found more at the apartment. First off, the jacket matched the skirt Hope was wearing, we're waiting for DNA confirmation on the blood and the sweat but blood type matches Hope's. There wasn't a lot of blood on the jacket so it most likely came from the split lip and bump on the head. And that's where the good news ends I'm afraid . . ."

"What do you mean?" J.J. demanded.

"Well if you weren't always interrupting me you would have heard what I was about to say," Marty gave J.J. a reproachful frown. "We found fingerprints and hairs in the apartment but so far everything looks like it belongs to Hope, her fingerprints are all over the place."

"All over the place?" J.J. repeated. "So not just on the pole where the ropes were found?"

"Light switch, benches, walls," Marty expanded.

"But nothing to identify the abductor?" Parker roused himself enough to ask.

"No," Marty confirmed. "And nothing to indicate he raped her there either. Nothing to say he didn't but I think he did it somewhere else before taking her there."

"And the girl still doesn't remember anything?" J.J. drummed his massive fingers on the table as he directed his question at Elisabeth.

"No, she still doesn't remember a thing," Elisabeth confirmed.

"We spent all afternoon with her, trying to prompt her memory with what we found at the apartment, but it didn't help," Parker explained, remembering the lost and helpless glint in Hope's eyes when she still couldn't remember anything.

"Is she faking?" J.J. asked.

"I don't think so," Elisabeth shook her head thoughtfully.

"She really has no idea who she is or what happened to her?" J.J. continued to look doubtful.

"It's possible following a traumatic event," Elisabeth told him.

"But not common," J.J. pushed.

"Amnesia's very rare," Elisabeth agreed.

"Okay, lets say she really is suffering from amnesia, when's she going to get her memory back?" patience was not one of J.J.'s strong suits.

"There's no specific timeline for things like this J.J.," Elisabeth reminded him.

"What about the owner of the building?" J.J.'s attention swiveled to him and Wyatt.

"The owner is a fifty-eight year old overweight man. He lives on the first floor and doesn't look like he's stepped foot outside his apartment in years," Wyatt responded.

"It didn't look like he'd showered in years either," Parker added, he still couldn't get the stench from the putrid apartment out of his nostrils. "I can't see him having anything to do with this. He said the owner of the basement apartment was his ninety-year-old aunt who passed away fifteen months ago. The place has sat there empty ever since because he can't be bothered going through the hassle of finding a new tenant. And there was no coat or scarf or gloves or anything in the apartment?" Parker directed his question to Marty.

"Nothing," Marty responded. "Which is odd considering the time of year. Maybe the abductor took them with him?"

"What I can't figure out is how she got free," Wyatt spoke up.

Parker could tell his partner was still mad at him, because Wyatt had taken a seat at the furthest end of the table. That suited Parker just fine since Wyatt wasn't his favorite person in the world right now either. At the moment it was his partner's ability to look calm and tidy after a long day that was annoying him. Every one of Wyatt's sandy blonde hairs was in place, there wasn't a wrinkle in sight on his white shirt or grey suit, and his emerald green eyes were clear and focused. In contrast Parker knew he was a mess. After a night spent sleeping in a chair his clothes were rumpled, and his black hair was a wild, woolly disaster. When he wasn't irritated with him, Wyatt usually brought him a clean change of clothes if he hadn't gotten home.

"The ropes weren't cut, right?" Wyatt looked to Marty for confirmation. When the crime scene tech nodded he continued, "and there were no cuts on her fingertips to suggest that she sawed through the ropes right?"

Parker couldn't help but remember finding Tessa just after she'd accidentally shot Dylan Riley. The psychotic maniac had tied her up in the hopes of convincing her to run off with him so the two of them could be together forever. Luckily, Tessa was always relentlessly prepared for every conceivable horrific incident that might occur, so she had on her a small razor and had been able to cut herself free. By the time Parker had found her, her hands had been covered in blood from the hundreds of tiny slices.

"So she didn't cut herself loose," Wyatt kept working his theory. "So how else could she have gotten out of those ropes? Could she have untied them?"

"If they were tied tight enough to restrain her then it would have been pretty difficult but probably not impossible given enough time," Marty replied.

"Maybe she had some help," J.J. suggested.

"What you mean someone found her tied up in there, got her free and then just let her run off into the night and never bothered to go after her or call the police to report what they'd found?" Parker raised an incredulous eyebrow. "That doesn't sound overly likely."

"Who knows, but since we don't really have much to go on at the moment we're not discounting anything at this point," J.J. decided. "Canvass the area and see if you can find out anything, take a photo of the girl to prompt people's memories."

"We don't even know how long Hope was tied up." Parker felt discouraged before they even began, and a little annoyed that J.J. kept referring to Hope as 'the girl', but judging his boss's mood he thought it best not to bring it up right now.

"Doctors best guess is between three and four days," Elisabeth filled them in.

"Okay," J.J. pounced on that, "lets work on that for now then. So we're working on the premise that three or four days ago this girl was abducted, then attacked either at the apartment or taken there later . . ."

"She was probably attacked somewhere else," Marty interrupted. Explaining quickly when he caught sight of J.J.'s glare, "there was no blood on the floor of the room. She bled enough from the head wound and split lip to lose a bit of blood and spatter the front of her jacket but there wasn't a drop inside that apartment."

"Okay," J.J. resumed his narrative, "so she was attacked somewhere else and taken to the apartment where she was tied to the metal pipe, with the cake and the water left out in front of her . . ."

"And the dripping tap," Parker added.

"Right," J.J. nodded. "Oh, I heard that the lovely Tessa met our mysterious stranger. Any insights on her part?"

"Why does it matter what Tessa thinks," Parker couldn't quite keep a pout off his face. "It's not like she's a qualified psychiatrist and you've already got Beth's opinion."

"No offense, Beth," J.J. gave the doctor's hand a pat, "but Tessa is the smartest person we know with an IQ of 178. Not to mention the extensive experience she's had dealing with, how shall we put it, unusual circumstances."

Beginning to regret the number of times he'd insisted that they listen to Tessa because of her uncanny ability to read people and situations. "Tessa thinks Hope smiles too much for someone with no memory," Parker sighed.

Chuckling, "I'll bear that in mind." J.J. stood, "okay, lets go people and try to make some progress on this case."

As they all filed out of the room the words Tessa had spoken at the hospital, as the door had swung closed behind him, floated into his mind. She'd warned him to be careful. But she needn't have bothered. Parker was never going to let things get out of hand again as they had with the Gina O'Hara case, where innocent lives at been placed at risk. Besides what harm could a young woman with amnesia possibly bring.

FEBRUARY 11TH

"What's going to happen to me?"

Parker looked into Hope's blue eyes and couldn't come up with a single thing to say. "We'll sort something out," he reassured her with a surreptitious glance at his watch. He was supposed to have been at Tessa's ten minutes ago and it was at least a half hour drive out to her estate. He'd intended to arrive early to talk with Tessa before they spoke with Winter, but he'd come by to visit Hope, meaning to spend only a few minutes however they'd got talking and he'd lost track of time.

"Do you have to go?" Hope asked a little forlornly.

"Uh, not just yet," he assured her, hoping that Tessa would wait until he got there before breaking the news to Winter. Parker wanted to be there to support not just his niece but his wife as well, he knew how badly Tessa was hurting over this.

"It's okay if you have to go," Hope gave him a shaky smile. "Dr. Bennett said she'd be here by lunch time so I won't be by myself for too long."

Hesitating, torn between his responsibilities with his family and his guilt at leaving Hope, who was already so alone. In the end, he was saved from having to make a choice when the door swung open and Elisabeth breezed into the room, baby Lucia in her arms.

"Morning, Hope," Elisabeth gave the young woman a warm smile. "Parker," she gave him a nod and he assumed he was still in her bad books.

"Oh," Hope squealed delightedly, "Dr. Bennett, is that your

baby?"

"Yes, this is Lucia," Elisabeth brought the baby over to Hope. "I couldn't settle thinking you were here on your own." She threw him another pointed look, "I thought Parker had other arrangements this morning."

"You did have somewhere to be," Hope looked dismayed. "You didn't have to stay with me. I hope it wasn't anything important."

"I uh, I still have time to get there," he avoided Elisabeth as she rolled her eyes at him.

"She's beautiful," Hope gushed unable to take her eyes off the baby. "Can I hold her?"

"Sure," Elisabeth gently placed the infant into Hope's outstretched arms.

Parker watched the young woman's eyes spark with genuine joy as she cradled the baby, letting Lucia's tiny fingers curl around her own. He couldn't help but think once again of Tessa and the baby they had lost and wondered if things would be different between them now if their baby hadn't died.

"She's so beautiful," Hope marveled again. "You must love her so much."

"I do," Elisabeth smiled and traced a finger across Lucia's silky black hair.

"When can I leave here?" Hope asked suddenly, her face gravely serious.

"Well," Elisabeth began nervously, both he and Hope stared at her suspiciously. "I'll be right back," she picked Lucia back up and hurried out the door.

"What's going on?" Hope demanded, turning panicked eyes to bore into him.

"I have no idea," Parker answered her honestly, wondering what Elisabeth knew that she hadn't told him.

Before they had a chance to speculate, Elisabeth returned, without the baby, and pulled a chair over beside the bed. "The doctors say that physically you're ready to go," Elisabeth began.

"But . . ." he prodded with a frown.

"But, while physically you're doing fine, psychologically is another story," Elisabeth continued. "It's been two days since you were found and you haven't had any memory flashes . . ."

"You said there was no time line for getting my memory back," Hope protested.

"And there's not," Elisabeth reassured her gently. "But your doctors and I were discussing the possibility that it may be for the best if you stay here in the . . . in the psychiatric ward."

"What?" he and Hope shouted in unison.

"I'm not crazy," Hope's dark blue eyes aflame with indignation. "I don't need to be in a crazy house."

"It's not a crazy house," Elisabeth soothed. "And no one is saying that you're crazy. We simply want to be sure that you're in a place where you have the most help available so that you can get your memory back."

"I don't want . . ." Hope started.

"You can stay with me," Parker blurted out before he realized what he was saying, the lost look in Hope's eyes was all he could think about.

"What?" Elisabeth exclaimed.

"Really?" Hope's face lit with delight.

"Really," he nodded, wondering how he was going to explain this to Tessa.

"Are you sure that's a good idea?" Elisabeth held him firmly in a reprimanding stare.

"Oh, Detective Bell, thank you," Hope threw her arms around his neck.

Returning the young woman's hug, Parker began to get the feeling that he'd just made a huge mistake.

* * * * *

10:53 A.M.

"He's not coming," Daniel came up behind her.

"He's coming," Tessa stated adamantly but inside she was a lot less confident than she'd been earlier this morning.

"He's well over an hour late," her brother reminded her.

"He promised he'd be here," she clung to Parker's promise.

"Yeah, well, your husband promises a lot of things he doesn't deliver," Daniel spat venomously.

"I don't understand what could be more important than being here for Winter," she began to wring her hands fretfully and forced herself to stop.

Daniel took her by the shoulders, his face softening. "Look, I know that you want to put off telling her because it's hard. But she's waiting for you and she knows something's up, we just need to do it. I know you know that."

"I do know that, but . . ."

"No, no buts," Daniel pulled her into a hug.

For a moment, Tessa allowed herself to lean on her brother while she gathered herself. Maybe Parker hadn't come because he was still angry about their argument at the hospital yesterday. She felt bad about throwing the Gina O'Hara disaster in his face but she'd wanted to hurt him as badly as he'd hurt her. Tessa knew they needed to tell Winter whether Parker showed up or not, but as much as she hated to admit she needed him here, she was terrified of telling Winter the truth, and having her husband at her side would make it the teensiest bit easier.

She had known from the beginning it was a mistake to learn to need someone, to become reliant on the fact that they would always be there, because she'd known it would end in disaster. If history had taught her anything, it was that invariably people you loved let you down. It was better to rely on yourself and yourself alone, that way you couldn't get hurt. But she'd let herself be drawn into the fairytale dream of marriage and a family because she had thought Parker was different. He wasn't though, he'd left her just like everyone else had, and she hadn't lifted a finger to stop him.

"Okay, lets do it," Tessa pulled out of Daniel's grip, she'd learnt how to be completely self-sufficient once before, she could do it again.

"Matilda and I are right here with you," her brother reminded her, taking her hand as they headed for the living room where Winter was waiting.

Despite her resolution to be strong and independent, Tessa squeezed Daniel's hand a little too tightly when she saw Winter sitting waiting for her. Her niece's smooth jet-black hair and glittering black eyes should have tipped her off immediately, but the possibility had never occurred to her.

"What's going on?" Winter demanded, eyeing her and Daniel suspiciously.

"We need to talk," Daniel answered.

"Something's wrong. Tessa, are you okay?" Winter watched her worriedly.

"I'm fine," she assured her niece. "There's just something important we need to talk about. Let's sit," guiding Winter to the sofa by the window.

"You're scaring me," Winter's black eyes were darting from her to Daniel. "Tell me what's going on."

"Okay," sitting down Tessa pushed all her emotions into a box in her mind and locked them up. "Last fall when . . ."

"When that man was stalking you and almost killed you," Winter inserted harshly. Daniel wasn't the only one who was angry with her for not calling to inform her family about what was going on last September.

"Right," she nodded, wanting to just rip the band-aid off and tell Winter everything before she lost her nerve. "When Dino had me on his boat I tried to distract him, to buy myself some time, by telling him something about his mother's death. Something I'd

61

found out a long time ago. Well he was thrown." Tessa remembered the shock on Dino's face when she'd told him his recovering drug addict mother hadn't relapsed and overdosed but had in fact been killed by his own brother. "But then he told me something."

Beginning to look wary, "what did he tell you?" Winter asked.

It still made Tessa feel sick when she thought of what Dino had revealed. "He told me that Jake didn't stumble upon me and Ellie accidentally. That he came after me on purpose. Because someone sent him."

"Who?" Winter asked but even before she finished the word understanding began to dawn. "She didn't really, did she?"

Trying to avoid her niece's horrified eyes. "I dreamt she was there, that first night I got home. Her face was a puzzle and I had to put it together before people started dying, only I wasn't sure it was her face. I only had that dream that one time until the Iceman case. I should have known then, only I didn't think she could be so cruel, so vindictive, so . . ." she trailed off when she felt Daniel's hands on her shoulders. "I'm sorry, Winter."

Winter's pleading eyes were filling with tears, "how could she do that? You were only eleven, how could she send a child trafficker to abduct you? She knew what he was going to do to you, she knew what was going to happen to you there. How could she do that? Your own sister? I'm sorry, Tessa."

"It's not your fault, Winter," she assured her, taking Winter's hand.

"She's my mother," the girl contradicted.

"Which doesn't make you responsible for her actions," Tessa reminded her softly, dreading telling Winter the rest.

"There's more isn't there?" Winter asked dismally.

Tessa opened her mouth to answer but not a sound came out.

"Yes, there is," Daniel replied, coming to her rescue, sitting behind her on the arm of the sofa, wrapping an arm across her chest, urging her to lean against him, and taking Winter's free hand. "Dino also told Tessa something about Jake. Something about Jake and Cordelia."

"What?" Winter's voice had dropped to a mere whisper.

"Jake is your father," Tessa blurted out.

Winter's face drained of all color, and for a second Tessa was sure her niece was about to pass out, but then the teenager spoke, her voice strained, "Jake Killinger is my father?"

"I'm sorry, Winter," Tessa pulled herself free from Daniel's grip and threw her arms around her niece, the girl didn't respond, sitting as still as stone.

"The man who abducted you and raped you and killed your friend is my father. The man who you were forced to kill to escape is my father," Winter's eyes took on a glassy faraway sheen.

"I'm sorry, Winter," she repeated.

"And my mother sent him to you. She sent the father of her child, who worked for a child trafficking ring, to kidnap her little sister, rape her and then sell her as a sex slave to a pedophile. You were eleven when you were taken. That's sixteen years ago. That means my mom was pregnant with me when she arranged your abduction. Even when she was pregnant with a baby of her own she could still do that to another child. My mother never loved me, she probably just used me to manipulate this guy. What would he have done to me if you hadn't killed him?"

"I don't know and Cordelia did love you in her own way," the words sounding hollow even to her own ears.

"But not more than she hated you. Hating you was the only thing she cared about."

Tessa couldn't argue with Winter's logic there. Her sister had hated her from the moment their mother announced she was pregnant. Had seen her as a rival for their abusive father's love. Their father had been sexually abusing Cordelia for years, and her mentally unstable sister had believed she was in love with him. In her crazy mind Tessa was a threat to her relationship. Arranging for Jake to kidnap her wasn't the only way Cordelia had tried to destroy her. She had been the instigator in Dylan Riley's murderous rampage, and the entire Iceman saga would never have occurred if not for Cordelia.

"I'm sorry," Tessa murmured again, mainly because she couldn't think of anything else to say.

"Why? It's not your fault," Winter's glassy eyes cleared. "I should be apologizing to you."

"You are not responsible for their actions," she assured her niece again, knowing that reason was the last thing on Winter's mind right now.

"That's easy for you to say," tears began to trickle down Winter's cheeks. "Your parents aren't psychopaths."

"Emilie tried to kill me and Patrick was sexually abusive." Tessa felt Daniel stiffen beside her. Now she was going to have to have a conversation with her brother about how she knew that. Patrick had only ever tried anything with her once, when she was six, and she had threatened to out him if he ever touched her again. She had also made sure that he knew that threat was still in place if he ever tried anything with his children from his second wife. "It doesn't matter who your parents are. That doesn't dictate what kind of person *you're* going to be. And you are the sweetest, kindest, most thoughtful girl I know."

Eyeing her doubtfully, Winter brushed angrily at the teardrops winding their way down her cheeks, her niece hated letting people see her cry as much as she herself did.

"It's going to be okay, Winter," Tessa attempted to console the girl.

"No, it's not. What they did to you ruined your whole life."

"No, it didn't," instantly defensive. "I'm fine, my life is fine. Right now I'm just worried about you."

"We all are," Daniel added.

"Well you needn't be." The last of the teenager's tears dried up as shock and horror were taken over by fury and disgust. "I always wondered who my father was and what he was like and what our lives would have been like with him around. Well not anymore. You did the world a favor, Tessa, when you killed Jake Killinger." She smiled defiantly, "wow, Cordelia and Jake make me actually with for Grant again," Winter stood and started for the door.

Bouncing up after her, "Winter . . ." Tessa began.

"I just want to be alone right now," hovering near the door with her back to the room.

Catching the small quiver in her niece's shoulders kept Tessa in her place. The desire to deal with things alone was one she understood perfectly. "Okay," she agreed, "but I'm here when you're ready."

Winter nodded once and then was gone.

As Tessa watched her go she could feel herself losing her own battle with tears. As Daniel engulfed her in a tight hug, she found herself wishing it was Parker's arms that she was wrapped safely up in. Shocked and hurt that her husband hadn't bothered to turn up when he knew how important today was and how much she needed him, hurt as much as if it were a physical blow. Sickened by having to recount the details of just what a monster her sister had been, Tessa let herself fall deeper into her brother's arms and for once let her tears flow freely.

* * * * *

2:11 P.M.

"Are you sure your wife isn't going to mind me staying with you for awhile?" Hope checked for the hundredth time since he'd opened up his home to her.

"Actually Tessa isn't staying here at the moment," Parker answered vaguely, very aware of the fact that Tessa was going to be furious with him for not turning up to help her tell Winter about Jake as well as for moving in a complete stranger.

"I hope everything's okay," she looked up at him anxiously. "I don't want to cause any problems for you."

"You're not, believe me," he assured her honestly, right now Hope was the least of his problems. "Here we are," he announced as he pulled into the driveway of the home he had grown up in, the home where he had dreamed about raising his own family.

"It's lovely," Hope gushed, taking in the two-storey home, the bare winter trees and patches of slushy snow in the front yard.

"I'll grab your stuff," Parker told her as he opened Hope's door for her then retrieved the bag of clothes Elisabeth had bought for Hope to wear.

She trailed along behind him as he led the way up the steps and across the small porch to the front door. Opening it wide they walked through into the long hallway that ran from the front door down to the kitchen at the back. "That's the study," he indicated the room on their left, then the one on their right, "and that's the dining room. The downstairs bathroom's in there, that's the living room, and this is the kitchen," he finished the tour, setting her bag down on the table. "Can I get you anything to eat or drink?"

"Umm," she rolled her eyes skyward as she thought. "Maybe just some water since I'm not really sure what I like or don't like."

"What about a soda," he suggested instead, rifling through the fridge and coming out with a bottle of Tessa's favorite diet soda. "Try this."

Hope nodded her agreement and took a seat at the table while he pulled two glasses from the cupboard before joining her and pouring them each a drink. Hope lifted the drink tentatively to her lips and took a cautious sip, but then smiled, "well I guess I can add soda to the list of things I like."

"Your memory will come back," Parker reassured her. There were certain parts of his past he would be only too happy to forget about but he couldn't imagine how strange it must be not to remember anything about yourself. They both lapsed into silence and he was just about to suggest making them something to eat when Hope looked up at him.

"Why doesn't Tessa live here? Is it because of me? Is she angry because you've been spending a lot of time with me?"

"Tessa and I have been having some problems for a while now. It has nothing to do with you. Honest," he gave her a quick pat on the hand and was about to stand when she grabbed hold of him.

"Are you positive? Because if I'm in the way I can . . ." Hope took a deep breath, "I can stay in the psychiatric ward like Dr. Bennett wanted."

"No, you don't have to do that, you're fine right here. Besides we don't know who hurt you or why or whether or not they want to come back and finish the job. As long as you're here I can keep an eye on you and you'll be safe," this was the excuse he was planning on giving Tessa, but in truth he didn't really know what had possessed him to ask Hope to move in.

Shivering, Hope cast an involuntary glance at her bandaged wrists, "do you really think whoever tied me up and left me to die might come back?"

"I don't know," he answered honestly. "But it's best to be prepared and have you someplace safe till we get this all figured out."

"Thank you," she whispered softly. "For everything you've done for me. Being there for me and supporting me and encouraging me and cheering me up. That's more than most people would do for a complete and utter stranger. Yet you even went beyond that and gave me a place to live. I don't know how I could ever repay you."

Parker's eyes were locked onto Hope's, her hypnotic voice drawing him in like a magnet and for one second he was sure she was going to kiss him before an icy voice broke the spell.

"I hope I'm not interrupting anything," Tessa stood in the kitchen doorway holding them both in a haughty glare.

Springing away from the table Parker felt like a child who had just been caught with his hand in the cookie jar. "No, you're not interrupting anything." He pasted on a smile and crossed to give his wife a kiss but she shied away from him.

"I wondered what was so important that kept you from coming this morning."

"I think I might just pop to the bathroom," Hope announced, clearly aware she was right in the middle of their personal problems.

"First door on your left," he reminded her. "Nothing was going on," he said again once they were alone.

"What is *she* doing here?" Tessa demanded, her eyes lighting on the bag that still sat on the table.

"She's staying here for the moment. Until we find out who she is," he answered lamely.

"She's staying here in our house?" Tessa repeated incredulously.

"It's not really *our* house, you moved out," Parker protested weakly.

"I moved out because I couldn't stand to be in the place where Lachlan Mountain was drugging me and spying on me," she shouted shrilly. "The house where I imagined every horrible thing that could have happened to you while you were missing, while I listened to our friends and family tell me over and over again that you'd just walked out on me."

Resisting the urge to point out the numerous times their positions had been reversed and he had been the one left to sit and wonder where Tessa was and what was happening to her.

When it came to getting into trouble his wife was an expert and he had long ago come to the conclusion that the genius gene replaced the gene for common sense. In fact, it was Tessa going off on her own with Dino Rollino, after she'd promised him she wouldn't, that had started their problems in the first place. At first he hadn't known that Dino had held a gun to her head and threatened to kill two innocent children if she didn't go with him.

Once he found out, though from J.J. not Tessa, it had been like a weight off his shoulders knowing that Tessa hadn't lied straight to his face and thrown herself in harms way once again. But by the time he'd found all of that out that damage had already been done and his and Tessa's relationship was already strained.

"The person who kidnapped her is still out there," he reasoned. "As long as she's staying here then she's safe."

"So rather than working on our marriage you move another one of your projects in here to 'keep her safe'?"

"That's not fair, Tessa," he hated how Tessa managed to twist things around to make herself the victim. "You're the one who won't open up to me, who shuts me out at every opportunity." Sighing, he was fighting a losing battle having this conversation again. "I'm sorry I wasn't there this morning, how's Winter?"

"Exactly how you'd expect her to be," Tessa snapped. "She just found out that both her parents were psychopaths."

"And how are you?" he asked gently, noting her red, puffy eyes, she'd clearly been crying earlier, something she hardly ever did.

"I'm fine," she huffed, but her aqua eyes refused to meet his.

Hooking a finger beneath her chin he tilted her face up, "I mean how are you really?"

"How could you not come?" vulnerability crept into her voice and his guilt took a surge. "How could you make me do that alone?"

"I'm sorry," he brushed his knuckles across her temple where a pale pink scar still lingered. "I meant to come. I was just going to pop by the hospital for a quick visit. But then Beth said that Hope was going to be moved to the psychiatric ward and then before I knew what I was doing I was inviting her to stay here."

"You promised," her chin trembled slightly. "And I needed you."

"I'm sorry," he said again, feeling like the most useless husband on the planet. It had been a mistake not to be there with his family this morning. He had hurt his wife, and despite their problems, he truly didn't want to cause her pain. "I'm sorry." Drawing Tessa into his arms, he was a little surprised, but pleased, when she didn't fight him, just wearily rested her forehead against his chest. Holding his wife, Parker felt for a moment like maybe everything could be okay, that they could get back to the way things used to be. But then they were interrupted by Hope clearing her throat.

"Sorry to interrupt," she smiled shyly, "if you just tell me which room I'll be staying in I'll take my stuff and get out of your way."

The spell was broken, Tessa pulled away, "don't bother, Hope, I need to be going anyway."

"Tess, wait," Parker tried to grab her arm but she quickly moved out of reach.

"I'm sure you've got plenty to do, I don't want to intrude," she headed off down the hall, a moment later the front door slammed shut behind her.

"I'm sorry," Hope spoke up immediately. "I made her mad."

"It's not your fault," he said once again. "It's mine. I should have told her myself that you were staying here, instead of letting her find out like that." He'd call Tessa later, once she'd calmed down a little, and try to explain things more thoroughly. "Come on, I'll show you to your room." Taking Hope's bag and leading the way upstairs Parker wondered whether Tessa would hear him out or whether his snap decision to move in Hope had damaged their relationship beyond repair.

* * * * *

4:26 P.M.

"Where's Parker?"

The way he was feeling right now Wyatt didn't care if he ever saw his partner again. "Who knows, who cares," he answered Marty Jenkins.

"What's going on?" the crime scene tech eyed him shrewdly.

Still unused to Marty's grey eyes being unobscured by his thick black glasses, "you haven't heard?"

"Heard what?" Marty's face crinkled in puzzlement.

"Apparently Parker has decided it's a smart idea to move Hope into his house," he spat out, still as furious as he had been when he'd found out.

"What?" Marty stuttered. "Does Tessa know?"

Rubbing weary hands across his face, "yeah. She went to find out why Parker didn't turn up when they told Winter about Jake and she saw Hope there."

Wincing, "how's she doing?" Marty asked.

"I don't know, she won't talk to anyone," Wyatt had already tried calling Tessa a dozen times.

"Why didn't you stop him?" Marty demanded. "Tell him it was a recipe for disaster."

"Because I didn't know," he growled, annoyed that Parker hadn't bothered to tell anyone what he was planning on doing. "I found out from Casey. Seemingly when Tessa came back from Parker's in tears, Daniel managed to drag out of her what had happened, he told Matilda, who called Casey, who told me."

"What is Parker thinking?" Marty had begun frantically rubbing at his eyes. "Moving a victim from a case into his house, and one who doesn't even know who she is or what happened to her, it's insanity."

"Tessa told Daniel that the reason Parker moved Hope in was to keep her safe since whoever hurt her is still out there somewhere," Wyatt was tired, worrying about Tessa was like a full time job.

"And Beth just let this happen?"

"When I talked to her she said she spent a couple of hours trying to talk him out of it but he was pretty adamant." His gaze drifted to the abandoned farmhouse behind them, "it's not that I don't feel sorry for Hope," he said softly. "What did you find?"

Following his gaze, "well this one wasn't so lucky, if we can call what happened to Hope lucky. Maisy's still inside," Marty began to walk towards the side door of the dilapidated house.

It seemed that the farmhouse had been sitting vacant for the last three years, ever since it's owner had passed away. The elderly gentleman had lived on this property his entire life but his two sons had moved to the city the second they were old enough and hadn't even bothered to return to sell the place upon their father's death. The house had a sagging roof, an overgrown yard and the walls that had once been painted a bright white with green trim were now weathered and peeling.

Stepping through the battered door to find the inside as derelict as the outside, he and Marty stood in a kitchen so thickly covered in dust Wyatt found himself sneezing. "Did you find anything in here?"

Indicating the areas where the dust had been disturbed, "Maisy took some fingerprints but this room looks like no one's been in here in years."

"Where is she?"

"Living room," Marty led him through the old narrow halls to the living room, which was as musty as the kitchen had been.

"Hey, Wyatt," Maisy Wallace gave him a somber smile. "I heard what happened with Parker, have you talked to him yet? Or to Tessa?"

Returning the pretty redhead's smile with one equally as solemn, "no and no. But you should call Tess, she might talk to you. How did you find out?"

"Casey." The twenty-eight year old returned her hazel eyes to the body in the centre of the room. "Do we have a serial killer?"

The room was icy cold and he slid his gloves from his pocket and put them on as he surveyed the scene before him. An open window was the source of the cold, a puddle of melted snow beneath it and the curtains that fluttered in the breeze were covered with a thin sheen of ice. A faded settee and mismatched armchairs were grouped in the centre of the room, an ancient television set off to the side, the wallpaper was peeling, the carpet threadbare, the family portraits that dotted the walls had faded so much you could barely make out the faces. And the lifeless body of a woman was chained to the fireplace.

The woman looked to be in her late thirties to early forties, with shoulder length chestnut brown hair, sunken grey eyes, cracked lips, and blotchy wrinkled skin. She was dressed in a white tank top and black business skirt, by the window laid a discarded black jacket and a pair of black pumps. Shivering in the cold Wyatt had to wonder whether the adductor had chained her to the fireplace as some sort of sick joke.

On the table sat a crystal jug filled with water, a glass and a plate of chocolate cake, Wyatt would bet anything that the table was just out of the woman's reach. The scene was eerily familiar to the one where they assumed Hope had been left tied up. The only difference was that this woman hadn't been lucky enough to escape.

"I hope not," he finally muttered in answer to Maisy's serial killer question as he crouched beside the body, but thinking that was more than likely the case. Gently he lifted the woman's hands and examined her ragged and bloody fingernails. Where the chain clamped around her ankle the skin was red and raw. Moving to the other end of the short chain where it had been fastened to a metal ring that had been anchored firmly into the brick fireplace, it allowed her about two feet of movement. The bricks around the metal ring were scratched and streaked with lines of blood, where the woman had tried desperately to free herself. "Any taps left on?"

"No, not this time," Marty replied.

"You found anything yet?" Wyatt asked Maisy.

Dragging her gaze away from the woman's face, "some

fingerprints but they were buried under layers of dust so I'm guessing they're from the deceased owner. Other than that there were some smudges around but most of the activity is around where . . ." she trailed off and waved her hand to indicate the area around the fireplace.

"No brown hairs this time?"

"Some," Maisy bobbed her head.

"Do we know who she is?" Wyatt asked.

"No ID on her," Marty answered.

"Who called it in?" Maisy queried.

"Anonymous caller on an untraceable disposable cell phone," Wyatt told her. "The 911 operator who took the call couldn't even tell if it was a man or a woman."

"I just don't understand what kind of sick mind could do this," Maisy's gaze became riveted once again on the woman's body. "Just chaining someone up and leaving them to die is bad enough but to then leave food and water just out of reach . . . how could someone do that?"

Unfortunately over the course of his thirty-seven years, close to twenty of those spent as a police officer, Wyatt had become jaded and was almost to the place where nothing human beings did to one another surprised him anymore.

"Why didn't anyone call me?" a voice demanded angrily from the door.

They all turned around to see Parker glaring at them.

Shrugging, "I left you a message. I assumed you were busy settling in your new houseguest," Wyatt answered. "Marty, I'm going to head off, try and identify the victim, call me if you find anything important."

Without a second look at Parker, he exited the house, leaving Marty and Maisy to fill his partner in on the newest victim in their case. Glancing at his watch he decided he'd go back to the precinct, then he'd try once again to call Tessa and find out how she and Winter were doing, after that he'd corner Parker and give him a piece of his mind.

* * * * *

7:42 P.M.

She'd just about got her tears under control, at least she thought she had, when the bedroom door swung open.

"Are you okay?" Detective Bell asked awkwardly.

"I'm fine," Hope tried to hide the last of her sniffles. "Just stubbed my toe," she fibbed.

Looking doubtful, and preoccupied, Detective Bell shrugged, "okay. I just need to make a phone call then I'm off to bed, I'll see you in the morning."

"In the morning," she echoed faintly, a huge wave of sobs building up inside her, threatening to burst out at any second, forcefully Hope held them back.

"Goodnight."

Hope tried to return the pleasantry but as Detective Bell began to close the door she couldn't hold it in anymore. The sense of aloneness so overwhelming, her emotions came bubbling to the surface and before she knew it, she was openly sobbing.

"What's wrong?" Detective Bell asked, laying a hand uncomfortably on her shoulder.

"I'm so scared," she managed through her tears.

"We'll find the man who hurt you," he comforted.

"That scares me, but . . ." Hope was scared of the man who had tried to kill her but right now she was more terrified of the sense of isolation that bore down on her.

"But there's something else," Detective Bell led her to the bed, sat her down, and put a self-conscious arm around her shoulder, holding her until her sobs finally ceased. "Talk to me," he said when she quietened. "Tell me what's going on."

He spoke with such gentleness that she almost burst into a

fresh batch of tears. "I feel so . . . so . . ." she wasn't quite sure how to put into words just how she was feeling, "so alone," she finished helplessly.

"You're not alone, you have me."

Staring into his warm, golden eyes Hope actually believed him. "Why did you ask me to move in here? Was it really to protect me?"

"You needed help," he answered simply.

"But me being here is causing problems for you with your family and friends," she reminded him.

"Not *causing* problems exactly."

"Well adding to them then," she modified. "Did you really find another woman?"

Surprised, "how did you find out about that?"

Embarrassed, Hope found herself squirming, "I overheard you talking to Detective Wyatt." The two men had had a heated argument on the doorstep earlier this evening. "I didn't mean to eavesdrop," she assured him. "I was just going down to the kitchen and I couldn't help hearing you guys. You were kind of screaming at each other," she added, catching the barely perceptible quiver in his eyebrow at the mention of his partner.

"Yes, we found another woman," Detective Bell nodded.

"Alive?" she asked half-heartedly, already knowing the answer but clinging to the hope that she was wrong.

"I'm sorry," he took her hand and squeezed it.

"But you think whoever killed her, it was the same person who . . . who tried to kill me?" Hope still couldn't quite believe there was someone out there who may want her dead.

"We think so."

"How did you find her?"

"We received an anonymous phone call."

Gaping, "you think from *him*? Whoever did this?"

"Maybe."

Taking all of this is in, "do you know who she is?"

"Her name was Henrietta Kendall, she was a forty-one year old mother of three, she worked in real estate, and she was planning a family vacation to the Bahamas' over the summer," he summarized briefly but Hope caught the sadness in his voice.

"You should go, make your phone call," she turned away and climbed under the covers. "I'll be fine."

Detective Bell hesitated, "are you sure?"

"I'm sure," she declared, although a glimmer of doubt was creeping up inside of her.

"Alright, see you in the morning," he patted her shoulder and once again made for the door.

Stopping him when his hand turned the knob, "Detective Bell?"

"Parker," he reminded her for the hundredth time. "What's up?"

Utter isolation was rippling at her toes, "do you think you could sit with me until I fall asleep?"

"Sure," he pulled over the desk chair and sat beside her. "Sweet dreams, Hope," he whispered.

Before she drifted off Hope knew it wasn't sweet dreams she was after it was revealing dreams.

* * * * *

10:21 P.M.

It had been a long day, a long *unpleasant* day.

Tessa yanked her unruly blonde curls into a ponytail and climbed into bed, not sure that she would be able to sleep after everything that had happened. When she'd returned from Parker's she'd been in shock after finding another woman living with her husband. In fact she had been in tears and so out of sorts that when Daniel had asked her what happened she'd told him everything. Her brother had been suitably furious about the situation and had threatened to go over there and throw Hope out. She'd talked him out of it then told him she just wanted to be alone, which is how she'd spent the remainder of the day, holed up by herself in her bedroom. She'd had to dodge phone calls from Casey, Skylar, Maisy, Marty and J.J. as well as Daniel and Matilda's many attempts to cheer her up.

Not that she was the only one who didn't want to talk to anyone. Winter had barely said two words to her since this morning. Tessa was very worried about the sixteen-year-old who had already been through more in the last couple of years than most people had to go through in a lifetime.

Just snuggling down under her quilt when the phone began to ring. Tessa tried to ignore it, leaving it for Daniel to get, but when it's insistent trilling continued, she assumed that her brother and Matilda had gone out and reluctantly reached out to answer it.

"Hello?"

"It's Parker," he announced unnecessarily.

She said nothing. Part of her had spent the day expecting him to show up and apologize for moving Hope in and beg her to come home with him.

"Tessa?" he ventured again when she didn't say anything.

"What is it, Parker? It's been a long day and I was just going to bed."

"I was worried about you, I just wanted to check you were doing okay after this morning."

Her husband sounded sincere but if he had been truly concerned about her there had been nothing preventing him from coming to see her before now. "You wanted to see how I was doing after this morning? You mean after I had to tell my niece that the man who raped me was her father and that her mother sent him to me? Or after I came to find out why you didn't come to help me with Winter after you promised you would and instead found you moved another woman into our house?"

Wisely refraining from once again telling her that it was no longer *their* house instead he tried for a more conciliatory path. "I thought I was doing the right thing."

"Right thing by who?" Tessa muttered under breath.

Either he didn't hear her or he chose to ignore her comment. "What was I supposed to do? Let poor Hope be moved into a psychiatric ward?"

"Well as long as you have your priorities straight," she jeered.

"I just wanted to make sure that she was someplace safe," he began in his slightly condescendingly patient voice that never failed to irritate her. "There's a possible serial killer on the loose who may not be too happy once he finds out that one of his intended victims didn't die. I wouldn't be doing my job if I wasn't trying to keep her safe."

"Is that why you were with me?" Tessa decided to confront Parker with her suspicions head on. "So that you could just do your job and keep me safe until you solved your own mystery and found out how Ellie died?"

"How could you even think that?" Parker sounded genuinely dismayed that she would suggest such a possibility. "You know that I love you."

"Really?" If she wasn't so tired her common sense would have told her to leave it there, but exhausted as she was she blasted onwards. "And how exactly would I know that? Because when we met you told me that you were never ever going to leave me, and then after two years of trying to find out about Jake when I finally tell you instead of being there for me you walk out because I didn't tell you about John Doe? Yeah, Parker, I can really tell how much you love me."

"I *do* love you," he insisted.

"As long as I tell you what you want to know," she goaded, Tessa wanted him to feel as mad as he was making her feel.

"He was there that night," beginning to get worked up. "You remember, the night I pulled you out of the water and then got shot by your psycho stalker. He was there, John Doe was the one who killed Dino, he was there and you let him walk away. I don't think it's unreasonable to want to understand why my wife would let a child trafficker just walk away free and clear."

"But you do think it's unreasonable to stay and support me?"

"You make it sound like I just abandoned you," his voice taking on an edge. "You're the one who refuses to open up to me. Who shuts me out at every opportunity. Who . . ."

She hung up before he could finish his sentence. Almost immediately it started to ring, climbing out of bed she bent down and yanked the phone cord from the wall, she was not in the mood to talk to Parker again tonight.

Flopping back down on the soft mattress, she pulled the covers right over her head and enjoyed the warm, dark space. Wondering to herself why she didn't just learn the lesson that no one could be trusted properly instead of repeatedly getting her hopes up and allowing someone into her heart only to have them dash her hopes to peaces and desert her. Well she'd spent the majority of her life before now on her own and it looked like the rest of it was going to be just as lonely.

FEBRUARY 12TH

9:00 A.M.

"Right on time," J.J. commended them. "I have a meeting in half an hour so lets get moving. Maisy, it's nice for you to be able to join us today, so why don't you begin."

"Okay," Maisy nodded vigorously sending her red ponytail bouncing up and down. "The victim was Henrietta Kendall. She was forty-one years old, happily married to Dimitri Kendall and dedicated mother of Liam, Larissa and Lucinda, ages eleven, nine and seven."

"Cause of death was multiple organ failure due to dehydration," Zak Fenton inserted. Zak was in his mid-thirties and before he became a medical examiner he had worked as a model. Despite the fact that he was very intelligent and brilliantly meticulous at his job Parker couldn't usually stand to spend more than a couple of minutes in his company because Zak was so over-bearingly vain. Zak had smooth cocoa skin and jet black eyes, he was good looking and he knew it, he also loved the fact that he left a trail of swooning women everywhere he went.

"Any idea on a timeline, Zak?" J.J. asked, he shared Parker's view on the medical examiner.

"It's hard to tell," Zak answered. "It depends on the temperature of the room she was in. But she'd lost almost fifteen percent of her body's fluid volume so I'd guess it didn't take her more than fourteen days to die."

"Fourteen days?" Parker repeated.

"Hey, I don't make the rules I'm just reporting the facts," Zak shrugged indifferently.

"She really could have lived fourteen days without water?" Wyatt's brow furrowed in disbelief.

"Death by dehydration can be affected by the temperature of the environment the person is in," Zak elaborated. "If a person's in a colder environment then they lose fluids more slowly and therefore they can live longer before succumbing to dehydration, and vice versa. She hadn't been dead more than a couple of days, but to pinpoint more accurately will be difficult because of how cold it was in the house. Also," Zak was on a roll now, his hands flying as he worked out his theory, "your killer could have turned up the heat in there to kill her more quickly, then come back and opened the window at a later date, to make it harder for us to get a complete sense of his actions. Same goes for rate of decomposition, it's hard to tell how long she's been dead because the room was so cold, it preserved the body, but she couldn't have been dead for more than about thirty-six hours."

"What did the husband say?" J.J. asked.

"That he wasn't sure when exactly his wife disappeared since she had been away at a conference for work," Wyatt answered. "Only when we spoke with her colleagues they knew nothing about it."

"Ah," J.J.'s brown eyes lit up, his bushy eyebrows arching excitedly, "maybe our perfect wife and mother has a secret to hide."

"We're seeing the husband later today," Parker added, annoyed that his partner had gone to speak with the Kendall family without him yesterday.

"What else did you find, Maisy?" J.J. returned his gaze to the young crime scene tech.

"There were short brown hairs on Henrietta's clothes, on the tank top she was wearing and on the jacket that was by the window. Henrietta has brown hair but it's the wrong shade and the wrong length to be hers. They match the ones that were on Hope's clothes so I guess it's safe to assume that they came from the same person, and that the same person attacked both women."

"The crime scenes were almost identical," Marty took over. "The chocolate cake and water left just out of reach of where the woman was chained up, just like with Hope, only this time he used a chain instead of rope."

"Her hands were all scratched and bloody," Maisy's hazel eyes were filled with pain at the knowledge of how the woman had spent her final days.

Parker too couldn't shake the image of Henrietta Kendall's lifeless grey eyes staring into eternity. At least the picture of Henrietta's empty eyes had pushed the picture of Tessa's angry, hurt eyes from his mind. He still felt terrible about their phone conversation last night. After she'd hung up on him, he'd tried calling back at least a dozen times but she'd disconnected the phone. He'd even considered getting in his car and driving over there but in the end he'd decided it would only make things worse, and besides he couldn't leave Hope alone.

"Fingerprints?"

"Only smudges," Maisy replied.

"So that's one difference," J.J. observed to no one in particular. "Hope's fingerprints were all over the apartment, so he obviously did things slightly different this time."

"There was no tap left on either," Wyatt added.

"But the window was left open," Parker reminded them. "Maybe there was a reason he did things differently this time, maybe it had something to do with the individual women."

"Was she raped?" J.J. asked Marty, every one of them understanding his underlying question.

In response Marty nodded gravely and a heavy silence hung over the room. Parker wondered what possible purpose it could serve to violate these women with a gun.

"Did he do it there?" J.J.'s voice brought them all back to life.

"Nothing to suggest he did," Maisy answered glumly. "Just like last time he must have raped her someplace else before taking her there to leave her to die."

"Did we get anywhere with the caller?" J.J. ploughed on.

Wyatt shook his head, "no, we couldn't trace the call and it sounds like the caller used a voice distorter. We're guessing that it was the killer who called it in because of the remote location. I also don't think we're likely to find any witnesses. We can check out the surrounding farmhouses, but that place was miles from anywhere so I don't think anyone is going to have seen or heard anything."

Parker became aware that everyone had started staring at him, "what?"

"So far we don't have anything concrete to go on," J.J. began.

"And?" he frowned getting the feeling he wasn't going to like where this was going.

"And so far the only real link we have is Hope," his boss continued.

"But she doesn't remember anything," he reminded them.

"Right," J.J. nodded vigorously. "But we were thinking that it might help her to regain her memory to take her to the apartment . . ."

"You mean the place where she was tied up and left to die?" flabbergasted that they could even suggest that. "Are you trying to traumatize her further? There's not even any guarantee that it's going to work."

"Right now it's our best shot," Wyatt looked at him directly for the first time this morning.

"Does Beth know about this?" Parker demanded, sure the psychiatrist would be as outraged as he himself was.

"Actually she does," J.J.'s usually self-assured face looked slightly sheepish. "She's talking with Hope about it as we speak."

"She's what?" When he'd come to work this morning he'd left Hope with Elisabeth who had told him she was going to take Hope out. Walk around, maybe do some shopping, try to get her doing normal things to hopefully spark her memory. "This is ridiculous, you're all ganging up against us."

"What us?" Wyatt glared at him. "You and Hope are not an *us*."

Ignoring him, "it's out of the question," he snapped stubbornly. "There is no way we're going to put Hope through the trauma of going to the place where someone left her to die." Parker wasn't really sure why he was so overcome with the need to protect and stand up for this woman whom he had known only a couple of days. "Besides her memory will probably come back on it's own. We just need to be patient."

"Patient?" Wyatt echoed. "There could be other women out there right now. Tied up in some remote location. Dying slowly of dehydration. And who knows how many more woman this man is going to attack. How can you not want to do whatever it takes to find him?"

"I do want to find him. Just not at the expense of Hope's sanity, she's already been through hell," he reasoned. "There has to be another way to find this guy than through Hope. There has to be," he insisted, Parker just wasn't sure he was even convincing himself.

$$* * * * *$$

9:43 A.M.

"Been avoiding me?" Wyatt finally cornered Parker in one of the small interview rooms. His partner was just putting away his cell phone, and he assumed Parker had been on the phone with Hope since she seemed to be the centre of his world at the moment.

"Of course not," Parker snapped.

Despite his partner's protestations Wyatt detected a slight tremor in his eyebrow that indicated Parker had indeed been avoiding him. "We need to talk."

"We already talked last night. Or rather *you* talked, you didn't really give me a chance to," Parker frowned reproachfully like he was the innocent victim in this mess he was creating.

"What is going on with you? Since when have you and Hope become an us?" Wyatt challenged.

"I didn't really mean it like that, it's just . . ." Parker trailed off thoughtfully.

"Just what?" after their confrontation last night on Parker's doorstep Wyatt didn't feel like he was a single step closer to figuring out what was going on inside his partner's head. "It's like you've fallen under a spell, all you can think about it Hope."

"I haven't fallen under her spell," Parker rolled his eyes. "I just like being around her. Besides she really needs someone in her corner right now . . ."

"And Tessa doesn't?"

"Tessa has never needed me, or anyone," Parker declared but Wyatt caught the glimmer of doubt in his amber eyes.

"Tessa is falling apart, Parker, and you're just too busy with Hope to see it," he shook his head in disbelief and his partner's naïveté. "All the progress that she made in the last couple of years is all falling away. She's reverting straight back into the withdrawn, defensive, emotionally closed off person she was when we first met her."

"Look, things are simple with Hope. It's a nice change to be around someone who isn't always planning out their next ten moves like some sort of emotionless cyborg . . ."

A sharp gasp sent both their heads swiveling towards the door where Tessa was standing staring at them in shock.

"Tessa," Parker gulped. "I . . . I . . . I . . ."

"You what?" Tessa growled, her turquoise eyes aflame with rage.

"I'm sorry. I shouldn't have said that. I don't really think that you're an emotionless cyborg. It's just that I get so tired of you never trusting me," Parker babbled defensively.

Throwing her hands up in the air in frustration, "I am so tired of hearing you say that I never trust you. I told you about Ellie, didn't I? I didn't tell Patrick or Emilie or Daniel, I didn't tell Anthony, and I didn't tell any of my friends from school, I told *you*."

"Yes, you told me about Eleanor and then you went flying straight into Wyatt's arms for comfort instead of coming to me," Parker huffed, then added emphatically, "your husband."

"You're an idiot," Tessa spun around.

"Tess, wait," Parker tried to stop her.

"Let her go," Wyatt grabbed Parker's arm and held him in place as Tessa flew from the room. "You really are an idiot."

"What?" Parker huffed. "It's true, Tessa did go to you instead of me after she told us about Eleanor and Jake."

"You want to know what she told me that day, when I took her upstairs? She told me that she was scared, terrified, to look into your eyes in case she saw that you were disgusted by her." Tessa had made him promise not to tell Parker that but Wyatt wasn't going to let Parker throw it in her face and use it as a weapon against her. He still remembered perfectly the look of weary devastation in her eyes as she'd told him she was so afraid that Parker wouldn't love her anymore now he knew what she'd done.

"Why would she think I'd be disgusted by her?" Parker looked stricken as he realized what a mistake he'd just made.

"Because she'd just told you that she'd been raped and that she'd killed someone, and she wasn't thinking clearly, but all you can see are things she hasn't told you not the ones she has. Hope is just a replacement for Tessa. An easier replacement because there's no strings attached," with a disappointed shake of his head Wyatt headed off to find Tessa.

He found her out the front of the precinct deep in conversation with his wife Casey, who at five foot ten towered over Tessa. Tess was waving her hands animatedly as she usually did when she was in argument mode.

"Are you okay?" he asked Tessa when he got close enough.

Whirling on him, "I'm fine. I was just trying to convince your wife of that but she's too busy trying to play doctor."

Casey had studied history at college and had gone on to be a middle school history teacher but following the death of their daughter she had become a doctor.

"You look pale," Casey stated firmly. "Doesn't she look pale, Wyatt?" Before he had a chance to confirm that he did think Tessa looked pale Casey ploughed on, "I bet you're not eating or sleeping properly."

"I'm fine, I just don't really appreciate being called an emotionless cyborg. I can't believe I was so stupid," Tessa shook her head in disbelief sending her mop of curls flying. "I was actually coming here to apologize to Parker because I felt bad about hanging up on him last night when he was actually making an effort."

"Come on, lets go and do some shopping then we'll have lunch," Casey took Tessa's arm.

"I really just want to be alone right now," Tessa pulled herself free.

Brushing irritatedly at her corkscrew curls, Casey was in the process of growing them and they were at that awkward stage where they were long enough to get in the way but not long enough to tie up. "Come on, Tessa, you don't have to be impossible all the time."

"Maybe it would be a good idea," he ventured, not wanting to push too hard or Tessa would shut him out completely.

"I hate it when you two fuss," Tessa moaned. "I'm fine and I just want to be by myself for a while."

"Tessa," Casey planted her hands on her hips, her black eyes giving off the same stubborn look they had when dealing with their kids. Wyatt had fallen in love with Casey way back in middle school when she and her adoptive family had moved into the area. Casey had been born in Sudan and adopted by and American family when she was fifteen months old.

"Look, I'll call you later if that'll make you feel better," Tessa offered. "But right now I just have something I need to do," she shot him a pointed stare.

Understanding what she meant, "let her go, Casey."

"Okay," Casey reluctantly relented, "but I expect to hear from you in one hour."

"Fine," Tessa scrunched up her nose in annoyance. "I'll call you in an hour."

"Wait, come here," Casey pulled Tessa into a hug. "You know I'm here if you want to talk."

"I know."

"Me too," Wyatt grabbed Tessa when Casey released her.

"Hey, Skylar," Tessa began, twirling her hair around her finger. "I know you're busy with work, and Sam and Stacey, and I know it's not your problem, but if you have some spare time, I was wondering, if it's not to much trouble, it's not for me . . ."

"Spit it out," he tried to hide his amusement that Tessa found it so hard to ask for help.

"I was wondering if you could come by and talk to Winter. It's just I think she needs to hear from someone other than me and Daniel that just because Cordelia and Jake were psychopaths doesn't mean that she's going to turn into one."

"Parker hasn't been to see her yet?" Casey looked astonished.

Tessa shook her head, "I don't want to be a bother . . ."

"It's no bother," he assured her. "I'll be over later tonight."

"Thanks, Skylar."

When Tessa was out of sight around the corner, Casey narrowed her eyes at him, "you know where she's going, don't you?"

"Yes."

"Is she okay, Wyatt?"

"She will be," he assured her.

"Well I'm glad that she can talk to you because she won't talk to me," Casey looked a little sad about that.

"Give her time, she'll get there." Wishing he could tell Casey what was going on with Tessa, but it wasn't his secret to tell.

"I am going to wring Parker's neck," Casey announced solemnly.

Slipping an arm around his wife's shoulders, "you'll have to stand in line."

* * * * *

10:02 A.M.

She still wasn't sure what she wanted to do.

For the last hour or so it had been all she could think about.

Should she say yes or no?

Hope honestly wasn't sure.

Part of her wanted to agree to go to the apartment where she had allegedly been tied up and left to die, but the other part wanted to run in the opposite direction as far and as fast as she could.

Dr. Bennett hadn't wanted to leave her alone earlier, but Hope had insisted that she needed some time to think through what had been asked of her. Plus she needed to talk to Parker.

In the last couple of days, ever since she had woken up all alone in that hospital bed, Detective Parker Bell had become her lifeline. Hope knew that by sticking by her he was causing himself problems with his family and friends. And even though she couldn't figure out why he was willing to risk everything to help her, she certainly appreciated it. She honestly didn't know what she would do without him . . .

"Hey!"

Hope stopped with a gasp as she realized she'd walked straight into someone, sending that person tumbling to the ground. "I'm sorry," she apologized immediately, bending down to help the person to their feet.

"Oh, it's you," the woman got to her feet, ignoring Hope's outstretched hand.

"Tessa," Hope was equally surprised but substantially less disappointed to have quite literally bumped into Parker's wife than Tessa appeared to be at seeing her.

"What are you doing here?" Tessa narrowed her greeny-blue eyes. "Are you sure it's safe to be out on your own?"

"I think I'll be okay." Hope was so touched by what she believed to be Tessa's thoughtfulness that she missed the other woman's eye roll. "I was just on my way to see Parker." Hope stared wistfully at Tessa, wondering what it must be like to have such a wonderful husband as Parker and what had driven a wedge between them.

"Of course you were," Tessa looked back over her shoulder and Hope assumed she had just come from the police station. "And what's so pressing you need to track my husband down at work?"

"Apparently they found another woman," Hope leant in closer to Tessa, stooping down to accommodate for the differences in their height. "Out in the country somewhere, tied up and left to starve to death, the same way I was," she hiccupped, and took a moment to steady herself. "Dr. Bennett asked me to go to the apartment where they think that I was tied up, to see if it helps me get my memory back," she explained. "I don't know what to do. I want to do the right thing and help them find this man, especially if he's hurting other women, but I'm scared, I don't know if I want to remember what happened to me. I was hoping to talk to Parker. He's so calm and logical and smart, I was hoping that he could help me sort things out and make a decision."

"And you can't make a decision without consulting my husband first?"

A little taken aback by the coldness in the other woman's voice. "I'm not sure what to do," she stammered. "I was just looking for some help."

"Don't you think you ought to be making your own decisions instead of involving my family in your mess?"

"I'm . . . I'm sorry," not sure what to say. "I didn't mean to take up so much of Parker's time, I'm really sorry that he missed your family meeting the other day."

"Parker told you about Winter?" Tessa's already large eyes growing even wider with disbelief.

Getting the distinct impression she'd just said the wrong thing Hope tried to backtrack, "no, he didn't tell me anything about your niece. He just said that he felt really bad that he missed something so important, he didn't tell me any details." Hearing that seemed to pacify Tessa, taking this as a positive sign Hope continued, "I hope everything is okay with your niece."

"That is none of your business," Tessa growled. "Why didn't you stay in the psychiatric hospital like Elisabeth suggested?"

Surprised, "I . . . I . . . Parker thought it was safer if I went to live with him."

"Safer?" Tessa raised a blonde eyebrow. "It was safer for you to spend all day by yourself while Parker's at work than it was for you to remain in a hospital surrounded by doctors and nurses and patients and their families?"

"Parker said that . . ."

"Parker said this and Parker said that," Tessa interrupted. "You seem to be awfully enamored with my husband. Don't you want to find your own family and friends, Hope? Find out who you really are?"

"Of course I do," she protested automatically, but even as she was saying the words a part of her realized that she wasn't quite ready to get her memory back. Getting her memory back meant giving up Parker and she wasn't sure she was ready to do that just yet.

"Well I don't believe you," Tessa said simply. "I don't believe you and I'm not falling for your games. Remember that." Turning on her heel Tessa continued calmly down the street, climbed into her car and drove off into the morning.

Watching her go, Hope wasn't quite sure whether she'd just been threatened by a jealous wife or whether Tessa actually believed that she was simply playing games. Deciding that for the moment she shouldn't risk going back to the apartment where she had been left to die. Right now, she didn't have anything except for the support of Detective Parker Bell and she couldn't do anything to risk that.

* * * * *

10:31 A.M.

Waiting anxiously on the doorstep.

"Tessa," Eric Abbott exclaimed as he opened his front door.

"Hi, Eric," Tessa returned his hug. "Is Charlie here?"

"He sure is," he held open the door to let her pass, "come on in."

Following him down the hall, she'd tried calling Charlie after leaving Casey and Skylar, but he hadn't picked up. She'd met Charlie Abbott through his brother Eric. Several months ago, while she and Parker had been dealing with Lachlan Mountain, Eric and his wife, Lila, had been dealing with their own living nightmare. Their five-year-old son, Joey, had been shot and killed and their infant daughter, Molly, abducted. Parker had worked their case with Skylar, until Lachlan abducted him. When things had calmed down for all of them she and Parker had caught up for dinner with the Abbott's several times.

Following their car accident last fall, Eric had given her his brother's number and asked her to seriously consider talking to him. Charlie was a psychiatrist, and despite her intense dislike for psychiatry, after finally coming clean on what had happened during her abduction, she had found herself calling Charlie almost against her will. However, she was impressed after their first meeting, and finally accepting the fact that she needed help, she had been seeing him regularly ever since.

"You look tired, Tessa," Eric commented. "Have you been sleeping?"

Eric was a doctor, and almost as bad at fussing as Casey was. "Not that well," she reluctantly admitted.

"You want me to write you a prescription for some sleeping pills?" he offered.

"No, but thanks," she smiled at him.

"Look who's here," Eric announced as they entered the kitchen.

"Tessa," Lila smiled, immediately coming to give her a hug.

"Hey, Lila," she returned the other woman's embrace. Tessa liked quiet, serious Lila. They'd talked many times about the loss of a child, and Tessa loved that Lila never made her feel bad for mourning the baby she had miscarried, while Lila herself mourned her five-year-old son.

"Hi, Charlie, Savannah," she greeted the room's other occupants.

"Hi, Tessa," Savannah returned. Tessa had only met Charlie's fiancée a few times, but she liked her.

"Everything okay, Tess?" Charlie was watching her closely.

Before she had a chance to answer, she looked down to find someone tugging at her leg. Little Molly Abbott had grabbed hold of the leg of her pants and was pulling herself up. "Hi, sweetie-pie," she knelt down to pick the baby up. "Oh my gosh, Lila, she's getting so big. I can't believe she's almost one."

"Me either," Lila grimaced. "She's into *everything* since she learnt to crawl."

Tessa laughed, and disengaged the baby's arms from around her neck so she could pass her back to her mother. "Charlie, can we talk?" she asked, growing serious.

"Of course we can," he stood instantly.

"I don't want to interrupt whatever you guys were up to," obviously they were in the middle of something, there were papers and books spread out all over the kitchen table and she didn't want to intrude.

"You're not," Charlie assured her. "It's just wedding stuff, we have plenty of time left to finish it off. And Savannah understands," he added, knowing what her next objection would be.

"I do," Savannah nodded her agreement when Tessa shot her a querying glance. "We can keeping going without Charlie, so talk for as long as you need to."

"Come on we'll go outside," taking her elbow he led her out the door and over to the patio table. "What's wrong?" he asked once they were seated. "You look upset."

Hesitating, she still wasn't so good at getting started. Luckily though Charlie was pretty good at reading her.

"What did Parker say to you?"

"That I was an emotionless cyborg," tears were pricking at her eyes, but she held them back.

"Why did he call you that?" Charlie's voice was calm but she caught the flash of outrage in his brown eyes.

"I don't know. I walked in on the end of the conversation." She sighed, "I'm guessing something along the lines of how I never trust him."

"Don't let him throw you, Tessa. You're working on your trust issues, and the reality is that Parker has his own issues with trust that have nothing to do with you. I'd consider helping him if he wants it but you're my concern right now."

"Charlie, you don't think I'm emotionless do you?" hating the quiver in her voice.

"No, I don't," he answered firmly. "But you try and control your emotions, we've talked about that before."

"It's all I know how to do to survive," she reminded him. If she hadn't perfected the art of controlling her emotions she would have fallen apart a long time ago.

"The problem is it's a false sense of control, you're not really controlling your emotions, they're controlling you. You've been through hell, Tessa," he said gently, "more than once. And you've never let yourself deal with it. You can't move on until you feel those feelings. I know you know this, Tessa. We've talked about it many times."

"I'm scared to," she said softly.

"I know you are. Look at me, Tess," he waited until she lifted her eyes to meet his, "tell me what you're scared of."

"I'm scared of letting go. I've spent so long literally holding myself together, most of my life, ever since Jake. What if I do what you want me to, what if I let myself feel everything, and then I fall apart? You have to understand how terrifying that is, Charlie, what if I let go of my control and then I can never get it back?"

"And what would be the worst thing that could happen if you lost control?"

"I'd be a crying, depressed mess."

"And?" Charlie prodded.

"Is that a trick question?"

Charlie merely raised an eyebrow and waited for her answer.

"I'd be a crying, depressed mess," she repeated. "I'd be useless."

"Like?"

"Like Emilie," she finished reluctantly.

"Because if your mom had been able to pull herself together and get control of her emotions then she would have known you were gone that weekend," Charlie elaborated for her.

"It wouldn't have changed anything," she said determinedly. "If she'd known Ellie and I were missing, it wouldn't have changed anything. She couldn't have known just how insane Cordelia was. She couldn't have known where Jake took us. She couldn't have stopped him from . . ." she still struggled to say this part, even though she and Charlie had talked about it before. He reached for her hand and squeezed it supportively, and she was able to finish her sentence, "from raping us. I still would have tried to escape, Jake still would have found us, he still would have killed Ellie, and I still would have killed him. It wouldn't have changed anything," she said again, a little desperately this time.

"But it would have changed what happened afterwards," Charlie reminded her gently. "You would have known that your mom loved you, that you weren't all alone. You might have been able to tell her what happened to you, she would have made sure you got proper help. You probably never would have met Dylan Riley, and none of that would have happened. It's okay to blame her, Tessa. She wasn't a good mom to you."

"I don't want to be like her, Charlie," tears were brimming in her eyes again, and she wasn't sure she'd be able to hold them back this time.

"I know you don't, honey, but letting yourself feel things is not the same as being like your mom. She was sick, she made the decision to drink and take drugs rather than get help. You're getting help. Lets say that you lose control, that you fall apart, why would that be so awful?"

The look she gave him must have been one of horror because he chuckled before continuing, "I'm serious, Tessa. It wouldn't be forever. And you have a ton of family and friends who would look after you."

"I guess," she agreed uncertainly. "But they shouldn't have to look after me."

"Why?"

"Because I'm an adult."

"So?"

"So adults look after themselves."

"And that means that they can't accept help when they need it?"

"I guess not," she shrugged.

"Then stop using that as an excuse. They want to take care of you, Tessa. They want to show you that they love you, but you have to let them. You have to accept that they really do love you. They do, you know they do." He must have noticed her wavering, "list them for me. Name all the people that would be there to take care of you."

"Charlie," she protested, she'd feel silly doing that.

"I need to convince you that you have lots of people who love you and will support you, so that I can convince you to trust me and try what I'm asking you to do. So come on, Tessa, tell me every single person that has your back."

Uttering a sigh, but complying, "Skylar and Casey, Daniel and Winter and Matilda, Maisy and Marty, J.J. and Elisabeth, Michelle, Lauren, Carrie and Melanie, Eric and Lila, you."

"You didn't say Parker," Charlie noted.

Blinking, sending the tears she'd been holding back spilling down her cheeks. Charlie moved to sit beside her, wrapping an arm around her shoulders. She would have been more embarrassed but Charlie had already seen her cry numerous times.

"Why didn't you say Parker, Tessa?" he repeated.

"Because I'm not sure anymore."

* * * * *

12:13 P.M.

"This just doesn't feel real."

Watching Dimitri Kendall wander aimlessly around his living room Parker knew exactly how the man felt. The hazy and surreal sensation that made it feel like you'd been thrown headlong into a nightmare. The disjointedness like you were no longer a part of the real world, or rather that the world had suddenly turned against you. The fear and terror and pain that stabbed at you with

98

each breath. At least he had always got Tessa back in one piece. Well maybe not back in *one* piece, each time another piece of her had been shattered. Unfortunately, Dimitri Kendall wasn't going to be lucky enough to get his wife back, in once piece or not. Whether his brain could process it or not his wife was gone forever.

"We just have a couple more questions," Wyatt gestured to the sofa on the other side of the coffee table where Dimitri had been sitting earlier.

"I don't know what else to tell you," Dimitri uttered helplessly as he perched on the edge of the settee.

Studying the man closely, his unruly red hair, his once ruddy complexion stained white by stress, olive smudges under his coffee colored eyes, Parker knew in his gut that this man had nothing to do with his wife's death.

Not that that meant they could positively count him out as a suspect.

According to Dimitri Kendall his wife had said goodbye to him and their children thirteen days ago to leave for her business trip. She had made a few phone calls and sent a few SMS messages, but in the last one she'd said things were pretty hectic and she may not be able to contact him again until she returned home. Dimitri had admitted that this seemed a little odd in retrospect but at the time he had been too busy with his own job and the kids to think too much about it. Since Zak had been unable to narrow down Henrietta's time of death they were unable to positively count the husband out, as he couldn't provide a definitive alibi.

"Your wife was away at a work conference, is that right?" Wyatt confirmed.

"Yes, I already told you that." Dimitri lurched once again to his feet, heading for the kitchen, "does anyone need a refill?"

"No, thank you," Wyatt stood and led the man back to his seat. The whole morning had been going like this. Dimitri Kendall looking for any excuse to keep from focusing his scattered brain, and them constantly trying to keep him on task.

"We spoke with your wife's colleagues," Parker told him.

"Okay," Dimitri nodded distractedly, obviously not picking up the tone in their voices.

"There was no conference," he announced.

Brow furrowing in confusion, "there was no conference?" Dimitri echoed.

"Your wife did not go away on a conference for work," Parker repeated.

"Well, where . . . what . . .?" Dimitri stammered. "Then where was she?"

"That's what we need to talk to you about," Wyatt explained.

"But she called us. And she sent emails and messages," Dimitri contradicted. "Besides where else would she be and why would she lie about it?"

"How would you describe your relationship with your wife?" Wyatt pressed on. "Were things happy between you or strained?"

Catching on immediately, a fire finally lighting in his brown eyes, "my wife was *not* having an affair."

"No one's saying she is," Parker soothed gently, "but she deliberately lied to you so that she could take a two week holiday on her own. Is there any possibility at all that she might be seeing someone behind your back?"

"No. Absolutely not. My wife and I are . . . I mean were . . ." Dimitri almost cracked but managed to regain control, "were very much in love and very happy together."

"Can you think of any other reason then that your wife might want to take a break from you and your kids?" he continued.

"Henrietta loved our kids, her family was her whole reason for being, she'd do anything for us," Dimitri broke off unevenly and moved quickly back to the kitchen under the pretence of refreshing his drink.

It was evident from the room where they sat that family was

very important to Henrietta Kendall. The living room was painted a bright, cheery yellow. No figurines or ornaments or other child unfriendly adornments decorated the room, instead framed artwork and award certificates hung from the walls. The TV cabinet was crammed with kids DVD's, and one half of the room was dedicated to shelves full of toys, and boxes full of toys, and toys scattered all over the floor. The kitchen, painted a paler shade of yellow, contained a whole row of colored glass jars, each containing a different homemade treat, there were cookies, and cupcakes, and fudge, obviously cooking was a favorite hobby of Henrietta's.

"So there's no male colleague from work, old boyfriend, neighbor or family friend that seems to take a particular interest in her?" Wyatt asked.

"No. I know all of Henrietta's friends, there was no one who she was involved with like that," Dimitri repeated.

"Dad."

All three of their head swiveled to the bottom of the stairs where three small faces peeped back at them.

"I don't think that's true," Liam Kendall announced seriously.

"What do you mean?" Dimitri demanded.

"Well . . ." Liam hesitated and shared a glance with his younger sisters.

"Whatever you can tell us could help us find the person who hurt your mom," Wyatt spoke up.

Apparently the children were convinced. They crossed to their father, the girls climbed onto his lap and Liam perched on the arm of the sofa.

"Do you know a friend of your mother's that your dad doesn't know about?" Parker asked, wondering if the seemingly perfect wife and mother was in fact having an affair. More often than not people weren't killed or raped by a random, psychotic stranger but by someone they knew and trusted.

"We didn't mean to be snoopy, daddy," Lucinda implored,

looking up at her father with round coffee colored eyes the same as her dad's, and fiddling with her lopsided pigtails that looked like the work of her older sister.

"That's okay, honey, whatever you did you're not in trouble," Dimitri did his best to offer the child a reassuring smile but failed dismally. Still the smile seemed to reassure the seven-year-old who settled back against him.

"What did you find, Liam?" Wyatt asked the boy, who was the spitting image of his mother; he had the same grey eyes, the same silky chestnut brown hair, and the same narrow facial features.

"Sometimes mom lets us play on her computer," Liam began seriously. "Only we're not supposed to go online . . ."

"We're only allowed to do that when mommy's with us," Lucinda piped up.

Her big brother nodded then continued, "but sometimes when she's busy she gets distracted and she don't, I mean doesn't, watch us too closely and then we like to look stuff up . . . nothing bad though," Liam looked to his father.

"That's okay, son," Dimitri patted the eleven-year-old's head but looked like he'd rather grab his son and shake answers out of him.

"What did you find, Liam?" Parker pressed.

Exchanging guilty glances, Liam opened his mouth to speak but Lucinda jumped in instead, "we found an email from mommy's secret friend," the little girl said in a rush.

Frowning at her, Liam expanded before anyone had a chance to ask anything, "I was looking up some stuff for a science project but mom had left her email open and while I was in the middle of doing stuff one just popped up on the screen . . ." the boy trailed off, clearly uncomfortable.

"Who was the email from?" Wyatt asked gently.

"It was from 'wild girl'," Liam answered. "The email said that the hotel was booked, that they were going to have fun and reminded mom not to tell dad or anyone else about the trip. Do you think the person who sent that email hurt my mom?"

"Maybe," Parker answered honestly, seeing no benefit in lying to the children who after everything they'd been through in the last couple of days had already been forced to grow mature beyond their years. "When did this happen?"

"A little bit before mom went away for work," Liam continued to watch them with a somber face.

"Did you read any other emails?" Parker asked.

"No, we just put the computer away after that," Liam replied.

"Why didn't you say anything," Dimitri snapped out of his daze.

Shrugging more childishly, "we didn't want to get in trouble," Liam explained.

"Mr. Kendall, can we take your wife's computer with us?" Wyatt asked.

"Henrietta took it with her when she went to her conference . . . Liam, can you please take the girls upstairs," Dimitri set Lucinda and Larissa down on the floor.

"Dad, I think I'm old enough to stay," Liam argued.

Standing to look Liam in the eye, at only five foot six he and his eleven-year-old son was almost the same height. "I think you're old enough to do as you are asked without arguing," Dimitri shot back. "Upstairs now."

Rolling his eyes Liam obediently took his sisters' hands and began to drag them towards the door.

"Hey guys thanks for your help," Wyatt stopped the kids before they disappeared.

"Do you really think we helped?" Liam asked.

"You were invaluable," Wyatt assured him.

"That means . . ." Dimitri started to explain.

"I know what it means," Liam snapped, glaring at his father before offering them a smile that was much too old for a child his age. Little Lucinda also offered up a shy smile as she continued to twirl her pigtail around one of her fingers. But middle child

Larissa, who had remained silent the entire time, simply frowned and ran for the stairs.

"I'm sorry," Dimitri apologized for the nine-year-old. "Larissa's taking it the hardest at the moment, she and her mom were very close. Come on you two, off you go," he ushered his remaining children up the stairs then rushed back to pinpoint them in a haughty stare. "That doesn't prove that Henrietta was having an affair."

"No," Parker agreed, thinking that it didn't really discount the theory either, "but it does prove that she deliberately deceived you when she told you she was going away for work."

"You didn't find her computer with her . . . her body?" Dimitri chewed on his lip.

"We didn't find her computer or her car," Wyatt responded.

"Could this 'wild girl' be a friend from your wife's childhood that she reconnected with?" Parker was pleased that they had gotten something helpful out of this interview and that he now had something else that might spark Hope's memory.

"Henrietta didn't have a lot of friends when she was a child. Her family struggled financially and she spent most of her time helping out in their hardware store. The kids could have misunderstood what they read," his brown eyes lit with a delicate hope. "It could have just been a joke with someone from her work."

"I might agree if it hadn't happened shortly prior to your wife going way, and the fact that we know for certain that she lied to you about where she was going and what she was doing. Besides, do you think that your kids would get it wrong? Your son seems like quite a bright young man," Parker knew it was better for the family if they all stayed on the same page. It wouldn't help the kids if they thought their father didn't believe them. Neither would it help Dimitri if he began to doubt his own children.

Deflated, Dimitri nodded, "Liam is a smart boy, top of his class. It's just that I don't know what to make of this," he began to wring his hands helplessly. "Henrietta's not someone who would have a secret life. The kids, me, her job, that's what's important to her. I just don't understand who this 'wild girl' is and what Henrietta was doing with her. I thought I knew my wife, I thought I knew what she was thinking and what she believed, but it turns out I know nothing about her."

Watching as Dimitri Kendall wandered into his kitchen and took one of the homemade brownies from a jar, Parker knew exactly how the man felt, this was exactly his problem with Tessa. He thought he had finally come to understand the way her brain worked but as it turned out, he had no idea what went on inside that blonde head of hers. For the first time since Tessa had had her miscarriage, he was thankful that the baby hadn't survived only to be caught in the middle of his and Tessa's problems.

"I'll leave you my card in case you or the kids think of anything else," Wyatt announced, placing a card on the kitchen counter.

Following his partner over, "Mr. Kendall, does this woman look familiar to you?" he held up a photo of Hope.

Turning to look at it with watery eyes, "no, why? Do you think this woman could be that 'wild girl'?"

"No, this woman is a victim too."

"Oh, I'm sorry, she doesn't look familiar," he answered absently, his mind clearly elsewhere, probably trying to figure out any signs he should have noticed that pointed to his wife's secret life.

"We'll see ourselves out," Wyatt patted the man's shoulder as they exited the kitchen.

Once outside Parker faced his partner, "well I think right now there are three options. Number one this wild girl was both Hope and Henrietta's lover and we're dealing with some sort of lover's quarrel. Number two wild girl is a friend of Hope and Henrietta and something went awry during a girl's holiday away. Or number three he or she is a predator, scouring the Internet in search of women to befriend and then trick into meeting as some sort of sick and twisted game."

"And our biggest problem," Wyatt added, "is not only don't we know who wild girl is but we also have no idea how many other victims are out there."

* * * * *

6:43 P.M.

"Did you talk to Winter?"

"Yeah I did . . ."

"And," Tessa prompted, cutting Skylar off in her desire to know whether he had been able to get her niece to open up.

"And she said she was doing okay," Skylar finished.

"Well you don't believe her do you? How could she possibly be doing okay?" Tessa demanded.

"No, I don't believe her. But I think I have about as much chance of getting an honest answer out of her as I do out of you." Skylar raised an eyebrow at her, "how are you doing?"

"I'm fine," she waved a dismissive hand at him. "I keep thinking that she's shutting me out on purpose, because of what happened with Dino last year. Then I think that I'm just being egotistical, this isn't about me it's about Winter. But then I think that I should push her, she shouldn't be going through this on her own she's only sixteen, she needs to talk to someone. Only then that makes me think that I ought to let her deal with things in the way she wants to . . ."

"Alright, alright, calm down, clam down," Skylar pushed her down into a chair and began to rub her shoulders. "This isn't just about Winter, it's about both of you."

Breaking away from him, "I don't know what to do, Skylar."

"Winter will be okay," he assured her.

"How could you possibly know that?"

"Because, my dear, Winter is you. Think of the hell you'd already been through by the time you were Winter's age. You learned to be strong, and as much as I wish you hadn't had to deal with all of that on your own, it's certainly made you well-equipped to help Winter through this."

Wandering over to the kitchen window which overlooked the tranquil back gardens. Beneath the shiny black sky, the clear expanse of neatly mown lawn was sprinkled with a dusting of white snowflakes. The trees that had once surrounded her cottage stood tall and proud in the winter night, like glittering angels beneath the moon.

"Cordelia loved the wintertime," she whispered absently. "Winter's worried that she's going to turn out like Jake and Cordelia."

"Tessa . . ." Skylar began warningly; he'd already had this conversation with her before on numerous occasions.

"I told her that DNA isn't everything," she continued. She and Winter had discussed that a lot since her niece had come to live with her but Tessa still wasn't one hundred percent convinced that she wasn't going to end up a product of her own DNA.

Grabbing her shoulders, Skylar turned her around to force her to look at him, "honey, you are not going to turn out like Patrick and Emilie," he assured her a little more forcefully than usual.

"Well I walked out on my family just like Patrick did to us," she retorted.

"No, Parker walked out on you," Skylar corrected.

Smiling at him gratefully, "thanks for saying that but you shouldn't have to take sides between us, Parker's been your best friend for over two decades."

"You're both my friends, and Parker's the one who left not you," Skylar insisted.

"He almost died because of me." She sighed, "maybe I just should have told him about Isaac and Rebecca."

"You know I think you should tell him, but not knowing every detail about that is not a reason for him to leave. How did your visit with Charlie Abbott go?"

"Charlie wants me to stop trying to control my emotions and just feel them," she answered. "He says I shouldn't be afraid of falling apart because I have a lot of family and friends who would look after me."

"He's right. On both counts, you do need to stop trying to control your emotions, and you do have a lot of people who are going to help you deal with things. I'm glad you're seeing him, he's good for you, you're doing really great, Tessa."

"Really?" she asked a little beseechingly.

"Really," Skylar assured her.

Before she became emotional, Tessa quickly changed the subject, "I saw Hope today, outside the station, she was on her way to see Parker," she rolled her eyes in disgust.

"You two have words?" Skylar released his hold on her shoulders and helped himself to some leftover quiche from the fridge.

"Kind of. Every word out of her mouth was Parker says, or Parker did, or I need to ask Parker, she's becoming obsessed with him."

"You want some?"

Skylar offered her the dish of quiche but she curled up her nose, she could never eat when she was stressed. However, she didn't want to hear another spiel from Skylar about healthy living so instead she answered, "I already ate earlier. It's not good for her, latching onto Parker like this," Tessa continued, she had spent all day trying to make sure her feelings about Hope were objective and not just jealousy.

"Well he's not really helping matters," Skylar added. "Moving her into his house, springing to her defense every five seconds."

"Something's not right with her, Skylar, and I'm not just being paranoid," she couldn't shake the feeling that Hope was not all she appeared to be. "I tried to tell Parker but he wouldn't listen.

He always lets himself get too emotionally involved and then he can't see straight. Just be on your guard around her okay, don't trust her, and don't let her hurt Parker. No matter how things turn out between us I don't want to see anything happen to him."

"Nothing's going to happen to him," Skylar assured her. "I'm watching out for him just like I'm watching out for you. So . . ." he gave her one of his stern gazes he usually reserved for when he wasn't about to take no for an answer. "You are not going to lock yourself away out here anymore, Casey has work tomorrow and the next day but after that the two of you are going to do something together. No excuses, no cancelling at the last minute, no doing a disappearing act, no feigning illness, or having something important pop up, absolutely none of your usual shenanigans. Promise me, I mean it, Tess, promise."

Feeling backed into a corner Tessa sighed reluctantly, "promise. But now you promise me something, promise me you're going to talk to Hope and try to find out what she's hiding."

"Deal," Skylar stuck out his hand.

Shaking on it, "deal."

FEBRUARY 13TH

2:18 A.M.

Deciding it wasn't worth tossing and turning any longer, clearly he wasn't going to get much sleep tonight. Parker pushed back the covers and threw on some sweat pants and sweatshirt, his bare feet padding along the floorboards; he decided he'd make something to eat.

It had been a long day. After their visit to the Kendall family home, he and Wyatt had spent the afternoon speaking with as many of Henrietta's friends, co-workers and neighbors as they could manage. Unfortunately none of their interviews had yielded anything helpful. No one knew anything about Henrietta's secret life nor had any clue who wild girl might be.

When he'd finally arrived home, somewhere around eleven, Hope had been locked up in the bathroom, and had refused to come out or answer him. Not in the least hungry, and with an unmarked car still parked outside he'd decided to go for a jog. Running mile after mile in the frosty night Parker tried to shut off his brain, tried to let the cold numb his guilt, but it did no good. All he could think about was what he'd said about Tessa while arguing with Wyatt.

He definitely did not really think that Tessa was an emotionless cyborg. He regretted saying it, and he regretted even more that Tessa had overheard him say it. He'd tried calling her at least two dozen times, but her phone had been turned off and he kept getting her voice mail. He had left a few messages apologizing, but he was yet to hear back from her. Not that he could blame Tessa for not wanting to talk to him. He'd really made a mess of things lately. Letting their problems pile up so high that now he didn't even know how to fight his way out from under them.

Parker wanted to though. He and Tessa needed to sit down and talk things through.

Reaching the kitchen, Parker rummaged through the refrigerator, which was severely lacking anything edible, and thought of how well stocked Tessa's fridge was bound to be. If he'd been at Tessa's house right now he could probably be helping himself to any number of homemade treats, instead he had to settle for a sandwich. Using the last two slices of bread from the loaf, spreading peanut butter on one and jelly on the other, he took his sandwich and was about to settle at the table when he heard a noise from outside.

Setting his plate down he moved tentatively to the backdoor. Wondering whether he ought to retrieve his gun from upstairs, Parker didn't really think it was anyone sinister in the backyard, but it was better to be safe than sorry. Sliding open the door he saw a white figure stretched out on the lawn in the middle of the yard by the oak tree where he and Tessa had spent many a summer evening gazing up at the great expanse of sky and discussing their future.

Relaxing, he went and retrieved his dinner, shrugged into a jacket, stuck his feet into a pair of sneakers and headed outside. "Couldn't sleep?" Parker asked as he plopped down beside her, leaning back against the old oak tree and taking a gigantic bite of his sandwich.

"My mind's too jumbled up," Hope answered, tilting her head sideways to look at him.

"I know the feeling. Want some?" he offered her the plate.

"No thanks," she curled her lip. "I'm not hungry."

"Tessa gets like that when she's stressed," he said before he thought, he felt strange discussing Tessa with Hope.

"I saw her today," Hope reverted her gaze back up to the inky sky, dotted with sparkling stars.

"Tessa?"

"Dr. Bennett told me about how everyone wants me to go back to the place where you think I was tied up in case it helps me get my memory back," her mind moving on to other topics.

"Not everyone."

She turned to study him, "why do you always stand up for me?"

"Because you need help and I know what it's like to be all by yourself and not know what to do to make things better." Parker thought of his time in foster care and how scared and alone he and Matilda had been. If it hadn't been for the love and support of his adopted parents and Wyatt then his life would have taken a completely different turn.

"I really appreciate everything you've done for me," Hope smiled shyly up at him. "I don't know how I'm ever going to repay you."

"You don't need to repay me," he smiled back, feeling a nervous fluttering begin in his stomach. Parker sincerely loved his wife, but he felt like things with Tessa were doomed. As long as he and Tess were together, her past was always going to be an obstacle between them because she couldn't leave it behind, but with Hope there was no past to contend with. He didn't love Hope; he liked her, he felt sorry for her, he was driven to help her, but he didn't love her, however maybe that was a positive. With Tessa he had jumped right in with his blinders on, completely ignoring the warnings of his friends. He hadn't thought things through, he'd fallen hard and fast and gone with his emotions. Things were different with Hope. Maybe she really *was* the easier option.

"Parker?"

Blinking he found Hope had scooted up to sit cross-legged and was staring at him anxiously.

"What?" embarrassed that he had zoned out on her. "I'm sorry what did you say?"

"I said," she repeated patiently, "that I don't know what to do."

"About going back to the apartment?"

"Uh huh," she bobbed her head. "I'm so confused, I want to do the right thing but I'm not sure I can."

"You also need to consider what's in your best interest," he reminded her.

"But there could be other women out there that he's hurt," she maintained miserably. "What kind of person am I if I do nothing to help them?"

"First of all, you don't even know if going back to the apartment is going to spark your memory, there're no guarantees. Second of all, I don't know what kind of person you were before, but I think I've got to know you pretty well and you are definitely a kind and caring person."

Offering him another shy smile Hope moved a little closer, "what do *you* think I should do?"

Drawing a deep breath, "I think that if it comes down to that then you'll know if you're up to it, but right now we have a few other leads, so lets just wait and see and cross that bridge when we come to it."

"Thanks."

"You're welcome, and whatever you decide to do I'll be there to support you."

"Thanks," she said again. "Thanking you just doesn't seem like enough considering all you've done for me."

Parker wasn't used to so much gratitude. Once again, with Tessa things were so different. When he and Tessa had gotten together, she had helped him as much as he had helped her, although he wasn't sure she had realized that. When things were going well between them he and Tessa completed one another so perfectly. It was only when things went awry that Tessa reverted to her old habits of shutting him out and facing everything alone.

"You're shaking," he announced, taking off his coat to drape it across Hope's shoulders. "I think we both need to get some sleep."

Offering her his hand, Hope took it and he pulled her to her feet. In silence, they entered the house and climbed the stairs, at the door of Hope's room they paused. "You're a really great guy, Parker," she looked at him wistfully. "Tessa's a really lucky woman." Standing on tiptoe she traced her fingertips down his cheek, then pressed a feathery kiss to his lips, before quickly disappearing into her room.

Sitting on his bed, phone in hand, Parker debated trying Tessa one last time. At last, with the feel of Hope's kiss still lingering on his lips, he put the phone back down, pulled the covers over his head, and finally drifted off into a fitful sleep.

* * * * *

9:32 A.M.

"You want any breakfast?"

"No, thank you, I already ate," Wyatt was trying his hardest not to let Tessa's suspicions completely cloud his judgment; he wanted to keep an open mind about Hope.

"Parker's in the shower," Hope continued, her smile permanently in place.

Wyatt had to agree with Tessa on this one. Hope did smile too much for someone who had just been through what she had. "I thought maybe we could have a little chat while we waited for him," he suggested.

"Sure," Hope nodded agreeably and despite his protestations that he wasn't hungry she set out a plate of cookies.

Unable to help himself from thinking that if it were Tessa she would have had freshly baked homemade treats instead of cookies from a packet. Pushing his pointless comparisons away he got down to business, "you still haven't had any memory flashes?"

"No," she shook her head sadly.

"Nothing at all?"

"Nothing at all," she echoed.

"You haven't been able to remember your name, or where you're from, or anything about your past?" Wyatt had to agree with Tessa that it was very unusual for someone to completely forget who they were. Over the years he'd seen victims who were unable to recall the events leading up to, during, and following their attacks, but never had he come across someone who could recall nothing about themselves.

"Not a thing," her smile remained, although took on a dismal glint.

"The other victim who was found in similar circumstances, her name was Henrietta Kendall, does that name mean anything to you?" Wyatt watched her closely for any hints of deception.

"I don't think so," her dark blue eyes studied him earnestly.

"It doesn't sound familiar?"

"No," she shook her head more firmly this time. "I definitely haven't met anyone with that name before."

Raising an eyebrow, "you definitely haven't met anyone named Henrietta Kendall before," he confirmed.

"Right," she agreed.

"So you do remember something?" Spending too much time with Tessa was starting to make him overly suspicious.

Confused for a second, "I'm sorry I thought you meant had the name helped me to remember anything. I didn't mean that I remembered not remembering it, if that makes sense," Hope gave a nervous chuckle. "Parker should be down at any second," she stood. "Can I get you something to drink?"

"No, thanks," he was starting to get the feeling that Tessa was on to something as far as Hope was concerned. "We can wait for Parker if you want before we continue."

"Oh, no, that's okay, I was just thirsty," she poured herself a glass of water and by the time she returned to the table her easy smile was back.

Before she had time to recover too much Wyatt forged on, "what about Dimitri Kendall, the victim's husband?"

"I'm sorry, that name doesn't sound familiar either."

"What about Liam, Larissa or Lucinda Kendall, they were Henrietta's three young children."

Eyes clouding over, "those poor little things. How awful for them to have to grow up without a mother."

Convinced that Hope looked genuinely disturbed about the fate of the Kendall children, and also genuinely unfamiliar with their names. "The children told us something that might help us find who killed their mother and also who tried to kill you."

"Parker said you had a possible lead," Hope inserted.

"He did, did he?" Wyatt had given his partner strict instructions to wait until today to speak with Hope about the emails.

"He didn't tell me what it was though," she added, seeming to sense that she had said too much.

"Henrietta's children mentioned that one day not long before she left on her trip they found an email on her computer. It was from someone called wild girl, and it was talking about the trip that they had planned."

"You think that wild girl is the one who killed her? The one who nearly killed me?"

"I think that wild girl is involved somehow," he answered. Truth be told he wasn't entirely positive just what role their mystery emailer had played, but he was positive that he or she was involved somehow. "Does any of this sound familiar to you?"

"No, I'm sorry," Hope clenched her hands into fists.

"The email also reminded Henrietta to lie to her husband and not tell him where she was really going."

"So you think that at least at first this woman went willingly to whoever hurt her?"

"Most likely."

"Which means I probably did too," Hope looked unsure how she felt about this prospect.

"And none of this sparks any memory?"

"No," Hope shook her head wildly sending her braids whipping around her head. "I don't know any Henrietta Kendall or anyone else in her family. I don't know any wild girl. I don't even know if I own a computer . . ."

"Everything okay in here?" Parker appeared in the doorway.

"Fine," Wyatt replied.

"Hope?" Parker turned his attention to the girl.

"Detective Wyatt was just asking me if I knew Henrietta Kendall or the person who was emailing her, but I don't know, I just don't know," she finished desperately.

Resting his hands on her shoulders, "calm down," Parker soothed. "We spoke with Henrietta's family, friends, neighbors, co-workers, no one recognized your picture, but at least we have something solid to work on at the moment."

Hope nodded and smiled up at Parker gratefully, "yeah, maybe you'll be able to figure out who I really am soon."

"Maybe," Parker smiled back down at her.

"Parker, could I talk to you for a moment, in private," he added with a pointed look at Hope.

"Sure," Hope tore her gaze away from his partner to shoot her perpetual smile his way. "I'll go take a shower, Dr. Bennett is going to take me out for lunch today."

Parker watched her leave but the second she was gone turned with a frown, "you couldn't have waited for me before interrogating her?"

"I wasn't *interrogating* her," Wyatt reminded his partner calmly. "And I thought I'd get more out of her if you weren't around. When you're there Hope seems to be a little . . . preoccupied," he finished.

Rolling his eyes, "I'm going to guess that you've been to visit my wife, and she's been feeding you another of her paranoid theories on what a threat Hope is."

"Look, Parker," Wyatt began seriously, "I'm not suggesting that Hope is a homicidal maniac, but I do think that she's hiding something. Earlier when I asked her did she know Henrietta Kendall she said that she had definitely never met anyone with that name. When I asked her if that meant she had remembered something she became nervous and quickly left the table . . ."

"That doesn't mean anything," Parker interrupted. "She's stressed, she has amnesia, she was almost killed, she's just edgy."

"Just hear me out," he placated. "What if Hope did know Henrietta, what if she is wild girl or maybe there was more than one person that Henrietta was meeting up with. We don't know exactly what they were planning on doing. Maybe they just got in over their heads, did something they shouldn't, and now Hope is scared to come forward because she thinks she might get in trouble. Or maybe Hope was just in the wrong place at the wrong time and saw something happen between Henrietta and wild girl and ended up as collateral damage and now she's afraid of this person. All I'm asking of you is that you just keep your eyes open, that's all we're all asking of you."

"I assume by *all* you mean you and Tessa," Parker scowled.

"Come on, Parker, Tessa's your wife and you're always complaining that she hates it when you look out for her, is it so awful that she wants to return the favor?"

"She kissed me," Parker said quietly.

"Who? Tessa?" Wyatt asked confused.

"Hope," Parker clarified.

"What?" he had to bite his tongue to keep from screaming it too loudly. "Are you insane?"

"Calm down," Parker said with an irritating calm. "It wasn't in a sexual way, she's just grateful. We were talking last night and she got a little emotional, it was nothing."

Staring in disbelief at a man he'd known most of his life, a man he'd considered a younger brother, a man who he'd thought he understood. "Are you kidding? You would really risk everything with Tessa, who I know you still love, over someone you've known for three days, someone who doesn't even know her own name? You know what, I don't want to hear it, I'll see you at work."

Before he had a chance to say something he knew he'd regret later, Wyatt stormed down the hall to the door. If his talk with Hope hadn't convinced him that Tessa was on to something then what Parker had just told him certainly had. He was now more convinced than ever that Tessa was right. He wasn't sure exactly what it was that Hope was hiding from them but he was positive there was something that she didn't want them to know.

* * * * *

9:32 A.M.

"Hey," Daniel dropped a kiss on Matilda's head and stretched out on the floor of her room next to the bed where she was perched reading a book. "You were out early this morning," he commented mildly.

"I went out for breakfast," Matilda answered vaguely.

"With *him*," he finished for her.

Setting her book down, "I'm sorry . . ."

"No," he interrupted forcefully, "don't apologize. I'm the one who ought to be apologizing to you. I shouldn't keep putting you in the middle. He's your brother, of course you want to spend time with him."

"I don't like what Parker's doing either," Matilda explained. "It's just that we were apart for so long and then when I come back everything falls apart."

"I understand, believe me, I understand," Daniel assured her. After their mother had tried to murder Tessa, he had left, convinced that as long as he remained in their home Tessa would always be in danger. By the time he returned things between himself and Tessa had changed almost irrevocably, even now, well over a year later, things still weren't quite the same as they once were.

"I wish you two could eventually learn to get along," Mattie sighed wistfully.

"I don't think that's ever likely to happen," he reminded her gently. For a while he and Parker had made an effort to get along for Tessa's sake, but then things had gone sour, Parker had started acting strangely, and then disappeared. Despite Tessa's insistences that something had happened to her husband, the rest of them believed he had simply walked out on his life. Unfortunately, Tessa had been right and Parker had been abducted by madman Lachlan Mountain. Once again, things had eased up between him and his brother-in-law, despite Parker's disapproval that he had started dating Matilda, until last fall.

Following a phone call from Wyatt, he, Matilda and Winter had rushed back from their holiday to both Tessa and Parker in the hospital. The arguments between his sister and her husband has started shortly after that, then bit by bit Parker had begun to phase himself out of Tessa's life. Daniel didn't think that he was ever going to forgive Parker for hurting his baby sister, but he was serious about his relationship with Matilda and he didn't want the fact that he couldn't get along with her brother to ruin things.

" . . . I just wish there was some way we could fix things," Matilda was saying. "I was talking to him again this morning, asking him what he thought he was doing with this Hope woman . . ."

Scooting over to rest his hand on Mattie's thigh, pleased when she didn't flinch away from his touch, Matilda's childhood had left her scared of a man's touch. "Honey, I know you want us all to be one big happy family, but that's just not in our future."

"I know. It's just that . . ."

"That things were so different when we were away," he smiled remembering the wonderful time they had had together on their holiday. It had been Tessa's idea for him to take Winter and Matilda on a trip through Europe. He had been several times already, as a teenager had even spent some time studying there, and it had been wonderful showing the girls all the places he loved. It had been a magical time, long walks through the countryside, visiting enormous castles and tiny cottages, beautiful hotels, great food, and plenty of time to get to know each other better.

"It was amazing," Matilda agreed, her sad face momentarily lighting at the memories. "But ever since we got back it's like things have gone from bad to worse. How are Tessa and Winter?"

"Both as stubborn as each other, and both firmly fixed on pretending that everything is fine," he shook his head, his sister and his niece were experts at driving him crazy. But as worried as he was about both of them right now he had other things on his mind. Climbing up on the bed he lay down, pulling Mattie against his chest, one hand tangling itself in her soft, wavy black hair. "There's something I want to talk to you about."

"What is it?" Matilda began to absently run her fingertips up and down his chest.

Catching her fingers before he continued, even through his shirt the feel of her hands on his body was stirring up feelings that if he responded to them were beyond what Matilda was ready to deal with right now. "I was talking to Tessie the other day and she said something that really got me thinking."

"What did she say?"

"She said that we really love each other, and that we make a great couple and . . ." he paused nervously, "and that I should think about proposing to you."

Matilda went completely still in his arms like she'd suddenly been turned into stone. "What?" she managed to croak.

Sitting up he pulled the small purple velvet box from his pocket, "Matilda Bell, will you marry me?"

Clambering to her knees, "Daniel, I don't . . . are we ready for marriage?"

"Who is ever ready for marriage?" he countered.

"It's not like my parents, or your parents were good at it. What if we have bad genes or something? I mean look at my brother and your sister, they've managed to make a mess of things in less than a year . . ."

Cutting off her babbling, "I don't care about that. All I care about is that I love you and I want to know that we're always going to be together."

For the longest moment Mattie just stared at him and he was terrified that she was going to say no, but then she began to cry and threw her arms around his neck.

"Is that a yes?" he checked as his arms circled her waist.

"Yes," she confirmed, laughing through her tears. "I really love you, Daniel." She lifted her head from his shoulder and grew serious, "I mean I *really* love you."

Taking her face in his hands he kissed away the last of her tears before his mouth found hers. As he gazed down at her, Daniel knew that this moment was only the beginning of what he was sure was going to be a long and happy life for the two of them.

* * * * *

2:01 P.M.

She was going to die.

Millie knew this. Had known it for some time. Just as now she knew that death was almost upon her.

She'd long ago lost track of time. It could have been days or weeks since she was tied up here and left for dead. At first Millie had been positive that her attacker would come back and set her free. Then she had been positive that someone would stumble upon her and she would be rescued. But she had long ago given up such fanciful ideas.

Now she knew that she was never leaving this room.

Alive anyway.

She couldn't believe how stupid she had been to get herself into this mess in the first place. It had been a terrible idea to join the group in the first place. Only she'd been bored one evening. Michael had been stuck at work late again, their two Siberian Huskies curled on the floor at her feet, and she'd decided to aimlessly browse the web. Looking for something fun to do with her time she had found a group where middle aged women such as herself chatted together about what they would do if they were completely and utterly free.

At first, she'd joined in as a bit of fun, but over the following weeks she had become obsessed with spending every second of spare time she had on the site. They chatted about their youth's, when they had been young and carefree, they talked about the burdens of their jobs and families, and before she knew it Millie had become dependent on the site to make it through the day.

It wasn't as though she were completely unhappy with the way her life had turned out. She had a husband who was wonderful and attentive, at least when he was around, but Michael spent every second month abroad for work. Still Michael was rich and he showered her with everything money could buy, but the magic of having expensive clothes and jewelry had long since dwindled when she realized it could not fill the deep hole in her heart. Despite years of trying they had been unable to conceive a child of their own, and after an adoption had fallen through at the last second after the mother decided to keep her baby boy, Millie had found herself lost, lacking any real purpose in her life.

When wild girl had suggested meeting in person at a central hotel she had jumped at the chance. Desperate for some excitement in her life, something to get her blood running and her limbs tingling, she had gone along with the plan to lie to her husband, who was conveniently on his month overseas, to attend the girls week away.

Things had gone sour almost immediately.

Wild girl turned out to be a psycho.

Then she was raped, drugged and dumped in the back of a van, driven here, drugged again, only to awaken in this dark, dingy, room. Millie guessed it was an old warehouse, abandoned years ago, it was dusty, piles of junk dotted about, the windows were all boarded up meaning only a miniscule amount of natural light peeped through.

Around her ankle was a metal clamp attached to an enormous iron ball. The short chain let her move maybe a foot, but no more, and nowhere close to reaching the chocolate cake and pitcher of water. She had put all her energy into reaching it at first. Had used all her strength to try to pull the heavy ball but had not been rewarded with even an inch of movement.

However, she had long ago given up hope that she would make it.

Millie knew she was dying of dehydration.

She'd gone through dry mouth, dizziness, tiredness, headaches, nausea, tingling in her arms and legs, muscle spasms, her skin had become wrinkly and shriveled like she'd been in the bath too long, her vision had dimmed and she'd become delirious.

Now however a sense of calm had descended upon her.

She was ready to give up.

She'd heard of elderly people who were able to hold on to reach a certain occasion, a wedding, a birthday, a birth, Millie herself knew of an old lady who had managed to hold on to celebrate her one hundredth birthday only to pass away two days later. The problem for Millie was that she had nothing to live for. She didn't think she really loved her husband; he was just someone who kept her from being completely alone. She didn't have any children or any other family. She didn't have any real friends. She didn't even have a job.

Just as Millie was letting go, she heard a noise just outside. A voice talking animatedly, and it was coming closer. "Think of the possibilities," it said. "All these warehouses could be turned into awesome apartments."

Those were the last words that Millie Waters ever heard.

* * * * *

3:06 P.M.

"Her body's still warm," Zak said sadly.

"How long's she been dead?" Parker asked, still staring at Millicent Waters' sunken eyes and thinking of how lucky Hope had been to escape a similar fate.

"She probably died while they were right outside," Zak gestured at the two young men hovering just outside the door of the warehouse.

"It's identical to the others," Wyatt stated the obvious. "Just this time he decided to go with a ball and chain."

"At least we know who she is," his thoughts still firmly focused on Hope, who had been edgy ever since her talk with Wyatt this morning.

"Do you think the killer left the driver's license here on purpose or by accident?" Zak asked.

"On purpose," he and Wyatt answered simultaneously.

"Any idea on how long she's been here?" he asked Zak.

Shaking his head, "the heater makes it harder to estimate," Zak looked over his shoulder at the large gas heater that had been set up facing Millicent's body, presumably to speed up her death by dehydration.

"Doesn't it say how long the gas bottle lasts?" he asked.

"It probably does, but we don't know if the killer came back and swapped it for another, they might have gone through one or ten," Zak replied.

"So far nothing," Maisy announced coming over to join them.

"Nothing even remotely helpful. The brown hairs again but I think that those are being planted. No fingerprints of fibers on the ball and chain, the heater or the windows. There were a couple of prints on the door handle but I'm pretty sure those are going to turn out to be from the two guys who found the body. This guy is really good, does that scare anybody else? Three victims, three crime scenes and so far we don't have anything to go on."

"We have the computer lead," Wyatt reminded them. "Hopefully we'll find Millicent's computer at her home, maybe that will finally give us a direction to move in. And we have Hope."

Parker caught his partner's piercing frown but chose to ignore it. "We're heading over to her house after here," he told Maisy.

"Well good luck," she gave them all a grim smile before moving to join her colleagues who were busily sifting through the piles of rubbish that filled the huge space.

"Well I notified the husband," J.J. growled, stalking over to them.

"And?" he prodded wondering what the source of J.J.'s anger was, knowing it was something more than just their three victims, lack of evidence and the fact that the media had now latched on to the case.

"And he's a despicable human being, when I called him I got his wife . . ."

"But his wife is . . ." Wyatt started.

"Well apparently this guy wasn't satisfied with just one," J.J. growled.

"Could Michael Waters be the killer?" he asked. "Maybe Millicent was on to him and he killed her to keep her quiet, then to cover his tracks he attacks two other women so we think we're dealing with a serial killer."

"No, he'd been out of the country for three weeks, due to come back in a little over a week. And he's been at this charade for going on twelve years. Wife number one didn't have a hint of wife number two," J.J. sighed and ran his hands through his bushy brown beard. "He sounded genuinely upset to hear about wife number one's death. Started bawling and telling me how he never stopped loving her, but they couldn't have kids, and he was away so much. After a while he and his secretary just happened to fall into bed together, she wound up pregnant, he got the child he always dreamed of and things went from there."

"So the second wife knew all along about the first?" Wyatt confirmed.

"Yes."

"So I guess she has no motive either," Wyatt frowned dismally.

"Maybe the husband hired someone else to do his dirty work," Parker knew he was clutching at straws but finding their killer was Hope's best chance at finding out who she really was.

"He's given us permission to check his back accounts, so I guess we'll see if anything pops up," J.J. started back towards the door. "Wyatt, Parker, you two go to the Waters house and find her computer. Zak, give me something concrete for these vultures out here. And you guys," he yelled to the crime scene techs, "find me anything. Come on people we need some answers. Who knows how many more women are out there waiting for someone to find them. Millicent Waters was almost found in time, lets not be too late next time."

FEBRUARY 14TH

10:42 A.M.

"Are you sure you're up to this?" Parker asked for the hundredth time.

"I'm sure," Hope nodded confidently.

Catching the slight hesitation in her voice, "this is your last chance to back out," he reminded her. He, Hope and Wyatt were sitting in Wyatt's car around the block from the apartment where Hope had been tied up and left to die. Last night, upon hearing about the latest victim, Hope had come to the decision that she wanted to try going to the apartment to see if it sparked any memories for her. He had protested that he wasn't sure she was ready, but Hope had been insistent, if there were more women in trouble out there and she did nothing to help them then she didn't think she could live with herself.

"Alright then, lets go," Wyatt restarted the engine.

"Wait, are you absolutely positive," Parker checked once more, he couldn't shake the feeling that this was going to turn out to be a bad idea.

"Parker, she said she wanted to do this, you seem to be the only one with a problem," Wyatt scowled disapprovingly.

"Dr. Bennett is going to be there right?" Hope checked.

"She should already be there," Wyatt answered. "We're running late."

Parker watched Hope carefully as they rounded the corner and pulled in across the street from the apartment. "Any of this look familiar?"

Wide-eyed, she shook her head, "I could swear I've never been here before in my life."

As the three of them crossed the street, Hope discreetly slipped her hand into his and squeezed tightly. Returning the gesture, Parker gently pulled her along as her steps slowed the nearer they got.

"You remembering anything, Hope?" Wyatt asked as they reached the front door, which sat slightly ajar.

"No, it's like I've never seen this place before." She took in the narrow steps leading back up to the pavement, "this is where I ran when I was escaping?" she asked distantly.

"That's what we think," he confirmed.

"I just don't remember it," she said sadly.

"Try to keep an open mind," Elisabeth opened the door fully.

"I am, Dr. Bennett," Hope nodded seriously.

"Alright then, you ready to begin?" Elisabeth stepped back to allow them access through the door.

Hope shuddered and took a deep breath, "I'm ready."

Stepping inside he gave Hope's hand a supportive squeeze and thought about how nice it was to have someone's complete and utter trust. Following Hope's gaze around the room it took him a minute to realize what was different. Someone had removed the boards that had previously covered the windows, which gave the room a brighter, airier feel.

Slowly Hope released her grip on his hand and began to wander around the room, stopping sporadically to examine things. Parker moved to follow her, but Elisabeth gave a slight shake of her head and held him back.

After a couple of minutes Elisabeth went to her, "Hope, how are you feeling?"

"Frustrated," Hope came to a stop in the middle of the room. "I don't remember any of this," she swept her hands around to include the whole room. "Where was I tied up?"

"Hope . . ." he started seeing no reason to upset her further.

Waving him quiet, "over by the pole," Elisabeth answered.

Hope crossed over to there, absently rubbing her wrists, scrutinizing the pole carefully. "How did I get free?"

"We don't know," Elisabeth answered.

"Did you find anything on the ground that I might have used?" directing her question to him and Wyatt. "Something to cut myself free, like a knife or a razor?"

"We didn't find anything here," he replied.

"Well there are no sharp edges on this pole, so how did I cut myself loose?" she demanded.

"Actually, Hope, the ropes weren't cut," Wyatt informed her.

"They weren't cut?" she echoed, brow furrowed in confusion. "Then how did I get away?"

"We don't know," Wyatt answered.

"Did I untie myself then?" she asked, then continued before anyone had a chance to answer, "how come if I could untie myself then the other women couldn't?"

"The other women weren't tied up with ropes," Wyatt told her. "They were restrained with chains."

Taking this in, "then why was I different?"

"I was wondering that," Wyatt agreed.

"There could be other women who were also tied up with ropes," Parker jumped in to reassure her. "We don't know how many victims are out there or what he's done to them."

"We found your fingerprints all over this place. Do you have any idea how they got there?" Wyatt enquired.

"None," Hope shook her head.

"It seems a like you don't even want to remember," Wyatt commented.

"Wyatt," Parker admonished, glaring at his partner.

"I can't help it," Hope began to cry, tears trickling down her pale cheeks. "I thought you said coming here would help me to get my memory back," she turned on Elisabeth.

"I said it *might*," Elisabeth corrected. "There are no guarantees with amnesia, Hope. You might get your memory back in days, weeks or months, or maybe not at all. Amnesia, like what's happened to you, is rare, there isn't going to be any magic answer, we're just going to have to wait and see."

"What if I never remember who I am?" Hope moaned.

"I was doing some research," Wyatt interjected, "and I was wondering whether Hope wanted to try hypnosis and that drug, Amytal. The article I read said that one or both of these can help some people recall lost memories."

"Is that true, Dr. Bennett?" Hope asked, brushing at her tears.

"It is," Elisabeth began a carefully. "But . . ."

"Is it something you'd be willing to try, Hope?" Wyatt persisted.

"I guess," Hope nodded doubtfully. "If Dr. Bennett thinks it's a good idea," she added.

"I would have thought you'd jump at anything that might help you to remember who you are," Wyatt raised an eyebrow reproachfully.

"I do. I mean I would," Hope protested defensively.

"Then even if the possibilities of hypnosis or drugs working are slim don't you want to at least try it?"

"Stop it, Wyatt," Parker jumped in. "This is stressful enough as it is for Hope. It's not like getting her memory back is going to be completely positive, she'll remember every horrible thing that was done to her. Her brain is just protecting itself right now, her memories will come back when she's ready to deal with them."

"And what if they don't," Wyatt obviously wasn't in the mood to give up easily today. "Have either of you properly thought that through? I mean Hope can't live with Parker forever. Not to mention the fact that we might have an unknown number of other victims out there with Hope as our best lead to finding them."

"We have Millicent Waters' computer," Parker pointed out. Thankfully, the computer had been there when they'd searched the Waters' house the previous evening, it was currently at the lab being thoroughly searched.

"It just doesn't seem like Hope is as anxious to regain her life as she keeps claiming she is," Wyatt stated adamantly.

"I think it's time to finish up," Elisabeth jumped into the fray before things got out of hand. "I don't think we're going to get anything else productive out of this."

"I'm sorry," Hope spoke up immediately.

"It's not your fault," Elisabeth assured her. "You were very brave to give it a try and agree to come back here. We all knew there were no guarantees it would help. Parker, why don't you take Hope home, and I'll catch up with you later. Wyatt, can you give me a lift to the hospital? There's an old colleague of mine I wanted to catch up with."

"Sure," Wyatt nodded and stalked towards the door.

"Detective Wyatt," Hope called out.

Wyatt stopped but didn't turn around.

"I really do want to remember everything," she implored.

Wyatt paused for a second then departed without a word.

"I really do want to remember," Hope repeated more softly before she too headed out into the cold winter morning.

"You know Wyatt's not completely wrong," Elisabeth stated once they were alone. "You haven't thought things through about what will happen to Hope long term. I hope you haven't made a mess of things for nothing."

When Elisabeth had gone and he was left by himself in the small, dingy room, Parker realized that Elisabeth was right, he had made a mess of things, and he resolved then and there to set things straight.

* * * * *

12:36 P.M.

"I hope you haven't eaten yet cos I brought your favorite

lunch," Parker smiled at his niece.

"Go away," Winter slammed the door shut.

Standing on the doorstep, Parker realized just how much things had changed since he'd moved out. The window boxes he'd planted had been removed, the curtains in the downstairs windows had been changed, and Tessa had added antique style lampposts to line the long tree lined driveway. Not that any of these things mattered. It was more that they symbolized the fact that this was no longer his home and that the people who lived here had moved on without him.

It wasn't just his relationships with Tessa and Winter that had fallen apart but also with his sister. Although Mattie had reappeared in his life with particularly bad timing, he was really glad that she was back. He had been devastated when Matilda had disappeared the day after they graduated high school with nothing but a note to explain her actions. All the years that he had been apart from his twin sister had felt like a little part of himself was missing, as children they had never spent a day apart. They'd been there for each other as they bounced from foster home to foster home, through the abuse, he'd been by her side when she'd shot a man, and then finally the move to the Bell house. Although he understood why Mattie had never been able to allow herself to be happy it still made him feel inadequate that he hadn't been able to help her.

Throughout their childhood and adolescence he had always been the 'good' one as Mattie used to call him. He'd been the one who'd looked out for her, the one who'd stood up for her and protected her, now it seems as if, at least in Matilda's mind, things had been reversed. Now whenever they caught up all he heard from his sister was what a mess he was making of his life. How he had everything they'd ever dreamed about when they were kids and he was throwing it all away. As a result, he'd been avoiding seeing her. And he knew she was limiting their time together too because she didn't want to upset Tessa, Daniel and Winter by spending time with the 'enemy'.

Still right now, he was here to make it up to his niece for not being there for her when she found out the truth about her parentage. Pulling out his key he let himself inside, and since they only ever used a few of the more than one hundred rooms in the mansion, headed straight for the kitchen. There he found Winter, standing at the fridge with the door open but staring blankly into space, apparently oblivious to the refrigerator's warning beep as the machine frantically tried to convince her to close the door.

When he came up behind her to close the fridge door she whirled around, "I thought you realized that you weren't welcome here," she spat out frostily, slamming the door closed. "Tessa doesn't want to see you . . ."

"Is she here?" Parker asked, not sure if he hoped she was or she wasn't.

"That is none of your business," Winter continued her rant, "don't you get that? You walked out, you left, and quite frankly Tessa is better off without you. So just go, no one wants you here, not even your own sister."

Holding his hands up in surrender, "actually I came to see you." He was sure what Winter had said about Matilda was true but it still hurt to hear.

Raising a skeptical eyebrow, "since when did I become so important?"

"Winter," he admonished, "you know that I love you."

"Really? And how do I know that? The same way that Tessa *knows* that you love her?"

"I do love Tessa, more than I love anyone else on the face of the planet, but I'm not here to talk about her right now, I'm here to apologize to you for not being there when . . ."

"When I found out," she interrupted, her voice jumping an octave, "that not only was my mother a homicidal maniac, but that she hated her eleven year old sister so much she seduced a child trafficker and sent him to abduct and rape her baby sister, and that man is my father."

Wincing, "I should have been there for you," he said lamely, knowing that there was no way he could make this up to Winter.

"No, no, no," Winter waved her hand dismissively. "You had much more important things on your mind," she sneered sarcastically. "Like moving a stranger into your house. I mean clearly that was much more important than being there to support your wife when she had to tell me that my father is the man who kidnapped and raped her and killed her best friend, and who she had to kill in order to flee. Honestly, Parker, Tessa is a mess, how can you not see that?"

"Tessa will be okay, she's always okay," he said with more confidence than he felt. He knew Tess tried to hide her feelings because she thought it made her look weak if people saw her crying or afraid, but maybe he had underestimated her strength. Winter wasn't the first one to tell him that Tessa wasn't handling things as well as she'd like everyone to believe she was. Maybe he was just convincing himself that Tessa would be okay because it was easier. Because dealing with her dramas was more exhausting than he'd thought it would be. And because dealing with her secrets was more hurtful than he'd thought it would be.

"You are an idiot, now go," Winter turned her back on him.

"Wait a minute. I came here to apologize to you for not being there for you like I ought to have been . . ."

"Well I don't accept your apology," she snapped.

Undeterred he continued, "and to check up on you, make sure you're hanging in there. I know this has to be horrible for you . . ."

Cutting him off, "don't you get it, Parker? I don't want anything from you, I just want you to leave me and Tessa alone."

"I need to know that you're doing okay," he persisted. Winter was making him feel at least a hundred times guiltier that he already had been feeling when he'd arrived here.

"Well then you can rest easy because I'm fine," she huffed.

Looking at his niece Parker still couldn't get over how alike she and Tessa were. In appearance they were night and day, Tessa was tiny, with huge turquoise eyes and big white blonde ringlets, whereas Winter was quite tall with dead straight jet-black hair and eyes as black as coal, but in personality they were identical. Both were stubborn to a fault, fiercely independent, and prone to going to extreme lengths to achieve their goals.

Remembering the tenacious way fifteen-year-old Winter had gone after her stepfather Grant Hamilton when she believed he was the serial killer the Iceman. Young Winter had not given up her suspicions even when Grant had beaten her to within an inch of her life. Still she had pursued her suspicions and ultimately given them the final piece of the puzzle they needed to reveal the Iceman's true identity. She went after what she believed in no matter what the personal cost. Just like Tessa, who even as a teenager had sacrificed herself to save her friends.

Suddenly overwhelmed with the need to see his wife, "is Tess here, Winter?"

"No," the girl stated firmly.

"Really?"

Winter's shuttered eyes didn't reveal anything. "I said no," she repeated. "And I think it's time for you to go," she turned her back on him once again, this time with an air of finality.

"When you see her," still unconvinced that Tessa wasn't hiding out in one of the many empty rooms, "tell her I miss her."

Stubbornly Winter refused to acknowledge him. Finally taking the hint that he was truly unwelcome here, Parker wandered through the long corridors back to the front door. Pausing at the car, he turned for one last look at the mansion and thought he saw the curtains in one of the upstairs windows flutter. Wondering if it was Tessa watching him, he raised his hand and waved, then climbed back into his car and sped off.

* * * * *

2:57 P.M.

His partner had been unusually quiet ever since he got back from lunch.

After driving Elisabeth to the hospital, Wyatt had come straight back to work, hoping there might be news on Millicent Waters' computer. There hadn't been, but Michael Waters had turned up, apparently he'd run straight to the airport last night, bought a first class ticket to fly back, then hopped in a cab and come right to the precinct.

Talking to the husband hadn't yielded anything helpful. The man knew surprisingly little about his wife. He couldn't think of any friend, neighbor, family member who might want to hurt him or his wife, no one here knew about his second marriage, and no one in Japan knew about his first. He had no idea of his wife's interests, hobbies, or how she spent her time. He bought her everything she wanted but he was away every second month and even when he was home he was busy with work. He had never heard his wife talk of a wild girl, or about any other group she conversed with over the Internet, in fact he didn't even know that his wife spent much time on her computer.

Ever since Michael Waters had left and Parker had returned, Wyatt had been avoiding his desk because his partner had set up shop there with Hope, who was apparently still worked up about their earlier visit to the apartment. It wasn't that he was unsympathetic to what Hope was going through, if indeed she was going through it, but Tessa's paranoia was most certainly rubbing off on him because he was definitely beginning to doubt Hope's sincerity.

As he watched Hope chatter away at Parker, the way she looked at him, the way she positioned herself close to him, the way she lit up every time he spoke to her. He also noticed something different in the way Parker responded to her. He seemed distant now, preoccupied, giving vague answers to Hope's questions. No longer did he stare at Hope as though keeping her safe was his single reason for existing. Wyatt wondered just what his partner had done at lunch that had changed things.

Thinking about what Tessa had said the other day, that he'd been friends with Parker for more than two decades. Wyatt remembered perfectly the first time he'd met ten-year-old Parker and Matilda. It had been the talk of the neighborhood that Luka and Laura Bell were going to adopt a set of abandoned twins. Half the neighbors thought it was a marvelous idea the other half thought it was a recipe for disaster. As it was it turned out everybody was right.

The day that the Bell's went to pick up their new son and daughter, his parents sat him down and gave him a talk about helping the children settle in. At the time fifteen-year-old Wyatt had wanted nothing to do with the kids his neighbors planned on adopting, he still fondly remembered little Taylor Bell. The child had been the picture of impish innocence, with a quirky sense of humor, a cheeky grin, and a bubbly personality, a real little light to all who came into contact with him. It had been a tragedy that the little boy had been struck down with leukemia at the tender age of five, finally succumbing to the disease after a two year battle.

Wyatt had been thirteen when Taylor passed away, but even to this day he could picture perfectly the little face, hear the boy's voice as he banged on their front door asking to retrieve his ball from their yard, or tagging around after him as he played with his friends. He'd been six years older than little Taylor, but as an only child the boy had looked up to him as a bigger brother, so Wyatt had taken him under his wing. Luka and Laura had wanted more children, but a bout of cancer just a year after Taylor's birth had left Laura unable to bear another baby, hence the reason they decided to adopt following their son's death. In the end it had been cancer that had taken Laura, just a couple of years after Matilda left and Parker began his career as a police officer, but every second of her life had been dedicated to her children.

Obediently that first day he had gone over to the Bell home, sat at the table with Luka and Laura, a terrified little girl, and a quiet, sullen little boy. They'd drunk lemonade and eaten homemade cookies then Laura had sent them all out to play. Wyatt had suggested baseball, Matilda had shrunk further away from him, Parker had kicked him in the shins, and it was from that second onwards that he had become determined to help those kids adjust to life in a happy home.

Now twenty-two years later it seemed like nothing had changed.

If convincing Parker that Hope wasn't what she appeared to be was what it took to help him get back on track with his wife, then that was what Wyatt would do.

In fact, he was already starting to formulate a theory.

Wyatt was starting to wonder if Hope might in fact be Rebecca Worthington.

According to Tessa, Rebecca was the daughter of Isaac Worthington, the head of the child trafficking ring that abducted Tessa when she was eleven. Through a series of events, Tessa had struck up a sort of mutual reliance relationship with Isaac, who had explained how he became entrenched in the dark, ugly world of stealing and selling small children.

Eight-year-old Rebecca disappeared one day without a trace. When the police had been unable to come up with any leads, Isaac had brought it upon himself to find out what had become of his daughter. Eventually he tracked down the child traffickers who had abducted Rebecca, and infiltrated them in a bid to find his missing daughter. When he came up empty, he had passed the job onto Tessa who had succeeded in finding his daughter. By the time Tessa found her, Rebecca was twenty-two, a drug addict and a prostitute, and in a bid to stop Isaac from ruining more children's lives, Tessa had lied and told him that his daughter was dead.

Wyatt was wondering whether it was a coincidence that Hope had turned up so soon after the Dino/Jake/Isaac debacle. It was possible that Isaac's daughter had returned and become jealous of Tessa, who appeared to have everything that she had lost. Tessa had been her father's replacement daughter, Isaac had looked out for Tessa, helped her, supported her, and even loved her in his own twisted way. It was also possible that Rebecca had decided to get revenge on those she felt had abandoned her and led to her life of misery by faking her abduction and amnesia. Besides that, Tessa was also the only one who knew where Isaac Worthington was.

He wasn't sure exactly how all of this fitted into their case. Or connected to wild girl, Henrietta Kendall and Millicent Waters, but Wyatt wasn't about to let that stop him. He'd see what he could find out about Rebecca Worthington and whether there was any chance that she could be masquerading as Hope, and then when he'd found out all he could on his own he'd go to Tessa.

Deciding he wouldn't float his theory with Tessa tonight. Since Casey was planning on bringing Tessa over for dinner tomorrow following their day out, if he upset her with his theory she'd back out, and she needed to start doing normal things again.

Besides tonight the kids were having a sleepover with their friends down the block, which meant he and Casey had the house to themselves for the first time in months. Tomorrow night after dinner he'd sit Tessa down and find out whether there was a possibility that Hope might be Rebecca Worthington out for revenge.

* * * * *

9:29 P.M.

"I knew you'd be back," Tessa looked distinctly unsurprised as she opened the door.

"You were watching when I left earlier," Parker smiled back at her, pleased he'd decided to come back out here tonight. "Can I come in?"

Tessa shrugged but as she retreated back into the house she left the door open. Taking this as permission to enter, he followed her to the living room, where she had flopped onto one of the sofas.

"Where is everyone?" he asked, secretly hoping that Daniel was not here. He had never particularly liked Tessa's brother, from the second he'd heard how Daniel had disappeared while twelve-year-old Tessa was in the hospital after their mother tried to kill her. Already sensitive to deserting siblings because of Matilda disappearing on him the day after they graduated high school, he had instantly hated Daniel Micah even though they had never met.

When Daniel had reappeared in the middle of the Iceman case, for a little while Parker had almost believed that his future brother-in-law was the serial killer stalking the city. After Daniel had helped save Tessa's life twice, he'd softened a little, and following his and Tessa's wedding had even made a concerted effort to get along with her brother. However ever since last fall when he and Tessa began having problems things had become strained between himself and Daniel once again.

"Daniel and Matilda are out on a date," Tessa replied.

Chewing on his lip to keep from making a snide comment, he did not at all approve of his sister dating Daniel. "And Winter?"

"Out. Sleeping over at a friend's. She gave you a hard time earlier, huh?" she asked with a half smile.

"Yeah, she did. She's pretty protective of you. She told me you're better off without me." All day he'd tried to think of just what to say to fix things but now that he was here, he wasn't sure that anything sounded sufficient.

"Winter didn't accept your apology?"

"No, she didn't," he said gravely. "But I didn't deserve to be let off the hook that easily. I should have been there for her . . . and you," he added crouching down in front of her.

"I'm fine," she smiled flippantly.

"No, don't do that," he countered sternly. "No excuses, I should have been there when you told Winter about Jake. I'm really sorry, Tessa," taking her hand in his, relieved when she didn't pull away.

"I know that you are," Tessa reached out a hand to smooth his wild black hair.

For a moment he was quiet, just enjoying things being peaceful between them. "What happened to us, Tess? Every time we're in the same room all we do is fight. How did things get to this?"

"Being with you I lost a part of myself," she told him with a rueful smile.

"That's the way marriage is supposed to be, Tessa," he growled hopelessly. "We join together, we become one life, only you never wanted that to happen. You know today is our anniversary. Our first anniversary. And look how we're spending it. Apart, both angry and hurt. Two years we've known each other and you still won't come to me when something's bothering you. If I want to find out what's going on inside your head I practically have to wring it out of you."

"You do exactly the same thing," Tessa countered evenly. "Before everything happened with Lachlan, you were planning on leaving me. You packed a bag, you left on your own."

Stunned into silence. Tessa had never before mentioned that she knew that. Not to him, not to the police, not to anyone. Parker hadn't thought that Tess knew how close he'd come to walking out on her and their life together. Ashamed, he stammered, "I was just going to take a break. I needed a couple of days to myself, to sort things out. I didn't know if I was ready to be a father." He wasn't sure whether this was true or not. At the time he hadn't planned on necessarily leaving Tessa for good, he hadn't even been sure he could leave her for a few days. But it worried him that he honestly didn't know what he would have done if Lachlan hadn't abducted him.

"And now you're doing it again," Tessa's eyes were so sad that for a second all he wanted to do was whatever it took to make her smile again, to take her pain away. "You're going to end up leaving me for her, aren't you?"

"You always do that, Tess," he snapped, immediately thrown straight back into anger mode, anger was easier to deal with than guilt. "You always make me out to be the bad guy."

"She's conning you, Parker, and you can't even see it because you have a hero complex, you always have to be the one to save everyone."

"Me?" he repeated incredulously. "What about you? I'm sick to death of worrying about what kind of trouble you're going to get yourself into next. Whether you're going to get yourself hurt or killed. You're the one who ran off on her own to confront Dino and was almost drowned so you could save those girls. You're the one who went off to confront the Iceman to try to save Hayley Geoffries. You're the one who was going to sacrifice herself to Dylan Riley to save her friends. And you're the one who got her own best friend killed trying to escape from Jake Killinger."

Tessa recoiled as if he'd slapped her and Parker instantly regretted saying the words he knew weren't true but which he also knew Tessa believed.

"Tessa," he tried to reclaim her hand but she flinched away from him. "I'm sorry. See this is what I was talking about, all we do these days is fight."

Frozen in place, her blue eyes aflame with pure fury, "no, you're right," she said at last, her voice as icy as the snow outside. "I did get Ellie killed trying to save us."

And then the anger left her eyes and she simply looked small and scared, vulnerable, exhausted and alone, and he was overwhelmed by a sudden need to hold her tightly, to cradle her in his arms, to stroke her hair, to make all the monsters in both their lives simply disappear. Before he realized what he was doing, he had grabbed her and dragged her up out of the chair and into his embrace. She stood stiffly, holding herself perfectly still. The second he released his hold on her she was gone, as though she possessed the ability to teleport, she was standing over by the window.

"I'm sorry, Tess," he begged her. "It's not true, what happened to Eleanor wasn't your fault, you were only a child. I didn't mean it, I was just trying to hurt you."

"Well congratulations you succeeded," she told him, but their was no malice in her voice only the weary sadness of one who has heard confirmation of something they always believed was true but always hoped was not.

He went to stand behind her, arms across her chest, hoping that she would turn and snuggle into his embrace like she used to, moving her ear around against his chest until she had positioned it against his heart. But she didn't, she remained as though made of stone, her reflection in the glass was so sad that it made his guilt as palpable as if someone had physically stabbed something into his chest.

"It's never going to be enough, is it? My love is never going to be enough for you," he murmured at last releasing his hold on her. Finally realizing that no matter how much he loved her, no matter how patient he was, Tessa was never going to truly trust him.

At last, she turned to face him, "you know why I find it so hard to trust people, to open up to them? Because of this," she waved a hand to indicate the space between them. "I've told you more about myself, trusted you with more of myself than I have with any other person and how does it end? With you throwing it back in my face."

Channeling his guilt into anger, anger he could deal with, anger was safe, anger he could use. "It's always all my fault isn't it? Perfect little Tessa is always right, always the victim, always the innocent one."

For the longest time she just looked up at him with her impenetrable aqua eyes. In fact she stared at him for so long that he began to squirm uncomfortably. Just as he had when he was a kid and he'd gotten into trouble, his mother would put on this calmly disappointed face, which always made him feel terrible.

"You know you're more like me than you want to admit," Tessa said at last. "I've been seeing Charlie Abbott since last September," she blurted out.

Shocked into silence. With the way Tessa felt about psychiatrists he never thought he'd hear her say those words. "So you can talk to Wyatt and you can talk to Charlie but you can't talk to me."

"You're the one who doesn't want to talk to me about Jake and Ellie," she said evenly. "You just want to fix it. But you can't fix it, Parker. It happened, and it nearly destroyed me. We both have to deal with that. You can't fix it," she said again, "you can't fix me. Only I can do that. And I have to do it at my speed, not at yours. I'm working on it, but I don't know how long it will take. I don't know if I can ever completely put myself back together. You have to decide if you can deal with that."

Too stunned to speak, he wasn't used to Tessa being so wise about psychological and emotional issues.

At last Tessa spoke, "you know I love you."

"And I love you."

"It's not enough is it?" she asked sadly.

"I don't know," he answered honestly. Then with an uncertain sigh he turned to the door, "you know what? I have to go."

Outside he stood for a moment, knowing he should go back and fix things with Tessa, but more confused now than ever after what Tessa had just told him. Instead he climbed into his car, gave a last look at the dark house and whispered, "happy anniversary, Tessa," before driving off into the night.

If he had of returned he would have heard Tessa whisper the

same words he had just uttered, "happy anniversary, Parker."

He would have seen the figure move quietly from the shadows, gun raised.

He would have seen the figure slam the butt of the gun into a distracted Tessa's temple, sending her crumpling to the floor.

* * * * *

9:59 P.M.

Maisy didn't want to add to Tessa's problems but she really needed her friend's advice.

For close to four years she had been dating Luke. Well that was partially true, Maisy thought to herself, they had been dating on and off for four years. That had been okay for a while, but now she was twenty-nine, ready to settle down, get married and start a family. She'd tried talking to Luke about it, asking him if he was prepared to commit to her and their life together. Safe to say the conversation hadn't gone well.

Now she didn't know what to do.

She loved Luke, at least she thought she did, but maybe they'd just been together for so long that she had convinced herself that he was the man for her.

Maisy remembered perfectly the first time they'd met. She had been walking home from a club one night with some friends when they'd come upon Luke stranded at the side of the road. Dressed in leather jacket and pants, his brown hair all spiky from his helmet, his blue eyes twinkling, Maisy had been instantly attracted to him. She had convinced her friends to stay and keep him company while he waited for a new tyre for his motorbike to replace the one he'd just punctured. By the end of the evening she was completely smitten.

From there things had developed quickly and a month later they had actually talked about eloping. Their plans had fallen through at the last minute due to a health scare with his mother, and suddenly Luke decided he wanted to slow down their relationship. Reluctantly she had gone along with it, having never felt about another man the way she felt about Luke, and that had been the beginning. Over the next four years they spun around and around on a merry-go-round of highs and lows. For a while, even though she had desperately wanted things to work out, she'd enjoyed the excitement. With Luke she never knew what was going to happen next, he was rash and impulsive and wild, and being with him made all the horror she saw on her job disappear.

But now things had changed. Or maybe she had changed. She wanted more out of life. She wanted the stability of coming home at the end of the day to a husband who loved her unconditionally, who was always there, who didn't change his mind about what he wanted every other month. As much as she wanted these things, Maisy couldn't make herself just walk away from Luke, and that was why she needed to talk to Tessa.

Her friend was perceptive, Tessa saw things that others never noticed, and right now that was what Maisy needed. She needed to know whether Tessa thought Luke was ever going to commit, and whether she should wait for him or cut her losses and move on.

Pulling off the road into Tessa's driveway, Maisy would have loved the huge mansion if she didn't know all the horrible things that had happened here. Still the enormous ivy covered stone structure was impressive. With it's intricately decorated stone pillars, large balcony, marble steps leading to the front door, and ornate lion statues positioned on either side of the stairs, it looked like something out of a period movie.

Climbing up the steps, Maisy pressed the buzzer and stood waiting. After a couple of minutes, when no one came, she rung the bell again. Starting to become alarmed when still no one answered, she gave it one last try then fished around in her purse for her key. Jiggling it in the lock, when at last she pushed open the heavy oak door she found herself surrounded by an eerie silence.

Uneasily she called out, "Tessa? It's Maisy."

Taking a tentative inside the dark house, she couldn't help but shudder. Originally owned by Tessa's paternal grandparents, the mansion had been decked out with large oil paintings on the walls, tables dotted everywhere with expensive vases or artifacts on them, even a couple of statues of armor graced the entry hall.

"Tessa?" she called again, closing the door behind her and heading for the living room. "Daniel? Matilda? Winter?"

Still there was no answer and Maisy was starting to wonder if everyone was out. Only Tessa hardly ever left the house these days. Resisting the urge to keep checking over her shoulder, when she reached the living room she found the door slightly ajar. Again this was odd, paranoid Tessa had a thing about keeping doors closed, she thought it gave her an added advantage if anyone tried to attack her.

"Tess?" she tried one last time.

Resting her hands against the door she slowly pushed it open. Her eyes roved the shadowy room in search of signs of life. At last, they settled on a figure on the floor, a familiar figure. With a gasp, Maisy threw on the light and ran to Tessa, dropping to her knees at her friend's side.

"Tess? Can you hear me?" At first, she thought that Tessa had simply fainted, but when she put her hand on Tessa's shoulder she noticed the red puddle around her head. "Oh my gosh, that's a lot of blood," she tried to fight the queasiness rollicking in her stomach; Maisy hated the sight of blood almost as much as Tessa herself.

Gently rolling Tessa onto her back, Maisy saw the huge gash on her temple and pressed her trembling fingers to her friend's neck, feeling her pulse fluttering weakly. Relieved, Maisy carefully brushed Tessa's blonde curls away from the sticky blood.

"It's going to be okay, Tessa," she whispered as calmly as she could manage. "I'm going to call an ambulance, we're going to get you to the hospital and fix you up. You're going to be fine. Once I call an ambulance I'm going to call Parker," she hoped this might actually bring her two estranged friends back together.

Unfortunately Maisy was so engrossed in juggling trying to pull out her cell phone with one hand while at the same time pressing her cardigan to Tessa's still heavily bleeding head wound with the other, that she didn't notice the black figure that had attacked Tessa enter the room.

It wasn't until she was about to dial her phone that she finally realized she wasn't alone. As she turned, she didn't even have time to scream before the knife plunged into her stomach. Hands springing automatically to cover the deep wound, Maisy had time to panic about the blood that was quickly drenching her clothes and covering her hands before everything disappeared into a red-hot haze.

"I definitely don't think we need to call Parker," the figure admonished the two unconscious women before it set about moving them and cleaning up.

FEBRUARY 15TH

8:31 A.M.

"Did you get a good night sleep?" Parker asked her as she shuffled into the kitchen.

"Not really," Hope rubbed at her bleary eyes, it had been about five before she'd actually fallen asleep. "You were out late."

"Yeah, I had something I had to do," he answered vaguely as he fixed her a plate of toast and set it down on the table in front of her.

Picking up a piece and absently nibbling on the corner, "you went to see Tessa?"

"Yes," he answered shortly.

Despite the fact that Parker clearly didn't want to pursue the topic Hope couldn't help herself, "it didn't go well?" she asked unable to help feeling a little gleeful that things between Parker and his wife were still on the rocks. She needed Parker, she had no one else to depend on, but Tessa had her family and friends. It seemed only fair that Parker's attention be on her at the moment.

"It's complicated."

Knowing she ought not to push it but unable to stop, "how?"

"It's just complicated," Parker snapped.

"I'm sorry," she gushed immediately, she didn't want to lose the one ally she had. "I just thought it might help to talk about it."

"Well it doesn't, okay, so leave it alone," he growled.

"Okay," she agreed quietly, feeling tears prick at the back of her eyes as she munched away on the rest of her toast.

For several minutes they both sat in silence. Parker staring blankly into space, while she fretted about the possibility that she

151

had just ruined things with Parker by being nosy. Over the last couple of days she had come to rely on him completely. It was only the fact that she knew he was asleep in the next room that allowed her to get through the night. It was only the knowledge that he was here, that helped her get up to face each day. If she lost that then she didn't think she would be able to function. She was so tired of being alone. So, so tired of being alone . . .

"Don't cry," Parker was awkwardly patting her shoulder. "I'm sorry I got mad."

Realizing that she had started crying, Hope let the floodgates fly open and threw herself into Parker's arms, sobbing wildly. A little taken aback, Parker hesitated for a moment before his arms circled around her. Burying her head against his shoulder, Hope clung to him tightly and let Parker's strong arms hold her up.

At last when her tears finally dried up, Parker set her back down in her chair. "I'm sorry," he said again. "I didn't mean to take things out on you."

"No, I'm sorry," she assured him. "I shouldn't have pushed. It's none of my business, whatever problems you're having with your wife. It's just that you've helped me so much I just wanted to return the favor, see if I could help you, but I went too far. I'm sorry, I won't do it again, I don't want to lose you," Hope knew that she was babbling but it was the only thing keeping at bay the tears that had built up again.

"Lose me?" Parker asked confused.

"You're all I have right now," she explained. "No one else likes me. Well maybe Dr. Bennett, but she has her baby to focus on, but Detective Wyatt and Lieutenant Jacobson and your sister and that woman with the red hair, none of them like me."

"That's not true," he protested, although not very convincingly.

"No, it's true," she repeated adamantly. "They don't like that you asked me to stay here with you, and they don't like that I'm taking up too much of your time and attention. They don't like me, especially Tessa."

"Tessa," he began carefully, "Tessa has issues that are not your fault."

"What do you mean?" she sniffed. "Tessa has everything that anyone could ever want, friends, family, a wonderful husband." Hope thought that her life would be perfect if she ever managed to have those things.

"Tess had a very . . ." he paused as he searched for the right word, "a very difficult childhood. Her parents were terrible and some really evil people hurt her very badly, because of all of that it made it really hard for her to trust people."

"Even you?" she asked wide-eyed, sure that she could never have met a more trustworthy person in her life.

"Even me," he nodded sadly.

Wondering where her own family was right now. Did she still have a mom and a dad, were they happy together or did they fight all the time, were they still together, or had they divorced? Did she have brothers and sisters, half brothers and sisters, stepbrothers and sisters? Nieces and nephews? What did they do? Where did they live? Did they think about her or was she a distant memory? She didn't know the answers to any of these questions but there was one thing she was sure of. "I wish I was Tessa," she sighed wistfully. "I wish I had a husband like you, so devoted, so caring, so thoughtful, so wonderful."

"Maybe you do, maybe you do have a husband who adores you."

"Then why hasn't he reported me missing?"

Parker gave no answer and she expected none. They both knew that if there was a loving husband somewhere out there then he would have moved heaven and earth to find her. Hope hadn't been able to forget the feel of Parker's lips on her when she had kissed him the other night. Or the safe and snug feeling she had just before when he'd held her against his strong, solid chest. She needed him, she wanted him, she wanted more than just his friendship, she wanted all of him.

"Thank you again for being there yesterday, when we went to the apartment," Hope was now positive that she had made the right decision by agreeing to go back there.

"You're welcome. You were really brave to agree to give it a try." He crouched down in front of her, his hands on her knees, "and don't let Wyatt try to bully you into giving hypnosis a go. Your memories will come back when you're ready to deal with them." Taking her face in his hands, "and I don't want you to ever worry about losing me," he gently kissed her forehead then gave her a sweet, goofy smile, "now I have to go get ready for work."

Watching him go she decided that if Tessa didn't want Parker, if she didn't appreciate him, than as far as Hope was concerned he was fair game, and she intended to make him hers for keeps.

* * * * *

9:57 A.M.

"When are we going to tell people?" Matilda asked, they were curled up in Daniel's bed, she was snuggled in the crook of his arm, and enjoying the way his hand brushed gently against her shoulder.

"Whenever you want. I can't wait to shout it from the rooftops," Daniel answered, and she could feel the smile in his voice even though she couldn't see his face.

"Let's tell everyone today," she exclaimed, excitement bubbling away inside her. Matilda had honestly never thought that she was destined for happiness. Had even spent most of her life trying to run away from it because she thought that she didn't deserve to be at peace. From the second she had killed Lachlan Mountain Senior, believing he was another one of her foster father's friends come to hurt her, then learned that in fact he was a social worker come to save her and Parker, she had believed that she was not worthy of happiness. She had taken the life of another human being and as such could see no reason why she deserved the things that other people took for granted. She hadn't wanted to go and live with the Bell's, instead she had wanted to stay where they were, knowing she would continued to be abused but thinking that that was what she deserved.

Young Matilda hadn't liked life with their adopted parents. Luka and Laura were too nice, too kind, too loving. All she had wanted to do was scream at them; I'm a murderer stop treating we nicely. Many a night she had lain awake contemplating running away, it was only the knowledge that it would devastate Parker that had kept her in her bed. At last she could bear it no longer and the night after graduation she had left.

Over the years she had looked for out of the way jobs where she wouldn't have to get to know people, she had avoided forming friendships, and always lived alone. But in the end the pull had been too great, she'd had to track down her brother, she needed to hear from him once again that what had happened was not her fault.

While she had returned with incredibly bad timing, when she saw that Parker had moved on from the horror of their childhood and was married, with a job he adored and friends to lean on, she had been inspired.

Or maybe it was Daniel.

The way he hadn't judged her, the way he'd been mad at her for blaming herself for something she hadn't meant to do, the way they'd argued about who had the worst family and childhood. Daniel Micah was everything she had ever dreamed of in a man, and being with him was . . .

"Mattie, you okay?" Daniel had wiggled around so that he was looking down at her, his face creased with concern.

"I'm perfect," she reached up her hand to trace his jaw line with her fingertips, "you make everything perfect." She was just starting to run her fingers down from his face and along his strong muscular chest, when the sound of footsteps in the hall emerged. "Did you hear that?"

"It sounded like footsteps," Daniel replied, amused. "It's probably Tessie, do you want to go tell her?"

"Like this?" she pointed from his naked body to hers.

"No, we should probably put some clothes on first," Daniel grinned as he got up and pulled on his pajama pants.

"But I don't have any clothes in here," she protested, her clothes were still in the bathroom, right where they'd left them last night when they'd returned from their date. They had had some fun in the shower before scampering down the hall naked to spend the night together in Daniel's room.

"Here borrow this," Daniel thrust her one of his shirts.

Slipping it on, then taking her fiancée's hand, "do you think this is the right time? I mean with the way things are between Tessa and Parker?" she asked with nervous anticipation.

"Honey, you are not wiggling out of it that easily," Daniel told her, pulling her towards the door. "I think you know Tess well enough by now to know that no matter what problems she's having with that jerk . . ." he trailed off and squeezed her hand apologetically. Sometimes Daniel seemed to forget that Parker was her brother, although she had to agree that at the moment her brother *was* acting like a jerk. "She's still going to be happy for us."

"Let's do it," she agreed, Matilda did know that Tessa would be happy for them even if Parker wouldn't be.

Together they opened the door, expecting to see Tessa but instead Casey Wyatt greeted them.

"Oh, Casey," Daniel said in surprise. "What are you doing here?"

"Tessa and I are spending the day together," Casey answered.

"You finally convinced her to go out?" she asked. Tessa rarely left the estate these days, spending most of her time in her room or out riding her horse.

"Wyatt spoke with her, she promised not to pull any of her usual tricks," Casey explained. "I was meant to be here an hour ago, but I got held up. I checked downstairs but she wasn't there. I thought maybe since she's been having trouble sleeping at night, she might have slept late."

"Maybe," Matilda agreed, trying to keep her left hand behind her back, as much as she liked Casey she kind of wanted family to be the first to know of her and Daniel's engagement.

All three of them traipsed down the hall to Tessa's room. "Tessie?" Daniel called, knocking. "Casey's here to pick you up, are you awake?" When he got no answer he knocked again, "Tess, I'm coming in, alright?" Already Matilda could hear the panic creeping into Daniel's voice.

Opening the door they found the room empty. Tessa wasn't in bed, neither had she passed out on the floor. In fact, the room looked as though she hadn't even spent the night in it. The curtains were open, the bed was perfectly made, everything was in its proper place, it looked just as it always did.

"What's going on?"

They all jumped at the voice, then turned to see Winter watching them warily from the bedroom door. "What's going on?" she repeated.

"Have you seen Tessie?" Daniel asked edgily.

"No, why?"

"Maybe she's in the bathroom," Casey suggested.

Spinning on his heels as though the idea had never occurred to him, Daniel took off for the bathroom, she, Winter and Casey trailing along behind him.

"Tessa!" Daniel's knock this time was a lot more forceful. "Are you in there?" He flung open the door when they didn't get an answer, only to be greeted by an empty room once again. "Are you sure she wasn't downstairs?" he demanded whirling around to face Casey.

"I checked the living room and the kitchen, she wasn't there," Casey seemed to be starting to catch Daniel's panic.

"What about the rest of the house?"

"You don't use the rest of the house," Casey reminded him tersely.

"I'm sure she's fine, Daniel," Matilda tried to reassure him. "She probably just went out."

"She promised she wouldn't pull any of her usual stunts," Casey protested. "She said she'd be here when I got here."

"She practically never goes out," Daniel whirled around again this time flying towards the staircase. "Was her car there?"

"I don't know," Casey replied as she ran downstairs after him, Winter at her heels.

Having to run to keep up with them, Matilda seemed to be the only one at the moment who wasn't jumping to wild conclusions about all the possible horrors that could have befallen Tessa. Catching up to them in the garage, as they stood beside Tessa's car, Daniel, Winter and Casey all wearing identical frantic faces.

"Maybe she just went out riding," she suggested, determined to stay calm until there was proof that something had happened to Tessa.

"No," Casey shook her head adamantly, "I saw her riding boots in the kitchen."

"And her purse and cell phone are on the table in the living room," Winter added worriedly, Daniel's panic was quickly spreading. "I saw them when I got home."

"Then she didn't just decide to go out somewhere," Daniel announced.

"We don't know that yet," she reasoned. "Let's not panic . . ."

"Not panic?" Daniel was back on the move, heading back inside and picking up the phone. "This is Tessa we're talking about. I don't know another person who manages to get into as much trouble as she does. Something has happened to her, she's gone, Tessa is gone."

* * * * *

10:42 A.M.

"What's going on?" Parker asked joining the gathering in the living room at Tessa's mansion. Matilda and a very stressed looking Daniel were sitting on the couch, Matilda tightly clutching his hand. J.J. was yelling into his phone. Casey and Winter were hovering together in the corner, deep in conversation. And Wyatt was pacing restlessly.

"Tessa's gone," Daniel growled accusingly as he leapt at him.

"Daniel, don't make things worse," Matilda jumped up with Daniel and rested a calming hand on his shoulder.

"What do you mean Tessa's gone?" he asked with a familiar sinking feeling in his stomach. "Gone like going away for a few days or like something happened to her?"

"Alright," J.J. hung up, "please tell me Marty found something so that we can officially report her as missing."

"He's done her bedroom," Wyatt answered, "but he didn't find anything, he's doing the kitchen now."

"What's he looking for?" Parker asked again, wondering why exactly it was that he'd been summoned here.

"We already told you Tessa is gone," Daniel repeated, glaring at him with a look of utter contempt.

When Wyatt had phoned him all he'd said was that he needed to come out to the mansion. In the middle of a conversation with Hope, who had been very vulnerable ever since their visit to the apartment, which he had known was going to be a bad idea, he'd dropped her off at Elisabeth's and come straight out here, not exactly sure what to expect when he arrived.

"Tessa and I were supposed to spend the day together," Casey explained.

"Well she probably just disappeared to avoid it then," he

answered confidently. If Tessa didn't want to do something then she'd go to great lengths to avoid it. After they had miscarried their child it had taken him months to coax Tessa out of the house, when she was dealt an emotional blow her typical response was to burrow herself in.

"I talked to her," Wyatt shot back. "She promised she wasn't going to make excuses, or cancel at the last minute, feign illness, or disappear," he finished emphatically. "We had a deal."

Wondering briefly just what Wyatt's side of the deal had been. "Maybe she just needed some time by herself," he suggested, remembering their last conversation and how badly that had ended.

"Why would you think that?" Wyatt asked with a suspiciously raised eyebrow.

"Things have been pretty tense lately," he answered lamely.

"Parker?" J.J. shot him a terse frown.

"Fine," he relented, "I came to see Tessa last night, to try and sort things out, but suffice it to say things didn't end well."

"You two fought again?" Winter sighed.

"I tried," he protested, wondering whether in fact he'd only pushed Tessa further than she could handle and she'd done something to hurt herself. He didn't think that Tessa would ever do something like that but the fact that she had been seeing a psychiatrist for months, given how she felt about them, was a pretty clear indicator of how much she was struggling. "Did you try calling her?"

"She didn't take her phone," Wyatt told him.

"Car?" he asked.

"Still here," J.J. replied.

"Her wallet?"

"Still here," J.J. said again, "but we want to monitor your accounts."

"Fine," he agreed, "but I'm sure Tessa has access to money I know nothing about." Parker still maintained that Tessa was fine, and had more than likely just gone away to sort things out. "Same goes for her phone, I'd be surprised if she didn't have more than one. Besides I'm sure she needs an untraceable cell to call her buddy John Doe," he gave Wyatt a pointed look. "I'm sure Tessa is fine."

"Of course she's not fine," Daniel broke free from Matilda's grip. "You think she just ran off without telling anyone, without her cell or any money, in the middle of the night, and without her car? You know when you disappeared Tessa never stopped believing in you, it didn't matter what any of us said. It's so nice to know you can return the favor," he finished sarcastically.

"Only something had happened to me," he reminded his angry brother-in-law. "And as far as any of us know Tessa is perfectly fine. She'll probably pop up at any minute, angry at all of us for making a fuss."

"What are you an idiot?" Daniel fumed. "Have you never met . . ."

"Okay," J.J. interceded, "lets try to work out a time line. Tell me what happened yesterday."

Still too furious to speak, Daniel let Matilda guide him back to the sofa. "Daniel and I went out about five," Mattie explained. "When we left Tessa was in here reading."

"Then she drove me to Vanessa's house," Winter filled in, "that was around seven."

All eyes turned to him, "I got here about nine thirty, when I left just before ten Tessa was fine."

"What time did you two get back?" J.J. turned his attention back to Daniel and Matilda.

Both their cheeks heated slightly, "maybe one or two in the morning," Daniel muttered.

It was blatantly obvious that the two of them had been out of a date. The thought of Daniel with his sister still made him sick, pushing these thoughts from his head, "she probably went out riding, she always does that to clear her head."

"Her riding boots are still here," Casey told him quietly.

"Did you see Tess when you got back?" J.J. asked Daniel and Matilda.

"We assumed she was in bed," Mattie replied.

"Casey, what time did you get here?"

"About ten, I was running late," Casey replied miserably.

"So we have a window of about twelve hours," J.J. pondered.

"I don't know why you're all getting so worked up," Parker told them exasperatedly. "Tessa has done this before, disappeared for a while, she always comes back just fine."

"Try to get it through that thick head of yours," Daniel spoke slowly, fiercely enunciating each word. "She didn't wander off. Something happened to her. Something related to that case of yours that you're so hung up on."

"You mean Hope's case?" he asked surprised, he didn't see why Tessa would be mixed up in that. "Well unless you think that Tess knows who the killer is I don't see what the case has to do with her."

"Of course she doesn't know who the killer is," Daniel snapped.

"Are you suggesting then that Tess is this wild girl?"

"You know we're not," Wyatt shot him a disapproving frown.

"Well I can't see Tessa chatting with someone called wild girl over the Internet, so again I don't see what Hope's case has to do with her."

"There's a lot we don't see about this case just yet, but we already have two dead women and no idea how many other victims may be out there," Wyatt reminded him. "This isn't just about Hope, we don't know how many women this man has already attacked, or how many women he has in his sights, but I'm going to do whatever it takes to make sure Tessa isn't one of them."

A vivid image of Tessa seeking comfort in Wyatt's arms after she finally confessed what had happened to her and Eleanor, flashed into his mind, followed by one of Hope throwing herself into his arms earlier today. He remembered the feel of her thin, fragile body crushed up against him. The way she clung to him, the way she wasn't afraid to let him see her express emotions, the way she'd been so scared of losing him because he was all she had. It was nice to be that needed.

Marty came bustling in, announcing, "before you ask, no I haven't found anything. Casey, can you close the blinds please?" he asked as he begun to spray Luminol around the room.

As he moved around the darkened room, sporadically spraying they all held their breaths, waiting for a reaction that might indicate that blood had been shed, but hoping none was found. Parker didn't really think that anything had happened to Tessa. At least he didn't want to think that anything had happened to her while things were so stained between them. He had meant what he'd said to her last night, he did still love her and he knew that she still loved him. But he had also meant it when he'd said that he didn't know if their love was enough to make things work between them.

All of a sudden, right where he had left Tessa when he'd walked out last night, a bright blue glow lit the room and everyone let out a collective gasp.

* * * * *

2:11 P.M.

Her head was throbbing.

The pain radiating out to every single cell of her body until it felt like a glow encasing her.

As she slowly started to slide back to consciousness, Tessa realized she had no idea where she was or what had happened to her.

The last thing she remembered was being at home in the living room talking to Parker, then nothing. She didn't remember him leaving, she didn't remember what she did next, and she didn't remember what had happened to make her feel so awful.

Prying open her eyes, which felt as though they'd been super-glued shut, Tessa lifted a hand to her head to try to find the cause of her pounding headache.

"Oh thank goodness," a voice spoke from the darkness.

Crinkling her forehead in confusion, then wincing at the fresh wave of pain that created, for the voice that spoke was Maisy's.

"Maisy?" she croaked, startled by how weak her voice sounded.

"I was beginning to think you were dead," came the reply.

"What happened?" she asked, desperate to know where she was and how she got here.

"I found you unconscious at your house," Maisy replied. "Someone hit you over the head. Whoever it was brought us here and keeps giving you tranquilizers to keep you asleep."

"Who did this?" she still had no memory of being attacked and knocked unconscious.

"I don't know, whoever it is always wears a mask," Maisy trailed off for a moment. "I keep trying to remember, I'm pretty sure I saw a face just before I was stabbed . . ."

"Stabbed?" alarmed, Tessa bolted up, and was immediately aware that this had been a bad idea. Her weakened limbs gave out and she fell back, her already aching head banging painfully against the floor, her vision fading to bright white, and nausea swelling in her stomach.

"Tessa?" Maisy called. "Tess? Come on, don't you dare pass out on me again."

Forcing herself to breath deeply and fight against the pain and queasiness. "Yeah, I'm okay," she managed. When she got a handle on things, she shuffled back slowly until she could feel a wall, then carefully eased herself up until she rested against the tightly packed dirt wall. "Are you okay?" she asked Maisy, breathing heavily from the exertion of moving.

"It's mostly stopped bleeding but . . ."

Noticing for the first time just how faint Maisy's voice was. Finally focusing her gaze away from the dirty ceiling, she turned to see her friend lying just feet away. Deciding it was better not to risk standing just yet, Tessa managed to crawl over to Maisy, who looked terrible.

"It's going to be okay, Mais," she soothed, as she focused her spinning head and began to inspect Maisy's wound. The cut seemed to be about two inches deep, but since Maisy was still alive also seemed to have missed all the vital organs, which meant their biggest problem was going to be infection. Already the skin around the wound was enflamed, and as she pressed her hand to Maisy's cheek she found it warm and sweaty.

"It's infected, isn't it?" Maisy asked, gazing up at her with tired eyes.

"Yeah, it is," she answered honestly, "but I'm going to do what I can." Tessa guessed that they had a couple of days before Maisy succumbed to septic shock, reaching for the bottles of water that had been left for them, taking one of the two bottles, she used about a third to clean out the wound. Then she pulled off her sweater, she hardly needed it in here anyway it was so hot, folded it up then slid one of the arms underneath Maisy before tying it together with its partner, tightly covering up the wound. "Here drink this," she offered the rest of the bottle to her friend, knowing it was important to keep Maisy hydrated after she'd lost so much blood.

"You need to drink too," Maisy said as Tessa helped her try to get comfortable.

"I'm fine," she assured her friend, they only had a limited amount of water and right now it was Maisy who needed it the most.

"Tessa," Maisy begun as sternly as she could manage, "you only have one kidney and a bad head wound. It's important that you keep yourself hydrated when it's so hot in here. Especially since we don't have much water."

Picking up Maisy's wrist to take her pulse, "I think that's the plan," she replied absently.

"You think it was the same person who hurt Hope and killed those women that attacked us?" Maisy asked.

"I don't know. But at least I'm pretty sure that Parker doesn't have anymore skeletons in his closet, and since I don't either, then I guess that's a little more likely than a random attack." She had an idea who it was who had locked them up here but she wasn't about to share that with Maisy just yet.

"How's your head?" Maisy queried.

"It's bleeding isn't it?" fighting back a whimper. Whenever she saw blood all Tessa could think about was Jake Killinger and how much blood there had been when she'd stabbed him.

"Uh huh."

"Then I guess we're both going to have to be brave," she tried to smile confidently for Maisy's benefit. Taking a proper look around the room where they'd been dumped, other than themselves and the water the room was completely bare. A rickety set of stairs was in one corner and against the opposite wall was an opening that presumably led to another room or rooms. "I'm going to check out the door," she announced, sure that it would be locked but wanting to gather all the information she could about their surroundings, since you never knew when it might come in handy.

"Can you make it?" Maisy asked worriedly. "That's a pretty awful knock to the head you got and then all those drugs."

"I'll be fine," she assured Maisy. Using the wall to help lever herself up, then clinging to it as a nauseating wave of dizziness rocked through her. Once it had mostly passed, she took a tentative step, pleased when she managed to remain upright.

"Are you okay?"

"I'm fine." Taking care not to move too quickly, she made her way over to the stairs. Finding she had to lean on the banister more heavily than she would have liked, as she dragged herself up. Reaching the top she found a fairly flimsy wooden door, trying the knob she found it was indeed locked, but wiggling the door it rattled a little and she determined that if she could find something solid she may be able to break through it.

Exhausted from the effort of crossing the small room and climbing the stairs, Tessa knew she needed to rest before she could look for anything to use to escape. Using the last of her remaining energy, she dragged herself back over to where her friend was lying with her eyes closed.

"Maisy?"

Eyes popping open, "did you find anything?"

"It's locked, but I might be able to bust it open. I just need to rest for a bit first," she sunk back down to the floor beside her friend.

"Yeah," Maisy nodded un-optimistically.

"I mean it, Mais," Tessa stated firmly. "I'll get us out of this. I have a great track record of getting out of sticky situations," she joked shakily.

"You get out," Maisy agreed, "but you only manage to just scrape through with your life. Besides your luck has to run out sometime."

* * * * *

3:05 P.M.

It was cold, so cold.

Meg just wanted to go home.

She wished desperately that she had never bought a new computer.

She wished that she had never heard of the Internet.

She wished that she had never met wild girl.

167

She wished that she was curled up in her own bed with the knowledge that her thirteen-year-old daughter was asleep in the next room.

And for the first time in years she wished that she was still married to her ex-husband.

Now she couldn't even remember why it was that they had divorced. She still loved him deeply, always had, but after that one indiscretion she had completely lost it and thrown in the towel.

Hadn't even listened to her husband's excuses.

Now more than anything, Meg wished that she had given him a second chance.

What was so bad anyway about him sending provocative text messages to that woman? He had told her it meant nothing, that it was just words and a few naked photos that he had used to help him 'work off his extra energy since she no longer let him touch her' to use his exact words. He had promised her that he would never have actually slept with the other woman, but at the time she hadn't cared. Cheating was cheating, and she classified his actions as cheating.

Growing up she had watched her father cheat on her mother time after time. Every time he got caught he was repentant. He hadn't meant to hurt his wife or kids, he promised he wouldn't do it again, and then a couple of months later he would be caught out once again. Watching her doormat of a mother take her cheating husband back, knowing he was going to do the same thing again, a young Meg had vowed that she would never put herself in the same situation.

If she had only agreed to at least listen to her husband, take things slowly, maybe see a counselor like he had suggested, then she would be at home with her family right now. Instead when wild girl had suggested this week away she had jumped at the chance, sent her daughter to stay with her father, telling her ex that she was off to visit her ailing aunt. Because of her lies no one knew that she was missing, no one knew that she had been attacked and left to die, and no one was looking for her.

She didn't want to die like this.

All alone in what appeared to be an abandoned stable, with her wrists tied together, the rope fastened to the wall above her head with a metal stud. Just out of reach sat a plate of chocolate cake and some water, but Meg had determined a long time ago not to look at temptation again, it helped to keep her in a more positive frame of mind. For a while she had tried like crazy to cut the ropes binding her, but now her arms ached from being help above her head for so many hours, or days, or weeks, or however long she'd been tied up here.

Picturing her daughter, and the second chance she would give her ex-husband if she made it out of this alive, she prayed that someone would find her before it was too late.

* * * * *

4:12 P.M.

Kelita didn't think she had any more tears left and yet here she was crying yet again.

She hadn't cried this much since her husband had died.

A widow by thirty, left to raise her two small children alone, there had been many a night that she had cried herself to sleep.

Now her kids were all grown up, eighteen and twenty and both away at college, and she was lonely.

That was why she had joined the group in the first place.

That and the fact that wild girl was so charismatic, even over the Internet.

She had been the first to arrive at their week away, and for the first few hours everything had been perfect. Each of the women were similar to herself. Middle aged, lonely, bored, yearning for some excitement. They had chatted, laughed, danced, had a few drinks, flirted with any man who came within striking distance, but then everything had fallen apart.

Wild girl had gone ballistic.

Then that man had raped her.

And she had ended up here.

Alone in this horrible old shack.

The walls were full of cracks through which the icy wind came whistling. Just inches out of reach sat a chocolate cake and a pitcher of water. And her feet were firmly locked in stocks. Real life stocks. Kelita hadn't even thought such a thing still existed outside of museums.

Wiggling to try to get comfortable, she wondered what Jordan and Sam were doing right now. Kelita wished that a gap hadn't grown between her and her boys. She'd been so hurt when Jordan had moved out of state for college instead of going somewhere close to home. And then when Sam had decided to move away as well she had blown up. Ashamed as she was about it now, Kelita had accused her boys of not loving her, of wanting to hurt her, of abandoning her just as their father had. It had been weeks since she had talked to them, and could still be weeks before they realized that she was missing.

Now if she could have just one wish it would be to see her children one last time. To tell them she was sorry and that she loved them. Kelita prayed that someone would find her before it was too late.

* * * * *

5:19 P.M.

She wasn't sad.

She wasn't scared.

Now Jacinta was just angry.

Angry that because of that crazy wild girl now she would never have the chance to get married, or have kids of her own, or do any of the things that she still so desperately wanted.

She was also angry at herself.

If she was about to die, which she strongly assumed that she was, without having achieved in life any of the things she wanted then she had no one to blame but herself.

At seventeen she had met the man of her dreams, a twenty-eight year old property developer, and had ignored the warnings of all her friends and family to become engaged. With wedding plans fixed for the day after her eighteenth birthday she could not have been happier. Unfortunately she had come crashing back to earth in the most horrible of ways when her fiancée never turned up to the wedding. Devastated at first, over time she worked on building a protective shell around herself, determined never to let anyone through again in case they ended up hurting her.

Because of this, Jacinta had never had many friends, socializing politely with the people at work but never taking things to the next level.

Neither had she had another serious relationship. She was too scared that things might end up the way they had the first time.

And now it was too late. Now she was going to die in this old amusement park. Chained up inside a fun house, with her wrist handcuffed to a creepy clown, in front of a distorting mirror, with a chocolate cake and glass of water tantalizingly out of reach.

Making a resolution with herself, if she somehow managed to get out of this alive then she was going to make the most of her life. She was only thirty-nine, she still had plenty of time to make friends and find a husband and have children. Now all she had to do was pray that someone would find her before it was too late.

FEBRUARY 16TH

6:11 A.M.

Wyatt could barely stand to look at Parker.

After what they'd found at Tessa's house yesterday afternoon he seriously couldn't fathom how Parker was still maintaining that Tess was fine and had just gone off somewhere to be by herself for a while.

They still didn't know exactly what Marty had found at the mansion yet, since he'd ended up kicking everyone out. When the blue glow had lit up the living room Daniel had gone ballistic, Winter had burst into hysterical tears, Casey had been close to tears, and J.J. had come dangerously close to smashing his hand through the antique mirror that hung above the fireplace.

Declaring that it was impossible to get anything done while they were there to distract him, Marty had thrown all of them out, with promises he would let them know the second he himself knew anything.

Wyatt couldn't even begin to sort out exactly how he was feeling. Terror that Tessa might be in the hands of a killer. Fear that she might be hurt. Fury at Parker for not being more concerned. Anger at himself for not protecting Tessa. Wyatt had always felt like Tessa was the little sister he'd never had and he would have laid down his life to protect her. He'd known that leaving her alone out on her estate had been a bad idea, he just hadn't thought it would end like this.

Neither did he know exactly what he thought had happened. When Tessa usually got into trouble it wasn't because she was abducted from her home in the middle of the night, it was usually

173

because she had gone running right to her attacker. Dylan Riley, Cordelia, Lachlan Mountain, Dino Rollino, the only reason these monsters had gotten their filthy hands on Tessa in the first place was because she had willingly given herself up to them.

Still he knew that something bad had happened to Tessa. Wyatt remembered the look in Tessa's eyes when he had made her promise that she wouldn't pull any stunts to avoid spending the day with Casey. She hadn't been happy about agreeing to the deal but she had honestly intended to honor it.

Despite the fact that in the past Tessa had disappeared without a word, he didn't believe that that was the case this time. When she'd done it before she had been out of her mind with fear because her husband was missing, but right now he couldn't see her just vanishing. She and Parker had been having trouble for months, so it made no sense that all of a sudden she would decide to leave.

"Did they find anything on Millicent Waters' computer?" Parker was asking calmly, his face relaxed as though he didn't have a care in the world.

Feeling physically sick at his partner's apparent lack of concern for his missing wife, Wyatt deliberately angled his face away from Parker. "Yeah I have the report," he answered, offering the paper to J.J. for him to read.

"No, you go," J.J. tossed the report back.

There was no need to read the report first since he'd already skimmed it earlier, Wyatt began to briefly summarize it, "the computer had been wiped clean . . ."

"What?" Parker looked devastated at the news. Wyatt presumed it was because now Parker was worried that they would be wanting to hypnotize Hope to find out what she knew.

"If you'd let me finish," he reprimanded before continuing, "you would have heard me say that the computer had been wiped clean *but* whoever did it did a pretty lousy job. Maxine was able to restore pretty much everything." Maxine Hingston looked about as far away from what you'd expect a computer whiz to look like as it was possible to look. Close to seventy, and very grandmotherly, Maxine was short and round and jolly, always wore her snowy white hair pulled back into a neat bun, never bothered with makeup and no matter the weather was always dressed in stockings, a skirt, blouse and cardigan. Until recently his daughter Stacey had been convinced that Maxine was actually Santa's wife Mrs. Claus, and Wyatt couldn't blame her, the computer tech did bear an amazing resemblance to the mythical woman.

"So we found what we were looking for?" J.J. asked, his brown eyes twinkling with hope.

"We sure did," he couldn't help returning J.J.'s smile. Finally they were making some progress on finding their killer, and therefore hopefully getting closer to finding Tessa. "Maxie found the chat room where they all met, and as we suspected wild girl seems to be the ringleader. It seems that he or she put out an ad looking for middle-aged women who were bored with life and after some excitement. Maxie wasn't able to tell how many responses there were but it looks like their little club ended up with six members, including wild girl."

"Do we know the women's names?" Parker asked.

"Not their real ones," he responded, refusing to meet his partner's eye. "Millicent Waters was going by 'little bear' and from the comments it seems Henrietta Kendall's name was 'flower maiden'. Then we have wild girl who may or may not be involved in whatever's going on . . ."

"So what *do* we think about this mysterious wild girl?" J.J. interrupted to ask.

"I guess it depends on the point of this little group," Parker replied. "Was it just an innocent group of women who wanted to spice up their ordinary lives who just happened to meet up with someone sinister on their holiday. Or whether the group was formed by wild girl and the holiday was his or hers way of killing these women."

"In the transcripts of the chats that Maxie could find there was a lot more information given about each of the other women than there was about wild girl," Wyatt informed them. "I think that wild girl deliberately formed this group for the purpose of providing him or herself with easy prey."

"You think that just because she didn't say much about herself that that makes her a serial killer?" Parker asked a little doubtfully.

"No, I think that wild girl is involved because in her emails to Millicent Waters she told the woman to delete everything and not tell anyone where she was going," he retorted.

"Is there any way to identify the other women?" Parker asked hopefully. Once again Wyatt assumed the purpose of his question was to ascertain whether they were any closer to helping Hope learn her true identity.

"The other names are 'DOOL1965', 'young&bold' and 'passionatelady'," he read the names from Maxie's report. "Going from the conversations in the chat room, it seems like one woman is a widow who's recently become estranged from her sons. Another woman's husband cheated on her. And the other is scared to date because of a bad experience from her past. None of this is going to help us to identify any of these women. There has to be thousands of women out there whose husband's cheated on them. These women could already be dead, or they could be tied up somewhere right now, or they could be blithely going on with their lives oblivious to the fate of their chat room friends."

"We don't know whether they met up with Henrietta and wild girl?" J.J. asked.

"The chat room suddenly went quiet about a month ago, right when Millicent Waters began receiving emails from wild girl," he explained. "The emails were all about meeting up for this exciting week away. I'm guessing since the Kendall kids said their mom got similar emails, then all the others got one too. We just don't know whether they met up all together or if wild girl met with them one on one, that might have been easier for wild girl to deal with. Unfortunately the emails didn't say whether all of them intended to meet up together . . ."

"I think I can answer that for you," Zak Fenton breezed into the room, folder in hand. "I think I found something that's going to make you all pretty happy."

"What?" J.J. demanded as they all turned to look at Zak.

"I wanted to find something so I took another look at the bodies," Zak took his time choosing a chair, settling into it, arranging his papers in a perfect stack. "I know you had this computer lead about some wild woman or something . . ."

"Wild girl," Parker corrected.

"Whatever," Zak waved a dismissive hand. "I know you heard from Henrietta Kendall's kids that she may have been meeting up with someone so I started thinking where might a forty-year-old married mom go that she wouldn't want her family to know about. And I wondered whether she might have met up with this wild friend of hers at a nightclub. So, I got out a UV light and checked her hand, and I found a stamp, you know one of those ones clubs use in case you go out then they know who to let back in. So I tried Millicent Waters too since they were presumably killed by the same person, and bingo, I found an identical stamp," he congratulated himself.

"Did it say what club they'd been at?" Parker asked hopefully.

"No," Zak's grin dipped slightly. "But it does have the date on it. As of February forth both Henrietta Kendall and Millicent Waters were alive and well."

"So we can check out Hope, she might have the same stamp," Parker babbled excitedly.

"Maybe," Zak drawled, "invisible ink doesn't wash off but if exposed to sunlight it will fade in about a week."

"It's been almost two weeks since the forth," Parker couldn't hide his disappointment.

"We can try," Zak smiled placatingly.

"Hope's too young," Parker continued. "The rest of these women were middle aged, Hope can't be more than thirty or so."

"We have no idea how old she is," he reminded Parker calmly. "Hope has no memories."

"Well we have three unknown women, and wild girl, Hope has to be one of them because so far we have no proof that anyone else was involved," J.J. mused. "Talk to her, see if any of those names sparks her memory. Then we're going to track down security footage from every nightclub in the city and see what we can find."

* * * * *

7:11 A.M.

Parker was still in shock.

He couldn't believe that it was happening again.

Once again, Tessa had disappeared without a trace.

Yesterday afternoon at her house when the luminol had cast it's ominous blue glow, for one horrifying second his heart had actually stopped, his airways had closed, and he'd been positive that he was about to pass out.

But then common sense had kicked in.

First of all they didn't even know if it was blood that had caused the luminol to glow since the substance also reacted to bleach. So it was possible that Tessa had spilt something in there recently and cleaned it up with bleach causing the luminol to light up.

Second of all, even if it did turn out to be blood, there was no one who had cause to hurt Tessa. He had no more skeletons in his closet, no one left, now that Lachlan Mountain was safely locked away, who might want to get at him by hurting Tessa.

Parker was also pretty sure that there was no one left from Tessa's past who might want to hurt her either. Dylan Riley was dead, so were Dino Rollino and Cordelia. And as much as he hated to admit it, it seemed unlikely that John Doe would risk coming back out of the woodwork to hurt Tess now.

That left only Hope's case. And he could see no logical reason why wild girl or whoever was prowling the Internet looking for women to tie up and leave to die would attack Tessa. It just made no sense at all.

Unfortunately at the moment what he thought was more likely to have happened was that Tessa had hurt herself. If it did turn out to be blood that Marty had found in Tessa's living room, and at this point Parker wasn't convinced that it was, then he believed there was a much higher probability that she had lost control and harmed herself in some way. Then embarrassed that people would think she was weak she had decided to disappear for a few days or weeks until she had recovered, then she planned on returning.

Now the Tessa he had first met would never have even contemplated injuring herself. However, from all accounts of Tessa's mental state the last few months it was clear that she had already well and truly reached her limits. Somewhere along the line there had to be a limit to how much Tessa could take before she finally cracked under the pressure of holding herself together, as he'd always been afraid she would. Everyone had warned him from the beginning that with a past like Tessa's she was bound to fall apart eventually. He'd warned her more times than he could count that holding everything in, pretending it never happened, relying upon herself alone, was never going to work. That sooner or later it would all come crashing down upon her. And he was very afraid that he had been the straw that broke the camels back and pushed her too far after their argument the other night.

Needing answers he grabbed his phone and dialed.

"Hello?" a voice answered on the second ring.

"Charlie, it's Parker."

"Do you have news on Tessa?" fear and concern laced the psychiatrist's voice.

"No."

Muttering something under this breath, then wary, "what do you want, Parker?"

"I . . . I . . ." not quite sure how to phrase what he needed to know.

"I can't tell you what we talked about, she's my patient," Charlie reminded him.

"I know that. I just wanted to know if," gathering himself, "if I'm to blame for her disappearance."

"You mean you want to know if I think she hurt herself."

"Yes," subconsciously holding his breath as he waited for Charlie's answer.

"In my professional opinion, no, I don't think she hurt herself."

Relief flooded through him.

"If that's all I'll be going now," Charlie dismissed him.

"Charlie, wait."

Irritated, "what do you want, Parker?"

"I just need to understand what was going on with her. She wouldn't talk to me," he added a little frustrated himself.

"Because you keep accusing her of not trusting you."

"She doesn't," catching the sulkiness in his voice.

"She does," Charlie contradicted. "Whether she knows it or not she trusts you. You want to know why you keep making such a big deal out of her trust issues? Because when you look at her you see yourself. You have the exact same problems with trust as she does."

Starting to see why Tessa had felt comfortable enough to open up to Charlie Abbott, he was calm and confident and straightforward. "Tess said that too."

A smile in his voice, "I'm glad she's been listening to me. It shakes her confidence when you keep accusing her of not trusting you, but she's working hard on dealing with things, you should be proud of her."

Wishing he'd given Tessa a chance to let him be part of this. "When did she start seeing you?"

"Right after she told you about Eleanor. She finally recognized that she needed help."

"Why won't she talk to me about that?" annoyed that Tessa could open up to others about her abduction, but steadfastly refused to talk to him.

"Because you won't let her. You can't deal with what happened to her. Every time you look at her you feel guilty because you can't fix it for her. But Tessa didn't . . . doesn't," Charlie corrected himself, "need you to fix it for her. She just needs you to be there."

Parker didn't know what to say to that. But he did know he was starting to feel worse and worse over how bad he'd let things get with his wife.

"Look, Parker, you need help just as much as Tessa does. Maybe you should consider seeing someone yourself. I'd offer but Tessa trusts me and I won't do anything to compromise that trust, but I can recommend you someone if you're interested." Charlie sighed, "Parker, I don't think you're a bad guy, but Tessa's not just my patient she's my friend too, and I'm protective of her. I don't want to see her get hurt again."

Wincing, assuming Tessa had gone to Charlie after the emotionless cyborg incident. "I don't want to hurt her."

"I know that. So sort yourself out, go find Tessa and let her know that you're there for her, she's waiting to hear it, she *needs* to hear it. Parker, there's one more thing you should know," Charlie hesitated. "I shouldn't be telling you this but I don't want to jeopardize her health. As part of her treatment for posttraumatic stress disorder, I have her on the SSRI antidepressant Paxil."

"Okay," he nodded slowly. Shocked, not by Charlie's diagnosis of PTSD, even he could have come to that conclusion, but by the fact that Tessa was allowing Charlie to treat her with medications. However, he didn't get why Charlie seemed so concerned about this.

"Parker, withdrawal symptoms from Paxil can be severe. I doubt whoever took her also took her medication. She's been off the drugs for over a day now, she's going to be suffering. When you find her make sure you have the Paxil on you, give it to her immediately. If you can't find her prescription, call me and I'll make sure you get some. I have to go now but keep me updated."

Lost in thought at he walked back to the room where J.J., Zak and Wyatt were still discussing the case. Parker was now more uncertain and confused than ever about his marriage. Tessa was obviously working hard to overcome her issues, surely he owed her the same. He wasn't sure what to think about Tessa's disappearance. Still unconvinced that anything sinister had happened to her, it still seemed a viable option that she just needed some time to herself, she was obviously dealing with a lot.

"Parker, are you coming?" Wyatt was scowling at him.

Obviously his partner was still mad at him for not flying off into a frantic panic when they had no proof whatsoever that Tessa had met some awful fate.

"Maisy's gone," Marty burst breathlessly into the room.

"What?" J.J. frowned at him.

"Maisy is gone," Marty repeated, the usual calm and in control crime scene tech looked wild and panicked. "Something has happened to her."

"What?" Parker asked, thinking that that was all they needed, for Maisy to have gone and gotten herself into trouble.

"Something bad," Marty continued, flustered. "Something dangerous."

"How did you jump to that conclusion?" Wyatt asked, confused.

"No one has seen her in two days," Marty wrung his hands nervously.

"And that adds up to her being in danger?" J.J. demanded wearily.

"No, the blood does," Marty replied.

"The what?" he knew his own face must look as shocked as J.J.'s, Wyatt's and Zak's did.

Marty threw his files on the table and made for the door, "I have to go find her."

"No, you have to sit down and tell us what on earth you are talking about," J.J. roared. "Now," he added when Marty hesitated.

Forcing himself into a chair, Marty took several deep breaths to calm himself before he began, "after you all left yesterday I decided to rip up the carpet. Sometimes a criminal will clean a crime scene with bleach thinking that they've got everything, but often blood will soak through carpet and remain on the floor beneath," the scientist calmed a little as he recounted facts. "When I ripped up the carpet in Tessa's living room I found two distinct blood patterns."

The news was a blow to his confidence. He'd been hoping that it would end up not being blood at all. Despite Charlie's opinion that he didn't believe Tessa would hurt herself, it didn't discount the possibility. "We don't know whose blood it is," he reminded everyone.

"I realize that," Marty began.

"Or how long it's been there," he added.

"I realize that," Marty tried again.

"Remember this is a house where Emilie and Cordelia lived. Who knows what those two crazy women might have done there."

"I realize that," Marty countered once more, this time with a warning frown. "But when Maisy didn't turn up to work today, which we all know is highly unlike her, I got worried and called Luke. He said that he and Maisy had been having problems recently because Maisy wants to get married and he's not sure he'd ready. Luke said he hadn't seen or heard from Maisy for two days, and the last time they spoke she told him she was going to see Tessa to find out her view on their problems. That was the same day Tessa disappeared. I'm running tests on the blood from the mansion to confirm its Tessa and Maisy's."

"Maybe Tessa and Maisy decided to get away from their problems for a while and take a vacation," he suggested, ignoring everyone's scowls and groans.

"Come on," Wyatt threw his hands up in disgust. "That doesn't sound like Tessa or Maisy. I think you're really grasping at straws now."

"No more than you are," he countered childishly and had to consciously refrain from pouting. "You're the ones who think that Tess and Maisy have been abducted by some mysterious fellow who may or may not be the man who's trolling the Internet in search of vulnerable middle aged women to tie up and leave to die. Not to mention the accusations you're hurling at Hope."

"What accusations . . .?" Wyatt began but J.J. waved him quiet.

"No one is accusing Hope of anything," J.J. held him in that cool unblinking stare that was usually only reserved for when the big man was very near the end of his patience.

"Earlier you said that Hope could be wild girl," he huffed, sick to death of hearing unfounded accusations about poor Hope. After his talk with Charlie, Parker was sure he wanted to fix things with Tessa, but that didn't mean he would turn his back on Hope. And it didn't mean that something awful had happened to his wife. If both Tessa and Maisy were having relationship dramas it seemed feasible that they might have taken off for a few days.

"And," he continued, "since Wyatt thinks that wild girl is the killer or at least helping the killer then it sounds as if you're all alleging that Hope is somehow involved in all of this. Hope had been nothing but helpful throughout this whole ordeal and has done nothing to suggest that she is a homicidal maniac. She's a victim. And we all know that Tessa has a history of disappearing when things get tough. It's completely plausible that since they're both having a hard time at the moment that Tess and Maisy decided to take a little break."

"I hear what you're saying," J.J. nodded coldly. "But Marty found evidence that two people were bleeding in Tessa's living room. And since no one has seen Tessa or Maisy in over thirty-six hours, and the last we know Maisy was headed out to Tessa's before they both disappeared without a word. So I think until we prove otherwise we have to work on the premise that both of them are in danger."

* * * * *

4:26 P.M.

J.J. was simmering, struggling to reign in the temper he knew was legendary. For the life of him he couldn't fathom why Parker continued to blithely support this Hope woman even when faced with evidence that suggested his wife had been attacked in her home.

From the beginning he had warned Parker that if he wasn't fully prepared for all that was bound to come with being involved with Tessa then he ought not to get involved. In fact he'd warned him of this several times even after Parker and Tessa had begun dating, and even after they'd gotten married. Both Tessa and Parker still bore the scars of their traumatic childhoods, whether either of them admitted it or not. And both of them were much better at diagnosing problems in the other's life than they were at addressing their own problems.

Once again, J.J. thanked his lucky stars for his family.

Jacob Jacobson was the third of four children, with an older brother and sister and a younger sister. His parents had remained happily married right up until the death of his father, his mother passing away just months later. Growing up his mother had been a homemaker, his father worked at a bank, they weren't wealthy but neither were they poor, comfortable their father always used to say. They went on family vacations to the beach each summer, they ate dinner together each night, his dad was always there to help him with his homework, and his mom was always there when he got home from school each day. His parents were firm but fair, and as he grew older he respected their decisions even when he didn't always agree with them.

As kids he and his brother rode their bikes, climbed trees, teased their sisters mercilessly, and remained close even into adulthood. After his brother died in a boating accident at the age of forty-two, leaving behind a wife and three small children the family had rallied. Through this tragedy J.J. had grown closer with his sisters, and if it were possible even closer with his parents, as they all worked to make sure their family was taken care of.

When other kids had told a young J.J. that his family was unique he had never believed it. He truly thought that every family was as close as his was. It wasn't until he entered the police force that he realized just how lucky he had been to grow up in a loving, stable environment with a family that supported one another through anything and everything.

Now there wasn't a day that went by that he didn't thank God for his parents and siblings, his beautiful wife of thirty-five years Linda, for whom his love grew almost daily, their four children and fourteen grandchildren. Picking up the framed family photo their kids had organized for his and Linda's Christmas present he felt his heart swell with love. J.J. knew what a blessing these people were in his life and he wanted to make sure that even in the midst of a world in turmoil, including the lives of people he cared about, he was never going to forget how lucky he was to have his family.

"J.J.," his office door burst open and a breathless Wyatt ran in, "we found her."

"Found who?" he asked confused. "Tessa? Maisy?"

Face falling, "no, we don't have anything on the girls yet. But Maxie started going through security footage from all the nightclubs that have sent us their tapes already and she just called me. She found her, on the tape."

"Found who?" he demanded, wishing Wyatt would fully explain what he was on about. "Henrietta Kendall or Millicent Waters?"

"Neither," Wyatt's grin grew again, "Hope. Maxie found Hope on one of the tapes."

"What's she doing on it?" he still wasn't sure whether he thought Hope was an innocent or somehow involved.

"I don't know," Wyatt shrugged. "I haven't seen it yet. When Maxie called me I came straight to get you."

"So what are we waiting for?" he pushed his chair back so vigorously he almost knocked it over.

"Absolutely nothing," Wyatt swung open the door. "Come on, Maxie's waiting."

"Parker coming?" he asked as they headed for the computer lab, not sure he was up to hearing another round of Parker's drivel about poor Hope.

"Maxie was going to call him," Wyatt replied indifferently. "So I assume he's coming. But we both know that Parker's more concerned about poor, sweet Hope right now than he is the possibility that something has happened to his wife."

Wondering why is was that even though they had all known Parker longer, everyone seemed to be on Tessa's side in this mess she and Parker had created. As J.J. knew from personal experience there was just something about Tessa that made you want to take care of her. Maybe it was her sad greeny-blue eyes, or her big blonde curls, or the fact that her life sounded more like one that belonged to a soap opera character than a real person. Whatever it was, it drew you into her stratosphere and filled you with a desire to protect her, to look after her, to make her happy. J.J. felt like Tessa was his daughter and when anyone hurt her it was hard not to see that person as the bad guy even when it was someone like Parker, whom J.J. considered a close friend.

"How's Marty?" Wyatt asked.

"He insisted on sending someone back over to Tessa's in case he missed anything," he answered.

J.J. had never seen the usually calm and collected crime scene tech so emotional. Arriving at the computer lab, J.J. knocked on the door, knowing Maxie hated it when people barged in on her.

"Come in," hollered a voice from inside the room.

"Hey, Maxie," Wyatt greeted enthusiastically as they entered.

"Wyatt, J.J.," Maxine greeted them both with equal enthusiasm, heaving herself out of her chair to come and kiss both their cheeks.

"I hear you have good news for us," J.J. smiled down at her.

"I surely do," she beamed, her rosy cheeks glistening, her blue eyes twinkling merrily. She crossed back to her computer and maneuvered her round frame, today clad in a bright red skirt and cardigan with ivory blouse, back into her chair.

"Show us what you've got," as he took the seat beside her J.J. couldn't help smiling at the woman who all of his small grandchildren were convinced was Mrs. Claus. It still amazed him every time he saw Maxine with her husband who looked about as anti-Santa as was possible to look. Trent was tall and as thin as a beanpole, with a stern, bony face and a head of thick brown hair despite the fact he'd recently celebrated his seventieth birthday.

"We're not waiting for Parker?" Maxine asked, placing her hand on the computer mouse.

"I'm sure he's got his hands full with his new buddy Hope," Wyatt answered snarkily.

"Actually Hope's with Beth right now," Parker appeared suddenly in the doorway. "So my hands are empty."

Wyatt shrugged unapologetically and refused to meet Parker's gaze as he joined the rest of them around the computer.

"Okay so this is from February forth," Maxine told them once everyone was seated.

"The same day we think Henrietta Kendall and Millicent Waters disappeared," he mused. "Any sign of them on the tape?"

"Not yet, but The Leopard has five rooms and the cameras from this one were the first I watched cos they were on top," Maxine moved the mouse and the screen sprang to life.

The frozen image showed Hope, dressed in a short black skirt, tight bright red halter-top and six-inch heels. She was pressed seductively up against a guy with spiky brown hair, which made J.J. remember the short brown hairs they'd found at each of the crime scenes, who looked like he was having the time of his life. As did Hope who had a huge smile on her pretty face.

"Looks like Hope's have a wonderful time," Wyatt commented snidely, with a sideways look at Parker.

Snapping out of his daze, "of course Hope looks like she's having a great time," Parker growled. "She doesn't know she's dancing with a man who is actually a homicidal maniac and is about to try and kill her and who knows how many other innocent women."

"He doesn't look like a homicidal maniac to me," Wyatt countered calmly.

"And Hope does?" Parker demanded.

"Well she certainly doesn't look like a bored and lonely middle aged woman who's hanging around a nightclub on a secret vacation to try and spice up her life," Wyatt argued. "She looks young and carefree and perfectly at home."

"So because she looks like she's having fun that makes her somehow involved in all of this?" Parker challenged. "I thought that was supposed to be the purpose of this little club, for these women to get away from their lives and have some fun."

"I think Hope looks like she's having more than fun," Wyatt gave a pointed look to the screen and the satisfied smile on Hope's face as she lay in the arms of the man.

"So what?" Parker insisted defensively and with a tiny hint of jealousy at the prospect of Hope enjoying the company of another man. "We don't know if Hope was married or involved with anyone, and none of that makes her a serial killer."

"No, but . . ." Wyatt started.

"Boys, boys, boys," J.J. interjected, feeling like he had jumped back in time to when he used to referee his sons shouting matches. "There's no need to speculate," he returned his gaze to the screen and the young man who had his hands all over Hope on the dance floor. "Because we just found someone who can give us all the answers we're after."

* * * * *

6:49 P.M.

"Here, drink this," Tessa held the bottle containing the last of their water up to Maisy's lips. Her friend drank greedily, and Tessa tried to hold the bottle steady but despite her efforts some of the precious liquid was wasted, trickling uselessly down Maisy's chin. "Better?" she asked.

"Yeah," Maisy settled back against the floor. "You should have some too though."

"Uh, I did," Tessa lied. "Earlier, while you were asleep."

If she had to guess, Tessa would estimate that close to forty-eight hours had passed since her argument with Parker and already they were out of water. In an effort to ward off infection in Maisy's wound for as long as possible she'd been washing out the cut every couple of hours, or at least what she guessed was every couple of hours. The rest of the water she'd given to Maisy to drink since right now her friend needed it more, but Tessa was beginning to feel the effects of dehydration. In addition to the overwhelming thirst, her mouth was dry, her head aching and dizzy, and as of the last couple of hours she had a bad case of insomnia.

As if dehydration and a head injury weren't enough, she was also suffering withdrawal symptoms from abruptly stopping her medication. Dizziness, headaches, nausea, muscle cramps, difficulty concentrating, chills or hot flashes, feelings of electrical shocks coursing through her body. Just some of what she may experience. Tessa wasn't sure she'd be able to hold it together to find a way to get herself and Maisy out of this.

It had taken Charlie a while to convince her to let him medicate her as part of her PTSD treatment. In her mind taking medication was associated with her mother. Emilie had been addicted to antidepressants, painkillers, sleeping pills, basically any prescription medications she could get her hands on. More than anything, Tessa didn't want to be like Emilie.

But Charlie had countered that taking advantage of all the treatment options available was simply being sensible and giving herself the best chance of recovering. So Tessa had put her trust in Charlie and agreed to start taking the Paxil, and had been surprised by the effects of the drug. Her nightmares had eased a little, as had her anxiety, and she hadn't had as many flashbacks. Still the medication wasn't a magic pill, and Charlie was also doing cognitive behavioral therapy, and exposure therapy with her. Tessa was working hard, attempting to do everything Charlie asked her to, because she wanted to get better. She wanted to be able to live a normal life.

"Tess?" Maisy's hand pressed weakly against her leg.

Wrapping up her own discomfort and making sure her face was calm and controlled but not falsely cheerful. "Yes?"

"How's your head?"

The stifling heat of the small room, dehydration, Paxil withdrawals, not to mention the blow her head had taken were making it feel like it wanted to explode but she answered, "it's fine."

"Liar," Maisy looked up at her reproachfully. "You probably have a concussion, your head has to be killing you."

"It's better since I slept," she answered truthfully. After trying the door when she'd first regained consciousness, she had passed out from exhaustion rather than fallen into a restful sleep. Ever since she'd awakened an hour or two ago she had been wired and edgy, but hadn't had enough energy to do much. She had gone back up the stairs and tried the door again, but she was already too weak to break it down. "I'm going to take a look around," she told Maisy. Despite her headache, curiosity was beginning to get the better of her; she wanted to know what lay beyond the other door.

"Take it easy," Maisy cautioned.

"I will," Tessa assured her as she used the wall to help heave herself up. Fighting dizziness, she rested against the wall for a moment before venturing across the room.

Managing to make it across the floor without falling, Tessa found herself at the dark opening in the wall. The dim light that allowed them to see didn't spill out into the narrow hall and she couldn't quite stop a shiver at the prospect of going alone out into the dark with no idea of what she was going to encounter.

"Everything okay, Tessa?" Maisy called.

"Everything's fine," she called back.

"Did you find something?"

"No, there's a hall," sticking her head through the opening and looking down to the end of the corridor where a small glow emanated from under a closed door. "It looks like a light down there."

"Be careful," Maisy warned. "We don't know what this maniac might have hidden away down here and you're hurt."

"I'll be careful," she promised, stepping out of the relative safety of the lit room and into the spooky shadowy hall. Keeping a hand on the wall, partly to guide her in the dark and partly to help keep herself upright, Tessa inched her way down towards the light. As she crept along she couldn't help thinking about that night, sixteen years ago, when she and Ellie had crept along the secret passage in Isaac's mansion heading for freedom. At the time Tessa had had no idea that it wasn't freedom waiting for them at the end of the tunnel but Jake. Or that Ellie was about to lose her life and her own life was going to be irrevocably changed.

Before she realized it she bumped into the wall at the end of the hallway, right in front of the door under which a little light tumbled out. Stretching out a trembling hand, she grasped the doorknob, and since there was no point in delaying, she quickly turned the handle and pushed it open before she lost her nerve.

Gasping as she took in the contents of the room.

The room was long and narrow, a single light globe the source of the light she had seen from the hallway. Both walls were lined with deep shelves, four to a wall, and stacked neatly with coffins.

There had to be at least thirty of them. As Tessa drifted down the walkway, her head swiveling from left to right and back again, trying to take everything in, she saw that each coffin was marked with a photo. Stopping midway, she peeled one of the pictures off at random. It was of a pretty young woman in skis, standing on the top of a mountain. Turning to grab another she saw an older man, his blonde hair streaked with snowy white, grinning at the camera from the front seat of a shiny new Porsche.

Head swimming, already beginning to slot things together, forming a picture of what was going on here, of who had kidnapped her and Maisy and why. Managing to make it to the desk at the end of the room before her legs gave out. Tessa plopped heavily down into a chair, resting her head in her hands, and trying to formulate a plan.

She always felt better when she had a plan. A plan meant you weren't helpless. A plan meant a chance at survival. A plan meant you were still in control, and losing control was what Tessa feared most, because she knew what it was like to have zero control over what people were doing to you.

Pulling herself together, the first step in any good plan was knowing everything you could about your opponent. Rifling through the desk drawers she stumbled across something that could tell her exactly what she needed to know. Settling down she cleared her mind and began to read.

* * * * *

7:53 P.M.

"We need to talk."

"Uh oh, that sounds serious," Hope's eyes grew wide with worry.

"It is," Parker took Hope's elbow and guided her to the settee, gently pushing her down before pulling up a chair and sitting in front of her.

"You found something," Hope said immediately.

"We found something . . ." he confirmed.

"Something bad," she continued.

"No, not really bad," he assured her. Still conflicted about the video Maxie had found of Hope flirting and dancing with that man at the nightclub. He didn't believe, as Wyatt and J.J. did, that the video proved Hope was involved in the murders, but it did give them some insights into who Hope had been before her near death experience. The Hope in the video looked bright and bubbly and outgoing, and definitely seemed to be lapping up the attention her young male friend was dishing out.

Parker wasn't quite sure why that bothered him so much.

He'd known that Hope had had a life before they'd met, possibly a boyfriend or husband, maybe even kids. But he had already come to take it for granted how much she depended on him, and even for some reason he couldn't explain, enjoyed it. Who knows, maybe Tessa was right. Maybe there was a part of him that always needed to play the role of the hero, rescuing some poor damsel in distress.

"Parker, you're scaring me," Hope was twisting her hands

194

together in her lap so tightly he was worried she was going to dislocate her fingers. "What's going on? What did you find? Did you find out who I really am? Did you find out who kidnapped me and those other women?" her questions coming tumbling out in a panic.

"Whoa," he soothed, reaching over to gently untangle her hands. "Just calm down and I'll explain everything to you, okay?"

"Okay," she took several deep breaths then steeled herself for what was to come.

"We were able to get a hold of Millicent Waters computer," he explained. Watching her carefully to gauge her responses in case they yielded any information about who Hope really was and what was going on inside her head. "Someone had attempted to wipe the computer clean . . ."

"Attempted?" Hope interrupted. "You mean they didn't do it properly? You were still able to find stuff?"

"Maxine Hingston, one of our best computer techs, was able to find everything," he assured her. "We found some old chat room conversations and some emails that suggest Millicent Waters found some friends on the Internet. Some friends who were just like her, bored and lonely and yearning for excitement. So they got to chatting and decided to meet up. The meeting appears to have been instigated by wild girl . . ."

"Who Detective Wyatt was asking me about the other day," Hope interjected.

"Right," Parker nodded, remembering well Wyatt's interview which had bordered on an attack, his partner had a real bee in his bonnet about Hope. "So when Maxie was going through the computer she found the names of the women in wild girl's group . . ."

"Their names?" Hope squealed excitedly. "So you know my real name?"

"No, no, not their real names," he corrected himself. "Their screen names."

"Oh," Hope's face fell.

"I'm sorry," he apologized immediately. "I didn't think."

"No, that's okay, it was my fault, I misunderstood." She pulled a smile back on, "so what were the screen names they were using?"

"Well there was wild girl, who we're still not sure how involved in all of this she actually was. Then there was Millicent Waters who was going by 'little bear', we think Henrietta Kendall was using 'flower maiden'. Then there were three other names, 'DOOL1965, 'young&bold' and 'passionatelady', one of which has to be you," he finished still watching her carefully but seeing nothing of importance flash through her face.

"But which one?" Hope asked mournfully.

"None of them sound familiar to you?"

Taking a moment to consider before shaking her head in disappointment, "no, none of them spark anything."

"That's okay," Parker assured her, a little disappointed himself. "At least we have a direction to move in."

"And two, maybe three, more women out there who could be dying as we speak," Hope considered sadly.

"We're doing everything we can to find any other victims before it's too late," he replied. Every available officer had been pulled in to track down Hope's dance partner from the nightclub.

"Where did they meet?" Hope asked. "You said that they all planned to meet up somewhere, did you find out where that was?"

Unable to put it off any longer, Hope's question was as good a lead in as he was going to get to ask his questions. "Actually, that was the second thing I wanted to talk to you about. Zak, one of the medical examiners, found some UV stamps on Henrietta and Millicent's hands. Like the kind that places like nightclubs use. The stamps were dated February forth . . ."

"A couple of days before I woke up in the hospital," Hope mused.

"Right," he agreed. "So we started collecting security footage from all the nightclubs in the city to see if we could find anything . . ."

"And you did," Hope interjected. "You found us right? Where?"

"A nightclub called 'The Leopard'," he replied. "Does that sound familiar to you? Do you think you've been there before?"

Brow furrowing, she chewed on her lip as she thought, "it doesn't ring a bell. Did you find Henrietta and Millicent on the tape too?"

"We found them," he confirmed. After they'd watched Hope getting intimate with their mystery man they'd all taken a tape, fast-forwarded to the corresponding time on Hope's tape and had spotted both Henrietta and Millicent. Unfortunately in all the footage they'd viewed to date, they were yet to see a single interaction between any of the three ladies. Which meant they were no closer to identifying their three unknown women.

"Well did you see anyone suspicious watching them, I mean us? Or talking to us?" Hope demanded.

Other than the man they were currently tracking down no one else had stood out as overly suspect. "No, but . . ."

"But what?" Hope snapped with more venom than he'd ever seen her use. "It sounds like you don't know anything. Again."

"Actually we do have one avenue to pursue," he answered, a little taken aback by Hope's sudden outburst.

"What?" she pouted.

"In the video you were dancing with someone . . ."

"A male someone?"

Nodding in confirmation, "it looked like the two of you were getting quite cozy."

"Maybe he was my boyfriend, or even my husband, or he could be . . ." she gulped, "he could be the man who tried to kill me. Did it look as if I knew him?"

"It looks like you met him there." On the tape they'd watched the young man trip and accidentally spill his drink all over Hope, then the two had gotten talking and things had progressed from there. If they hadn't already known how things had ended up, they might have thought they were watching a sappy romantic comedy. Still until they located this guy they had no idea whether the apparently chance meeting had in fact been staged and Hope's clumsy date may be less innocent than he seemed.

"Well did he spend time with the other women? Did I leave with him?"

"We didn't see him spend any time with Henrietta or Millicent, and you didn't leave with him."

"So he could be nothing," she threw her hands up hopelessly, tears welling up in her eyes. "And we could be right back where we started which was nowhere."

In addition to seeing no interactions between Hope, Millicent or Henrietta neither had any of the women left at the same time. Maybe this whole mess was just one big coincidence and even though these women had been connected on the Internet they had been picked entirely at random. About to make some sort of lame consoling comment to Hope when someone cleared their throat.

"Is this a bad time?" Daniel asked, scowling at them with unconcealed hostility.

"No, not at all," Parker answered, willing himself to remain calm.

"Good, glad to see you're not losing any sleep over your missing wife," Daniel sneered sarcastically.

"Daniel," Matilda warned. "We won't take up much of your time, we have some news . . ."

"On Tessa?" he interrupted before he thought, then realized that if Daniel and Matilda had news on Tessa, Daniel wouldn't be standing quietly at a distance seething with rage he'd be up close and personal, and busy with his fists. Tessa may bottle up her emotions inside until it consumed her but her brother preferred to let things fly.

"No, not about Tess," Matilda replied.

"Then what?" His sister was acting a little nervously and Parker began to wonder what exactly was up.

"Just tell him," Daniel huffed.

"Tell me what?" he repeated exasperatedly.

Matilda began to raise her arm and as he glanced at it he couldn't help but notice the sparkling diamond ring adorning her left hand.

Following his gaze, Matilda nodded, "Daniel and I are getting married. He proposed a couple of days ago but then Tessa went missing and we haven't told anyone else yet. We wanted you to be the first to know. Parker? Parker? Parker, say something."

But he found he couldn't say a word. He was completely and utterly speechless.

FEBRUARY 17TH

"Why am I here?" Pete Hastings demanded the second they opened the door. "Am I being charged with something?"

"Right now you're just helping us with our enquiries," Wyatt informed him, taking a seat opposite the man.

"Then why am I here in a police station inside a cell?" Pete frowned.

"Interview room," Wyatt corrected.

"Whatever," Pete's frown deepened. "Why am I here? What am I supposed to have done?"

Wyatt had to admit the young man did not look like a potential serial killer. A baby face, clean cut and suavely dressed, still as he knew all too well looks could be deceiving. In the wee hours of the morning, at the same club where he had been dancing with Hope just a fortnight ago, they had located the man they had been looking for, one Pete Hastings. Aged thirty-three, Pete was currently single, worked as a travel agent and spent the majority of his free time hanging out at nightclubs and hooking up with beautiful young women.

"You're here about the recent spate of murders," Parker explained.

Unable to completely hide his smirk at Parker's apparent jealousy for the man with whom Hope had been so obviously interested in getting close to. "You know," Wyatt added, "the three women who were chained up and left to die."

Chocolate eyes growing wide in disbelief, "you think *I* killed those women?"

"I think you're somehow involved," he confirmed. "I just

don't know how deeply."

"I'm not involved," Pete declared.

"Prove it to me," Parker settled back in his chair.

"Huh? What? How?" Pete Hastings spluttered.

"Prove it to me," Parker repeated.

"I can't. I just didn't do it. I never killed anyone. I'm a vegetarian," Pete uttered as though that were the final word.

"I don't think that the fact that you don't eat meat excludes you from being a murderer," he smiled.

"Look, I'm serious," Pete began in earnest. "I didn't kill anyone, I would never kill anyone. Sure I can be a little wild, sure I've hurt a lot of women emotionally, sure I'm young and irresponsible and self-centered, but you have to believe me I would never ever, in a million years, take another human being's life." The edgy young man's chocolate brown eyes darted backwards and forwards between him and Parker, trying to gauge if they believed him or not.

Actually, Wyatt did believe that this man had not killed Henrietta Kendall and Millicent Waters, but he was still going to remain cautious. "Okay," he nodded agreeably, "say we believe you, then can you explain why you were dancing with one of the victims on the day she was attacked, at the same club on the same night where the other victims also were?"

"I was at the same club as the victims?" Pete asked astounded.

"The Leopard, February forth," Parker supplied.

"What? I don't know, I go there a bit, I meet a lot of girls there but I never pay too much attention. I'm not looking for anything serious just a great night."

"Maybe this'll help," he laid a picture of Hope entangled in Pete's arms down on the table in front of the man.

"Oh my gosh . . ." Pete Hastings's tanned face turned an unnatural shade of grey.

"You remember her," Parker's caramel eyes lit with hope at the idea of finally discovering who Hope really was.

"Oh yeah," Pete's head bobbed emphatically. "This woman is insane."

"You know her? You know who she is?" Parker looked just shy of clapping his hands and jumping with excitement.

"I know she's a crazy person," Pete shoved the photo away. "But I did not kill that woman."

"She's not dead," he informed Pete. "She managed to escape."

"Great, then she can tell you I never hurt her," Pete beamed but it quickly turned into confusion. "If she's okay then why don't you just ask her who tried to kill her? Just ask her, she'll tell you I never did anything to her."

"Unfortunately it's not that easy," Parker countered.

"What do you mean?" Pete asked suspiciously.

"Hope has amnesia, she doesn't know who she is, let alone who tried to kill her," he explained.

"Her name's Hope?" Pete asked.

"Not her real name, but Hope is what we've been calling her," Parker replied. "We were hoping you could tell us her real name."

"She never told me," Pete shrugged.

"You were making out with a woman and you didn't even know her name?" Parker asked skeptically.

"I asked her what her name was," Pete countered defensively. "But she wouldn't tell me, just said I could call her wild girl."

Parker froze as though the revelation had turned him to stone, but for Wyatt it was simply confirmation of what he'd already suspected. It seemed that once again, Tessa had been right on the money about Hope, and he was glad that this time he had listened to her.

"That means something to you," Pete studied them perceptively. "The name wild girl."

"We think the victims were all part of an online club led by someone using the name wild girl," he explained.

"Well I don't know anything about an Internet club but," Pete picked up the photo of himself and Hope and tossed it at them,

"I know that this woman was crazy."

"Why do you keep saying she was crazy?" Parker demanded, perplexed.

"Because it's true," Pete answered simply. "She was wild, and she was all over me from the second I spilled my drink on her. She would have gone home with any man there. She wanted sex and she didn't care who is was with."

"Hope wasn't just tied up and left to starve to death she was also raped," Parker informed him.

"Well I certainly didn't rape her," Pete looked outraged at the suggestion.

"But you did have sex with her," he stated.

"Of course I did. But let me assure you not only was it completely consensual but your friend Hope was begging for it."

"A lot of rapists say that," Wyatt couldn't count the number of times a rapist had told him that his victim was asking for it.

"Yeah?" Pete was beginning to lose his temper, "good for them, but I am no rapist and I did not rape that woman. She was all over me at the club. I thought she was going to insist we did it right there and then. And when we finally did get someplace more private we were barely in the door before she began to tear my clothes off. Then once we started she kept insisting she wanted it rough. She was begging me to hurt her, saying it was the way she liked it. It made me uncomfortable but she was hot," Pete shrugged as if to say what was a guy to do. "I didn't do anything to that woman that she didn't ask me to."

Wyatt noted how crushed Parker looked at hearing the truth about just what kind of person his precious Hope actually was. It was turning out to be a bad twenty-four hours for his partner. Not only had he learned some hard truths about Hope, but he'd also found out that his twin sister had just become engaged to his least favorite person in the whole entire world. Daniel and Matilda had called him late last night to tell him the news, and while he and Casey had been happy for them he knew that Parker would definitely not have been.

Repulsed by Pete Hastings' glib attitude, Wyatt had an easy solution to see how involved Pete was in this. "At the crime scenes we found several short brown hairs. Let us take a sample of your hair, compare it to what we have and see if we can clear things up." It was a simple request, especially for someone proclaiming his or her innocence, so he was surprised when Pete refused.

Running his hands through his spiky hair Pete shook his head, "no, I don't think so. And I'm not saying another word until I call my lawyer."

* * * * *

10:18 A.M.

"Do we have anything on Tessa and Maisy?" Wyatt asked Marty as he entered the room.

Parker lifted his head to hear the answer. He was beginning to get the feeling that he had been wrong and that in fact Tess and Maisy's disappearance was not voluntary.

"No, nothing," Marty dropped exhaustedly into a chair.

"Tess must have been unconscious when she was taken otherwise she would have found a way to leave us some sort of clue," he mused thoughtfully.

Raising a surprised eyebrow, "I thought you believed Tessa had just gone on vacation," Wyatt snapped.

Shrugging, maybe it was because his illusions of Hope had just been shattered that had finally made him wise up. A part of him still believed that Pete Hastings was lying. He certainly had reason to, if he was the killer it would help to throw attention off himself by claiming that it was Hope who was the psychopath. Unfortunately the other part of him had seen how Hope behaved on that tape and wouldn't be surprised if everything that Pete

Hastings had told them was accurate. Still that didn't mean Hope was a killer, it just meant that she was, or rather had been, wild. Whatever the truth was with Hope it didn't change the fact that he loved Tessa, and whether they were together or not he needed to know that she was safe.

"We didn't find anything else at the mansion," Marty added. "And since we have no idea who or what we're looking for it's like shooting arrows in the dark, you have no idea if they hit the target or not."

"Actually I think I can help with that," Wyatt smiled. "I have a theory but, Parker, I don't think you're going to like it."

Beyond caring at the moment, "if it helps find Tessa and Maisy then I'm all ears."

Wyatt nodded approvingly and began, "I don't think that it's a coincidence that Hope showed up now."

"What do you mean?" J.J. demanded.

"I mean I don't think it's a coincidence that Hope showed up so shortly after John Doe's child trafficking ring was broken up," Wyatt clarified.

Suspicions confirmed. For weeks Parker had suspected that Tessa had told Wyatt the truth about the mysterious John Doe. "You know who he is," he accused.

"Do you Wyatt?" J.J. whirled on him. "Do you know who John Doe is?"

Sighing resignedly, "Tessa told me a little, the rest I found out on my own."

"You could lose your job for not disclosing this," J.J. was glaring.

"I know," Wyatt nodded calmly. "But Tessa said she wouldn't back me up, claim that she was in shock and that she didn't know what she'd been saying. It was the night Dino shot Parker and almost killed her, she *was* in shock, or she wouldn't have told me. She begged me not to say anything, I reluctantly agreed."

Fury crackling, if Tessa had been here this second he didn't know what he would have done. He didn't understand how she could confide in Wyatt while blatantly refusing to reveal anything to him, her own husband. "Why didn't she tell me?" he demanded.

"She didn't think you'd understand," Wyatt replied. "Or be able to let it go. She was scared you'd make it your quest to find him and punish him for everything he'd done."

"And why would she have a problem with me punishing a man who made a living out of stealing little children and selling them to pedophiles?" For the life of him, Parker couldn't figure out Tessa's reasoning on this particular subject.

Uttering another sigh Wyatt elaborated, "maybe once I tell you the whole story you'll understand a little better. John Doe's real name is Isaac Worthington. He was originally from England, and he used to be a happily married family man until the day his eight-year-old daughter was abducted . . ."

"By child traffickers," immediately seeing where this was heading.

"Right," Wyatt confirmed. "So when the police made no progress in his daughter's case he took it upon himself to find Rebecca."

"And let me guess, to do that he had to join a child trafficking ring but by the time he finally found his daughter it was too late to give it up because he'd already lost his mind," Parker sneered. Isaac Worthington's sob story was having little impact on him and he couldn't quite figure out why is had had so great an influence on Tessa. Just because his daughter had suffered was no excuse for Isaac to hurt more children.

"Just let me finish," Wyatt said reproachfully. "Actually Isaac never found Rebecca. The night after Tessa got home from the hospital she went back out to the house to look for Eleanor's body and found Isaac. She remembered that he'd watched and let her get away after she'd stabbed Jake . . ."

"Isaac saw that and he let her get away?" Parker asked.

"Apparently Tessa reminded him of Rebecca, and since he couldn't have his daughter, he transferred his feelings onto Tessa. And since Patrick had dumped his family and run off to Paris to start a new one and Emilie barely left her room, Tessa was all too happy to finally have a parental figure," Wyatt summarized. "She was just a little girl, and she was so scared, and all alone, and Isaac made her feel safe."

"Okay, I can buy that," Parker nodded reluctantly, finally beginning to get a glimmer of what had possessed Tessa to find something redeemable in this man. "But Tessa wasn't a terrified child when she went to him for help when Lachlan abducted me," he pointed out.

"No," Wyatt agreed, "she was a terrified wife who was scared out of her mind that she was going to lose another person that she loved."

Exhaling slowly, "well what's her excuse that she didn't turn him in five months ago?" he demanded.

"We had just made her relive the worst days of her life. Parker, stop trying to make sense of it. It's not logical for her. He was there for her when she was in desperate need of someone, so she cares about him. They formed some sort of tentative bond, and when Tessa needed help with Dylan Riley so she could get Tanner safely away . . ."

"She went to Isaac Worthington," J.J. finished.

"And in return Isaac asked Tessa to try to find Rebecca for him. By this time she was a twenty-two year old drug addict and prostitute," Wyatt explained. "Tessa wanted to come up with a way to stop what Isaac was doing without turning him in to the police so she told him that Rebecca was dead. She thought that if Isaac believed Rebecca was dead then he would have no reason left to keep taking children and selling them . . ."

"Only Isaac didn't stop," he reminded Wyatt.

"But Tessa didn't know that until last fall when you two found Clara. She was devastated but she still couldn't bring herself to turn him in after everything he'd done for her over the years."

Unfortunately, Parker was now beginning to understand and even sympathize with Tessa's reasons for protecting Isaac Worthington, and that only made him feel worse about his and Tessa's problems. Logically he couldn't understand her reasoning, since she herself was a victim of Isaac's. But, as Wyatt had pointed out, for Tessa it wasn't logical. She had been a traumatized child with no one to turn to. No one but Isaac. And since it wasn't logical for Tessa, then it wasn't logical for him either, because he loved Tessa.

"And Isaac saved both of you from Dino," Wyatt added.

"You risked everything for Tessa," Parker was staring at his partner in shock. After Tessa had finally admitted what had happened to her and Eleanor, he had been so full of anger over what had happened to her, and so scared that he wouldn't be able to ever get the haunted look to leave Tessa's eyes. So he'd done the only thing he could. He'd buried himself in his work. Determined that finding the men who hurt her would do more for Tessa than holding her hand and letting her know he was there for her. Charlie Abbott was right. He'd avoided her because he couldn't deal with the fact that he couldn't make things better for her. But while he'd been a coward, Wyatt had remained right by Tessa's side, giving her what she needed; unconditional support. As much as it hurt that his wife hadn't opened up to him, Parker was beyond grateful that Wyatt had been there for her. "Thank you," he met Wyatt's eye for the first time, the words didn't seem like enough.

"You're welcome," Wyatt nodded.

"While this is all very enlightening," J.J. interrupted. "What does it have to do with Hope, and Tess and Maisy disappearing?"

"I'm getting to that," Wyatt informed him. "I don't think that it's a coincidence that Hope popped up so soon after Isaac's empire collapsed. I think that Hope is really Rebecca Worthington."

"You think what?" Marty exclaimed.

"That is impossible," he protested.

"Where's your proof?" J.J. challenged

"My proof," Wyatt replied calmly, retrieving a photo from the file in front of him and laying it down on the table, "is this."

Immediately Marty and J.J. leaned over to peer at it, both gasping in shock. Parker wasn't sure he wanted to look at it but Marty passed it over and as he drew his unwilling gaze to the picture. He saw instantly what had caused the others to gasp. "This isn't really proof," he protested weakly.

"Come on, Parker," Wyatt reasoned sensibly. "That is a photo of Rebecca Worthington. Are you telling me you don't see the striking similarities between her and Hope?"

"Rebecca is only a child in this photo," he knew he was clutching at straws but he still couldn't believe that Hope was Rebecca Worthington.

"Tessa told me about Rebecca. She was kept locked inside an apartment with her abuser for eight years. Kicked out when she was only sixteen so that he could up-grade to a younger model. Forced to sell herself because it was all she knew how to do to survive. Living on the streets she got hooked on drugs. Her life ruined because of the men who abducted her. It's sad, it's traumatizing and it has to have affected her. Tessa found Rebecca so she knows that Tessa knew her father, she probably also knows how Isaac felt about Tessa. Is it such a stretch to think that she could have come to believe that Tessa had stolen her life? And that to be happy all she needed to do was the same thing, take over Tessa's life?"

Parker didn't know what to say. He didn't want to admit it but Wyatt's theory did make sense. Still he couldn't match up the sweet, innocent, Hope he knew to the psychopath Wyatt was describing.

"It wouldn't have been hard to track Tessa down after all the press coverage she's gotten the last few years. If she's been watching you two she would have known that you were having problems so what better time to strike. All she had to do was invent her little Internet club so she had some other victims to throw us off her track, set up her own abduction, and then wait to be found. Faking the amnesia ensured sympathy and was a great way to manipulate you, and you can't deny she's also been using it to drive a wedge between you and Tessa."

Still he couldn't believe that Hope could do all these things.

"Okay, I can see you're still skeptical." Wyatt pulled out another photo, "maybe this will change your mind."

This time Wyatt handed the photo directly to him so he had no choice but to look at it. What he saw made his heart plummet, "where did you get this?"

"I'm sorry, Parker, but I found it at your house, in Hope's room," Wyatt looked genuinely dismayed.

Reverting his gaze to the photo he held clutched in his hand. One of his and Tessa's wedding photos. At least it had been one of his and Tessa's wedding photos until someone had cut out Tessa's face and replaced it with Hope's.

* * * * *

12:34 P.M.

She hadn't slept in hours.

Exhausted as she was, sleep continued to remain tantalizingly out of reach.

Tessa knew it was because her mind was spinning from everything she'd read in the diary. She'd been busy going over every detail, examining it, turning it over inside her head, arranging it all so that when the time came it would serve the greatest purpose.

Beside her Maisy groaned uncomfortably in her hazy slumber, and Tessa knew that if someone didn't find them soon then Maisy wasn't going to make it.

It wasn't like she was doing so well either.

She was tired and thirsty and in pain and every time she tried to stand up it felt like her brain was jumping off a diving board. Dehydration and withdrawals were hitting her hard but she couldn't afford to let it throw her off her game. She was sure that Skylar would figure things out. She was pretty sure he was already on the right track, so all she had to do was keep herself and Maisy alive a little longer . . .

"Morning ladies," a bright voice sing-songed from the top of the stairs.

"Morning, Hope," Tessa returned, shielding her eyes from the bright light that shone through the open door.

"Ah, you figured it out," Hope clapped her hands gleefully.

Narrowing her eyes, "you know I never believed you really had amnesia," as she spoke, she eyed the open door, weighing up her options. She was weak, it was doubtful that she could make it up the stairs before Hope caught her. Even if she did attempt to make a run for it there was no way she could drag the unconscious Maisy with her, and if she left her friend behind Hope was certain to kill her immediately. For the moment it seemed her only option was to try to talk her way out of here.

"How come?" Hope asked with seemingly genuine curiosity. "What tipped you off that I was faking?"

"Honey, when you've met as many bad people in a lifetime as I have you learn to sense it," Tessa explained. "Oh, and the fact that you smiled too much. No person who had just been through what you supposedly had and didn't know who they were or where they came from would smile as much as you did."

"You have no idea about bad people," Hope griped, stomping down the stairs, hands planted firmly on her hips, a pout fixed on her lips. "I saw that awesome house you live in. You grew up there, right? Probably had everything your little heart desired, toys, clothes, holidays, a pony, anything money could buy."

"You know material possessions aren't everything." As a child, Tessa would gladly have given up every single one of her expensive toys for a mom and dad who actually wanted her.

"You know who says that?" Hope growled. "Someone who has always had the luxury of having everything they want. But that's all about to change. For once I'm going to end up with everything I ever wanted, with everything I spent every night dreaming about, and you are going to be left out in the cold. As if having a perfect childhood wasn't enough you then get the most wonderful, caring, thoughtful, kind, loving husband in the whole entire world," Hope got a dreamy, faraway look in her eyes as she spoke about Parker. "You have everything I ever wanted and you just threw it away as if it wasn't good enough for you. Well now you don't have to worry, with you out of the way I'm going to end up with your husband."

Wishing more than anything that she hadn't been stubborn and had just told Parker the truth about Isaac from the beginning, Tessa knew that regrets weren't going to help her now. "Parker doesn't love you, Hope, he just feels sorry for you," she said gently.

"No, it's you he feels sorry for," Hope contradicted. "You blink those big blue eyes and its like he's hypnotized. You've got all of them wrapped around your little finger, you say jump they all ask how high. Now with you out of the way Parker's going to realize what its like to be with a real woman, because you're nothing but a spoiled, selfish little girl."

"I read your diary," she informed Hope quietly.

"Well you had no right to read that," Hope roared but then smiled, "still I guess that means you also found my little collection."

Determined not to get sidetracked by the room full of coffins, of which she'd counted thirty-four. Thirty-four people that Hope had killed in her quest for happiness. "It's terrible what happened to you. Awful that any person could do that to another human being, especially a helpless child. But killing me to get my husband is not going to give you what you want and it's not going to replace what you lost."

"Getting Parker is going to make me happy," Hope protested adamantly. "All my life all I've dreamed of is a family of my own, and Parker is even better than all the white knights I ever imagined riding in to save me. He's my prince charming."

"No, Hope," she shook her head sadly, "you were abused, you suffered terribly, you missed out on being a part of a real family, on having a real life. Nothing is going to make up for that. Murdering me and trying to make Parker love you is never going to give you peace. Believe me, I know . . ."

"You know?" Hope screeched launching at her, fists spiraling madly, one connecting painfully with her cheekbone, the other almost knocking her shoulder out of it's socket. "You don't know anything. Your life was perfect, you don't know anything about suffering."

Attempting to fend Hope off, Tessa was too weak to accomplish much. It wasn't until Maisy stirred beside them that Hope finally went still.

"Tess?" Maisy struggled to open her eyes.

"Its okay, Mais," she soothed immediately, she needed her friend to remain calm.

"Oh my gosh, Hope?" Maisy caught sight of their captor. "You were the one who kidnapped us? Why?"

"She wants Parker," Tessa filled her in, "but in order to get him she had to get me out of the way. Unfortunately you were just collateral damage."

"You want Parker?" Maisy asked clearly confused. "But Parker is in love with Tessa."

"Not for long," Hope gloated, "not for long. Well ladies it's been fun but its time for me to go. Parker will be missing me if I'm not back soon, he does so worry about me when we're not together."

"Hope, wait," she called out. "It's me you're angry with, its me that you need to get rid of to get Parker, why don't you just let Maisy go, drop her off at a hospital. She has nothing to do with any of this, besides she's lost a lot of blood and her wound is infected. Just let her go, you don't need her you still have me. Don't let her unnecessary death weigh on your conscience."

"Your problem my dear little Tessa, is that I just don't care," Hope raised an indifferent shoulder. "I don't care if your friend has to die so long as I end up with what I want."

"At least give us some more water then," she pleaded. "It doesn't have to be a lot, just enough for me to bathe Maisy's wound and give her something to drink. Come on, Hope, please."

"Uh," Hope tapped her chin and pretended to think. "No, I don't think so," she turned and headed back up the stairs.

"Please, Hope," she tried one last time, refusing to believe that things had become hopeless. "You weren't always like this. You were once a sweet, loving, sensitive child, it's not too late to find that little girl, it's not too late to go back to who you used to be. Let me help you, if you let us go I'm sure the courts will understand. They'll get you the help that you need, I'm sure Elisabeth would be willing to help you. Your prince charming is out there somewhere, let yourself get better and then you can have all those things that you dreamed about."

For a second Hope wavered and Tessa allowed herself to believe that the woman was going to have a change of heart, but then she strode through the door, letting it fall shut with a terrifying air of finality.

* * * * *

2:47 P.M.

"You okay?" Wyatt asked plopping down beside Parker who was huddled on a bench at the park just down the street from the precinct.

It had started to snow again, the tiny flakes flittering on the breeze, before gently coming to rest indiscriminately on everything below. Wyatt remembered how beautiful the snow had been on the night Tessa and Parker had been married, just over a year ago, and how happy they had all been then. Tessa had recovered from the gunshot wound that had almost claimed her life, Winter and Daniel had just entered their lives, and the future had looked bright for all of them. It seemed almost impossible that in such a short space of time so much could have happened, that they all could have lost that joy and peace. He wondered whether it was too late to get it back or if it had escaped them forever.

"I still can't believe that Hope would fake amnesia, that she would set up all of this, killing those innocent women," Parker answered dazedly. "I can't believe that she would hurt Tessa."

"That photo that I found wasn't the only one, there had to have been over a hundred of them," he told Parker sorrowfully. As mad as he was at his best friend for his recent behavior and treatment of Tessa, he could see that the light had finally switched back on inside Parker's head and he was thinking clearly again. "It looked like she'd gone through your album and picked out any photo of you and Tessa together then cut out Tessa's face and replaced it with her own. She'd put together a new album and named it 'Treasured Memories'. It was really creepy, Parker."

"When did you find it?"

"Yesterday, after we watched the video of Hope at the club," he replied, it hadn't taken him long to find them. While Parker had been busy reviewing more footage he'd simply slipped quietly away, arrived at Parker's house to find it empty, let himself in with his key and headed straight for Hope's room. The photos hadn't been hidden very carefully; in fact he'd found them in the very first place he'd looked, just tucked away under the mattress. "But I'd had my suspicions from the beginning . . ."

"Because of Tessa," Parker surmised dismally.

"Yeah. Then I started thinking about what she'd told me about Rebecca . . ."

"Why did she tell you and not me?" Parker frowned in frustration.

"It's not like she willingly came to me and spilled her guts," Wyatt explained. "You know what happened that night, she was a mess, it all kind of just came tumbling out, she collapsed in my arms minutes later. I wanted her to tell you but she got it in her head that you wouldn't understand and that you wouldn't rest until you'd hunted Isaac down. I think she was ashamed that she loved him but . . ."

"But he was the one person who was there for her and he helped her and he let her escape even though he saw her kill Jake," Parker finished.

"I think part of her wanted desperately to tell you," he added, wanting to make Parker feel better but also sure that this was true. "She was just scared."

"I shouldn't have pushed her away," Parker moaned miserably. "I wanted to hurt her like she'd hurt me by not confiding in me and so I let Hope get too close. It was just nice that Hope needed me so much, that she trusted me so implicitly, that she wanted me to help her. It was alluring; it was so different from Tessa. You know this could all be a set up," Parker looked like he knew he was stretching but couldn't help himself.

"Who would set her up?" he queried, he was willing to keep an open mind but only so long as there was some credence to the theory.

"The only person who has something to gain, Pete Hastings."

Raising a doubtful eyebrow, "I don't know, Parker . . ."

"Come on," Parker's golden eyes began to shine with excitement as this theory wound him up. "What a perfect way for Pete, the real killer, to deflect attention from himself. It's brilliant, he blames Hope, who can't contradict him or defend herself because she has amnesia and doesn't remember any of it."

Not really buying this as overly likely, "don't forget that Pete Hastings said Hope wanted to be called wild girl . . ."

"So what?" Parker countered. "We still don't even know if wild girl was involved in any of this. On the tapes we didn't see any interactions between Hope and Henrietta Kendall or Millicent Waters . . ."

"Which in and of itself is a little suspicious," he put forward. "We know that wild girl was the instigator of this little gang of lonely housewives, from both the email the Kendall kids saw and the transcripts from Millicent's computer. Do you think that there were two wild girl's at The Leopard that night?"

"Maybe when Hope was talking to Pete she meant to call her wild, not wild girl," Parker was obviously bent on clutching at straws today.

"Well she certainly sounded wild from the way Pete described her," Wyatt agreed.

"Or maybe Hope really is wild girl but her whole club is completely innocent. We don't really have any evidence that it is anything but what it appears, a group of like-minded women complaining about how mundane their lives have become and wanting to spice things up a little. Maybe they did meet up at The Leopard, but that doesn't have to mean anything suspicious was going on. It could have been completely by chance that Pete Hastings stumbled upon them and tried to kill all of them," Parker garbled.

"Maybe," he conceded skeptically, he believed that Hope was Rebecca Worthington and that she had master-minded this whole thing in order to get her hands on Parker. However if this malarkey was what Parker needed to believe right now to make it through the day then fine, he'd let his partner have his delusions for the moment but he wasn't about to jump on board. "Or maybe it was Hope who was using Pete Hastings," he suggested.

"What do you mean?" Parker frowned.

"Well if she is the one behind all of this, it would certainly help her out if we ever tracked her to the club to be able to point the finger at Pete and imply that he was the killer."

"That's kind of risky."

"Maybe," he agreed, but sure it was true. "Plus it gave her someone to have sex with so that we would assume she was raped, that gains her a lot of extra sympathy."

"Wyatt, do you really think that Hope is capable of doing these things?" Parker asked, looking more vulnerable than he had since the first day Wyatt had met him.

"I think," he chose his words carefully, "that we don't really know anything about her."

"That's not really an answer," Parker gave him a half-smile.

"Okay," he smiled back and elaborated, "I think that if Hope really is Rebecca Worthington and she was ripped away from her happy home at the age of eight to be smuggled into another country. Kept who knows where and in what conditions, and then sold to a pedophile to live the next eight years as his sex slave only to then be discarded for a younger girl, then who knows what she's capable of."

Parker nodded solemnly, trying to process everything he'd learnt today. "It's just . . . it's so evil," he uttered helplessly. "Imagine the planning that would have had to have been put in to this to pull it off. Setting up the Internet club and getting people in, finding out enough about each person to choose which women were going to be gullible enough to do whatever she suggested. Convincing the women to lie to their husband's and family's. Luring them into a seemingly fun and innocent week away where they would all have the time of their lives. Somehow getting them all tied up and then leaving them there to die, with food and water just out of reach. Finding all those different remote locations where her victims would have enough time to die before their bodies were found."

"Rebecca never learnt to care about others, she never learnt how to form meaningful bonds, all she knows is how to survive. And that it's okay to hurt others to get something for yourself."

"But to hurt herself? I mean she tied herself up and stopped eating and drinking for five days. It's one thing to be able to leave these other women to starve to death but to be able to do it to herself. And then faking amnesia, pretending that she didn't even know her own name. And for what? Just to get me?"

"This woman has probably been watching you and Tessa for a long time," he murmured quietly.

"That's just creepy," Parker shivered at the thought.

"I know, it doesn't make any sense to us, how someone could do these sorts of thing to another person. But you have to remember that Rebecca's been traumatized, her brain just doesn't know how to love anyone but herself."

"I just can't comprehend it. I just can't comprehend that Hope could . . ."

"Hang on," Wyatt pulled out his trilling cell phone and answered. A smile grew on his lips as he listened to J.J. on the other end. "Well my friend," he hung up and faced Parker with a grin, "it seems you might be about to get some answers. Pete Hastings has spent the last couple of hours conferring with his lawyer and it seems he's decided that he's ready to cooperate."

* * * * *

4:02 P.M.

"Okay," Wyatt was asking calmly, "what did you want to talk to us about?"

Parker wasn't sure he wanted to hear another word out of Pete Hastings' mouth. What he really wanted to do was bury himself under a rock and pretend that the last couple of weeks had never happened. Scratch that, he thought to himself, what he really wanted was to jump back in time a couple of months to before he

220

and Tessa started having problems and then never let things get this far.

"I didn't kill anyone," Pete eyed them both defiantly, daring them to disagree.

"You told us that already," Wyatt moved to stand.

"Wait," Pete exclaimed, stretching across the table to try and clutch at Wyatt's arm, ignoring his lawyer's pleas to sit still. "I just want you to know that I didn't kill anyone, but I want to help you, so you can ask me anything you want and I'll do my best to answer it."

Exchanging a glance with Wyatt, "had you ever met Hope before that night at The Leopard?" he asked.

"No, never," Pete shook his head emphatically.

"So the first time you saw her was when you accidentally tripped and spilt your drink all over her?"

"I didn't accidentally trip," Pete looked baffled, then wary as though they might be trying to trick him.

"We saw you on the tape," he informed Pete. "We saw you trip and spill your drink all over Hope and then the two of you got talking."

Pete laughed, "that was no accident . . ."

"You did it on purpose then," Parker pounced on that happily. He wanted desperately to believe that Hope was nothing more than an innocent bystander in this whole mess. That she had absolutely nothing to do with Tessa's mysterious disappearance. "You deliberately spilt your drink on her so that you had an excuse so start chatting her up."

"No, no, no," Pete looked stricken. "You've got it all wrong. I wasn't the one who deliberately tripped over, that girl Hope was the one who deliberately tripped *me*," he exclaimed.

"Hope made you trip?" he asked doubtfully, determinedly hanging onto his skepticism.

"She stuck her foot out and deliberately made me fall," Pete clarified. "Then she immediately started hitting on me. I told you," he repeated as though they were idiots, "this woman had a plan and I was just a means to an end."

"What do you mean?" he demanded, if he was going to believe Wyatt's accusations then he needed to hear in detail what Hope had done.

"I already told you," Pete moaned, obviously frustrated that they weren't able to read his mind and obtain every detail of what happened during his night with Hope.

"Be specific," Wyatt smiled dryly.

"Fine," Pete sighed but obediently began to recount what had transpired that night. "Like I said already, she stuck out her foot on purpose so I'd trip and spill my drink all over her and then she'd have an excuse to hit on me. The first thing she said to me was 'oh silly me, did I make you fall?'. She wasn't even bothering to try and hide that she'd done it on purpose. I could tell from that second that she was wild, there was just a look in her eyes."

"You could have just walked away," Wyatt pointed out.

"Are you kidding?" Pete asked incredulously. "She was flirting with me and she was hot. I mean she was *really* hot, you saw what she was wearing right? That tiny little skirt with her long legs. That tight top with her breasts practically falling out. I mean come on, what's a guy to do? You know what I'm saying right?" Pete's focused on him.

"Continue," was all Parker could muster. He hated guys who treated women this way, as just an object to use then discard, and it was even worse when women allowed themselves to be treated in this way.

Shrugging as though they were both a lost cause, "I apologized, she asked me if the champagne made her top transparent. I laughed, she asked if I wanted to dance, I said yes, so we headed to the dance floor. While we were dancing she had her hands all over me, under my shirt, in my hair, and she had her body pressed seductively right up against me," Pete shivered at the memory, a dopey smile lighting his face. "Then she started asking me all these weird questions . . ."

"What kinds of questions?" he couldn't help interrupting, he didn't want to hear about Hope behaving this way, the Hope he knew was so sweet and innocent it was hard to picture her as wild and sexy.

With a withering frown Pete resumed, "all these questions about sex. How many women had I had sex with, where and how, what was my first time like, what was my wildest time like, had I done it in a public place, had I ever been in love, had I ever paid anyone for sex. Like I told you earlier by the end I was sure she was going to throw me down on the floor, rip my clothes off and do it right there and then with all those people watching."

"But she didn't," Wyatt pointed out.

"No, she didn't," Pete agreed with a smirk. "She was getting me really turned on with all this talk about sex, not to mention her busy hands, besides it had been a couple of days since I'd had any. So I asked her if she wanted to meet me outside, in my car, and she went absolutely bananas," he still looked puzzled about this.

"Maybe she didn't want to have sex in the back seat of a car," Wyatt suggested.

"No, it wasn't that," Pete disagreed. "She was the one who couldn't stop talking about sex. And it couldn't have been the location because she was the one who would have done it right there. I think she went crazy because she didn't want to be seen with me."

"Why do you think that?" Wyatt asked.

"Because she started hissing at me about how we couldn't leave together because someone might see us and it might ruin her reputation."

"Did she say why she didn't want anyone to see her with you?" he asked. A look at his partner confirmed that Wyatt had taken this as more proof that Hope was involved.

"No, I assumed it was because she had a boyfriend or husband or something and she didn't want to risk anyone she knew seeing her with another guy." Looking a little sheepish for the first time, "to be honest, I didn't really care. I was all turned on and all I was thinking about was how great it was going to be between us."

"You said she asked you all these questions about your sexual history, did she tell you about any of her past . . ." he could barely make himself say the words, "sexual encounters?" It still felt like they knew nothing more about Hope than they had before. Even if she was really Rebecca Worthington as Wyatt claimed, they still knew next to nothing about her life between the time she was sixteen and now.

"No, she never told me anything about herself at all," Pete replied.

"So what happened next?" Wyatt asked.

"She told me to leave and go and wait in my car, and that she would be out in about twenty minutes, so I did," Pete began to look troubled.

"What's wrong?" he had a feeling he was going to like what Pete said next even less than he liked what he'd already heard.

"Well Hope and I did it, and like I said she wanted it really rough. Then when we were done she . . ."

"She what?" Wyatt prodded.

"She brought in these other women. But I didn't know that she was going to kill them, I swear I didn't know anything," he'd gone from cool and collected to nervous and edgy in less than a second.

"These women?" Wyatt laid out the photos of Henrietta Kendall and Millicent Waters that Zak had taken in the morgue.

Pete slowly picked up the pictures as tentatively as if he were handling a poisonous snake. "Yeah, this is them, but there were three others."

"How did you not hear about this on the news?" he inquired incredulously. If Pete Hastings had come forward when Hope or Henrietta had been found then they might have been able to find Millicent in time to rescue her.

"I don't really listen to the news," Pete replied. "The alarm on my cell phone wakes me up, I like to sleep late since I'm usually out at night, I go straight to work, listen to my iPod not the radio in the car, then after work I usually grab dinner out before hitting a club. I don't have time for TV and I don't read the newspapers."

"Do you know the names of the other women?"

"No, wild girl, I mean Hope," he corrected himself, "never told me their names."

"What did she tell you to do with them?" Wyatt looked almost afraid to ask.

Casting an unsure glance his lawyer's way, the slightly pudgy middle-aged man nodded reassuringly. Pete sighed deeply but continued, "Hope told me to sleep with them."

"You had sex with them?" Wyatt's emerald green eyes were wide in horrified shock.

"Hope said that they were her friends," he explained defensively. "She said that they had all recently been divorced or widowed and were looking for someone to have meaningless sex with. I thought it was kind of creepy but she was so insistent, threw a fit when I said I wasn't sure I wanted to do it."

"What did the women say?" Parker was sure that Henrietta, Millicent and the other women would have been as far from willing to sleep with Pete Hastings as it was possible to be. He also wondered, if this was all true, how Hope had managed to force the women to go along with her plan. There were five of them and only one Hope, so how had she managed to get them all to sleep with Pete?

"Actually looking back they kinda looked scared but at the time I didn't really notice. I was sort of focused on Hope," Pete said sheepishly.

"You said there were three other women," Wyatt checked.

"Right," Pete nodded.

"But you don't know their name?"

"Right," Pete nodded again.

"But you do know what they look like?"

"Right," a little hesitantly this time.

"So I'm sure you'll be more than happy to work with one of our sketch artists and try to come up with images of them so we can hopefully identify them?"

It was a rhetorical question but Pete nodded vigorously, "of course, of course."

They weren't going to get anything more out of Pete Hastings so Parker stood and headed for the door, Wyatt at his heels. Before they could leave, Pete stopped them.

"Wild girl, or Hope, or whatever her real name is, she's crazy, completely and utterly crazy. I sincerely hope that she doesn't have any other victims in her hands because she is capable of anything. And I mean anything."

Thoughts immediately jumping to Tessa, Parker ran from the room, ignoring Wyatt's pleas for him to wait, and didn't stop until he was in his car. Revving the engine, he sped off into the afternoon heading directly for the one place he hoped might give him some insight into what had happened to his wife.

FEBRUARY 18ᵀᴴ

2:13 A.M.

"Do you think Hope's coming back?"

Hesitating, Tessa knew that Maisy didn't have long left, and while she was positive that Skylar would eventually figure out who Hope really was she was beginning to lose hope that he would find them in time.

Other than Charlie, Skylar was the only person who knew that she was on Paxil. For some reason she wasn't quite sure of, she trusted Skylar implicitly and told him everything. She hoped when he finally put the pieces together and came to rescue them he would bring her medication. She needed it badly. Tessa just prayed that Skylar figured it out soon. She and Maisy couldn't last much longer without help.

"Tess?" Maisy prodded.

Relenting, "no, I don't think she'll be back."

"Did she give us any more water?"

"No," despite her pleas Hope had refused to leave them any more water.

"And we don't have any left?" Maisy shifted uncomfortably, wincing at the effort.

"No. I'm sorry."

"It's not your fault," Maisy murmured.

"Yes it is," Tessa continued stubbornly, they were lying side by side so she turned her head to study her friend carefully. Maisy's skin was an awful grey color, her hazel eyes were sunken, her cheeks stained with red from the exertion of remaining alive. "It's all my fault. This whole entire mess. If it wasn't for me then Hope would never have concocted this plan."

"That's not true," Maisy took her hand and squeezed it. "Not every bad thing that happens in the world is your fault, Tess."

"Maybe," she chuckled half-heartedly, "but this one definitely is. Hope was probably watching us for months, planning all of this out, and I gave her the perfect opportunity to think that getting Parker was an option. I should have just been honest with Parker in the beginning and told him whatever he wanted to know about Isaac."

"Isaac is John Doe?" Maisy looked confused.

"I should have just told him about Rebecca," she continued, barely hearing Maisy. "Now I can't even remember why I didn't want to tell him. Parker would have understood, he would have understood why I couldn't turn Isaac in. After Isaac let me escape and he never told anyone what I did to Jake, he helped me with Dylan, I couldn't let the police throw him in jail. Skylar understood. At least I think he did. How could I have thought that my own husband wouldn't have understood? I pushed him away on purpose, and now it's too late, Hope is going to ruin his life," she knew she was rambling but she was too tired and thirsty and scared to care.

"What?" Maisy looked completely lost.

"I'm pregnant," she blurted out.

"What?" Maisy repeated.

"I'm pregnant," restlessly she sat up, wanting to pace but she didn't have enough energy left to do so.

"I thought I heard you wrong but I guess I didn't," Maisy was fighting to keep focused. "You're pregnant?"

"Yeah, at least I was," her hand pressed to her stomach, much longer without water and she knew her baby couldn't survive. Neither could she.

"I would say congratulations, but," Maisy's eyes roved the room, "considering where we are, I guess I'll just say I hope we get out of here before it's too late for any of us."

"I told you, Mais, Skylar will figure Hope out and find us," she was going to maintain this belief until it was literally too late.

Raising a doubtful eyebrow, "how far along are you?"

"Eight weeks," Tessa knew the exact day the baby had been conceived since she and Parker had only been together once since last fall. On Christmas Eve Parker had apologized to her for thinking that she lied to him and deliberately went off with Dino despite her assurances she would wait for him. His apology had been sweet and heartfelt and the two of them, caught up in the magic of Christmastime, had fallen into bed.

"Does Parker know?"

Shaking her head miserably, "no. I wanted to tell him. I was *planning* on telling him. When he came out to my place to see Winter, I knew he'd be back and I promised myself that I would just come right out and tell him. But then he got there and before I knew it, we were fighting again and I just couldn't make myself say the words. Then he left and Hope knocked me out, and now . . ." her emotions were beginning to tumble out despite her attempts to hold them firmly in place. She didn't want to lose Parker, she didn't want to lose another baby, she didn't want to die here in this hot little room while her husband thought that she hated him. "And now it's too late, now we're going to die here and I'm never going to get the chance to tell Parker that I'm sorry and that I love him." Then Tessa did something she practically never did, she burst into a fit of uncontrollable sobbing.

"Shh, it's okay, Tess, it's going to be okay," Maisy soothed. "Parker knows that you love him."

"How? How could he know that with the way I treated him lately?" she cried helplessly.

"He knows, honey," Maisy stroked her hair, "he knows how much you love him, I promise you he does. He knows that you've always loved him and he knows that you'll never stop loving him. He knows that you were just tired and scared and stubborn," Maisy joked.

As Maisy comfortingly rubbed her back, and her tears slowly

cleared, Tessa noticed the thin sheen of sweat on Maisy's face, and her common sense slowly returned. "I'm sorry, Maisy," she sniffed, brushing away the last of her tears, "you're hurt, you should be resting not trying to console me."

"Sometimes its okay to lean on other people, Tessa," Maisy said seriously. "You've helped me all you can, now let me help you. Come on lets try and get some rest. If the three of us," Maisy rested a trembling hand on her stomach, "are going to have any shot at getting out of here then we need to keep our strength up. Besides your head must be killing you, especially since you never drank any of that water."

Surprised, "you needed it more," she protested as she helped Maisy ease herself back down against the cold floor.

"Yeah well, if I'd known you were pregnant I never would have let you do it," Maisy's eyes were already drooping closed, her remaining strength sapped.

"We can all last a little longer," she reassured Maisy, but her friend had already drifted back into unconsciousness. Stretching out beside Maisy, Tessa said a little prayer that her words might be more than empty consolations and they all really could last a little longer.

Then her mind crashed and she joined Maisy in unconsciousness.

* * * * *

6:26 A.M.

"You didn't come home last night, is everything okay?"

Hope tried to keep the neediness out of her voice but it kept creeping back in. She hadn't spoken to Parker in over two days. Ever since he's asked her questions about that idiot Pete Hastings from the club. She had continued to feign innocence, claiming she still just couldn't remember a single little detail, and she thought she'd kept him convinced, but now she wasn't so sure. It had been a calculated risk to include Pete Hastings in her plan. A step she'd never taken before in any of her other failed endeavors to secure a husband, and she hoped it wasn't going to be her undoing.

"Oh, I've uh, been busy at work," came Parker's reply down the phone line.

The vagueness in his voice let her know immediately that he knew she was behind the whole thing. "You found that guy right?" It couldn't hurt to give it one more shot. Maybe she would get lucky and she'd already got him to fall out of love with Tessa and into love with her. "The one from the club you said I was at."

"Hope . . ." Parker sounded disappointed.

"Did he confess to killing those other women? Did he confess to tying me up and leaving me to die?"

"Hope . . ." Parker tried again.

Finally she relented, "you know, don't you?"

"Why?" Parker pleaded, sounding like the last little bit of hope he'd been clinging too had just been dashed.

"What did Pete Hastings tell you?" she didn't want to divulge anything that he didn't already know, she still desperately wanted to salvage her relationship with Parker.

"That you deliberately tripped him over at the club. That you were all over him. That you were obsessed with discussing sex. That you wanted him to call you wild girl. That you threw a fit when he wanted to leave with you. That you arranged to meet him. That you insisted on rough sex. And that you made him have sex with Henrietta Kendall and Millicent Waters," Parker fired at her.

"Darn," she muttered to herself, that stupid Pete had blabbed *everything*.

"I know what you did, Hope, I just don't know *why* you did it," Parker spoke softly.

"I did it for you," she pleaded. "I did it for you, so that we could be together." In all her life Hope had never met anyone like Parker Bell. When she had been a little girl, alone and scared and in pain, she would curl up in a tiny little ball and dream about the man who would one day save her and make her happier than she could ever imagine. From the second she had seen the newspaper article of Parker rescuing Hayley Geoffries, one of the Iceman's victims, she had known that he was the answer to her prayers. So for the next year she followed him around, diligently studying every aspect of his life, and becoming increasingly frustrated by the way he was treated by his so called wife, Tessa. She wanted to make him as happy as she knew he was going to make her, so she had set the wheels of her plan into motion.

"You did it for me?" he echoed.

"I love you," she blurted out.

"You love me?"

"I love you more than *she* does," she spat our vehemently.

Parker was silent for a moment. "You mean Tessa?" he asked at last.

"Yes," she affirmed. "You deserve so much better than her. She doesn't love you like she should, she takes advantage of you, she expects you to drop everything to go running to her rescue. She's no good for you."

"Hope, you know I love Tessa, but . . ." he trailed off, paused, and then ploughed on, "but she's dead right?"

"Right," she agreed, or at least she will be soon she added to herself.

"And you did that for me? You killed Tessa for me?"

"You would never be happy as long as she was around," she maintained adamantly. Forcing herself not to get over emotional, she needed to keep her cool so she could evaluate Parker's every word in case he was just playing her.

"You killed Maisy too?"

"She showed up at the wrong time," she explained, hoping that he wouldn't be mad that she had stabbed his friend. She didn't care that Maisy Wallace had ended up as collateral damage but she knew Parker's huge, warm heart would be saddened by her death. "I followed you that night to Tessa's house. I listened to her say those horrible things to you and I just lost it." She hadn't gone there planning to abduct Tessa, but she just couldn't stand to see her treat Parker that way for another second. "I was just so mad that I couldn't hold it in and I just smashed Tessa over the head," even speaking about it got her blood boiling again. "And I was just cleaning up when Maisy showed up. She found Tessa unconscious, I didn't have any choice, I had to take her too."

"Were they still alive when you took them?"

Growing tired of this line of conversation, "you love me too, I know you do. Otherwise you wouldn't have asked me to stay in your house with you, you wouldn't have been so nice to me, you wouldn't have let me kiss you. I'm right aren't I? You do love me, don't you?"

"I . . ." once again he lapsed into silence, "I do care about you Hope, but if you want anything to develop between us then I need to understand why you would do all of this. Why you would fake amnesia and your own abduction, and why you would kill those innocent women."

Honestly she didn't feel the least bit remorseful for killing those other women, they were simply a means to an end and nothing more. "I had to," she explained, "how else could I have got your attention?"

"You could have just come up and talked to me."

"That wouldn't have gotten you away from her," she protested immediately, she knew her only shot at Parker was to get Tessa out of the way first. That was why she had waited until a rift had formed in their relationship before she had set her plan into motion. And now that Tessa was taken care of there was no longer anything standing in the way of her getting Parker. "You and I are destined to be together," she gushed. "I knew it from the very first time I laid eyes on you. We're going to be so perfect together, we're both going to be so happy, our lives are going to be so wonderful."

"Pete Hastings also said that there were three other women there that night," Parker spoke up. "Are they still alive?"

"Who knows?" she managed to stop herself from adding 'and who cares' just in time.

"Can you tell me their names," he pressed.

"I can't remember," she replied sullenly, she didn't care about those women's names and never had.

"They might still be alive," he continued relentlessly. "If you could just tell me where you left them then we could maybe find them in time and . . ."

"And nothing," she raged, losing her temper. She wanted Parker thinking about her and her alone, not Tessa, not Pete Hastings, and not those stupid, gullible women. "I don't care about any of that, I don't care if they're alive or not. Why do you care about any of that? I only did it for you, everything I've done in the last eighteen months it was all for you, for the life we can build together, but we can't do that if you keep holding on to things that aren't important."

"Hope, I don't want to make you mad but I know there's a good person inside of you no matter what you've done," he spoke with genuine gentleness. "I know a little about your childhood. I know how rough things were for you back then."

She didn't want to think about that now. She wanted to be happy, and when she thought about her childhood it made her anything but happy, and when she wasn't happy she did crazy things. If she could have just one wish it would be to change her whole life story, to take away all the hurt and pain she'd suffered at the hands of that horrible, horrible man.

"It must have so awful for you," Parker was saying, "so young and vulnerable, unable to protect yourself. You were just an innocent little girl then but you're not anymore. Now you're an adult. You have to take responsibility for your actions. If you do the wrong thing you have to own up to it and do whatever it takes to make it better. You have a chance to do that. It might be too late for Henrietta Kendall and Millicent Waters, and Tessa and Maisy, but there's still a chance for those other women. You can do the right thing Hope. We can do it together, we can make things right together. I want to help you, you had a terrible childhood and I want to try to make it up to you."

"You really want to help me?" she asked in a small voice, she couldn't remember a time when anyone had wanted to help her. "You really want to make things up to me?"

"I really do," Parker repeated.

Beginning to get the uneasy feeling that Parker was holding his breath, and that their conversation was being eavesdropped upon.

"Just tell me who those other women are and where they you left them," he prodded.

"Where are you?" she asked her temper beginning to flare dangerously.

"What?"

"I said, where are you?"

"I'm . . . I'm . . ."

"You're at her house aren't you? I love you and you can't even let go of her even though she's dead."

Ignoring Parker's pleas she slammed the phone down, then threw herself down upon her bed, determined that she wasn't going to let all of her hard work be for nothing. Formulating a new plan. One that was sure to ensure that she and Parker would be together forever. Chuckling a wicked sort of chuckle, she stood, dressed, and marched out the front door, ready to face her destiny.

* * * * *

7:15 A.M.

It felt odd to be in this room. In the whole time he and Tessa had lived here, he had never been inside this room. Tessa's childhood bedroom had a creepy sort of feel. Like a lingering presence of pain, loneliness, sadness, remained even though the room had laid empty for close to ten years.

Parker surmised that when he had stopped sleeping here Tessa had moved back into her old room as a way to torment herself. After two and a half years he thought he had a fair idea of the way Tessa's mind worked. And the way it liked to work when she was stressed was to punish itself because that was the only way she knew how to deal with trouble.

Wandering over to the bed, where the sweet scent of Tessa's perfume and shampoo still lingered, across the pillow rested a few strands of her white blonde hair. He felt so close to Tessa here. He could almost feel her arms slipping around his waist, her head resting against his chest, her hair tickling his nose, the whoosh of her breath against his neck.

Sitting propped up against the pillow was the teddy bear he had given Tessa for the first birthday they had celebrated together. He'd chosen the bear because it's warm caramel fur was the same color as his eyes, and the turquoise ribbon around its neck was the same color as Tessa's eyes. Parker knew that Tessa had dreamed of giving this bear to their firstborn child, and for a while after their miscarriage had been unable to even look upon it, now he despaired that their dreams would ever become a reality.

"I made a huge mistake, Wyatt," Parker said when he became aware of a presence behind him. "I made a huge mistake in trusting Hope."

"It's not too late to fix things with Tessa," Wyatt consoled.

Clinging tightly to the teddy bear, as though that might somehow connect him to his wife, "we don't know if Hope has killed her already." From the way Hope had described it he wasn't even sure Tessa had still been alive when Hope removed her from the house. Thinking back to their conversation yesterday about why Tessa hadn't told him about Isaac and Rebecca. While everything Wyatt had told him sounded reasonable as to why she hadn't told him the feeling still remained that there was more to the story. "Is there another reason that Tessa didn't want to tell me about Isaac and Rebecca?" he asked, finally turning around to face Wyatt.

"Tessa got it into her head that she didn't want to pressure you."

"Didn't want to pressure me?" he repeated, confused.

"She thought if she told you the truth about Isaac then that would be pressuring you to be with her. I don't know," Wyatt shook his head, "you know what she's like when she gets an idea in her head, that wife of yours is beyond stubborn."

"Yeah, she really is," he smiled fondly, recalling the many times he'd been frustrated beyond words by his wife's amazing obstinate streak.

"I tried to convince her to tell you but changing Tessa's mind once she's already made it up is like changing the sunrise from east to west."

"And now its too late," Parker clutched the teddy bear a little tighter, remembering Marty's warning that if he didn't step up and make the first move then he would live to regret it. At the time he hadn't taken the words seriously, he'd just been annoyed that once again he was being made out to be the bad guy while Tessa was the perpetual damsel in distress. But now he may really have to live out the consequences of that decision. "Tessa is already dead."

"We don't know that," Wyatt countered.

"Hope said she was dead," he reminded his partner.

"But Hope can't kill face to face, so she probably locked Tessa and Maisy away someplace and left them to die of dehydration. She's only had them for a little over three days, there's still hope that they're alive," Wyatt pointed out.

Parker hadn't thought of that, he'd been too focused on

Hope's words that Tessa was dead.

"And," Wyatt added, "you played along with Hope on the phone so she had no reason to run off and do anything drastic."

Playing along with Hope on the phone had been the hardest thing he'd ever had to do. Pretending that he didn't care that Tessa was dead, and that he did have genuine feelings for Hope, had taken every ounce of strength he possessed. What he'd wanted to do when Hope had called was to scream at her to give him his wife back. But he knew that doing that would be signing not only Tessa and Maisy's death warrants but also those of the other three unknown victims.

"Even if she is still alive," he uttered miserably, "she's locked away, dying slowly, and thinking that I hate her."

Shaking his head adamantly, "Tessa knows you love her, Parker."

"No. She doesn't. She thinks I abandoned her, she thinks I chose a murderer over her, she thinks that once again she's all alone in the world. She's scared and injured and fighting for her life, and she's doing it thinking that I don't love her anymore." His heart physically hurt with the thought that his precious wife, who he would give his own life for in a second, might die while believing that he no longer loved her. "You know she's been seeing Charlie Abbott for months."

"Yes. You should be really proud of her, Parker, she's doing great, and she's trying so hard."

"Charlie said that too." Wishing he hadn't walked away from Tessa, that he'd been there to support her and comfort her, as she worked towards overcoming her demons.

"You talked to Charlie?" Wyatt looked surprised. "When?"

"Tessa told me she'd been seeing him before Hope abducted her. I guess given her history it was so hard for me to believe that I needed to hear it from Charlie. He said that I pulled away from Tessa because I felt guilty that I couldn't fix things for her. I think he was right. He also said Tessa's on Paxil, and that we should make sure we have some on us when we find her because the withdrawal symptoms can be bad. I looked it up, Wyatt," his scared eyes found his partner's and saw that Wyatt already knew that Tessa was on medication and what she would be going through having been abruptly taken off it. "She already has a head injury, and Hope's probably left her without food and water, with the withdrawal symptoms on top of that, I'm not sure she can survive too long."

"Right now we just need to believe that she and Maisy are still alive."

"Why does Tessa talk to you, Wyatt? How do you always know what to say to her? Why does she trust you so implicitly?" Parker wanted to know how Wyatt managed to get through to Tessa so he could do it too.

"She talks to me because it's easier for her than talking to you. Because she loves you so much she's scared of saying or doing the wrong thing and pushing you away."

"I want her to be able to talk to me, about anything. I don't want her to be scared that I'll leave her. I want her to trust me like she trusts you. She said she didn't talk to me about her abduction because of me. Because I wouldn't let her." Casting a cautious glance at Wyatt, "she wanted to talk to me about it didn't she?"

Pained, "I'm sorry, Parker."

"This is all my fault," he groaned.

"No," Wyatt said adamantly, "it was *both* of your fault. Tessa could have told you what she needed."

"But things wouldn't have gotten so bad between us if I'd been there to just listen to her," Parker almost couldn't breathe as he realized just how much Tessa had needed him.

"Tessa knew you couldn't deal with what Jake did to her. She didn't want to make you have to go through it with her."

Hating himself, "after every despicable thing that man did to her, Tessa shouldn't have had to worry about me. The night Hope kidnapped her, she told me she was seeing Charlie, she was giving me an opening, an opportunity to make things right, to talk to her about everything."

"Most likely," Wyatt reluctantly agreed.

Heart thundering so hard he wouldn't have been surprised if it beat itself straight out of his chest, "after five months of me pushing her away she was still willing to offer me a chance to be there for her. And I walked out. If I'd stayed, if I hadn't been such a coward and just stayed and let her talk, then she'd be here, safe and sound, right this second. I told her I could handle it. I told her whatever had happened to her and Eleanor I could handle it and I'd be there to help her deal with it. When we met I told her that I'd never leave her, that she could trust me, but I walked away when things got tough." A thought occurring to him, "would she have told me about Isaac?"

"I don't know."

He'd known Wyatt most of his life and caught something in his voice, "Wyatt? Come on, you know everything that's going on with her. She told you everything. Would she have told me about Isaac?"

Hesitating, "if she thought you'd understand, if she thought you wouldn't hate her for not turning him in, then yes, she probably would have told you. Look, Parker, having someone to talk to, someone who'd listen to her, wasn't something she was used to. When you pulled away from her, she backed down, she wasn't confident enough to go to you and tell you what she needed."

"So she went to you instead," this time Parker said it without a hint of jealousy, he'd pushed Tessa away, he hadn't deserved her confidence.

"Maybe I only made things worse," Wyatt looked troubled. "I was the easy answer. Having me there meant she didn't have to attempt to talk to you. Maybe I should of backed off, insisted that she go to you."

"No," Parker shook his head adamantly. "Tessa deserved

someone who was unconditionally there for her. I'm glad you were, Wyatt. She would have fallen apart without you. You gave her everything she needed, everything I didn't. I'll never forgive myself for hurting her. How am I going to live with myself if she dies?"

"Tessa and Maisy are still alive," Wyatt countered a little desperately.

"We need to face facts, they may both be dead already, or they may be by the time we find them. We can't live in denial."

"Yes we can," Wyatt said firmly, "we have to, *I* have to."

Going to the closet, he opened the door and reached up to the highest shelf, sliding his hand along until he found what he was looking for. Pulling down a large bag, he carried it with him back to the bed. His fingers shaking so badly it took him several attempts to undo the knot. When at last the bag slid open, Parker reached a hand inside to feel the contents, then tipped it upside down, emptying everything out onto the bed.

"What's all that?" Wyatt asked.

"These," he began to arrange them so all the pieces fitted together, "used to be Tessa's teddy bears when she was a little girl. The night that she buried Eleanor, I guess the night she also met Isaac, she came back here, got a pair of scissors and cut them all to pieces. But she couldn't bring herself to throw them away so she put them in a bag and buried them away in her closet."

"She told you that?"

"Yeah, Christmas Eve." The only night that they had spent together in months. After finding out that Tessa hadn't willingly gone with Dino Rollino, he had gone straight to her house, apologized profusely then the two of them had made love. Then they had gone out into the snowy night and while gazing up at the millions of twinkling stars, Tessa had shared a little about that night when she had felt so alone and scared that the only way she had been able cope with her feelings had been to destroy all her teddy bears. Unfortunately after she had shared that, he had been stupid enough to ask her once again to tell him John Doe's true identity so that they could put an end to this once and for all. Tessa had gone ballistic at him and stomped off and from there things had quickly continued their downhill slide. "I never seem to get it right," he returned the teddy bear arms and legs and bodies and heads to their bag.

"Get what right?" Wyatt queried.

"Who to trust and when," Parker replied. "I trusted Hope, big mistake. I didn't trust Tessa, big mistake. And I trusted Gina O'Hara, another big mistake."

"Parker, Gina was . . ."

"Gina was a psychopath," he finished honestly. "And I truly believed that she was just a good kid who had been through a horrible ordeal and needed someone to be there for her," it was hard to admit how gullible he had been regarding the murderous teenager. "I really wanted to be that person for her. That person to believed in her, who supported her, who gave her the courage to be whatever she wanted to be. I wanted to do for her what my parents did for me. They were always there for me, they just simply believed in me and loved me, and that was enough to help me let go of everything that I'd been through before I met them. I really wanted to do that for someone else."

"Parker, your dad had just died," Wyatt reminded him, "of course you wanted to carry on his legacy, you just picked the wrong person."

"I tried to do it for Tessa too," he continued. "I thought if I just loved her then it would undo everything that Patrick and Emilie, and John Doe and Dylan Riley had done to her. Only I thought it didn't work, but I was wrong," cradling the broken teddies, "it *was* enough for her, it really did break through all her barriers. I just pray it's not too late to find her alive."

* * * * *

10:38 A.M.

Pete Hastings really wanted to help. Well he *really* wanted to get out of here but he did want to help too. He just wasn't sure what he could offer to get the cops off his back. He really hadn't had any idea that this Hope was really a murderous psychopath so he didn't know what he could tell the police that would help them.

Pacing nervously around his condo, he hadn't gotten home until an hour or so ago. He'd been at the police precinct all night trying to recall exactly what the women Hope had brought with her had looked like. He'd done his best to remember their faces, but that night he hadn't really been paying attention to them. All he'd been focused on was Hope, how beautiful and enigmatic she had been, not to mention the awesome sex.

His doorbell chimed, for a moment Pete debated opening the door in his current disheveled condition but then he decided he was too tired to care and threw it open. "Not you again," he groaned when he saw who was on the other side.

"May we come in?" Detective Wyatt asked with a cheery grin.

"Whatever," he disappeared back into the kitchen and poured himself a large glass of milk, as a child he loved to drink an icy cold glass of milk no matter what the weather. Returning to the living room he found the two detectives lounging on his sofa. "What do you want? Haven't you tortured me enough already."

"Yeah, I'm sorry that the death of two women and the lives of five other women who are hanging in the balance are such an inconvenience," Detective Wyatt rolled his eyes.

Exhaling slowly, feeling only slightly repentant for his self-indulgence, "fine. What do you want?"

"We just have a couple more questions," Detective Wyatt set out the three pictures he'd spent the night with the sketch artist compiling.

"I already told you I don't know who they are," Pete insisted.

He was exhausted, he hadn't slept or showered in over twenty-four hours, and he just wanted to stand under the hot spray of the shower then fall into bed.

"I know, but we thought maybe if you took another look at them and we told you the computer names they were using it might spark your memory and give us something, however small, to go on," Detective Wyatt explained.

"Fine," he relented, "shoot."

"From the transcripts of the chat rooms we got three names, 'passionatelady', 'young&bold' and 'DOOL1965' . . ."

"Days of our Lives," he put in immediately.

"You remember something?" Detective Wyatt's green eyes lit up.

"No, but DOOL is a nickname for the soap opera Days of our Lives, plus the show started in 1965, so one of your women is definitely a soap fan."

"You watch soap operas?" Detective Wyatt couldn't quite hide a snicker.

"No, at least not any more. I used to watch with my Nan." Time spent with his Nan watching soaps were some of his all time favorite memories from his childhood. Following his Pa's death his Nan had come to live with him, his parents, and his brother and sister. Aged eight at the time, with both his mom and dad working, he had enjoyed having someone at home to give him a glass of milk and a plate of cookies when he got back from school. On every holiday or whenever he was home sick from school, he would curl up with his Nan on the sofa in their den and watch soap operas with her.

"Do you know which of the women might have used that name?" Detective Wyatt pressed on relentlessly.

Chewing on his lip as he scrutinized each picture, his gaze lingering on one drawing in particular. The woman was pretty, in a plain sort of way, with soft brown eyes and shoulder length chestnut hair, a defined chin and high cheekbones. Pete thought he remembered her as being even quieter than the others, he also thought he remembered her crying quietly as he'd had sex with her.

"This one I think," he jabbed angrily at it, wishing that he could get his hands on Hope or whoever she really was, and wring her neck for what she'd made him do. "But I don't really know. I'm not even sure that she told me their names, even fake names, or anything about them."

"Okay," Detective Wyatt collected up the pictures, "well it was worth another try."

"What are you going to do with the pictures?" he asked curiously.

"Put them on the news," Detective Wyatt replied. "Hopefully someone who knows them will come forward and at least we'll know who they are even if we don't know where they are."

"But if that Hope doesn't tell you where they are then you might never find them, right?"

"Right," Detective Wyatt agreed sadly.

"So I was the last person, other than their killer, to see them alive," Pete couldn't stop a shiver from coursing through him. "That's kind of creepy. I'm sorry I can't be more helpful. I just wish that I hadn't been so obsessed with sex."

"That's why she chose you," Detective Wyatt consoled. "Because she knew that in the event we ever connected you to this and tracked you down you wouldn't be able to give us anything."

"Thanks," he nodded appreciatively, feeling a little better about being so useless.

"What if we bring one of our CSU techs over here to see whether we can find anything helpful?" Detective Bell piped up for the first time.

"Why would you do that?" he asked puzzled.

"What do you mean?" Detective Bell looked equally as puzzled.

"I never brought Hope and her friends back here," he explained.

"You never what?" Detective Bell bellowed.

Noticing for the first time the poorly concealed panicked glint in Detective Bell's eyes, wondering what that was about. "We didn't come back here. Hope wanted to meet at some house in the middle of nowhere."

"Where?" Detective Bell practically jumped out of his chair, probably would have if his partner hadn't placed a calming hand on his shoulder.

"I don't know. It was some sort of farm, I saw some cows and sheep, and a few horses." The only reason he'd even noticed it was a farm was because it reminded him of the one his Nan and Pa used to live on before his Pa's death.

"Well you must know how you got there," Detective Bell looked wild, bordering on manic.

Detective Wyatt's words finally dawning on him, "wait a minute, you said that the lives of five women were hanging in the balance." Pete looked at the folder containing the pictures of the women he'd slept with. "There were only three other women that Hope brought for me to have sex with, so who are the other two women you're talking about? Did she get her hands on more victims?"

"She kidnapped my wife," Detective Bell answered tightly. "And one of our good friends who ended up in the wrong place at the wrong time."

"Kidnapped her? What does she want like a ransom or something?"

"She wants me," Detective Bell replied flatly. "She thinks she's in love with me so she wanted to get Tessa out of the way."

"Is that why she did all of this?" he was flabbergasted at the length this insane lady had gone to just to snag a man. "She set me up, she faked amnesia, she killed two women, she kidnapped your wife, and she did it all just to make you fall in love with her?

I told you she was a crazy person."

"Yeah, she is a crazy person," Detective Bell agreed. "But right now I don't care about Hope all I care about is finding my wife before it's too late. You said she told you to meet her at a farm, that could be where she's holding Tessa right now, I need to know where that was."

"I'm sorry," he threw up his hands in helpless frustration. "I told you I don't know. I just followed the directions she gave me." Catching the two Detective's hopeful glances. "She texted me, but I already deleted the message. I guess you could take my phone and maybe do something to it to retrieve the message," he pulled his cell phone from his pocket. "Or maybe the GPS in my car recorded where I went, you could take that too if it'll help," he volunteered.

"We'll do that," Detective Wyatt smiled gratefully. "We'll see ourselves out. You should grab a shower and some rest."

"You might not care about Hope right now," he spoke with a surprising cool calm that seemed to wash over him, "but I hope you find her. I hope you find your wife and your friend and those other women, and then I hope you find Hope before I do. Because if I find her first I'm going to smash her pretty little head in for turning me into a rapist."

* * * * *

1:57 P.M.

"Come on, Maisy," Tessa pleaded with her.

Roused from her comfortable sleepy haze by her friend's panicked voice. She was so tired but for Tessa's sake, she forced open heavy eyes.

"Thank goodness," Tessa gushed. "Come on, Maisy, you have to hang on just a little longer."

"I can't," she breathed heavily.

"Yes, you can," Tessa insisted. "You can't give up on me, Maisy."

"Tess, you have to face it, I'm going to die here," she said as gently as she could. Maisy could feel what was happening to her body. The wound in her stomach was infected, an infection that had now spread into her blood. Her body continued to valiantly fight the infection that was killing it, causing a raging fever, and while at first it had given her relief from the hot room by making her cold, now it was only adding to her discomfort in this horribly stuffy place.

Pressing her hands over her ears, "I don't want to hear talk like that, Maisy," Tessa admonished. "You're going to be fine."

"No, I'm not," gazing up at her friend, who didn't look like she was doing very well either. "I'm sorry, Tess."

"Don't do this to me, Maisy," Tessa implored. "Don't give up on me."

"Hope's not coming back," she was struggling to keep her mind on track. "Wyatt, Parker, J.J., Marty, they don't know where we are. They might not even have figured out that Hope's behind this."

"But they might have," Tessa persisted, grabbing her hand and squeezing it tightly. "I told Skylar from the beginning that I was suspicious of Hope. He knows I'm usually right about stuff like that, he'll figure it out."

"Maybe," she agreed, "but it doesn't matter anyway. Even if they know Hope is the killer they'll never find us in time. There's no hope for me. I can feel what's happening to my body, I'm dying."

"I don't want to hear that," Tessa begged.

"I know you don't," she mustered a smile for Tessa who appeared to be teetering on the edge of hysteria. "I know you want to believe that you can fix everything, but you can't, Tess, and you don't have to try. You're not responsible for the whole world."

"I don't think that," Tessa huffed.

"Yeah, you do," Maisy smiled fondly, she was so lucky to have been able to have such a loyal, caring friend like Tessa, who would do everything in her power to help someone in need. "I'm so glad that I got the chance to be your friend. The time we spent together was so wonderful. You've taught me so much about being strong and dealing with adversary. I'm really grateful. I just wanted you to know that."

"Don't talk like that," Tessa snapped. "You can do it, Maisy. You can hang on until Skylar gets here."

"Can you do something for me?"

"What?" Tessa asked sullenly.

"Can you tell Luke that I love him?"

"Tell him yourself," Tessa all but screeched. "When you see him next you can tell him that you love him yourself."

"It's kind of funny," she hardly heard Tessa's words.

"What is?"

"I went to your house to get an answer and now I have it."

"What?"

"I was going to your house to talk to you about Luke," she explained. "You're so smart, and I don't mean just because you have an IQ of 178, but you're so good at reading people. I wanted to ask you if you thought Luke was ready to commit to me. I wanted to see if you thought I should persist with him or give it up and look for someone else. But now I know that I love Luke and I would wait forever."

"Luke loves you, Maisy," Tessa seemed to re-gather her cool.

"Really?" she already believed this but hearing it from Tessa made her feel even more convinced.

"Really," Tessa nodded firmly. "The two of you will be really happy together."

Watching as Tessa pressed an uncertain hand to her stomach. Maisy knew how much her friend had suffered when she'd miscarried her first baby. She also knew how insecure Tessa was regarding her abilities to raise a child. "You and Parker are going to be really happy too," she placed her hand over Tessa's. "All three of you. You're going to be a great mom, Tess."

Tessa shook her head doubtfully, "I don't know how to be a mother. Emilie really wasn't the ideal role model and neither was my grandmother."

"It doesn't matter, you already have all the qualities you need to be the best mom," she reassured her friend. "You're patient, and caring and no one could love a baby more than you. I just wish that I was going to get a chance to be a mom too."

"I thought we'd finished with talk like that," Tessa reprimanded.

"I never realized how much I wanted to get married and have kids until it seemed like I never would. Now as I look death in the face it's my biggest regret," she spoke dreamily now, half lost in the haze that would soon consume her. Maisy wasn't in any more pain as she had been earlier. Now she felt peaceful, resigned to what was going to happen. Now she mostly just felt sad at all she would never have the opportunity to experience. "It must be so amazing the first time you hold your baby in your arms. Looking down at it and knowing that it's yours. Feeling those tiny fingers clasp your own. I don't think anything on earth could compare to that feeling of knowing that you are responsible for such a perfect little creature."

"You can still have that, Maisy," Tessa murmured softly.

Her foggy mind lurching from one idea to another, "I can't believe it was Hope who did this to us," she marveled.

"I know."

"You were right about her all along."

"Being paranoid has its benefits," Tessa smiled wanly.

"I just can't understand why she would kill those women, and fake amnesia, and lock us up here."

"Hope's childhood was pretty rough . . ."

"So was yours," she inserted. "And you didn't turn into a serial killer."

"Different people react in different ways I guess."

"But to take another human being's life and to not even feel remorse," Maisy just couldn't comprehend that and she didn't think it was just because her brain seemed to be quickly turning to goo.

"Hope's past taught her how not to get weighted down by emotions."

"Tess?"

"Yeah, Maisy?" Tessa pulled her into her arms, tears glistening in her greeny-blue eyes

"Can you tell Luke that I love him?" Maisy knew she was fading fast and she wanted Luke to know that he was the love of her life, and that her final thoughts had been about him.

"I'll tell him," Tessa assured her, tears spilling from her eyes and rolling down her cheeks, splashing down onto Maisy. "Don't worry about it, Mais, I'll make sure he knows how much you love him."

Contented Maisy nodded and then let go and slipped quietly away.

* * * * *

4:43 P.M.

"We need to talk," Parker announced uncomfortably, he hadn't just let Tessa down by his stubborn refusal to listen to their warnings about Hope, but every single person in this room.

"What's wrong?" Daniel asked suspiciously, not even bothering to hide his loathing.

Parker couldn't blame Daniel for hating him; the guy was just being protective of his baby sister. Not to mention the fact that everything his brother-in-law had accused him of doing he *had* done. He had pushed Tessa into confronting her past with Isaac and Jake when she clearly wasn't emotionally ready to deal with the fallout. After learning every horrid detail of the suffering she had endured at the hands of Jake he had abandoned her to deal with it on her own. And as if all of that wasn't bad enough he had chosen to support Hope, a women he didn't even know and whom he had clearly misread, over supporting his own wife. Now they might all have to live with the consequences of his actions, and he just prayed that the price of learning his lesson was not going to be Tessa's life.

"Parker," Matilda's voice snapped him back into the moment, "you're scaring us. What's going on?"

"Let's sit," he suggested, wanting to delay telling Matilda, Daniel and Winter about Tessa for as long as possible.

"Let's not," Daniel growled. "What do you need to tell us?"

While Daniel was clearly still clinging to the anger route to deal with Tessa's disappearance, Winter however no longer looked mad, now she just looked plain terrified. "Please, let's sit." To get things started he took a seat in one of the armchairs. Reluctantly the others joined him, first Matilda, then Winter, and finally, with an exasperated sigh, Daniel.

"Okay, we're sitting," Daniel snapped immediately, but Parker could tell he was scared because he slipped his hand into Matilda's. "Now tell us what you know about my sister."

Trying hard not to get worked up about his own sister's engagement, just because he and Tessa had made a mess of things didn't mean that Daniel and Matilda were going to. And he *did* know how happy Daniel made his sister . . .

"Parker," Matilda prompted, "did you find out something about Tessa?"

Knowing he couldn't delay forever he clenched his hands together and reluctantly began, "Tess was attacked . . ."

"I told you," Daniel sprung to his feet. "I told you that Tessa wouldn't just walk off. We all told you," he waved his hand to include Matilda and Winter.

"Daniel," Matilda soothed, gently tugging on his arm to get him to return to his seat. "Parker, do you know who took Tessa?"

"It was Hope," he let the words tumble out before he could back out.

"That freak who you moved into your house?" Daniel shouted. "The one that Tessie was suspicious of?"

"Wyatt thinks that Hope is really Isaac Worthington's daughter Rebecca," he explained.

"Who's Isaac?" Winter asked.

"Isaac was John Doe," he informed them.

"The man who ran the child trafficking ring that abducted Tess and Eleanor," Daniel frowned. "She finally told you about him?"

"No, she told Wyatt," Parker tried really hard not to let that hurt him. "Who told the rest of us when it looked like Isaac's daughter was masquerading as Hope."

"I don't understand," Matilda looked baffled. "Why would the daughter of the man who ran the child trafficking ring who abducted Tessa when she was a child attack Tessa now?"

Deciding he might as well tell them everything, "when Tessa killed Jake to escape someone saw her, Isaac Worthington. When she went back to bury Eleanor's body Isaac was there. He told her about his daughter, Rebecca, who had been abducted by child traffickers when she was a child, which was the reason why he had given himself over to a life of crime. Tessa felt sorry for him, and also grateful that he let her escape, so she never turned him in. In fact she went to him for help several times over the years. The two of them formed some sort of precarious bond and Wyatt thinks that Rebecca has come back to get revenge on Tessa for stealing her father's affections."

"That is insane," Winter murmured.

"Yeah, it is," he agreed.

"So this Rebecca came back jealous that Tessa had a father/daughter relationship with her dad?" Daniel still looked puzzled.

"That's Wyatt's theory," he replied.

"So why did she fake amnesia?" Matilda asked.

"It was all part of her plan," he explained.

"Her plan to get revenge on Tessa?"

"Not just to get revenge on Tessa because of her relationship with Isaac, she also wants me," Parker added.

"She wants you?" Daniel looked as if the idea was about as far-fetched as if he'd just suggested Hope was really a polar bear in disguise.

"She thinks that she's in love with me, but in order to have me she has to get Tessa out of the way first."

"And you actually know this for sure?" Winter clarified.

Nodding, "I spoke to Hope on the phone, she told me that she has Tessa," he confirmed.

Completely losing his cool, "so all this time that you were maintaining that Tessa simply decided to take a vacation because she was upset over you, this lunatic was actually holding my sister prisoner?" Daniel roared. "Look how much time we've wasted because you wouldn't believe in your own wife. That delay could cost Tessa her life. Do you get that? If you had of just believed in her like she did for you then she could be home here safe and sound this second. Do you know how lucky you were that Tessa never doubted you, even though you gave her every reason to, when Lachlan kidnapped you? It didn't matter how many times we begged her to look at things logically and accept that you had walked out on her, she never gave up on you."

"I do know how lucky I was that Tessa never gave up on me," Parker agreed softly, contemplating just what would have happened if Tessa thought he had simply left like the rest of his family and friends had. If Tessa had of given up on him then he would surely not be alive this second. Tessa's fate would have depended on whether she could convince Lachlan Mountain that she was in love with him. Even if the maniac hadn't killed her he would have spirited her away and kept her secluded from the rest of the world. The one positive would have been that their baby would probably have survived, but it too would have been doomed to a life of imprisonment.

"You know how lucky you are to have Tessa do you?" Daniel continued his rant. "Then why wouldn't you make sure she knows that she's the most important person in your life? If she dies," his voice breaking, "if my sister dies, it's on your head."

With that Daniel stormed from the room, Matilda hot on his heels, calling a quick apology over her shoulder. Deeply hurt by Daniel's words, but unable to find fault with them. If Tessa died it would be no one else's fault but his own.

"It's not true," Winter spoke up, her blacks eyes shining with unshed tears. "If Tessa dies it's not your fault."

"I should have believed in her. I should never have left her alone here in the first place," he protested.

"Maybe," Winter agreed, "but the only person to blame if Tessa dies is that Hope woman."

Softening he crossed and sat beside his niece, placing a tentative hand on her shoulder, "I'm really sorry I wasn't there for you, Winter."

Shrugging his hand off, "I don't care about that now," the teenager's tears began to flow. "I don't care that Jake is my father. I just want my aunt back so I can tell her that she's the closest thing I've ever had to a mother and that I love her."

Pulling the crying girl into his arms, she resisted at first but then relented and fell into his embrace, clinging to him tightly as she cried. As her tears soaked through his shirt, Parker stroked her hair, and murmured reassuringly in her ear. Reassurances he knew she didn't believe and that he didn't either.

At last she pulled back, still sniffling, "Tessa told me not to tell you but I think you have a right to know."

"Know what?" he asked, more fear stabbing his heart.

"Tessa is pregnant."

The world began to spin dizzyingly, the walls swirling around him, the chair beneath him seemed to rock from side to side.

"Parker?"

Winter's worried face came back into view as the world began to return to normal.

"Parker, are you okay?"

"Why didn't she tell me?" he asked shakily, if he had known about the baby he wouldn't have let Tessa out of his sight, much less have moved out of their home.

"Tessa thought the baby would make you feel pressured to be with her, and she didn't want that. The only reason she wanted you to be with her was because you wanted to not because you felt obligated," Winter explained. "I'm sorry, Parker, I told her she should tell you but you know how she is once she gets an idea in her head."

As his brain slowly climbed out of its pit of shock, Parker realized that the baby didn't really change anything. He still loved Tessa, baby or no, and he still wanted to fix things with her, baby or no. The only thing the baby added to the situation was another reason to hate himself if he was too late to find Tessa alive.

FEBRUARY 19TH

3:45 A.M.

"Why don't I see any driveway?" Parker felt like he had ants in his pants, he just couldn't keep still. They were so close to Tessa yet still so far away, he wasn't going to rest until he was cradling her safely in his arms. He was, however, trying to prepare himself. More than likely Tessa wasn't going to be in good shape when they found her, he needed to be ready for that.

"It has to be here somewhere," Wyatt reminded him patiently.

"I'm with Parker," Daniel jumped in. "We followed the directions to the letter, we should be there by now."

"Exactly," Wyatt continued in the frustratingly calm voice Parker had heard his use a hundred times when refereeing his kid's arguments. "We did follow the directions to the letter, therefore the farm has to be here somewhere."

"Well I don't see anything," he couldn't help pouting. The second they'd received the directions pulled off Pete Hastings' GPS unit, they had jumped in the car and sped up here. Only now that they were here there didn't appear to be any farm. "I'm calling Pete." Yanking out his cell he dialed the number, waiting impatiently for the phone to be answered. "There's nothing here," he spoke the second Pete picked up.

"What do you mean?" came the reply.

"I mean we followed the directions only there isn't a farm house within sight," he returned. "We've driven up and down but there is no driveway here."

"No, there's no driveway," Pete told him. "See the line of big elm trees?"

Staring out the front window he could just make out a line of trees in the thin light of the headlights. "Yeah."

"Between the two big ones in the middle, there's a little track, it leads straight up to the house," Pete described.

"Thanks," he garbled before hanging up. "Between the two big trees there should be a track," he told Wyatt, who immediately aimed the car in that direction.

Within a minute they had located the track and were crawling along it cautiously. Partly because of the dark and partly because they didn't know what was awaiting them at the end. After another couple of minutes they reached the house. A small but tidy weatherboard cottage, with a neat and well-trimmed garden, sparkling clean windows, and a bright red front door. No light spilled out of any of the windows, no car sat in the open garage, and no signs of life emerged from the still property, yet they needed to remain cautious.

"You wait in the car," Parker told Daniel sternly.

"Yeah right," Daniel sneered, then before they could stop him he jumped out of the car and ran to the house.

Muttering a curse under his breath, Wyatt climbed quickly out, "I told you we should have left him at home. He's not a cop, he has no idea what he's doing, he's pumped high on emotion, he's going to get himself, or Tessa and Maisy, or all of us killed."

"He's Tessa's brother," he countered as they reached the front door.

"And you feel guilty," Wyatt shot him a disapproving frown as they followed Daniel inside.

"He would only have followed us here anyway," Parker shot back. "At least this way we can keep an eye on him."

"Yeah, we can keep an eye on him while he gets us all killed," Wyatt muttered.

"Wyatt, Parker, you got to see this," Daniel's horrified voice yelled from somewhere within the dark house.

Diligently scanning every corner of the house as they made their way towards where Daniel's voice was coming from.

Eventually finding him standing in the middle of a large room, the walls of which were covered, floor to ceiling, in photographs.

"Oh my . . ." Wyatt's eyes grew wide.

Parker was sure his own eyes must have grown just as wide, as his heart skipped a beat, and the hand holding his gun dropped uselessly to his side. Adorning the walls were thousands of photos of himself. Photos dating back eighteen months when he and Wyatt had been working the Iceman case. Photos of him and Tessa. Photos of him and Wyatt. Photos of him and Matilda. Photos of him in his car, at the mall, at church, jogging in the park, at the gym, at the movies, out to dinner. Even creepier were the ones of him taken inside his own home. There were ones of him cooking, eating dinner, watching TV, in the shower, and even asleep in bed.

"This is too weird," he mumbled, walking around the room, he came to a stop in front of the far wall. Covering this space were pictures of Tessa. Newspaper clippings dating back to when Tessa had been kidnapped by Jake at the age of eleven, and chronicling every ordeal she'd been through right up to nearly being drowned by Dino Rollino five months ago. More disturbing than that were the drawings. While technically proficient they depicted Tessa in hundreds of different torturous predicaments. There was one of her being burned alive, another being stretched on the old-fashioned torture device the rack, there was one of her being strangled, another of her having her fingernails pulled out, one of her being buried alive, one of her having scolding water poured over her, and another of her being raped by the devil.

"I didn't realize how much she hated Tessa," Parker uttered weakly, even more afraid now over the fate of his wife and unborn child.

"Don't lose it just yet," Wyatt placed a comforting hand on his shoulder.

"I'll check the rest of the house," he hurried from the room, unable to spend another second in there where so much hate for

Tessa was so blatantly and unashamedly obvious.

Since they had already cleared the downstairs, he headed up to the small attic, thinking that it would be a perfect place to stash a prisoner.

"Tessa?" he called as he rested his hand on the doorknob and turned. "Tess? Maisy?"

No answer greeted him as he pushed the door open. Expecting to find a dingy, dusty storage room but was met instead by a bright, airy bedroom. Floral drapes adorned the windows, thick pale pink carpet covered the floor, a bookcase stuffed full of romantic novels sat in a corner, beside it a tall lamp and an old rocking chair. Artwork adorned the walls, in the same style as the hideous drawings of Tessa downstairs so clearly drawn by the same artist. Only these pictures were full of princesses and knights on white horses, of couples on the beach and walking in the moonlight. These were obviously Hope's dreams for her future.

An enormous sleigh bed filled the middle of the room, the covers still mussed, and as he took another step into the room, closer to the bed, the unmistakable scent of sex drifted off the covers.

Without a doubt this was the room where Hope had brought her five victims, and lured Pete Hastings with the promise of wild sex. Determined not to think about that until he knew that Tessa was safe, he quickly checked under the bed, and in the closet, which was full of nothing but expensive clothes and shoes. Disappointed, Parker headed back downstairs and was met by Daniel and Wyatt.

"Did you find anything up there?" Wyatt asked.

"No," he joined them in the hallway, "but that was the room where Pete Hastings slept with Hope's victims. Did you guys find anything?"

"The kitchen's full of food," Daniel volunteered, "fresh food."

"Hope was definitely living here before she cooked up her little scheme," Wyatt observed. "And she's been here recently."

"The upstairs closet is full of clothes," he told them, then groaned in frustration, "but none of this helps us find Tessa. I was so sure she would be here."

"She still could be," Wyatt consoled automatically.

"We've checked the house from top to bottom . . ."

"Outhouses," Daniel interrupted, his eyes, identical to his sister's, sparkling with excitement. "This is a farm. There has to be at least a couple of barns, stables, work sheds, whatever. Tessa and Maisy are probably in one of those."

* * * * *

4:31 A.M.

Tessa was so tired.

Too tired.

The kind of tired that took hold of every single part of your body and refused to let it go.

The kind of tired that had her drifting in and out of consciousness.

The kind of tired that made even breathing seem like running a marathon.

The kind of tired that told her she didn't have long left to live.

It had been moving Maisy's body that had wiped her out. Sapped the last of her strength and left her empty.

She hadn't wanted to move Maisy's body. It had made her feel like she was betraying her friend. But neither could she sit for another second and stare at Maisy's cloudy eyes.

When Maisy's body had finally succumb to infection and she'd fallen from this life into whatever stood beyond, Tessa had sobbed hysterically for what felt like hours. She had done everything within her power to save her friend and yet it had been useless.

She had been useless.

And even as the cold waves of death splashed at her toes, Maisy had tried to encourage and reassure her that her qualms about becoming a mother were unjustified.

Tessa didn't quite believe Maisy words that she would be a good mother. Her own mother had been a drug and alcohol addict who spent most of her time locked away in her room, in a world of her own, painting. Emilie had not even noticed when she'd been kidnapped. And that maternal failing had hurt her more than any other neglectful thing her mother had ever done.

The only other maternal figure in her life had been her grandmother. While not a cruel lady, her grandmother had been cold and distant, not interested in raising her grandchildren and not happy with the burden of them coming to live with her.

Aside from all of that, her previous encounter with motherhood, however brief, had not had a happy ending.

Almost a year later Tessa still thought of her lost baby every morning when she arose and every evening before she fell asleep.

She thought of all that she would never get to do with her child. She never got to give it a name, in fact she didn't even know if it was a boy or a girl, although Parker had always insisted that it was a girl. She hadn't got to hold it, or see it smile, or hear it's contented little gurgle. She hadn't gotten to touch its soft silky hair, or tickle its pudgy little tummy.

It was her fault that she had miscarried that child.

She knew that.

She hadn't told Parker about that baby because she had been scared that he would confirm her fears that she would be a terrible mother. She had put herself, and her own selfish needs and desires, above her child's and her baby had paid with its life.

She had deliberately placed herself and her unborn baby in harm's way because she had been positive that it was the only way she could find and save Parker.

And now she was doing it all over again.

Her first baby's death had apparently taught her nothing.

She hadn't learnt her lesson at all.

Tessa hadn't told Parker about this baby either. Deluding herself into believing that it was because she didn't want to pressure him to come back to her, but that was a lie and she knew it. The reason she hadn't told Parker about their child was because she wanted to punish him. She wanted to punish him for walking out on her, for not fighting for their relationship, for giving up on her when she needed him the most.

Now she and her baby were going to die and Parker would never even know that she had been pregnant. She'd been so busy being childish that she'd lost sight of what was really important.

She was an idiot.

When she had dragged Maisy's body to the room with the coffins, she had found something most disturbing. She had found a coffin that Hope had prepared in advance. A coffin that had been prepared just for her. On one of the coffins down the end of the room near the desk Hope had stuck a photo of her. Not just a photo of her, but one with a baby drawn crudely in her arms. Somehow Hope knew that she was pregnant and even that wasn't enough to change her evil machinations. Even the life of an innocent baby wasn't enough to break her cold, hardened heart.

Sinking to the floor, Tessa wanted to cry for her baby's lost life, she wanted to sob wildly for her own lost dreams, but she was unable to shed even a single tear. Dehydration had robbed her of even that small comfort.

Now that Maisy was gone, she didn't bother trying to bottle away her pain. It was severe. Coursing up and down her body relentlessly. As if the pain wasn't enough, she was swinging from chills to hot flashes courtesy of her body protesting the sudden stop of her medication.

Death was all she could think about.

Suicide lingering in her mind. Whether because of the hopelessness of her situation, dehydration induced delirium, or Paxil withdrawals, she wasn't quite sure. It didn't really matter anyway. She didn't have any strength left to take her own life. All she could do was lie here and wait for death to find her. It shouldn't be long. Already unconsciousness was hovering over her.

"I'm sorry, sweetheart," she cradled her stomach.

Somewhere above her something clunked.

"I'm sorry I wasn't stronger for you."

Another clunk.

"I'm sorry I couldn't fight harder for you." Tessa let her eyes fall closed, and allowed herself to be washed towards the inky black ocean that would bring her and her child eternal peace. "I really do love you, you have to believe that. I love you more than I ever thought I could love someone."

Another clunk, louder this time, at last prompted her to peel open her eyes one last time.

"Tessa?" a voice yelled.

It was Parker's voice. But he couldn't be here. Could he?

"Tessa? Can you hear me? Maisy?" Skylar's and Daniel's voices melded with her husband's.

She must be hallucinating again.

She let her eyes fall closed.

"Tessa?"

The door at the top of the stairs jiggled.

Was it possible that she wasn't hallucinating? That somehow Parker had managed to find her? With strength she hadn't known she had, Tessa managed to drag herself to her feet.

"It's locked," Parker's muffled voice spoke.

"Well break it down," Daniel's equally muffled voice replied.

A second later a loud crash sent the door shattering into a hundred splintered pieces and light filled the dim room.

Squinting, she looked up but all she could see was a shadow.

"Tessa."

The shadow took a step down the stairs and the features slowly became visible.

It was Parker.

He was here.

He had found her.

But it was too late.

She had fought for as long as she could, but exhaustion had overwhelmed her and she couldn't muster another ounce of strength to keep herself going.

With a smile at Parker, Tessa collapsed.

* * * * *

5:09 A.M.

"Tessa!" Parker screeched as he launched himself at his wife who had just dropped to the concrete floor with a terrifying thud. Flinging himself down on the ground beside her. "Tessa? Honey? Come on baby, can you hear me?" His trembling fingers tried to steady themselves enough to search her neck for a pulse, almost fainting with relief when he found one. "Sweetheart? Come on, Tessa. Don't give up on me. Not now, honey, not when I just got you back."

Miraculously Tessa's eyelids began to flutter and then before he knew it he was gazing down into her sunken eyes. "Parker?"

Her voice was faint and raspy but it was still the most beautiful sound he had ever heard. "I'm here, Tess," his thumb gently stroked around the ugly red lump on her temple. "I'm right here, I got you, you're safe now. Everything's going to be okay. I love you. I love you so much."

"Are you real or am I hallucinating?" her bottom lip trembled.

"Baby, I'm real," he assured her, easing a hand gently beneath her head, bringing his mouth down to her face, kissing it all over, her eyelids, her cheeks, the tip of her nose, her chin, eventually finding her lips and pressing against them softly. "You're going to be fine. I'm going to take care of everything. It's going to be okay.

You just have to hang in there a little while longer. Paramedics are on the way. We're going to get you to the hospital and fix you up. And then we're going to go home." He cast a glance at Wyatt for confirmation that an ambulance *was* on the way.

"Medevac," Wyatt confirmed.

Even better, Parker thought. It would take them at least an hour and a half to get Tessa to the hospital by road, but with the chopper she would be there in minutes. "See, everything's going to be fine."

"She's dehydrated, I'm going to go get some water," Daniel pressed a kiss to his sister's forehead and then disappeared up the stairs.

"Water . . . not enough . . . asked Hope . . . her wound . . . gave it to her . . . she needed it more . . . Hope wouldn't bring more . . . I tried . . ." Tessa began to babble incoherently.

"Shh, it's alright," Parker pulled Tessa into his lap, cradling her against his chest. Holding her in his arms felt every bit as good as he'd been imagining.

Grimacing, Tessa groaned, squeezing her eyes shut, her breath coming in gasps.

"What is it, honey?"

"Pain," she whimpered. "Cramps and it feels like . . . like electrical currents . . . up and down my body. I hurt so badly," she moaned pitifully.

Feeling unbelievably helpless, "dehydration and withdrawals. Just hold on, baby."

"I'm not doing so good, Parker," she murmured. "I'm so tired."

Desperation strangling him, he wanted to help Tessa but he didn't know what to do for her. "I know, honey, I know, just hang in there," he pleaded.

Eyes focusing she looked up at him, "I'm so sorry, Parker," she was crying but too dehydrated to produce any tears. "I'm so sorry. I was just being stubborn by not telling you about Isaac. I was testing you. I wanted you to prove that nothing would make you leave me."

"And I failed," he said dismally, hating himself for letting her down.

A smile lit her cracked lips, "no, you didn't, because you're right here by my side." Her face clouded over once more, "I'm so sorry, Parker," she whispered again. "I don't hate you. I love you more . . ." she hiccupped, "I love you more than I can say."

"I never thought you hated me, honey," he stroked her tangled hair soothingly. "And I'm the one who should be apologizing to you. I'm the one who walked out on you, on us. I'm so sorry I wasn't there for you when you needed me to be. I was afraid. Afraid that you'd think I was useless because I couldn't fix everything for you. I'm the one who was stupid, an idiot, a fool, a moron, a jerk, a dope . . ."

The string of synonyms elicited a small chuckle before her face grew serious again, "Parker, I'm pregnant."

"I know, sweetheart, Winter told me," he placed his hand on Tessa's stomach.

"You're not mad?" Tessa's dusty, tear stained, blood streaked face remained creased with concern.

"I'm not mad," he assured her. "I'm happier than I ever thought I'd be. You, me and the baby, we're a family, Tessa, and we are going to be so happy together."

"A real family," Tessa's eyes began to get a faraway gleam. "We're going to be together forever."

"Forever," he echoed, "I am never going to leave your side again."

She gave him a weak smile.

"I mean it," Parker squeezed her tightly, he didn't ever want to let her go again. "I am never ever letting you out of my sight again, not for a second. You, me and our baby are going to be glued together. I talked to Charlie, he wouldn't tell me what you talked about but he said that you're doing great, that I should be proud of you. I am proud of you, Tessa. So, so proud of you. I'm going to start seeing someone too. Not Charlie because he doesn't want to jeopardize your trust in him, and not Beth because we're too good a friends now for her to be objective. But Charlie said he'd recommend someone. We're going to fix this mess we created and we're not ever going to let things get like that again."

"That's good, Parker," her voice had gone even fainter, and her head drooped against his shoulder, eyes falling closed, she was shaking uncontrollably.

"Come on, Tessa," brushing his lips against hers to rouse her. "Don't give up on me, stay with me just a little while longer. I know you're tired and in pain, but the paramedics will be here soon. I have your medication with me, as soon as Daniel gets some water you can take it. You just need to hold on. Please, Tessa," he begged.

"Parker, about Isaac . . ." she began

"It's okay, Tess," he assured her. "Wyatt explained everything, I understand."

Relief washed over her face, and with it a sort of peace. Like she had needed to hear that he understood why she hadn't been able to turn Isaac in to the police. Like she had needed to hear it so she could let go. Let death wash her away.

"Keep fighting, Tessa," he said sharply. "Don't you dare give up on me. You stay with me, okay?"

"Don't leave me," she whispered.

Clinging to her tightly, "I won't leave you."

"Tessa?"

Parker jumped at the sound of Wyatt's voice, he'd forgotten that anyone else was in the room.

Lifting her head wearily and prying open her eyes. "Skylar," Tessa smiled.

Cupping her face in his hand, Wyatt gently stroked her cheekbone where a purple bruise was slowly taking shape. "Honey, where's Maisy?"

Tessa's face immediately clouded over, and Parker realized guiltily that he had been too focused on Tessa to even notice that Maisy wasn't in the room.

"I tried," Tessa's dry cry returned. "I did everything I could. I used all the water we had to clean her wounds, and I gave her the rest to her to drink. I really did try," Tessa's eyes stared up at him imploringly, "I did everything I could."

"Shh, I'm sure you did. It's alright . . ."

"No, it's not," Tessa interrupted. "Maisy died. Her wound got infected. I tried to keep it clean, but there wasn't enough for me to work with. I begged her to hold on. I begged her not to give up, but she died. She died in my arms," Tessa broke off into hysterical sobs that wracked through her already weakened body.

Clutching her close, "shh," he murmured against her hair and prayed the paramedics weren't much further away. He couldn't lose Tessa now. Not when he had just got her back. But she was in bad shape. She was dangerously dehydrated, she was breathing too quickly, her heart beating too fast, still shaking, hovering on the edge of unconsciousness. She was hanging on by a mere thread.

"Here, give her this," Daniel reappeared beside him, glass of water in hand.

Holding her with one hand, with his other, Parker pulled the bottle of Paxil from his pocket, retrieving a pill he popped it into her mouth then took the glass from Daniel's outstretched hand, and held the straw to Tessa's lips. "Drink, honey," he urged her. She took a shaky sip, swallowed the pill, but then pushed the glass away.

"Sweetheart, where's Maisy's body?" Wyatt asked.

Having regained some composure, Tessa raised a weak hand to point towards a small opening in the adjacent wall. "She has a room filled with bodies . . ."

"With bodies?" Parker repeated.

"All in coffins, about thirty of them." Her scared eyes found his, "she had one for me, Parker. For me and the baby," she shivered violently.

Taking the blanket Daniel had brought with him, he wrapped it around her. "And you put Maisy in there?"

"I couldn't look at her anymore. I felt too guilty." Tessa's eyes closed with exhaustion but she continued to speak, "she's done this before. Killed people to try to get a man." Forcing her eyes open to look at Wyatt, "I knew you'd figure it out. I begged Maisy to hang on because I knew you'd figure out who Hope really was."

"Who would have thought that Rebecca Worthington . . ."

"Rebecca?" Tessa looked puzzled.

"Hope is Rebecca Worthington. Isaac's daughter."

"No, she's not," Tessa shook her head then winced at the movement. "I found Rebecca again, just before Christmas. I called Isaac and told him, I had to make it up to him for lying. Rebecca and Isaac were reunited and they disappeared together. I don't even know where they are. Hope isn't Rebecca, I found her diary, her real name is Charlotte Lainie. Rebecca would never do anything like this. She was a good person, before I found her she was even working on getting her life together. She'd stopped taking drugs, she had a job, things were looking up for her."

"So we were wrong all along?" Wyatt looked dumbstruck. "Well if Hope isn't Rebecca Worthington and she didn't have this horrible, traumatic childhood, then why did she do all of this?"

"It's all in her diary," Tessa mumbled, snuggling against him and starting to look very sleepy.

"Where's the diary?" Parker asked. Since they still had no idea where Hope was, the diary might be the only proof they had against her, and the only key to tracking her down.

"In a desk, in the room with the bodies," Tessa replied in a flat voice he didn't like one little bit. She lay limply in his arms. She was fading fast. "My head hurts," she whimpered quietly.

"I know it does, baby, just hold on a little while longer.

Paramedics will be here soon, they'll give you oxygen and painkillers and fluids, and fix you all up. Stay with her," he instructed Daniel, gently maneuvering Tessa into her brother's arms. "I'll be right back, okay? I love you," he gave her one last kiss before following Wyatt into the dark passageway.

Even though Tessa had prepared them for the room, actually seeing it still took his breath away. Floor to ceiling, the coffins were packed in like sardines. All neatly labeled with a photo, presumably so Hope, or Charlotte Lainie, could keep track of which of her victims was where.

Studying each photo as he made his way down towards the desk at the far end of the room. Parker felt his anger growing stronger for this evil woman who had tricked him and nearly cost him everything he held dear.

Remembering Pete Hastings last words as they left his condo. He had said he hoped that they found Hope first because if he found her he was going to smash her pretty little head in for turning him into a rapist. Well the way he was feeling right now, Pete would have to step in line, because when he found Hope he was going to do a lot worse to her than just smash her pretty little head in.

Reaching the end, tacked to the last coffin in the row was a photo of Tessa on which Hope had drawn a baby. If it wasn't for Wyatt's relentless refusal to believe that Hope wasn't as innocent as she was making herself out to be then this would have been Tessa and their baby's final resting place.

Dragging his eyes away from the picture, they rested on an equally grim site. Maisy's body lay on the floor about a foot away. If he hadn't known better he would have thought that she was merely sleeping. Tessa had closed her eyes, and in this half-light her skin lost the awful pallid color of death. If it wasn't for the blood soaked clothing he would never have thought she was dead.

"Guys, hurry up," Daniel's voice called through to them. "Tessa's unconscious, I can't wake her up."

"Lets find the diary," Wyatt rose from where he'd been hunched beside Maisy's body and resolutely faced the desk, grabbing at the first drawer his hand reached.

As the drawer slid open they both heard the ominous click.

"Was that what I think it was?" he asked.

Peering over and lifting up a thick notebook with a puppy on the cover, "yes. Run."

Not needing any more prompting, Parker turned and ran, screaming as he went, "Daniel, grab Tess and run."

"What?" came Daniel's confused response.

"There's a bomb, grab Tessa and run," he yelled again.

By the time he and Wyatt reached the main room Daniel was scooping an unresponsive Tessa into his arms. Together the three of them clattered up the stairs, out of the barn, not stopping when they burst out into the cool pre-dawn. Continuing across the freshly cut lawn they had made it a couple of hundreds yards when the barn exploded with a deafening crash. Throwing themselves onto the ground as burning debris was flung through the air, coming to rest all around them. Parker's only concern was for Tessa and he flung his body protectively over hers.

When things seemed to settle, he, Wyatt and Daniel raised their heads, taking in the flames that leapt and curled, lighting the sky and quickly consuming what was left of the barn. They were lucky to escape the burning inferno with their lives. When he'd first met Tessa her life had been in jeopardy and she'd nearly been burned alive in her own home.

Parker vowed that his would be the last time anything or anyone would try to harm her. He would do whatever it took to keep her safe. He would quit his job, he would move back to her mansion, he would move to the ends of the earth, whatever it took to keep Tessa and the baby from harm he would gladly do.

Right now only one person stood between his family and peace and he wanted to make sure that person was no longer a threat. "Did you get the diary?" he asked Wyatt.

"Oh yeah," his partner held up the notebook, a huge, goofy grin covering his dirt streaked face.

"She's not breathing," Daniel's panicked voice spoke behind them.

"What?" Turning around, Parker saw Daniel hunched over Tessa, his hands pumping her chest, his mouth forcing air into her lungs.

* * * * *

6:51 A.M.

The sun was beginning to rise like a giant golden paintball, splattering fingers of red and pink and yellow into the pale sky. It was an almost unspeakably gorgeous morning and Charlotte Lainie felt privileged to be a part of it.

It was beautiful up here, the place she had always escaped to when she was a child, to drink in enough nature to keep her going until the next time she had opportunity to sneak away. Charlotte loved painting the spectacular scenery up here. From the time she could remember she would find any scrap of paper she could and any pen or pencil lying around then climb up the hill right to the top. To this spot here where the ground just disappeared in front of you into the sharp cliff face, then perch herself right at the edge and just draw.

This had been her favorite place growing up, and long after she reached adulthood, and she could think of no better place to end it all.

For this was the only way she could think of to ensure that she and Parker would be an entity for eternity.

The icy wind rustled her thin white dress. A dress she had been saving for her wedding day, but could think of no better use for it than to be worn when she tossed herself and Parker off the cliff.

A part of her brain told her that she should be cold. That the snow covered hills and the freezing wind should leave her shivering violently. But Charlotte felt none of that. A bonus from years of training herself not to feel pain and humiliation, had soon led to her teaching herself not to feel anything at all. Then there had been the tuition from her father, who when he wasn't beating the pulp out of her or raping her until she bled, had loved to tell her about the benefits of throwing away your conscience.

At night when he returned from work and eaten the dinner she had prepared, he would rip off her clothes, pull her onto his lap, and while he played with her he would say; if I just evolved from a monkey Charlotte then I can do as I like just as a monkey does.

Over the years Charlotte had bit by bit come to understand that this theory made sense. And eventually she had adopted her father's theory as her own. If, as so many people believed, that the universe simply created itself, and that each animal evolved from another, and that anything that wasn't fit to survive simply became extinct, then she saw no reason why she shouldn't cut down anything and anyone that stood in the way of her happiness.

And so her quest for happiness had begun.

Her first venture had been an unmitigated disaster. Deciding since she had grown up poor that money might make the difference, she had secured a job at an up-market gentleman's club, zeroed in on the oldest, richest man there, and within a fortnight had ended up in his bed. With years of practice under her belt, she had given him the best sex of his life, and was rewarded with a marriage proposal.

Of course his three grown children had gone berserk. Accusing her of being a gold-digger. Which was completely untrue. She wanted someone to love her not to buy her things, she just thought it would be super if she could have both.

Her elderly lover had been attentive, had even agreed to give her a child, and she had thought that she had finally found happiness. But then she had overheard him telling his snooty daughters that he had merely married her to impress his friends and that she was nothing more than a trophy wife.

Furious, she had completely lost her temper, as she was frequently prone to do, and threatened to blow his little grandchildren's heads off if he didn't write a suicide letter and let her overdose him with his heart medication. Unfortunately along the way she had been forced to kill one of the daughters and a small grandson, a chauffer, one of the maids and one of her husband's closest friends. Charlotte had tried to be creative with the deaths, and never ever left a body behind, but even so suspicions eventually fell on her and so she had disappeared and moved on to another part of the country.

Her second venture to obtain happiness had only fared slightly better. Determining this time not to go for old and rich, she had set her sights on a sweet neighbor, close in age to herself and who clearly had a crush on her. Sure that this time she was on the right track, she had thrown herself headlong into the relationship, focusing all her time and attention on Adam.

This however proved to be her downfall. Adam was freaked out by her constant phone calls and visits, her obsessive need to know where he was every second of the day, and her constant pleas to consummate their relationship. In the end, driven to despair, Adam had ended things with her, with a stern warning that if she didn't leave him alone he would take out a restraining order. Driven into a frenzy she had broken into his house that night and shot him in the knee while he slept, then tied him up and a night of one sided passion ensued, as morning neared she had dragged him to the bathtub and electrocuted him.

By her third venture, and now nearing her late twenties, she decided to try a toy boy and hand picked one of her art students from the community college where she worked. Charlotte had been undeterred by the fact that her young suitor was already involved in a committed relationship, with a pretty young thing named Annie. She had gone about setting up the young woman with another young man from her class who she knew was hopelessly in love with Annie.

Young Chet had been devastated when he saw what he thought was his girlfriend having sex with someone else, and Charlotte had swooped in to console him. Chet was completely uneducated in the world of sex, a virgin who had taken a pledge to remain so until marriage, but a bottle of champagne, some candles and romantic music helped and she had had her way with him the first night.

After the joining of their bodies Charlotte had expected Chet to fall head over heels in love with her but the young man had continued to pine away for Annie, so she had been forced to rid Annie from the equation permanently. A midnight visit to Annie's home with some rope and a bottle of superglue had led to a very interesting evening. Tying up the girl, then supergluing her lips together, Charlotte had put a peg over her nose and then watched in fascination as Annie slowly asphyxiated. Forging a letter saying Annie was ashamed and had left town for good finally convinced Chet to believe that he and Annie were over. While he did date her for a while, his heart was never in it and she was forced to kill him too, his body placed beside his true love's in her underground cavern.

The forth venture had by far seemed to be the one that was finally going to give her what she dreamed about. She began an affair with a middle-aged talent agent. Thornston was unhappily married with two teenage children. He had showered her with genuine love and affection, and bit-by-bit she had managed to separate him from his family. Everything had been going swimmingly, Thornston even proposing marriage, until his seventeen-year-old son was diagnosed with bone cancer in his leg. Thornston became convinced that his son's ailment was his punishment for abandoning his family to be with her, and so he broke off all contact. Thrown into another of her rages she had cut the brakes on Thornston's brand new Porsche and watched with glee as the car ploughed into a tree killing her lover, his wife and their sixteen-year-old daughter. Once again the three bodies were added to her collection.

And that had brought her to Detective Parker Bell and her biggest scheme by far.

By time number five she had finally learnt that sex was not the answer to winning a man's heart, so she had devised a completely different tactic. What seemed to attract a man was that his woman was vulnerable, fragile, and in desperate need of a big strong man to swoop in and make everything better. So she had made herself as vulnerable and fragile as it was possible to be, a victim of violent crime who had lost her memory, and it had worked like a charm. At least it would have if that horrible Tessa hadn't been around.

A sly smirk lighting her lips, Tessa Bell would no longer be a problem. By now she should be blown into a million pieces by the bomb Charlotte had set late last night. When she had been there earlier Tessa had still been alive, although slumped in unconsciousness, but Maisy Wallace had already passed away. Charlotte had resisted the urge to slice and slice and slice at Tessa until all her anger had dissipated, but time wouldn't permit that so she had settled for setting her bomb and coming up here to await Parker's arrival.

Tingling with anticipation and the thrill that was to come, she reveled in the successfulness of her plan so far. Tessa was dead, Parker would be hers and she was finally going . . .

"Hello, Charlotte."

* * * * *

7:46 A.M.

"Hello, Detective Bell."

Charlotte Lainie turned to face him, her blonde hair whipped around her pale face, her dark blue eyes filled with a near insane glint, her white dress fluttered in the wind, she looked like an evil goddess.

"Are you now unattached?" Charlotte asked.

Knowing that seizing Hope, Charlotte he reminded himself, depended entirely on him, and that if he distracted himself with worry about Tessa this would all likely end in disaster. The Medevac chopper had arrived mere seconds after Tessa stopped breathing. The paramedics had shocked her heart into restarting and put a tube down her throat to breathe for her, her condition remained precarious. Daniel was with her, and Winter, Matilda and Casey were going to meet them at the hospital. While Parker knew that even if he were with her, there was nothing he could do for her he still ached to be by her side. The only thing keeping him from being there was that he knew Tessa would want him to take care of Charlotte before he joined her at the hospital.

"You set a bomb," he decided to stick to honest, albeit vague, answers for the moment. "Last I saw it the barn was still smoldering."

Clapping her hands excitedly, "now there's nothing stopping us from being together."

"We need to talk," he told her seriously.

Charlotte's enthusiasm dipped slightly, "about what?"

"About your past," he had read the diary on the drive up here, and even knowing all the terrible things Charlotte had done he couldn't help but feel sorry for the horror she had endured as an innocent child.

"What about my past?" she asked sullenly.

"Your childhood."

The change in her demeanor was as instantaneous as it was terrifying, "no," she shrieked. "I won't. I don't want to. You can't make me."

Holding up his hands calmingly, Parker took a tentative step towards her, not wanting to spook her while she perched so close to the edge of the cliff. He wanted Charlotte to have to face what she had done not plummet to her death. "I think we have to. If we're ever going to have any chance of being together I need to understand why you are the way you are, why you've done the things you've done."

That seemed to placate her for the time being, "you really mean you still want to be with me? Even though I killed your wife?"

Squeezing his hands into fists so tightly he could feel his nails pierce the skin, "Tessa had problems. She didn't love me the way I loved her. She didn't love me the way that you love me."

"I do love you," Charlotte gushed. "I've been searching for you my whole life."

"You really felt alone when you were a child. Unloved by everyone. Abandoned by everyone. You've spent your life trying to find someone who would simply love you," he ploughed on carefully, pushing as hard as he dared, he had read her diary detailing every single one of her previous attempts to snag a husband.

"Everything I've ever done was to find my one true love," Charlotte had gone still, her voice dropping to a mere whisper he had to strain to hear.

"They never loved you, starting with your mother."

A spark of fury flamed in her eyes, "she never even fought for me. She just let them give me away. To *him*."

"They shouldn't have done that," he agreed.

"How could she do that?" for a second Charlotte looked small and vulnerable, but then her temper flared again, "I don't care that he raped her, I was her child, how could she just give me up so easily."

"Maybe she didn't want to," he suggested. "Maybe she had no choice, maybe they forced her to do it."

"She was my mother," Charlotte maintained.

Parker had to admit it was hard to understand. Charlotte's mother had been a young nun, aged only twenty, when she had been viciously raped one night while walking from choir practice back to her room. The rape produced a child, and when baby Charlotte was born the sisters at the nunnery had given the infant to her biological father, her mother's rapist, a priest.

"And she gave me to *him*," Charlotte spat. "I hated him so much."

"He hurt you."

Bursting into a peel of laughter as though he'd just said the funniest thing she'd ever hear. "That is the understatement of the century."

"You were just a helpless little girl."

"I was no little girl," she shook her head wildly. "He started raping me when I was three and continued to all through my childhood, my adolescence, my young adulthood, right up until the day I killed him. That was the first time I took another person's life," she turned thoughtful. "At the time I didn't really want to do it. I just knew that if I didn't then it would never stop, that he would continue to rape me up until the day I died."

"It was self-defense," he said softly, if Charlotte had simply left it there then no jury in the world would have convicted her of murder.

"I didn't feel bad," she continued, "I just felt a sense of peace."

"He was a bad man."

"He was an evil, wicked, despicable man," Charlotte corrected. "Do you know how many mornings I woke up with my insides so ripped and shredded from him pounding into me that my sheets would be drenched in blood? And still I would hobble downstairs to make his breakfast. Sometimes he'd want to do it again before he went to work, and I would lie there in so much pain I thought I would die. And then he would go to work and I'd curl up in a ball and cry until I had no more tears left, and I'd promise myself that this was the day I'd run away, but I never did. No, I was a good little girl. I would scrub the house from top to bottom, then cook his dinner, timing it perfectly for his arrival home. I'd sit beside him while he ate, then clean the dishes, all the time knowing what was coming, but praying that tonight might be different. It never was. Every night was the same, more torture."

"I'm sorry, Charlotte," he murmured truthfully.

"It was better the nights he was really tired," Charlotte continued. "Then he would just rape me and go off to watch TV, but the nights he was energetic, those were the worst, those were the ones when he wanted to play. Pretend you're a nun, Charlotte, pretend you're a nurse, pretend you're a prostitute, pretend you're a schoolteacher, pretend you're a princess, pretend you're a dog . . ." she shuddered in revulsion. "Can you believe he actually made me do that? Take off all my clothes and put on a collar and crawl around and eat from a bowl on the floor. That was my father, the priest, the man who raised me, that was what he thought was fun."

"I'm sorry," he repeated, not sure what else to say.

"Every day from the time I was three until I was twenty-two," she dropped down onto the grass.

While she was distracted Parker seized the opportunity to move closer. "Why did you rape yourself with a gun? After you were found, the hospital did a rape kit on you, Marty found gunpowder residue."

"That was another of his games," she replied with a mirthless smile. "He would load his gun then make me lie on the floor while he pushed it inside me, he said it was the only way that I would learn that he decided if I lived or died."

"You did it to the other women too."

"They had to learn the same lesson I did."

Stopping just a couple of yards away from her, "why didn't you go for help after you shot your father? The police would have understood, anyone would have understood, they would have gotten you help, you could have had a normal, happy life."

"Yeah right," Charlotte scoffed.

"But you chose the wrong path. You took it upon yourself to

play god with other people's lives and that changed everything."

"I was trying to find happiness," she corrected him. "Is that so awful? Isn't that what everyone is searching for?"

"Most people don't kill others to try to get what they want," he reminded her.

"I tried everything I could to find happiness. I tried old men and young men, rich men and poor men, married men and unmarried men, but it didn't make any difference, it always ended the same way. They never loved me as much as I loved them, so I had to kill them."

The straight-faced, matter of fact way Charlotte stated that was truly terrifying. "And how many innocent people got caught in the crossfire?"

Shrugging indifferently, "they were in my way."

"You could have gotten my attention without resorting to killing Henrietta Kendall, Millicent Waters and the others."

"It would have brought too much attention onto me. I had to include those other women. It took a lot of work you know," she said proudly. "Setting it all up, timing things, adjusting the temperature in the rooms to try and give each of the women a different time of death. Then you hadn't found any of them so I had to give you a little helping hand."

"You were the anonymous caller that led us to Henrietta."

"I wanted it to work this time. From the second I saw you carrying that girl to safety, one of the Iceman's victims, I knew that you were what I'd been looking for my whole life. You are so perfect. You're everything that I spent all those years dreaming about, and I can't lose you, I won't. Now that I know what I need to be happy I'm not going to let it go."

"Give yourself up, Charlotte," Parker took another step towards her, but she stood and backed closer to the edge of the cliff. "I can get you the help that you need, I won't walk away from you, I'll stand by you and make sure that you get help. I called you Hope because I wanted you to figure out who you really were, it's not too late to lose that hope, we can still find out who you really are."

A serene smile grew on her lips, "I know that you'll never leave me," she said with a horrible calm that chilled him to the bone. Before he had a chance to react Charlotte had produced a gun, "I love you, Parker," she smiled sorrowfully yet tranquilly as she fired.

The bullet seemed to rocket through his heart in slow motion, he could feel every rip and tear as scalding hot pain swept through him like a tidal wave.

The last thing Parker saw was Charlotte, arms thrown wide, face tilted to drink in the soft sunshine, fall backwards off the cliff as though she were a bird that would swoop off into the morning.

His last thought was that he loved his wife and prayed that Tessa survived.

FEBRUARY 20TH

11:24 A.M.

"How can this be happening?"

Casey's face was as streaked with tears as he knew his own must be. Wyatt hadn't seen his wife cry so much since Serena's death. "I don't know," he wrapped his arms tightly around her, still in shock from the events of the previous day.

They had come so close and yet it had all fallen apart at the last minute. Managing to find Tessa still alive, and all escape the barn before it exploded into flames, only for Tessa to stop breathing. And Parker almost had Charlotte Lainie talked down before she pulled out a gun and shot him, then threw herself off the cliff.

His gun had already been drawn throughout Parker and Charlotte's conversation but it had all happened so quickly. One second her hand was empty and she looked like she might be being persuaded by Parker's words the next she was firing her gun. Wyatt too had fired, but before his bullet could reach her, she had stepped calmly off the cliff and was floating soundlessly to the bottom. It had been very surreal watching her fall. Charlotte had looked so serene, so peaceful, that it was hard to believe she was plummeting to her death.

"Wake me up, Wyatt," Casey begged. "Pinch me and wake me up and let this all be a terrible nightmare."

"It's the worst kind of nightmare," tightening his grip on his wife. "The kind that never ends."

"How are we going to tell Sam and Stacey?" she looked up at him with her huge black eyes. "They're going to be devastated."

"Speaking of telling people," Daniel and Matilda materialized behind them, looking as exhausted and rumpled as only a night in the hospital could leave you. "We have to figure out which one of us is going to in there and break the bad news."

They all turned automatically to look at the hospital room door, each of their hearts aching for the person unconscious on the bed inside.

"I'll do it," he said immediately. "Parker's my best friend."

"Tessa's my sister," Daniel objected. "I should do it."

"Maybe it would be better coming from a woman," Casey brushed away her tears. "Tessa is my best friend, I think it should come from me."

Shaking her head, "Parker's my brother, I'll do it," Matilda joined in.

"As if it matters which one of us does it," Winter leaped out of the chair on which she'd been huddled for hours. "It's not going to make this any easier. We're telling Tessa that her husband is dead."

The reality of why they had all been huddled in the hospital for over twenty-four hours crashed once more against their already battered brains.

Wyatt could still smell Parker's blood on his hands. His best friend had bled out in seconds, had probably been dead before he hit the ground. But that hadn't stopped Wyatt from trying frantically to try and prevent more blood from joining the every-growing pool around them. Nor had it stopped him from going ballistic when the paramedics finally arrived only to refuse to perform CPR. Reminding him gently that a bullet, shot at close range, piercing the heart and ripping through it, was not a wound from which one recovered. Neither had it stopped him from collapsing against a tree and sobbing wildly, completely oblivious to the uncomfortable yet sympathetic glances of the cops and paramedics who had showed up too late to be of any use.

Turning up at the hospital the news had not been any better. Tessa had still been in critical condition, barely clinging to life. She'd lost almost fifteen percent of her body's fluids and her doctors were struggling to stabilize her as her failing organs refused to come back to life. Throughout the night the doctors continued to attempt to rehydrate her and early this morning her scrambled body had ever so slowly begun to return to the land of the living. Still her doctors had been at pains to explain that there were no guarantees. That she might or might not ever wake up, that even if she did she might have suffered brain damage from lack of oxygen.

Tessa was a fighter and a couple of hours ago had begun to breathe on her own again. Her doctors had taken her off the ventilator and she continued to grow stronger.

As bad as it had been telling Matilda and Daniel and Winter and Casey and everyone else about Parker, Wyatt knew it was going to be infinitely harder to tell Tessa. And he also knew that he should be the one to tell her.

"Wyatt should do it," Casey announced, seemingly reading his mind.

"I agree," Matilda nodded her assent.

"What?" Daniel glared at his fiancée. "Tessie's my sister it makes sense that I should be the one to tell her."

"I don't want to hurt your feelings, Daniel," Casey looked like she couldn't give two hoots about Daniel's feelings at the moment. "But Wyatt is the one Tessa trusts the most. This isn't about us, this is about Tessa, she's the one who's about to learn her husband is dead. She should hear it from the person who's going to make her feel the most comfortable."

"Fine," Daniel relented reluctantly, "but you come get me the second you've told her. I haven't been there for Tessa in the past but I'm going to make up for it this time. I am going to be there for her whatever she needs."

Wyatt could see the genuine pain in Daniel's eyes as he thought of all the times he'd let his sister down, and the desperation to support her through this. This he understood perfectly, because this was the exact same way Wyatt was feeling.

Parker and Tessa were like his little brother and sister and he should have done more to prevent this whole mess from happening. He should have gone with his instincts and told Parker about Isaac. He shoulder have forced Parker and Tessa to sit down and sort out their problems. He should have insisted that Charlotte Lainie remain in the psychiatric ward of the hospital where she would have been unable to continue with her macabre plan.

There had been one bright spot last night.

Charlotte's diary had been most specific. Detailing all her previous plans as well as this current one. Including the locations of the three remaining victims. Unfortunately Jacinta Owens, a quiet unmarried forty-four year old, had already been dead by the time the police had arrived, and Meg Stevens, a divorcee with a thirteen-year-old daughter at home, had died in the arms of the first officer on the scene. But unbelievably one of the women had still been alive. Kelita McNamara, a widow with two estranged grown sons, was recovering down the hall from Tessa, her sons on their way.

"I'm going to go in and sit with her," Wyatt announced. "I don't want her to be alone when she wakes up."

"Tell her we love her," Casey squeezed his hand, knowing how hard it was going to be for him to tell her.

"Come get me the second, the second, you tell her," Daniel reminded him.

"I will," he assured them.

Now that the time had come, he actually had to force himself to walk to the hospital room door, turn the handle and go through. Inside Tessa's pale face blended in with the white sheets, her white blonde curls rested on the pillow and framed her sleeping face. Part of him wished she could stay that way forever. Peacefully asleep and blissfully unaware of her husband's death.

Tessa wasn't moving and she didn't indicate that she had registered his presence, so he pulled the one chair in the room over to the bed. Leaning over the guardrail to take hold of Tessa's frail, thin hand, Wyatt could no longer fight the tears that had been pricking at the back of his eyes all morning. He had been holding them back, trying to be strong for the others, but now that he was alone he let them fall freely.

All the things he should have done and would have done differently if given the chance. He should have convinced Parker to accompany Tessa in the chopper. He should have convinced him that they could come back for Hope later. He should have convinced him that Tessa would want him by her side, even though they both knew that she would want him to take care of Hope first to ensure that she didn't get away to remain free to hurt more people.

His life had been reduced to a series of should haves. Wyatt had been here before when his daughter had been killed by a murderer he'd been trying to track down who had decided to make things personal and steal his car with his child inside. He knew that it was a pointless game. That no one could change the past. You only got one shot at life and you had to make it count.

Overwhelmed with sorrow and anger and guilt, so intense that he couldn't deal with it all, and it made him want to rip out his own brain.

* * * * *

10:17 P.M.

"Where are we going?"

Tessa had to shield her eyes as she looked around at the bright blue ocean, and the equally bright blue sky. Staring into the distance she couldn't even tell where the ocean stopped and the sky began.

"Parker?" she drew her eyes from the mesmerizing blue to look at her husband who was concentrating on rowing their little boat. "Where are we going?" she asked again.

"You're not going to like it," he said at last, still refusing to meet her eye.

"Why?"

He refused to answer, pretending to be consumed with rowing.

"Parker," she demanded, resisting the urge to plant her hands on her hips and stamp her feet like she used to when she was a child. "What's going on? Where are we going?"

"I'm taking you back."

"Back where?"

Finally looking at her, "home."

"Why is that so terrible? Why wouldn't I like that? It's exactly what I want. For you and me and the baby to all go home together."

"I'm not going with you."

For the first time she noticed the tears glistening in his golden eyes, "why not?"

"Tessa, I'm dead," he told her gently, reaching out a hand to brush her cheek.

Laughing, "no you're not, you're right here." To prove it she threw her arms around his neck and pressed her body closely against his hard, strong chest.

"I'm sorry, honey."

"I don't believe you," she pressed her eyes closed. After a while, when Parker still hadn't spoken she opened her eyes to see that they were no longer out in the middle of the ocean. Now they were on the sandy beach and Parker was carrying her in his arms. "I don't want to go home," she entwined her arms around his neck. "I want to stay with you."

"You can't, sweetheart," his voice rumbled in his chest. "Our baby needs you."

"Well I need you," she countered. "Parker, I don't want to leave you."

"I don't want to leave you either, but I have to, it's not your time, but mine is up."

He was starting to waver, growing transparent. Tessa tried to meld her body against his so he would have no choice but to take her with him. "But I love you," she cried.

"I love you too, Tess. Always . . ."

"Tessa?"

That wasn't Parker's voice. It was Skylar's.

"Tess? Can you hear me? Wake up, Tessa."

But she didn't want to wake up. She wanted to stay right where she was.

"Tessa? Wake up now. Please, honey. I need you to wake up."

His hand on her shoulder gave a gentle shake that seemed to pop her eyes involuntarily open.

"Hey."

Skylar's smiling face looked down at her but she could see in his eyes that something was terribly wrong. Something she ought to know. Something she was sure her dream had told her, but the dream had already vanished from her mind.

"You couldn't believe how happy I am to be standing here talking to you."

Tears were sparkling in Skylar's eyes and since she had never seen him cry before her anxiety jumped up several notches. Opening her mouth to ask what was wrong, Tessa was surprised and unnerved when no sound came out.

"It's okay," Skylar soothed immediately. "Drink this."

He brought a straw to her lips and as she sipped a couple of mouthfuls of the icy water a hazy image came to mind. Back in Charlotte's basement, after Parker, Daniel and Skylar had found her, Parker had given her a drink of water. She wanted to see her husband, convince herself that the ominous presence that hovered in the room was unjustified. Wondering why it was Skylar sitting at her bedside instead of Parker.

Licking her dry lips, she attempted once again to talk, managing only one word, "Parker?"

A dark shadow splashed across Skylar's face, and after only a split second hesitation he spoke, "I'm so sorry, Tessa."

"No," she whispered, clinging determinedly to denial. "Where's Parker? Did Charlotte hurt him? Is that why he isn't here?"

Lowering the guardrail on one side of her bed Skylar sat, and Tessa realized for the first time that she was in a hospital. Skylar clasped her hands, "Charlotte shot him."

Bolting upright, "is he here too? In the hospital? I want to see him."

Grabbing her shoulders and forcing her to lie back against the mattress, "Tess, honey, listen to me. Charlotte shot him in the heart, he bled out in seconds. I'm sorry, Tessa, I'm so sorry."

Skylar tried to pull her into a hug but she shoved him away, turning her attention to ripping the IV from her elbow and the wires from the heart monitor off her chest. Skylar did his best to stop her but she had completely flipped out. "I need to find him," she screeched. "I need to find Parker."

"Sweetheart, he's gone," Skylar was trying to get a hold of her squiggling form.

"I don't believe you," she screamed and beat her fists wildly against Skylar's chest. Parker wouldn't go and die on her and leave her all alone. He just wouldn't do that. "I need to find him," she begged.

The room began to fill with anxious healthcare professionals anxious to make everything all better with their pills, but Skylar waved them back. "Tessa, listen to me," closing one of his hands over hers and pinning them against his chest, the other gripped her shoulder firmly. "You can get through this."

A thought occurring to her, "the baby?" she asked through her tears.

"The baby survived," he told her. "I don't know how it did but it's a miracle."

Tessa didn't think it was a miracle. She wanted her husband

not a child that she would have to raise on her own. Luckily, she was still groggy enough to refuse to believe that what Skylar had just told her was true. "You're lying," she half yelled half cried, feeling like she was drowning. It couldn't be true. She wouldn't let it be true.

"I wish I was," Skylar once more tried to pull her against him and this time she let him.

The pain welling up inside her was too strong, too powerful, too overbearing, she didn't know what to do with it. She needed to get it out somehow, before it smothered her, she just wasn't sure how. Then she thought of the needle that had been in her arm, delivering fluids to her parched body. If she could just release the pressure in her heart then everything would be better.

Keeping the rest of her body still so as not to alert Skylar, she moved her hand across the bed until it located the needle. Wrapping her fingers around it, she brought it towards her heart and was about to stab it in when a hand clamped around her wrist.

"Tessa, what are doing?" Skylar exclaimed with horror.

"I just need to make it stop hurting," she screamed hysterically. Trying to yank her hand free from Skylar's grip but finding she no longer had enough energy to function.

When one of the doctors came at her with a syringe full of sedatives, she didn't fight it instead she welcomed it. As the medication began to take effect, she felt Skylar settle her gently back against the bed, the doctors reattaching their machinery.

Before sleep took hold Tessa pasted a picture of Parker in her mind, hoping that she could force herself to dream that her husband was still alive and they were both happily anticipating the birth of their child.

FEBRUARY 28TH

9:19 A.M.

"Hi. I know this is a stupid question but how are you doing?"

Looking up blankly it took a moment for the blurry image to morph into a recognizable identity. "Hey, Elisabeth," Tessa gave a half smile and resumed her mindless staring into space.

Seemingly undeterred by her mindless staring Elisabeth joined her in the small room at the church into which she had fled to escape the many well-meaners who had turned up for Parker's funeral.

Right now Tessa just wanted to be alone. Something she hadn't been since regaining consciousness in the hospital. Awakening after Skylar had told her about Parker, Daniel had been at her bedside. Her first thought was that it had all just been a horrible nightmare, but one look in her brother's eyes had confirmed that it had all been true.

Someone had stayed by her side every second of the three days she spent in the hospital. When she'd been released and gone back home Daniel, Matilda and Winter had made it their mission to make sure she was never alone.

Coming home had been a lot harder than Tessa had thought it would be. She hadn't anticipated any real difficulties since Parker hadn't been living at the mansion for weeks. It had been Parker's house that she knew she couldn't face. The house where they had started their lives together, the house where that evil woman had stayed, but the mansion she had expected to be a breeze. Well maybe not a breeze exactly, but she had been completely unprepared for the rush of emotions she got when she'd climbed out of Daniel's car. They had hit her with the force of a tornado, and caught out without her usual barriers in place, she had fainted into Daniel's waiting arms. Which had inadvertently solved her problem since she had regained consciousness inside.

After that someone made sure they were with her all the time. Especially at night. She couldn't face the bedroom, neither her childhood one that she had resumed using when Parker moved out, or the one that she and Parker had shared when they'd lived here together, so she had taken to sleeping curled up on a chair in the living room. Although she hated to admit it, it was comforting when she awoke panting, sweating, shaking, screaming, to have someone by her side. Winter, Daniel and Matilda took it in turns to spend the night with her, and even though she'd only spent seven nights at home at least half of those Skylar or Casey had come over. Once they'd even brought the kids who loved roaming the large, empty halls, and choosing one of the many vacant bedrooms to sleep in.

Tessa was also pretty sure that part of the reason that everyone was making such a concerted effort to ensure she was never alone was that Skylar had told them of what she'd tried to do at the hospital just after she'd learnt of Parker's death. She wasn't quite sure whether she had just wanted to let out some of the pain that was smothering her or whether she had wanted to end her life and join Parker. But she knew that Skylar was terrified that grief might swamp her and she would try it again so he wanted her to be watched every second. He needn't have worried though, as appealing as the idea was, she knew that Parker would be so disappointed in her if she took her own life.

While she appreciated, and even though she would never admit it actually enjoyed, the fact that her friends and family wanted to look after her, right now she just needed to be by herself for a while.

"Tessa?" Elisabeth was peering at her anxiously.

"Yeah?" she blinked and tried to focus, something that she found increasingly hard to do at the moment. She was so tired.

Sleeping only because of the sleeping pills Daniel gave her each night. Wondering absently whether the prescription had come from Elisabeth, Casey, Charlie or Eric, and whether her four doctor friends had had to draw straws for the privilege of medicating her.

Eyeing her carefully, "I just wanted to check up on you," Elisabeth slid onto the sofa beside her. "And don't tell me that you're fine," she added, "because we all know that's a lie."

"I don't feel anything right now," Tessa hated how hollow her voice sounded. "I'm just empty." She was still in shock Charlie kept patiently explaining every time he came to check up on her. He'd been to see her every day and Tessa knew it was as much to closely monitor her mental stability as it was because they were friends.

Elisabeth said nothing for a full five minutes before cracking, "I think you were right, Tessa."

"About what?" she asked without the tiniest hint of curiosity.

"About psychiatrists."

"What about them?" she was only partially paying attention to what Elisabeth was saying.

"Tessa," Elisabeth exclaimed exasperatedly, "I think you were right all along that psychiatry never helped anyone."

Blinking in surprise, that was the last thing she had expected to hear Dr. Bennett say. She had been expecting a long spiel about how talking about how she felt about her husband's murder would somehow make him less dead. "Maybe it's not that psychiatrists never helped anyone maybe its just that some people can't be fixed."

"I'm really sorry, Tess," Elisabeth began to babble earnestly. "About believing Charlotte, I feel like this is all my fault. Parker only asked her to move in with him because I told him that I believed that she was really suffering from amnesia. I should have been more cautious. I should have insisted that she remain in the psychiatric ward. I should have done *something*. If I hadn't fallen for her trick then none of this would ever have happened. Parker and Maisy would still be alive, and maybe those other women would be too. I'm so, so sorry, Tessa."

Staring at the shrink in amazement, "it's not your fault, Elisabeth, it's Charlotte's. She was the one who chose to kill people to get what she wanted. No one else is responsible for her actions." Studying Elisabeth's guilty eyes, "I've been seeing Charlie Abbott," she confessed. "Ever since last September."

"Eric Abbott's brother?" Elisabeth looked positively astounded. "The psychiatrist? *You* have been seeing a psychiatrist?"

Shrugging, "he diagnosed me with posttraumatic stress disorder, but you already knew that's what was wrong with me," she cast a glance at Elisabeth, who nodded. "He has me on medication, and he's doing cognitive behavioral therapy and exposure therapy with me," Elisabeth again nodded, approvingly this time. "Charlie has been telling me for months to just do whatever it takes to fix things with Parker. So has Skylar, Casey, Matilda," she checked them off on her fingers, "Winter, J.J., Maisy, you . . ." she chewed on her lips to keep her tears in. "We're all responsible for our own choices."

"Oh, Tessa," Elisabeth threw her arms around her, "somehow we'll get you through this."

"I warned Parker," her mind was drifting back in time two and a half years.

"Warned him about Hope?" Elisabeth asked remorsefully, still radiating guilt for her part in aiding Charlotte Lainie in her devilish scheme.

"No, I mean before, when we first met. I warned him that every single person who gets involved with me winds up getting hurt, and look how things ended up. Maybe Parker would have been better off if we'd never even met." Tessa had known from the beginning that it was a bad idea to risk forging a relationship with someone else. After years of hopping from one bad experience to another, causing pain and heartache to everyone who befriended her, she had locked herself away on the estate, where she couldn't cause harm to anyone else. But then she'd met Parker and she'd let him convince her that she wasn't actually bad luck and that the two of them would end up together and happier than they could ever imagine.

"Honey, you know that's not true right?" Elisabeth shook her gently. "You completed Parker, I've never seen him happier than when he was with you. He also left you with an amazing gift," her eyes strayed to Tessa's stomach.

Ever since she'd miscarried her first child Tessa had dreamed of getting pregnant again, but not like this. "How did the baby even survive?" she marveled. "I was clinically dead." Apparently, she had been resuscitated four times between Parker and the others rescuing her and eventually waking up in the hospital.

"It's a miracle," Elisabeth smiled.

"I'm not ready to be a mother," Tessa whispered guiltily. "I put the baby at risk by not telling Parker I was pregnant. I'm still putting the baby at risk because I'm still taking Paxil, it can cause birth defects."

"You're taking your medication because you need it," Elisabeth assured her. "Because you and the baby are at greater risk if you go off it right now given your PTSD and everything you're dealing with."

Remaining unconvinced, she and Charlie had talked about it, but since she'd already suffered such severe withdrawal symptoms he didn't want to take her off it again. They'd also discussed changing medications, but he had been concerned about trying to find a new one that worked while she was so emotionally unstable. Between her already existing posttraumatic stress disorder, and now also dealing with being abducted and her husband's death, Charlie didn't want to do anything to put her further at risk. Logically she understood Charlie's reasoning, and she'd gone along with it because she trusted him to do what was best for her, but it didn't change the facts that her baby could suffer birth defects because of her medication.

"Does it make me a terrible person if I said I don't want the baby?" she dropped her head into her hands. "That I would rather have my husband back than our child?"

"It doesn't make you a terrible person," Elisabeth comforted. "It makes you a person who is grieving the loss of their husband."

"Parker knew we were doomed," she whispered, "that night when we were at the station, when Parker and Skylar were trying to find out about Dylan Riley. I thought he was going to kiss me but then he didn't because he knew that we would never work out. But then I freaked out after I accidentally shot Dylan and then Parker felt sorry for me so he felt like he had to stay around."

"Tessa, you know that's not true," Elisabeth told her reproachfully.

Tessa did know that it wasn't true. She knew that Parker had loved her completely, and that she loved him the same way. She also knew that even if she'd known how things were going to turn out she still would have married Parker. But right now she didn't want to think logically she wanted to wallow deliciously in a huge pool of self-pity.

"I'm angry at him," she said softly.

"At Parker?" Elisabeth slipped an arm around her shoulders.

"Mmm hmm," she nodded.

Waiting patiently for her to continue, Elisabeth stroked her hair soothingly.

"I asked him to stay with me, when we were in the basement. He said he would. But he didn't. He had to go and find Charlotte. He had to fix it. He always has to fix everything. But I didn't need him to fix it, I just wanted him to be with me. If he had of gone to the hospital with me then he'd still be alive," tears pricking at her eyes again she rested her head on Elisabeth's shoulder.

Tightening her grip, "you're grieving, honey," Elisabeth

reminded her again. "It's normal to feel angry. Parker went after Charlotte to keep you safe, as long as she was out there then you were in danger."

Lying in Elisabeth's arms, too drained to move, Tessa let Elisabeth's gentle smoothing of her hair ease her jangled nerves. "I like you Elisabeth. I have ever since I told you and Parker and Skylar about Ellie's death. You were so good with me, so gentle, and patient, and what you said to me, it was the first time I ever doubted that what happened was my fault. You're a good friend, I'm sorry I didn't tell you so before now. I'm sorry," she repeated. She'd messed things up with Parker because she hadn't just said how she felt and now she'd lost him. She didn't want to make the same mistake again with the friends and family she had left.

"Shh," Elisabeth soothed, "it's okay, sweetie. I don't want you to worry about that now."

"It's my fault, Elisabeth," Tessa began to cry.

"No," Elisabeth said forcefully. "No, it's not, Tessa."

"I let us drift apart because I was hurt and angry at him, and that gap between us was what Charlotte used to get to him. It's all my fault," she clung to Elisabeth, desperately wishing the woman could do something to ease her pain.

"Oh, baby, no, that's not true. Look at me, Tess," Elisabeth gently sat her up.

Tessa stared unseeingly through the psychiatrist, swamped by guilt and overwhelmed by pain.

"*At* me, Tess," giving her chin a shake, Elisabeth waited until she was looking at her. "What happened was *not* your fault. Like you told me before, it was Charlotte's fault, and Charlotte's alone. I will keep telling you that as many times as you need to hear it until you can believe it. Come here, honey," Elisabeth pulled her into a hug again.

A knock at the door announced that the funeral service was about to begin.

"You going to be okay?" Elisabeth asked her anxiously.

"No, not even close," she replied as she pulled herself together and prepared to farewell her husband.

"Are you ready?" Casey asked, blocking her exit as she opened the door.

Rolling her eyes when she saw her friend had her doctor face firmly in place. "Ready as I'll ever be."

"Have you been eating? Sleeping?" Casey queried with a raised eyebrow that indicated she wanted the truth. "I don't want you passing out on me in there."

To Tessa, unconsciousness sounded like bliss. "I'll be okay," she assured her friend, even though they both knew that wasn't true.

Reaching out to tuck a strand of hair behind her ear, Casey studied her carefully, "yeah, you will be."

Casey took her hand and was about to lead her through the door when Skylar suddenly appeared. "Tessa, we need to talk. Now," his face was serious.

Wondering what was so important it couldn't wait until after the funeral. "What's wrong?"

Taking her arm Skylar led her to a corner of the room, "Charlotte Lainie was shot," he told her gently. "She didn't throw herself off a cliff, she was shot and fell off the cliff."

Tessa could feel the color draining from her face. "Isaac," she murmured, suddenly lightheaded.

Gripping her arms before she could topple to the ground, Skylar lowered her to a chair. "That would be my guess."

Casey and Elisabeth materialized beside her.

"What's wrong?" Elisabeth asked.

"Is she okay?" Casey knelt at her side

"He said he was going away," she mumbled tonelessly.

"It looks like Isaac Worthington may have killed Charlotte Lainie," Skylar explained, his hand on her shoulder kneading gently.

"He said he couldn't be around to help me anymore," Tessa

whispered, more to herself than anyone else. Part of her numb brain noting that both Casey and Elisabeth were a hairsbreadth away from beginning to treat her as a patient, and she wondered which would be the first to reach for her wrist to check her pulse.

"Do you think Isaac is here now? At the funeral?" Casey asked Skylar.

"I don't know."

"But you know what he looks like, so go see if he's here. Come on, Wyatt, now's your chance to finally arrest him. What are you waiting for?" Casey demanded.

"I have some photos from two decades ago, I'm sure he's changed since then. Tessa is the only one who knows what he looks like now," Skylar explained patiently.

"So you're going to do nothing?" Casey was incredulous.

"What exactly do you want me to do?"

"I want you to do *something*, Wyatt," Casey snapped.

"You want me to go out there and make a scene? Make her more upset?" Skylar was angry now.

Only vaguely listening to them, Tessa became aware of the fact that she was struggling to breathe, sucking in one shallow breath after another. If Isaac hadn't left her like he said, then she wasn't all alone. Tessa hated that the thought comforted her.

"Tessa?" Elisabeth was peering at her, alarmed.

Casey's attention snapped immediately from her argument with Skylar, to her. "Breathe, Tess," she commanded gently.

"I can't," she gasped. The room doesn't have any air left, she added to herself.

"Yes you can," Casey soothed.

"Her pulse is through the roof," Elisabeth held her wrist.

"She's having a panic attack," Casey murmured.

"You want me to call an ambulance?" Skylar asked, shrugging out of his jacket and draping it over her shaking shoulders.

"Beth and I can handle it," Casey replied curtly, then gently, "Tessa, honey, lets try to slow your breathing down, okay?"

"I can't," she whimpered, with each gasping breath it felt like her lungs were getting smaller and smaller.

"Shh," Casey stroked her hair, "yes, you can. We'll do it together. I just want you to concentrate on me, okay? Forget about everything else. We're going to breathe in and out really slowly, okay?"

Concentrating all her energy to focus on Skylar's firm grip on her shoulders, on Casey's calm face hovering before her and her soothing voice directing her breathing. These things were solid and real. Her panic was not.

After a couple of minutes of deep breathing, Casey glanced at Elisabeth, "how's she doing?"

"Pulse is still elevated, but she's doing better," Elisabeth answered.

"You're doing great, Tessa," Casey gripped her hands. "Let's try and calm you down a little more though."

"I'm scared," tears were pricking at her eyes again, and she did so hate to cry in front of people.

"I know you are, honey," tears were glistening in Casey's eyes too. "And I wish I could make everything better for you but I can't. But you are strong enough to get through this, Tessa, you just have to believe it."

"I don't want to be strong anymore," Tessa was so tired of always having to be strong. Parker had promised he would be her strength but he was gone now. Throwing herself into Casey's arms she began to sob, her friend's arms squeezed tightly.

Eventually Casey pulled back, holding her at arms length, studying her carefully, "Tessa . . ."

"What's wrong with me, Casey?" she asked softly. "How can Isaac coming back make me feel better about Parker being gone? How can it make me feel like I'm not completely alone?"

Grabbing her roughly and dragging her from Casey's arms and to her feet. "Don't do that, Tessa," Skylar's voice was fiercely angry.

"Wyatt," Casey warned.

"No," Skylar cut off his wife, "she is not going to do that."

"Wyatt, let her be, she can't handle this now. Do you want to give her another panic attack?"

Casey reached for her but Skylar dragged her away, his grip on her arms so tight she knew it would leave bruises. "No, Casey. She is going to hear this. It's for her own good. You are not going to push us away, Tessa. You are not alone. Whether Isaac is back or not, you are not alone."

The anger in his voice caught her off guard and she sobbed again, wanting to get free of his grip and let Casey's comforting arms soothe her again. She had wanted to cope with this day so well but now she was a complete mess.

"Look at me, Tessa," Skylar commanded.

She didn't want to look into Skylar's usually calm green eyes and see anger bubbling there.

"Tessa, please," his voice softer now.

Reluctantly she raised her eyes to meet Skylar's, and in them she saw the pain she knew clouded her own.

"I failed him, Tessa," tears dripped down his cheeks. "I couldn't save him. I failed you too. I should have made you tell Parker the truth from the beginning. But I am not going to fail you again. I am not going to let you go on believing that you are alone. I promised Parker if anything ever happened to him that I would take care of you, and I intend to keep that promise. You are not alone, Tessa, you have all of us, we care about you, we love you, and we are not going anywhere."

"Parker said that too." She'd never seen Skylar cry before and it shook her. "He promised."

"I know he did, honey," releasing his grip on her arms to gently brush away her tears. "And I know it took everything you had to believe him. Now you're scared to believe it again. But Isaac is not the answer. You know that, Tessa. *He* knows that. It's why he told you he was leaving. He knows that he can't give you what you need. I don't want to admit it, but he loves you, he wants to know you're safe, but that's it. He knows that you need more than what he can ever give you."

Tessa didn't want to hear this now. She wanted Isaac to be able to make everything better. But Isaac wasn't God. He couldn't give her what she wanted.

Tipping her face up so she was looking at him, "let us help you, Tessa," Skylar begged. "You said that you don't want to be strong anymore, then let us be strong for you."

Wavering, she wanted to let Skylar and her friends help her but she was so scared. Isaac was the only person who had never let her down. And yet she knew what Skylar had just said was true. Isaac could never give her what she really needed. He couldn't bring her dead husband back to life.

"Tessa?" Skylar was watching her imploringly, his hand held out.

Slowly, hesitantly, she reached her hand towards Skylar's. He took it and squeezed gently, then he pulled her against him, lifting her feet off the floor. Tessa wrapped her arms around his neck and clung to him, crying. When her sobs finally ceased he didn't release her, so Tessa tucked her face against his neck and just allowed him to comfort her.

"I'm sorry, Casey," Skylar kept hold of her with one arm, with the other he drew his wife close.

"Me too, Wyatt. I don't want to fight with you. I'm just so worried about her," Casey placed a hand on her back. "Parker is gone and I don't know how to help her. I don't want to lose her too. Tell me we're not going to lose her too, Wyatt," Casey pleaded desperately.

"We're not going to lose her, Casey," Skylar's voice was strong and confident. "We're going to give her whatever she needs to get her through this."

Usually Tessa hated when people talked about her like she wasn't there, but today . . . today she was willing to let them take care of her. Because they loved her.

A knock suddenly sounded at the door, and her head snapped up, panicked. She couldn't deal with her husband's funeral right now. Again her chest tightened and she couldn't draw enough oxygen into her lungs. "I can't do this now. I can't, I can't," she babbled, bordering on hysteria.

Skylar set her back down on the floor, Casey and Elisabeth immediately grabbing her arms and easing her into a chair.

"Deep breaths again, Tess, just like we did before, okay?" Casey murmured.

"Her pulse is racing again," Elisabeth added.

"Concentrate on your breathing, Tess," Casey commanded

With each shallow breath her vision was blackening and blissful unconsciousness was edging closer. Both Casey and Elisabeth were doctors, they'd take care of her once she fainted, and then she wouldn't have to worry about anything.

"Her pulse isn't slowing," Elisabeth sounded panicked.

A few more gasps and her brain would be lacking enough oxygen to let her pass out.

"Tessa! Tess, come on! Focus!" Casey was nearing hysteria now. "Wyatt, it's not working, I can't help her."

Her limbs were starting to go limp. Casey cradled her head as it drooped.

"I'm going to call an ambulance," Elisabeth announced.

"Tessa?" Skylar's voice remained calm, and she felt rather than saw him crouch in front of her. "Honey, you know letting yourself lose consciousness is not the answer. This is your last chance to say goodbye to Parker. And you're scaring Casey. Beth too. I want you to try to calm yourself down. If you don't we're going to have to call an ambulance, take you to the hospital, and you'll miss your husband's funeral. I know you're scared, but I want you to just listen to my voice and breathe slowly with me."

Skylar's logic pierced her barely functioning brain, and reluctantly she let his voice calm her down. Her vision cleared, and she could breathe a little easier. Skylar smiled at her and took her face in his hands, pressing a kiss to her forehead. Still anxious, both Casey and Elisabeth took her wrists to check her pulse. Both of their concerned faces eased a little, presumably her pulse had slowed enough to please them.

"Tessie?" Daniel came barging into the room. "Everyone is waiting to . . ." he trailed off. "What's wrong? You look terrible," he rushed to her side.

Giving her brother a weak smile, "I'm okay," she assured him. "Just a couple of little panic attacks."

"Is she really okay?" he directed the question to Casey and Elisabeth.

"No," Casey replied, "but I think she's as well as she can be given the circumstances. I love you, Tessa, you know that right?"

"I know you do," she assured her best friend. "I'm sorry I scared you."

"Apology accepted. But don't you ever do that to me again," Casey crushed her in a fierce hug.

When Casey released her she turned to Elisabeth, "sorry I scared you too." She held out her arms for a hug, and after a moment's hesitation Elisabeth's arms wrapped around her.

Daniel took her hand, "it's time, Tess. You ready?"

"I guess," she answered uncertainly, she didn't want to have to admit that Parker was really gone, that he was really never coming back.

Four sets of hands gripped her as she rose on shaky legs, and Tessa realized just how many people she had to love and care about her. She was halfway to the door when she froze. "Skylar, wait," she reached for his hand.

"We'll meet you in there," Skylar told the others.

"Tessa?" Casey raised a questioning brow, apparently still a little concerned about leaving the two of them alone after Skylar's angry outburst.

"It's okay, Casey," she assured her friend.

Reluctantly giving her a hug, "I'll be waiting just outside the door, call if you need me. And, Wyatt, don't upset her again," she gave her husband a warning glare.

"I'm going to be just outside too," Daniel squeezed her tightly.

"You really promised Parker that if anything ever happened to him you'd look after me?" she asked once they were alone.

"The night Dylan Riley died," Skylar took her hands. "You were in the hospital, you told Parker to go, to leave you alone, he watched through the door as you cried. On his way home he came by my house. He told me that you were it for him, you were the woman he wanted, and that nothing was going to keep him from you, including you. He told me that when he finally broke through your defenses and you learnt to believe in him, that if anything ever happened to him, you'd shut yourself off even more than before. He didn't want that for you. He wanted to spend the rest of his life making you feel special and loved, but if he couldn't then he at least wanted you to know that you weren't all alone in the world, he knew that was your greatest fear. So I promised him. I promised that if anything happened and he couldn't be there for you, then I would make sure you were okay."

"What would I do without you?" she murmured, honestly unsure how she would have even gotten this far without Parker's best friend by her side.

"You don't have to worry about that because I'm right here," Skylar assured her.

"But you can't be by my side twenty-four hours a day," Tessa reminded him, pulling Skylar's jacket, which she still wore, tighter around her shoulders.

"You need me to take time off work, I'll do it. You need me and Casey and the kids to come and stay with you for a while, we'll do it. Tessa, Parker was my family, maybe not biologically but in every other way that matters, and so are you. Tessa, I'm a police officer and I couldn't save my daughter, I couldn't save my best friend, helping you makes me feel like I'm not completely useless. You are not alone, Tessa, please believe that."

"Okay," she whispered. Grabbing the front of Skylar's shirt and pulling till be bent down, pressing a kiss to his cheek, "thank you. I'm really lucky to have so many people who love me so much. Who are going to love this baby so much."

Wiping her tears, "you're going to be okay, Tessa," Skylar assured her, dropping a kiss to the top of her head. "Now together we are going to walk through that door, and we're going to do what we're both dreading and terrified to do."

Once again she froze halfway to the door, "Skylar, you're not completely useless, you already saved Parker when he was a little boy, and because you saved him, he saved me."

Squeezing her hand tightly, "thanks, Tess."

"If we help each other, maybe we can both get through this."

Bringing her hand to his lips he kissed it, his tears dripping onto both their hands. "Maybe we can," he agreed.

Together they made their way out the door, where their friends and family pressed around them. As they all made their way into the small chapel, Tessa wondered if it was true. Whether she ever would be okay again, or if she had ever been okay in the first place.

The funeral passed in a blur. She didn't really hear a word the minister said, instead she replayed in her head every wonderful memory of her time with Parker. She half heard Skylar's beautiful eulogy. She half remembered Daniel guiding her up to the coffin but she couldn't make herself say goodbye.

Before she realized it they were at the gravesite, and she was watching the coffin get lowered down into the hole that was going to keep her from Parker forever.

"Tess, this is your last chance to say goodbye," Skylar hovered beside her.

"I can't," she whimpered.

"You'll regret it if you don't," Casey gave her a hug.

"I still can't," she muttered helplessly.

"We'll leave you alone," Elisabeth gave her a purposeful look.

"Maybe I should . . ." Daniel started.

"She'll be okay," Matilda assured him. "And we'll be waiting right over there."

"I don't know. I don't want her to have another panic attack," Daniel hesitated. Her brother took his big brothering responsibilities very seriously since he'd found out what had happened to her when he'd been absent from her life.

As much as she didn't want to stand alone next to her husband's grave, partly because she knew that it would force her to face reality and partly because the thought of another panic attack truly did scare her, even if it did lead to lovely unconsciousness. Still she knew this was something that she needed to do if she was ever going to have any chance at living, and she owed her baby that. "I'll be okay," she assured her brother.

Reluctantly they all hugged her then disappeared to a safe distance. Far enough away to give her space, but close enough to swoop in if she fell apart again.

They weren't the only ones watching her carefully.

Tessa had seen Isaac earlier, both at the funeral and here at the graveyard. She didn't care what Skylar had said, even if Isaac couldn't give her everything she needed, it was comforting to know that he was looking out for her, even if it was from a distance. She was glad that he had killed Charlotte, she just wished he had been a little quicker and taken her out before she killed Parker.

As if on cue the phone in her pocket began to trill. Carefully Tessa pressed answer and speaker phone, she didn't want the others to know she was talking to someone.

"I don't have long, they're watching you," Isaac spoke urgently.

"They aren't the only ones watching me," she murmured, "you are too."

"Always," he said fiercely. "Always, Tessa. I'm not going anywhere." Then his voice softened, "oh, Tessa, my sweet little angel. Whatever shreds of humanity are still left in me are only there because of you. Tessa, there's something you have to know," the urgency was back in his voice. "Rebecca is here with me, so you have to know that this is the truth. I love my daughter with every fiber of my being. I love you the same way."

Tessa had never before allowed herself to say the words that were now on the tip of her tongue. Never even allowed herself to think them because she had been afraid it made her a bad person. A worse person than Isaac. Maybe even worse than Jake. But now she didn't care. She didn't care if it made her a terrible person, because it was true. She loved Isaac.

"I love you too, Isaac."

Tessa heard the small sigh of relief and realized that he hadn't been entirely sure she felt the same way about him. That he still loved her despite his doubts made his feelings all the more meaningful. "If you ever need me, Tessa, I'm there. Even if it means the police catching me. You say the word and I'll be there. I'll take you away with me, if it's what you want. I'm sorry, Tessa, I'm sorry I didn't get there in time to save your husband. I have to go now, sweetheart, but I love you, and you know how to find me if you need me."

Tessa stood for several minutes listening to the empty dial tone before disconnecting. Then her gaze drifted back to Parker's headstone. She wanted to say something meaningful, something profound, something that was fitting for a pregnant widow to say at her husband's grave, but her mind remained frustratingly blank.

It was all so unfair.

She and Parker were so young and they'd wasted so much time, they should have had their whole lives ahead of them. They should both be here eagerly anticipating the birth of the baby they had both longed for.

A single tear escaped and began a long journey down her cheek and chin. She could feel it weaving its way along her skin, leaving a wet, salty line in its wake. Before a whole deluge of tears could swamp her, she took another step closer to the grave, staring down at the shiny wooden lid of the coffin.

"Goodbye Parker," she said at last. "I love you." Her hand moving to cradle her abdomen, "we love you."

Just before she turned to rejoin the others Tessa felt a hand press on hers. And then like a wisp of smoke when you blow out a candle it was gone.

EPILOGUE
FIVE YEARS LATER
FEBRUARY 19TH

6:08 A.M.

Scrambling wildly up the bank as only a small child could, four-year-old Parker Bell Junior knew that if he didn't get home soon his mother would be in a complete panic.

Even at four, PJ knew that his family was different.

Different because his father had died before he was even born. Different because his mother was so terrified of losing him too that she kept them both locked away out here on this enormous estate. Not that he minded living out here in the peace and quiet. PJ never felt completely comfortable around lots of people. It made him feel on edge, like any one of those people might suddenly change into the bogeyman if you weren't careful.

PJ also knew that he was different. He wasn't like the other little boys his mother occasionally arranged for him to play with. He didn't like the same games, he didn't like the same toys, he didn't think about the world in the same way they did. His mother said it was because he was gifted, which meant his brain had developed quicker than most children his age. His mom was gifted too, PJ knew this, and while people told him he looked exactly like his father, he knew inside he was more like his mother.

PJ loved his mom so much and it made him so sad that he couldn't make her truly happy. She always told him that he was the most precious gift she'd ever been given, and he knew without a doubt that his mother loved him more than life itself, but many a night he'd been awakened by the soft sound of her crying. Creeping to her room he'd see her curled up in a chair by the window, clutching a teddy bear, and crying so sadly it always made him start to cry too. PJ wished he could take her pain away almost as much as he wished he could take his own pain away.

He had often wondered how it was possible to miss someone he'd never met, and had come to the conclusion that he wasn't missing Detective Parker Bell the person but Detective Parker Bell the idea. He loved and missed the idea of a dad, and wondered what his and his mom's lives would have been like if his dad hadn't died. PJ knew that it had been a bad person who killed his father, and that same bad person had tried to kill his mom and him. He didn't know all the details but he knew it was a miracle that he and his mom had survived, and he knew that he hated that woman who had taken his dad from him.

Breaking through the tree line to the large grassy lawn he saw them all there waiting for him. Uncle Wyatt and Aunt Casey and their children Sam and Stacey, Uncle Marty and Aunt Rachel, Grandpa J.J. and Grandma Linda. None of these people were his real aunts and uncles and grandparents, but he loved them just as much as he loved his real relatives. They were there too of course, Uncle Daniel and Aunt Matilda and their one-year-old twins, his cousin Winter and her fiancée, and his mother.

His mother looked beautiful. Standing alone in the dawn light, her blonde curls blowing in the gentle breeze, the picture of calm and patience even though he knew inside she would be churning with fear that something awful had happened to him.

When she saw him she lifted a hand and waved, and PJ snapped instantly from the quiet, observant child, wise beyond his years, into a normal, scared little boy who needed his mother to comfort him. He didn't want to remember that it was five years today since his father's murder. He didn't want to see his mother cry as she continued to mourn the love of her life. He didn't want to hear everyone tell him how wonderful his father had been and how much like him PJ was.

All he wanted was to be in the safety of his mommy's arms where he could as least pretend that the world wasn't such a terrible place.

Reaching her he did just that. Flung his arms around her waist and burst into noisy sobs. Without a word, Tessa knelt, pressed his wet little face against her neck, and enfolded him in her warm embrace. It took PJ a long time to realize that she was crying too.

One day he was going to help her to stop crying.

One day he was going to take away her pain.

One day he was going to make everything better for her.

One day he was going to make sure she never suffered again.

One day he'd make everything perfect for both of them.

Jane has loved reading and writing since she can remember. She writes dark and disturbing crime/mystery/suspense with some romance thrown in because, well, who doesn't love romance?! She has several series including the complete Detective Parker Bell series, the Count to Ten series, the Christmas Mysteries series, and the Flashes of Fate series of novelettes.

When she's not writing Jane loves to read, bake, go to the beach, ski, horse ride, and watch Disney movies. She has a black belt in Taekwondo, a 200+ collection of teddy bears, and her favorite color is pink. She has the world's two most sweet and pretty Dalmatians, Ivory and Pearl. Oh, and she also enjoys spending time with family and friends!

For more information please visit any of the following –

Amazon – http://www.amazon.com/author/janeblythe
BookBub – https://www.bookbub.com/authors/jane-blythe
Email – mailto:janeblytheauthor@gmail.com
Facebook – http://www.facebook.com/janeblytheauthor
Goodreads – http://www.goodreads.com/author/show/6574160.Jane_Blythe
Instagram – http://www.instagram.com/jane_blythe_author
Reader Group – http://www.facebook.com/groups/janeskillersweethearts
Twitter – http://www.twitter.com/jblytheauthor
Website – http://www.janeblythe.com.au

sic enim dilexit Deus mundum ut Filium suum unigenitum daret ut omnis qui credit in eum habeat vitam aeternam

www.ingramcontent.com/pod-product-compliance
Lightning Source LLC
Chambersburg PA
CBHW071102250626
47159CB00002B/559

9 780099 241805 2